Tracee A.

Carl Roach

The Fall of Avalon

A novel.

COMING SOON
Novels by CARL ROACH

Book 2
The Prequel
RITE TO RULE
(Glorianna and Author)

Book 3
The Finale
RISE OF A NATION

THE
FALL OF
AVALON

CARL HOUSTON ROACH IV

Book one in The Lineage Series.

Bella Tracee Books

CARL HOUSTON ROACH IV

THE FALL OF AVALON

For more information contact:

Bella Tracee Books,

BellaTraceeBooks@MissTracee.com

First Edition AUGUST 2018

Copyright © 2018 Carl Roach

All rights reserved.

ISBN-13: 978-1723379727

ISBN-10: 1723379727

Edited by Tracee A. Hanna

Cover: Original art by Roxana Macias

Printed in: The United States of America

To Shellie, Please enjoy this book and keep on smiling!

Carl W.

DEDICATION

To the one who thought I was nothing:

Ex cineribus resurgam.

Table of Contents

Carl Houston Roach IV

CHAPTER 1   UNEXPECTED GUEST

He came upon them in the cover of night, carried by the fury of the wind. He was not a stranger to these lands, though its people had forgotten him.

In the land of Androma four kingdoms co-existed peacefully. Zolabar to west, a kingdom of artisans and craftmanship and brotherhood. Although, they were not a wealthy people, they were content. Kilbin, to the south, along the river leading to the sea, was a kingdom of tradesmen, sailors and scholars. They charted the stars, sailed the waters, and established trade routes amidst Androma and beyond. Eramar to the east, nearest to the sea, was a kingdom of warriors. Their system of law followed a strict code of ethics founded upon principles of strength set forth by the founders over 1,000 years ago. Eramar fostered treaties and non-aggression pacts with the other kingdoms as a means of fostering wealth and solidarity among them. Of these kingdoms, however, none could hold a candle to the roaring flame that was the Kingdom of Avalon.

Avalon, the shining city in the land of Androma, revered as the jewel among stones. Clean streets of cobblestone rolled between alabaster stone buildings free of blemish betwixt well kept, wooden vendors and houses. Black iron torches lined the streets in a staggered fashion, lit every night so the city was never without light. Overseeing it all was

The Fall of Avalon

the Ivory Palace of Glorianna, the first ruler of Avalon.

The palace itself was magnificent, a work of architecture the likes of which had no equal. Immense, rounded pillars held up the grand arch of the foyer. Polished mahogany doors with gold decorations opened to a hall furnished with purple tapestries bearing the national symbol of Avalon: a golden eagle with a serpent clutched in its talons. Black marble from the northern mines was the material of choice for the flooring and the stairs that led to the golden throne adorned with wings extending from the back.

The halls themselves were well lit with the finest of scented candles. The soothing aroma of lavender and vanilla sifted through the air like a light glaze on a pastry. Faces of dukes and duchesses, marquess and marchioness, earls and countesses throughout Avalon's history - all the way back to its founding - served as decorative tapestries along the walls. Intermixed among them were portraits of the Paladins, warriors of the line of Arthur, the greatest warriors in Avalon's history.

This night was special for the all the people in the land of Androma. So special , in fact, Titania, Queen of Avalon, hosted a ball every year. All the royals and nobles throughout Avalon, and her allied kingdoms, were invited to attend. For this was the seventh anniversary of the destruction of Ravana - one of the twelve Lords of Evil - who once wreaked havoc in the ancient world.

The music was festive and well suited for dancing. The barrels of wine, ale, rum, and whiskey overflowed. A hunting party dispatched earlier that day had returned with enough game: wild boar, deer, fowl, and bundles of the best fish from the rivers and lakes to prepare a bountiful feast for hundreds of people. Gifts of fine jewelry and jewel encrusted swords were given at the door for each guest who arrived.

The ladies laughed and danced about as the strings and flutes played. The men scurried about and chased the women around the ballroom. Joyous laughter and shouts of jubilee filled the air. Glasses clanged together as toasts were made. The noble men and women recognized the heroes from the various regions who had fallen that fateful day to protect the kingdoms from the wrath of that primordial threat.

Queen Titania sat petulantly in her seat as she panned the room. The kings and queens of the other kingdoms could not bother themselves to join the celebration, she fumed. Despite the presence of their most significant subordinates, the rulers' absence was an insult. Queen Titania deliberately rose to her feet, the picture of elegance and grace. Her raven hair cascaded down her dainty figure to the base of her back. Her flawless countenance made most believe it was carved by the angels themselves. Her figure resembled the rolling hills of the east, bountiful and enticing.

The Queen spoke with a voice like her mother before her: full of power and authority, and yet serenity and grace were not lost in her tone. Prismatic eyes, inherited from her father, Oberon, carried in them the resolute will of a ruler. All eyes

The Fall of Avalon

moved to her as she prepared to speak. "My dear friends, welcome once again to Avalon. It is my tremendous honor to host this celebration tonight. Tonight, we celebrate that seven years ago, on this day, the terrible calamity Ravana was destroyed by the great Company of Heroes!"

Applause rang out. Titania paused, and watched the crowd with a completely stoic face. Though it had been seven years ago to the day, she could still remember seeing those 100 warriors assembled in that very ballroom as if it were only yesterday. She remembered how they ate, drank, and made merry for what, in the end, had been their last night on Earth. Two of them were once her great champions. The first was Argus Nox, descendant of the great wizard Merlin. He was the most powerful sorcerer in Avalon at that time. He served as Titania's advisor during times of war, as well as peace. He was wise, kind, and courageous. No man in Avalon held a position of prominence equal to Argus.

Mifuné Tahaka was the second great champion of Avalon. The last of the Lotus Tribe, Mifuné came to live in Avalon after the desolation of his people. He became Argus's disciple, and trained under him for most of his young life. In that time, he became the greatest swordsman in the history of Avalon - since the days of Arthur over 1000 years ago. He brought honor and pride to the memory of his lost people.

"One-hundred of the finest men and women sat in this very room. Though they feared it may have been their last night at home, still, they went and bravely fought against the Ravana and its terrible evil." Queen Titania took solemn pause. "The Company of Heroes was lost, but their sacrifice was not in vain... For Avalon and her allies are still here!" Queen Titania proclaimed with pride.

More applause rang out. Titania paused again and waited for it to settle.

"My fellow royals, stand with me. Let us drink to their sacrifice, and never abandon their memory, or what their blood has bought for us."

Calls of "Here, here!" rang out from the men and women alike as all rose to their feet to drink to the fallen ones. Each face carried with it its own emotional expression. Some faces were heavy, burdened with sadness for a fallen brother, sister, friend, compatriot. Some light, beaming with hope and gratitude for the lives they continued to live because of the fallen warriors' sacrifices. Even Queen Titania's husband, Colabion, who had never met the great heroes of Avalon, of Zolabar, of Kilbin, and of Eramar, shed a tear or two in reverence.

The Queen bore no emotion at all. She remained completely serene as she gracefully descended back into her seat. She appeared to have no interest in celebrating at al which was nothing new, though. Queen Titania had always been noticeably reserved on that night, every year.

Once the feasting concluded, the party resumed in full swing. Traditional dances from Avalon, as well as the surrounding kingdoms, erupted across the dancefloor. The crowd, completely stirred into a drunken frenzy, relished in the excitement and fun. Sexual tensions began to rise, as several lords and

The Fall of Avalon

ladies were seen attempting to steal away hand in hand with lechery in their eyes. This did not hold true for the Queen of Avalon. No amount of drink, food, or music could alter Queen Titania's stoic expression. She could not stave off the lump growing in her throat, nor could she explain, even to herself, what was causing it.

"My love," Colabion began, sliding the side of his right index finger up and down Queen Titania's bare arm, "it is a party after all. Would it not be a terrible shame if you and I could not have a dance this evening, at least once?"

Colabion was not the most handsome of men the Queen had been with in her long life. He had a plain face, free of any remarkably distinguishing features. His dark brown hair was short cut and well kept. Deep-brown eyes, as common as they come in Avalon. Light, fine stubble adorned his upper lip and his jawline. Though he was past his 30th year, some would say of him that he resembled an adolescent child.

"I would rather not," Queen Titania said dismissively. She did not bother to turn her head to look at him.

Having been married to Queen Titania for seven years, Colabion had learned her many faces and facades. He could tell, just by looking at her, when she was genuinely happy, or when something was amiss. It was completely transparent to him in that moment; it made him wonder if she really believed that he would not notice something was upsetting her.

Carl Houston Roach IV

Colabion positioned his chair in front of his queen and rendered himself the focus of her attention. He took her hands gingerly in his and detected the faintest tremble. He knew her delicate temperament was not uncommon for her on the anniversary of the destruction of Ravana, Moreover, he particularly hated seeing her in such a state, as he did not know the cause. It was a subject she adamantly avoided, even seven years later.

"My dearest love, you are the envy of the night, the most beautiful woman in the realm, and yet you cannot even bring yourself to smile once this night?" asked Colabion.

Queen Titania gripped his hands lightly. "You do not know what this night is to me. No one does. And no one can." Her eyes, and her tone, were heavy, laden with sentiment akin to guilt. My beloved wife must hold herself responsible for the deaths of the Company of Heroes, Colabion pondered.

"I could if you would just tell me. Please." Colabion ran his hand down the side of her face gently. "We have been married for seven years. Can we not make tonight the night for no more secrets?"

From the balcony, suddenly, a wicked wind blasted into the ballroom. The doors to the balcony were thrust open, as the ballroom door leading to the palace slammed shut. Those outside on the balcony were forced back into the ballroom. The people who attempted to escape into the palace were pulled back away from the door, as a horrid vortex had encircled them. The torches were extinguished. The music ceased. Women screamed.

The Fall of Avalon

Men protectively put themselves in front of women. Guards drew their swords and scanned their surroundings, desperately attempting to pierce through the darkness, seeking a cause for this anomaly.

Like a twister, the circling wind focused in the center of the ballroom. Frightened and confused, the royals and nobles stared on at the concentrated cyclone that occupied the middle of the room. It howled and shrieked like some unholy demon. Just as suddenly as it appeared, the cyclone dissipated all at once, and took with it the voices of the spectators. All looked on in terror at what they saw before them, unsure of what the rest of this night would hold. Queen Titania rose to her feet, as the lump in her throat sank to the deepest part of her stomach.

A figure stood in the middle of the room. It was impossible to determine exactly who or what it was, though it appeared to be a man. It kept its head bowed, as if it were staring at the floor. It was completely still, which only increased the tension in the room. Fear was so palpable it drowned out the scent of the feast. The interloper was about to make a move. Its arm raised up slowly, to shoulder level. Hearts began to race like war horses in full retreat. A sharp, snapping sound echoed throughout the room and the candles reignited all at once. With the advent of light, it became apparent that the figure was indeed a man; but this revelation did not ease the tension in the room, nor settle any fears.

He was dressed in attire foreign to everyone in the room. He wore a round hat on his head that appeared to be made of straw, which concealed his eyes. On his torso he wore a loose-fit, black tunic with long, loose sleeves that folded over itself just beneath his chest. It was cinched at the waist by a red sash. His lower half was covered by pale gray pants, also loose fit, and on his feet, he wore simple, wooden sandals. Most frightening of all about this man was the weapon he had seated in his sash: a long, slightly curved sword with gold emblems along the sheath.

The interloper's head rose, slowly, like a hunter stalking prey. To those in his immediate line of sight, his gaze pierced through them like a thousand arrows. It was an experience unlike any other. Although there was no rage or ill-intent apparent in his eyes, the calmness of his face did not stay the sense of foreboding danger his presence created.

"Queen Titania," the interloper spoke, which caused everyone around him to take an immediate step back, "I have returned."

All eyes once again went to the Queen. Upon inspection, her face had certainly changed from her previous stoic demeanor. Her naturally light skin waxed pale as death, as if she was looking upon her own grave. Colabion watched with morbid curiosity as this powerful woman he loved so much, quaked inside like a frightened child. He would watch no more.

"Guards, seize him!" Colabion commanded.

A dozen soldiers clad in heavy armor clamored towards the man in the center of the room. The royals and nobles cleared the way as best as they could to make the path for the guards. Each man shouted some order of 'halt' or 'surrender' as they approached, but the lone swordsman did not bother to acknowledge them. Rather, he began to approach the Queen slowly, steadily.

Before the swordsman could reach her, six guards were upon him: three from the front, three from his left flank. As they came just outside arm's reach of him, the interloper took hold of his sword handle. No one saw what happened next, but without missing a step, the samurai continued forward, as the six guards fell to the floor. His sword tore through their plate armor like a knife to butter. Each man was dismembered, slashed, bloody, and dead. Screaming erupted from nearby onlookers splashed with soldier's blood. The remaining guards kept their distance. They knew they were out matched.

Colabion did not know what else to do, without a moment's hesitation, he positioned himself between the swordsman and his beloved wife. His heart trembled, but he set aside his fear. He would protect his wife, as he had vowed to do on the day of their wedding. He sucked in a deep gulp of air and held his breath, all the while thinking, any moment following this decision may be his last.

The swordsman stopped before him. His presence was overwhelming. Colabion knew in his heart if he had not taken that previous breath, he would be starving for air in that moment. Though he was afraid, he held his composure as best he could. Much to his surprise, the interloper did not cut him down, nor did he make the effort to engage him.

"Step aside," the man uttered, perturbed.

Carl Houston Roach IV

"I will not! I am Colabion, King Consort of Avalon! And I will not allow you to do as you please, here! I command that you leave Avalon at once, and never return!"

The swordsman wasted no more time than that with Colabion. He placed his hand squarely centered on Colabion's chest and delivered a forceful thrust. Colabion was pushed from where he stood and sent barreling towards the wall behind him. His back struck the ground and he slid well out of the way.

Queen Titania's eyes were locked with the swordsman's. What was left of her composure was stained by hot tears streaming from her eyes. Her arms visibly shook. Her breath was stifled. She, too, felt overwhelmed in the swordsman's presence. The lump that had sunk into her stomach churned like a maelstrom churns the waters of the sea. Everything around her seemed to shrink, until it was drowned out by the darkness she could see emitting from this man.

"Queen Titania," he began, "say my name." He spoke softly, but there was intensity in his voice.

Queen Titania's eyes went wide, as though she were in a living nightmare. Seemingly, a terrible skeleton had found the keys to escape the closet she tried so desperately to keep closed. Some part of her believed this day would come, as no secret can be buried forever. The larger part of her so desperately wanted to believe that it would not, but the day of reckoning was upon her.

While there was some confusion from the onlookers as to the stranger's motive, it was

The Fall of Avalon

unquestionable from the haunted look on the queen's face that she knew the man. She knew his name. There had to be a reason that she would not say it. The popular growing suspicion among the spectators was that the reason Queen Titania knew him and the reason why he had appeared were one in the same.

"Say my name!" he shouted. Every person flinched away and slammed their eyes shut, but only for a moment. All eyes quickly turned back to the Queen, poised to see what would happen next. Her lips pursed and trembled, much like the rest of her. Her shaking hand rose up to her chest. She clutched the piece of her dress over her breast, as if to still her racing heart. "Say it! Tell them who I am!" he screamed.

Queen Titania's breath escaped her like a whisper at first. In her heart, she sensed granting his request would be her only salvation. His rage, his malice, would not be contained by her tears. It would not be satiated by her trembling trepidation, not without a greater price, or a greater sacrifice would he leave her be. More than anything, she wanted to survive that night, a night she had hoped would never come to pass.

"Mifuné. Mifuné Tahaka, the sole survivor of the grand Company of Heroes that slayed Ravana."

"Come now, your Majesty. Do not try to deny me my right." His voice lowered to its original tone. "Tell them the truth."

The Queen shrugged off her fear, blinked away the tears from her eyes, and in her typical authoritative voice, she declared, "You are my former guardian, and protector of Avalon. Mifuné Tahaka, the man who slayed Ravana seven years ago."

Shock reverberated throughout the crowd. Whispers went around the nobles over what they just heard. Whispers of doubt and confusion.

"It is as you say," the swordsman replied as he offered a half bow, which silenced the muttering in the crowd.

Mifuné walked away from Queen Titania to the nearest table. He noticed a half-full glass of drink. He raised the glass off the table with his right hand and put it just under his nose. He sniffed the glass to properly identify its contents, a potent concoction. "Rum from Zolabar, my favorite," the warrior said in a tone distinctly more light-hearted than his previous tone. "The brewers there really know how to mix in the spices just right." He tilted the glass to his lips and sipped. The sound of each swallow was like a nail being driven into Queen Titania's heart.

Shocked by this revelation, Colabion rose to his feet. "Titania, what is he talking about?" He stepped closer to her. "You said that all the warriors who fought against Ravana died that day. Who is this man to claim such a right?"

Queen Titania could not reply. She looked down and away, only able to stare at the ground, overwhelmed by the revelations brought on by that night. He is not supposed to be here, she thought; he is supposed to be safely locked away The Queen's world shook apart as her nightmare continued.

"Yes, Titania. Tell them. Tell them all what happened when last we spoke," Mifuné indignantly insisted. He set the empty glass down and seized another.

Silence was the Queen's response, as if her voice had been stolen out of her throat. Her spirit waned under the exposure, which begat shame that pressed down on her in the light of the malice and contempt the swordsman held for her. She felt like releasing everything in her stomach at once as she watched him casually swallow all the rum from the second glass in a single gulp.

Mifuné held the glass out in front of him in the direction of the people now huddled away from him. Their reflections changed as he turned the glass in his hand. He could see the fear in their eyes; the suffocating anticipation that gripped them was almost more than they could bear.

"My patience has run out, Queen Titania," said Mifuné.

Mifuné released the glass from his hand. The crowd watched it fall to the ground. Before they could react, Mifuné launched a fearsome attack against them. With his blade, he sliced them apart like a scissor to ribbon, spewing blood and flinging meat into the helpless crowd. By the time the glass hit the ground and shattered into dozens of fragmented pieces, Mifuné had cut down five more people. The bodies were mangled beyond recognition, and pools of blood formed on the floor. Screaming, shrieks of fear, and cries of sadness rang through the air. Queen Titania sank into her seat and began to cry bitterly. The surviving group bunched up together and backed away from Mifuné. They stacked themselves shoulder to shoulder, such that

Carl Houston Roach IV

no one could fit between them. Silence overtook the people once they were away from the swordsman. The sound of the fresh blood that dripped from his blade sent a chill to their bones.

"Perhaps you will not tell them for my sake. Perhaps instead you should answer to them why these people have died!" His scream evolved into a roar like a raging dragon. "It is no longer my time you waste, but their lives, Titania!"

"Enough!" Queen Titania shot up out of her seat. "I will answer you. Spare them, and I will answer you. Please!" the Queen begged desperately.

"Tell them in earnest, Titania, Queen of Avalon. What happened to your faithful servant when he returned? What happened to me?"

The Queen's voice shook as she choked back bitter tears. "You and I were to be wed upon your return from the battle against Ravana. I promised I would await the day of your homecoming, yet I did not. I married Colabion long before I received word of your return."

"Now tell them what you did to me upon my return. Spare no details." Mifuné pointed the tip of his sword at her. "Let them all see who you really are this night. Tell them how the divine and generous Queen of Avalon rewarded my efforts."

"I sent an emissary to invite you to meet with me at the Tower of Galahad. When you arrived, I would not let you hold me. I told you I had already been married to another. Once I had spoken my truth, I could sense darkness radiating from within you. I had my sorcerers strike you down with

The Fall of Avalon

powerful magic, as I feared that you were not yourself anymore," the Queen replied innocently.

Mifuné, who had paced back and forth in front of this crowd of nobility and royalty, suddenly stopped. His eyes went wide and his pupils dilated. In a flash, his blade flew through the crowd again. Four people lost their heads practically simultaneously. Blood gushed from the necks of the severed heads and showered those near them. The fallen bodies splashed into the pools of blood formed on the floor.

"Tell me, Titania, shall I kill them all now so that you may cling to this lie?! Are their lives so worthless to you that you would sacrifice them like sheep!?" Mifuné roared. His voice echoed through the ballroom and shook the palace.

"Please! No more! I beg of you. I will tell them the truth. Stay your sword, Mifuné," the Queen pleaded.

"I will play no further games with your Majesty." In an instant, Mifuné was gone from her sight. She heard Colabion grunt. Her heart sank into her belly as she turned her head. Her husband was on his hands and knees. Mifuné's sword lay over the back of his neck. Fresh blood dripped onto the nape of his neck and stained as it ran down the back of his tunic.

"His will be the next life you forfeit should you hide the truth any longer," declared Mifuné.

Please... do not hurt him, she thought. She could see no mercy in his eyes, though. The part of him that loved her all those years ago was gone. Wrath, deeper and darker than any she had ever experienced in her long life, had taken its place. He had become a monster of her own making. A monster she was now powerless to stop.

"My sorcerers attacked you because I told them to. I did not want you anymore, but I feared one day you might turn against me. If your might was great enough to fell Ravana, who could stop you? I had no choice..." She released a few tears. "I had them imprison you with great magical restraints beneath the tower so that you could never escape. There you would remain bound..."

"While you lived the life you promised me would be mine," Mifuné interrupted. "You used me, and when you had no further need of me, you cast me down and locked me away. You lied to cover your own treachery, and left me to pay the price, while you reaped everything you wanted. And you gave it all to him!"

Mifuné kicked Colabion over to her. He coughed once, but he was not severely hurt. She knelt beside him and cradled him in her arms, as if hoping to shield him from Mifuné's fury. The Queen held fast to her husband as Mifuné approached, sword still in hand. She refused to close her eyes. She refused to show any fear of dying with the one that she loved.

The truth about the Queen had been revealed, all else was dust now. She showed no signs of terror. Death was not something that terrified her. When the tip of Mifuné's sword eyed Titania, only inches from her face, her countenance fell. Rather than slit her throat and kill the man at his feet, Mifuné oriented his blade away from Titania and pointed it

The Fall of Avalon

towards the crowd. The fear that they had felt towards him began to be replaced with something else. For he was not a senseless man overcome with rage intent on killing them all. He was a man who had come to deliver a message, and the message had been received.

"Take heed, all of you! The Tower of Galahad is mine. That is where I shall be for those who wish to find me. And, I shall remain there for seven days. On the eighth day, I shall return to Avalon," Mifuné paused to turn back to Queen Titania, "and I shall take away everything from you, just as you took everything away from me." He turned back to the crowd. "For those of you who renounce your loyalty to Titania and to Avalon, I shall spare you. Those who do not will share in her fate."

The room was quiet. All eyes were fixed on the swordsman, but no one said a word. His sandals clacked against the floor, reminiscent of war drums beating outside the walls of a city under siege. He casually lifted another glass of rum from a different table and raised it to his lips. The sound of him slurp the rum out of the glass sent shivers down everyone's spine, everyone except the Queen. Then, a magnanimous sound caught their attention. A sound Queen Titania had been waiting for since Mifuné arrived. The doors to the ballroom were forced open. Queen Titania's ever faithful protector; the Paladin of Avalon with unrivaled power, Virgil, had come to her rescue. Finally, her worries were at ease. Virgil would dispatch Mifuné swiftly and decisively, as he did any enemy of Avalon. The threat of undermining her kingdom, her mother's kingdom, would vanish that night and forever more. Never again would she be haunted by the looming threat of Mifuné's return, or so she thought...

The door to the ballroom crashed against the wall how the winds of a maelstrom crash against a mountain. The hinges roared like the sound of a war horn. Queen Titania's heart radiated with joy, briefly. Rarely did she admit it, but she loved seeing Virgil clad in the armor akin to his forebears. Sterling silver armor covered his chest. Magnificent pauldrons over his shoulders secured the royal red cape that whipped in the wind. Vambraces and grieves marvelously complimented his cuirass. No helmet covered his handsome, smiling face – the proud, heroic smile of a true descendant of Arthur. Donned in his armor, he was the image of a champion, and as fine a Paladin as Avalon had ever seen.

That uplifted moment was brief. Indeed, it was Virgil who had entered the ballroom. It was clear his intent was to engage the enemy that appeared, as he was carrying a sword in hand, but something was very wrong. Queen Titania expected her champion to burst through the doors, radiating with the Light of the Paladin. His voice would fill the ballroom like thunder fills the sky in a storm. By his great power, Mifuné would be brought to nothing, and never pose a threat to the Queen or her kingdom ever again.

Virgil limped as he entered. His armor, normally shimmering with the Paladin's Light, and sturdier than any Dwarven forged mithril, was cracked and broken in places. His golden blonde hair was stained reddish brown. His right eye was swollen almost completely shut. His red cape was tattered, cut, and pierced. The tip of his sword he carried scraped across the ground. He clutched his midsection with his unarmed hand.

"My Queen," he called out with a weak voice, "are you hurt?"

"So, you finally made it," Mifuné said. He finished the rum from the glass he had picked up. "I wondered if you would you attempt to pursue me after you woke up." He set the glass back on the table and faced the beaten Paladin.

"I will not fail in my duties. I will protect the Queen from any threat! Even you!" Virgil shouted with what strength he could muster.

"Such effort is wasted on a master like her, Paladin. Had she no need of you, she would cast you away just as she did me. You will not listen to me, but I know this to be true," Mifuné stated straightforwardly.

Mifuné casually strode towards the balcony. Virgil lunged forward, determined. "You are not going anywhere!" He raised his sword to Mifuné.

Mifuné heard Virgil's sword come up through the air and shook his head. "Put it away. It is not worth your losing again." Mifuné took a deep breath, then exhaled. "We will face each other again before this is over, Paladin. Regain your strength and clean yourself off before trying to face me once more," Mifuné uttered confidently.

Mifuné stepped onto the balcony. Virgil did not pursue him, but he watched intently to see what Mifuné would do next. To Virgil's surprise, Mifuné vanished like a shadow into the darkness of the night. Unable to do anymore, and having exhausted all that remained of his strength, Virgil fell to a knee and collapsed onto the ground.

The crowd of royals and nobles stirred amongst themselves, growing louder and louder as they pondered the situation in which they found themselves thrusted. The situation in which the Queen of Avalon had knowingly and selfishly placed them. They roared into a frenzy, both angered and frightened. There was naught that Queen Titania could do to control the situation that had developed. Her greatest warrior was beaten and bloodied, her husband lay at the ground beside her, and her allies expeditiously made up their minds to abandon any, and all alliances with her and with Avalon forever.

As her guests frantically fled the Ivory Palace in droves, Queen Titania watched her life fall apart, and said only, "How did it come to this?"

The Fall of Avalon

The last son of the Dragon had returned to Avalon. The legacy of the Lotus bloomed once again in the land of Andromach.

Dawn, The Ivory Palace was silent as a graveyard. Neither Queen Titania nor her council could have anticipated the events of the night before. Although, if her majesty was completely honest, the horrors of that evening were the realization of her seven-year nightmare. They had convened in the Queen's chambers in the west wing of the palace to discuss all options available to them, so that they might develop a strategy to afford them their best chance for survival, as their continued existence, their perseverance was paramount, and time was not on their side. The Queen expressed no optimism. Her every thought was consumed by the burning wrath she saw in the eyes of the man who once loved her. It was as clear to everyone in the room as the vacant expression on her face.

The council talked frantically amongst themselves. Some were hysterical, some were composed. All were oriented toward the same goal. None of them, however, could orient the discussion in a functional direction. They had depended on Queen Titania's direct guidance toward order for so long, that her silence only fed the chaos that the Samurai had stirred.

Carl Houston Roach IV

"We have received countless letters this morning from our allies across the lands. I am afraid none of them will stand with us against this threat," Councilman Methis said.

"He is but one man! Can they truly be afraid of what this one man is capable of?" Councilman Peter roared over the crowd.

"Nonsense! They're just frightened from the display he put on last night. Surely, they will come to their senses soon and repledge their loyalty."

"Can we wait for such an opportunity?"

"Of course, we can. We have the Paladin. Your Highness, I advise we deploy the Paladin to engage this threat. Hold Mifuné back until we can devise an alternative solution to deal with him."

Titania paid little attention to the deliberations going back and forth between the men and women in the room. The fear was so engrained in her that she had not stopped trembling since the previous night. She saw them all as fools, blind to the truth that locked its icy grip around her throat and intended to choke away her life. Little did she know; her days were already numbered.

"Your Highness?" the councilman asked again.

The Queen's blank gaze drifted towards the man speaking to her, but she could scarcely see him. Nothing in front of her came into view. No sounds were clear to her. Even the sound of the heart beating in her chest was a foreign instrument she was unable to recognize. The breaths she took did not fill a living body, no, the air that entered her lungs sustained a living corpse.

The Fall of Avalon

"My Queen?" the councilman asked again, sounding a bit frustrated.

"I refuse to live under this threat," Queen Titania stated emphatically as she regained focus. "What is the council's verdict?" she asked.

An older woman stepped forward and centered herself before the Queen of Avalon to properly address her. She knew the woman well, her name was Maribeth, a kind woman that Queen Titania had watched grow up in the palace, from a sweet little girl to a well-respected woman, with influence and power. Maribeth always knew how to talk to her Queen to calm even her worst fears. She spoke with such a soft voice, and with such optimism. Seeing Maribeth immediately put the smallest touch of light back into Queen Titania's heart.

"The Council has agreed upon a course of action, your Majesty. We believe our allies will return to aid us in due time, but we must demonstrate, not only to them, but to this man who has threatened our kingdom, that we will not sit idly by and allow him to do as he pleases. Deploy the Paladin. Have him hold back this threat until we can assure our allies that we can shield ourselves, and them, from his tyranny."

Titania was silent, her countenance unchanged. Her heart sank at the thought of sending out Virgil to face Mifuné. She had known Arthur, the very first Paladin, and each Paladin that followed, after Arthur ascended to the realm of the gods. The might of the Paladin was strong, the strongest power in Androma, second only to her own. No Paladin, however, was as strong as Arthur, not even Virgil.

Carl Houston Roach IV

For Mifuné to have bested Ravana, he must have had strength that rivaled or even bested Arthur himself. And if that were true, it would not be possible for Virgil to defeat Mifuné.

"What say you, your Majesty?" Maribeth asked.

"No. Virgil will stay here and guard the Citadel with the knights."

"Your Majesty, we cannot simply sit and wait for…"

"Am I not still the ruler of this kingdom?" Titania fired back.

"It is as you say, your Majesty."

"Is my word not still law in this land?" Titania asked again.

"Y-yes, your Majesty," Maribeth replied.

Titania aggressively rose to her feet. "Then it shall be as I say! Virgil and the rest of the knights are to remain here to protect the palace. Place them on high alert! Assemble them in groups of no less than four. Position them at every entry point to the palace!" She shifted focus. "General!" she called out.

"Yes, your Majesty," he replied.

"Collect the garrison at the wall. Position them between the Citadel and the city. They shall form a buffer to hold back anything that comes their way!"

"What of the defense of the wall?" the General replied.

"Dispatch your Captains and Lieutenants to gather our troops from the countryside. They will take the place of the garrison at the wall of the city."

"It will be done, my Queen." The General bowed and left the room immediately.

The Fall of Avalon

"Councilman Donovan!" she called.

"Yes, your Majesty?"

"Our treasury is abundantly overflowing. Offer whatever promise of riches or gold you must. Bring in the best and the strongest mercenaries money can buy. As many of them as you are able!"

"It shall be as you say, your Majesty."

"The rest of you, leave me, I wish to be alone. If I have need of you, I will send for you."

Each councilman and woman bowed to Queen Titania and departed the room. They muttered amongst themselves their concerns for her decisions. It all seemed like so much effort for just one man. Despite what some of them had seen the night before, they could not fathom how one man could possess such power as to be worthy of such extreme measures. Each one of them, however, knew better than to go against the wishes of the Queen of Avalon. It was not uncommon, even amongst the nobility, for her opposition to go missing. It was best to keep one's head down in the Queen's presence. The last of the councilmembers closed the door behind him, and the room was completely silent.

Queen Titania cradled herself as she glided through the room to look out the window. Avalon was such a beautiful place. Verdant fields of lush grass painted over wide planes reaching all the way to the horizon. Fair temperatures, cool breezes, and never a shortage of resources, it was paradise Glorianna chose a wonderland on earth to establish Avalon over 1000 years ago. Lost in a hellish reverie—obsessed with images of her beloved

Carl Houston Roach IV

homeland burning, the incubus haunted Queen Titania. It was a nightmarish sight she could not stave off. She could see crimson flames devour the natural beauty surrounding the kingdom. The stone walls which protected the city were shattered. The voices of her people, cried out, rang in her ears. She could almost feel the fire begin to burn her flesh.

There was a sudden knock at the door, the Queen flinched. First one, then a second, followed by a third. She turned to face the door, still cradling herself. Virgil came through the door gallantly. She was overjoyed to see him and pleased at how well he had healed thus far from his bout with Mifuné the previous night. His hair was clean, once again resembling the golden rays of sunlight she adored so much. The skin around his eye was still enflamed from the injury he sustained, though the swelling had gone down. His eyes, those emerald green eyes that had always beset her heart, held not an ounce of fear or terror for what may lay in wait for them. He had but one care, and it was the woman standing just before him.

Queen Titania ran to Virgil and fell into his strong arms. Her head rested gently against his solid chest, which she could feel the bulk of even through his tunic. She felt her tensions ease as his fingers brushed up and down her arms. Her heart lifted as his head rested atop hers. He tenderly wrapped his powerful arms over her and held her close. Softly, she kissed his arm at the point closest to her face and nuzzled her head firmly against his chest.

Virgil slid his index and middle fingers up her arm, gently caressed her shoulder, and traced up

The Fall of Avalon

Titania's neck to her cheek. She felt goosebumps form all over her body. Her face leaned against his fingers, as she had longed for his touch. Her arms slid around his waist, and she gripped his back as if some force were attempting to steal him away from her. Slowly she looked up into his eyes, and he looked back into hers. Virgil pressed his lips against hers, longingly, passionately. With his hand at the small of her back, he pulled his queen closer to him, tightly pressing her to himself. His cupped the side of her face, and she kissed him in kind. She dug her nails into his flesh as she pressed her lips to his in true lovers' fashion.

A fire erupted within her which chased away all her fears in that moment. Physical ecstasy coursed through her, all the way to the tips of her fingers and toes. She set her hand behind his head and clutched fistfuls of hair. His lips separated from hers and set to her neck. She exhaled a sigh of pleasure as she leaned in and cradled his head against her neck. She continued to sigh louder and louder as he transitioned between his lips, tongue, and teeth. With every bite, she pulled the handful of hair locked in her grip, enticing him to continue.

Her body's curves rolled like the hills in the east. The sight of the Queen's bare breasts drove him wild. They were easily more than a handful, even for Virgil's generously proportioned hands. His teeth visibly gritted as he eyed her body with unrelenting hunger. She could not wait any longer. She pulled him off her and pushed him onto the couch. He watched intently as she pulled the ties that held her dress in place until they unraveled. The dainty dress fell to the floor, revealing her bare skin. To describe her in the eyes of Virgil is to say she was the object of any man's desire.

Titania straddled him seductively. Carnal desire painted her face. She wasted no time removing his tunic with excessive effort. Virgil's chest was wide and thick, mostly free of body hair. His shoulders were round and solid, as were his arms. His core possessed the best cuts and definition of any man she had ever seen, even Mifuné's. He was far beyond the physical scope of her husband, or any man in Avalon for that matter. She pressed her lips against each part of his torso, beginning with his powerful chest. She preceded each kiss with a lick, the slightest bit of contact from her tongue to his muscular physique. With each kiss, she felt a heat growing within her. It grew in intensity and fervor as her lips came closer and closer to his belt line.

Of all the pleasures he had ever experienced, nothing compared to her body against his. He sighed from the ecstasy of her lips against his skin. Her hands caressed his body which made his eyes roll back in his head. He reached for her head and took handfuls of her hair in his grip. She dropped to her knees and began to remove his trousers. When they were off, she straddled him again, leaning in for a kiss. Time stood still. The world around them faded to black. In that moment, it was only the two of them, locked together for just a time, but also forever, bound in an act of physical pleasure, ecstasy, and the intertwining of the souls.

໒໐

The Fall of Avalon

Colabion, the King consort, had his own agenda for the day. He had waited until he was sure that his wife was sealed away in the Queen's Chamber with the council before he stealthily snuck out of the palace into the city. He wore a brown hood that covered his face. In his belt, he carried a small purse of gold coins, should he find need of anything. Colabion hoped, though, where he was going, he would have need of nothing.

Colabion came to a doorway in a back alley near the market district in Avalon. A foul odor, which commonly sifted through the air, was present, and plagued the King-Consort's senses. It felt as though it worsened the ache along his side from where Mifuné had kicked him. He looked to his left, and he looked to his right to make sure he had not been followed before knocking on the door. Once. Twice. Then a third time.

The door opened, and, standing behind it was a tall, burly man. His jaw was wide, and his face was chiseled. Groomed, dark facial hair ran along the bevels of his masculine face. Most peculiar about this man was his eyes. One eye was faded gray, the result of an accident the man suffered when he was a child. The other was a shimmering blue, a hue that rivaled the Queen's splendid, prismatic eyes for beauty and intensity.

The man looked into Colabion's eyes with soft care. Before he could speak a word, Colabion fell against him and clung to his thick arms, which wrapped around him. Colabion shook as he wept, much the way a frightened child weeps in his father's embrace. The man stroked Colabion's back tenderly and pulled him closer still.

"Are you alright?" the man asked, rife with concern. "Tell me, please."

"May I come in? Is your master home?" Colabion muttered pitifully.

"No, she left out into the city early this morning. I am not sure when she will be back, but for now we have time."

The man delicately led Colabion through the door into the tiny space he inhabited. Colabion felt his touch leave as he went to light the candles and provide some illumination.

"Wait!" Colabion shouted.

"What is it?" the man asked.

"Did you cover it? You know how I hate to see that thing," Colabion inquired.

The man strolled over to his King Consort and cupped his face with his strong hands. Colabion's eyes closed as he felt this powerful man's gentle, serene touch. He felt the man's lips purse against his forehead, and a wave of warmth and love washed over him. "Of course," he assured Colabion. "I would never do anything to upset you."

The man continued to light the remaining candles in the room. It truly was a small space. The only furniture there was a table in the center of the room beside the stone fire pit. A cauldron of frightening construction hung over it from a black iron bar, but the man had covered it with a tarp so that it was completely concealed. He pulled out a seat from the corner of the room and set it beside the chair tucked under the table.

The Fall of Avalon

Colabion graciously accepted the seat. As his body bent, he grunted and gasped in pain, feeling his body fold over his bruised flank. The man flinched, his eyes flickered with concern. "Are you hurt? Did something happen to you?" he probed innocently.

"A warrior came to the palace last night..." Colabion uttered as the man lifted his tunic. Colabion's whole right side was purple and red from the bruising where he had been kicked. The man gasped and pulled away. "He did this to me," Colabion finished, lowering his tunic.

"I have a remedy," the man answered quickly. A tinge of anger was evident in his tone. He sifted through the contents on one of the shelves in the tiny room, searching for the ingredients he needed. "It will make you good as new again in no time." His voice was urgent. Colabion's heart sunk. He knew why the man before him was so insistent on healing his wound. The King Consort rose from his seat and hugged the man from behind.

"It is not your fault," Colabion assured him. He could feel the man's search begin to slow until he stopped and wrapped his powerful hands over Colabion's soft, royal fingers. "It was that Samurai, that Mifuné!" Colabion grunted, as though he were spitting the name out of his mouth.

The man suddenly took in a slow, deep breath. Colabion could feel his wide torso expand to its full girth and released his hold. The man faced Colabion with a spark of interest in his eye. It was beyond any form of arousal he had ever seen in his lover's eyes. He was almost excited, with a vast array of other positive responses that Colabion did not understand. Before he could inquire, the man spoke.

"Did you say 'Mifuné Tahaka'?" the man asked forcefully.

"Yes, that was what Titania called him. He did not deny the name, either," Colabion answered, his tone gruff.

"Colabion..." the man said as he helped Colabion take a seat, "Mifuné Tahaka has returned to Avalon, are you sure?" he pressed.

"Yes! Why are you so interested in this man? I do not understand..." Colabion's voice trailed off.

The man dwarfed Colabion's dainty hands as he held them in his. "When we met, those years ago, I promised I would make you a king, to make your greatest wish come true. Do you remember that?" he asked in earnest.

"Yes, of course. It was the sweetest thing you had ever said to me." Colabion's eyes glittered with nostalgic tears.

"I did make you a king, did I not?" the man asked again.

"Yes. I have ruled beside Titania these past seven years. I have greater wealth status than any of my older brothers. I want for nothing. Nothing except you." Colabion clasped his hands around one of the man's hands.

"I know, my love." His lover's voice turned severe, his tone cold and grave. "This samurai warrior could threaten what I have given to you. I need to know everything that you know. Can you do that for me?" he brushed the side of Colabion's face.

The Fall of Avalon

"Yes, of course I can, Sebastian," Colabion replied. He took in a deep breath, and imparted all that he knew of the night before.

⸏❧

Far away, outside the city of Avalon, the Tower of Galahad baked in the light of the sun. It stood as a lookout beside the beginnings of the forest that led to the Kingdom of Zolabar. Named after one of Arthur's great knights, Sir Galahad, the structure served as a watchtower should enemies approach Avalon from the west. The tower was stone, inglorious. In its prime, it could have housed potentially a hundred or so troops. Unfortunately, it had been deemed needless, and had fallen into disrepair over the course of the past one-hundred years. Moss and ivy had overtaken the base and the walls of the tower. It was a staunch reminder, to those who had seen it, of some of the lost grandeur of Avalon's history.

Mifuné sat alone in the highest room and overlooked the space between the tower and the city. His rage from the night before had settled, but his decision would not change. He would bring down his retribution upon the whole of the city, in time. There was a knock at his door, behind him. He did not address it. He continued to stare out the window, occasionally closing his eyes to the caresses of a cool summer breeze that snuck in through the window.

"Master," a voice said, softly, "are you there?"

No answer.

"We did not hear you come back last night. I wanted to see if you were here."

Carl Houston Roach IV

The door creaked open, slowly. Through the crack in the door, a young woman's head poked in. She saw him, her master, seated cross-legged on his bed, facing the window. The tip-end of the sheath for his sword rested on the ground. The length of it ran up at an angle. The handle rested on Mifuné's shoulder. He seemed so peaceful to her, sitting there alone. It almost seemed a crime to intrude.

"Do you want to be alone? I-I know it could not have been easy seeing her again, after all this time. After what she did…"

"Titania was as beautiful as she ever was, Naomi," Mifuné said, "but even the timeless beauty of a rose can be tainted by the thorn that pricks you."

Naomi could sense the pain in his voice as he spoke about his love, his queen. The sound was hollow, like something inside of him was broken, possibly beyond repair, the way that wind sounds when it passes through a potter's broken vase.

"Master?" Naomi asked softly, "may I sit with you?"

Mifuné did not open his mouth to reply. Instead, he shifted himself slightly toward the headboard. There was just enough room for Naomi to take a seat. Despite his gesture, she felt a little uneasy about joining him in such an intimate setting. Even so, she stepped into the room and sat on the bed beside him. Though he tried his best not to show it, she could feel the intensity of his heart wrenching pain—devastating emotional agony. It grieved him beyond her comprehension to see the queen again; to see her in the splendor, enjoying the life that he

The Fall of Avalon

bought for her though his deeply personal prostrating sacrifice: her life paid for with the deaths of his friends, her life that stole his freedom, her life which cost him his life.

"Master, are you alright?"

"To some, sacrifice can be such a meaningless thing. For seven years I have contemplated it, but I can never understand how someone so fair could prove to be so treacherous. Or how I could have been so blind."

Mifuné turned his gaze to Naomi, his sworn disciple, and took in everything about her. There was innocence in her eyes. Upon first glance, anyone could see that she was everything Titania was not. The woman beside him had short-cut blonde hair, barely past her ears. Her eyes were plain, pale green. She wore a figure-fitting black blouse with long sleeves over a short skirt that passed her knees. On her feet she wore knee-high black boots with one heel worn down, laced up with dingy stained white laces. Around her neck, a red hood was fastened with a cloak that hung down to the backs of her knees. Mifuné never said it aloud, but he found her hood quite charming.

In the months since he was released from his prison, Mifuné had not smiled, not even once. Naomi longed to see her Master smile again. Once, when she was a young girl, he gave her a smile. Even after all the time that had passed, she could not forget that smile. He was so consumed with this betrayal, Naomi feared he had lost who was. More than anything, in her heart, Naomi wished she could steal the pain in his heart away.

Carl Houston Roach IV

As Mifuné glanced away from Naomi, her eyes locked on him. She longed to put her hand on his, although he tightly gripped his sword. Slowly, she reached over, fingers outstretched, to touch his hand. As she did, she could hear the faintest sound of whispering. The closer her hand came to his, the more intense the susurration became. It mesmerized her. Naomi could not make sense of the soft voice that seemed to emanate from the sword. It was a curious thing, and equally frightening. Naomi pondered: Is this real or am I imagining a phenomenon? If this is really happening, can Mifuné hear the whispers as well? And if he can hear the whispers, does the sword's hushed message make any sense to him? Regardless, she continued to reach forward. Naomi was unaware, though, that her hand changed its trajectory, from her Master's hand to the sword he clung to.

Just before her hand could find its place, he fervently jerked the sword away from her. The whispers suddenly vanished, and she could see her fingers pointing at the handle of his sword, rather than his hand. His head shot toward her, and their eyes locked. A ferocious, animal-like intensity came over him. A feral scowl twisted his normally calm face.

"Do not touch my sword." His voice was as sharp as a knife.

Naomi's eyes went wide in fear. Her hand retreated from his and continued to inch back as far from the sword as possible. Her heart began to pound out of her chest. Her breath locked itself at the base of her throat. She knew he was protective of his sword, but she never expected such a reaction.

Mifuné reared back, as if shocked by his own words. He blinked rapidly and shook his head. The fearsome look that had overtaken him faded. His eyes returned to their normal, calm stasis. He stood up from his bed and fixed his gaze out the window. After a moment, he mustered up the will to speak.

"How are the others?" Mifuné asked.

"Oh! They are fine," Naomi replied reluctantly. "Desmond went out fishing, and Gabrysia is meditating downstairs."

"Has she been able to store more power, like I taught her?"

"It is hard to say for sure. I am not that skilled at sensing another person's power just yet. I could not even tell when you came back last night. I am afraid I am not as good at this as Gabrysia."

"You are too hard on yourself, my pupil. You did not sense me because I did not want you to. I am able to mask my presence and location from anyone." Mifuné paused. "You must believe in yourself, and in your abilities. Once you do, I am sure you will become something much greater. I have faith in you."

Naomi smiled and blushed. She raised her hood to conceal her face from her teacher. "I think I should go, Master. You must need some rest after last night. Even the sharpest blade will dull if it is not cared for," she chuckled nervously. Naomi shuttered to think she may have offended him, as a student is not permitted to lecture the Master. More than anyone, she knew exactly what the man was capable of. His aura and power radiated with the same wrathful intensity as it did the night before. Mifuné's brow was as firm as ever.

As he rose slowly to his feet, the furrow in his brow softened. Hearing his father's proverb cited back to him set a light in his heart. A look of pride overtook his countenance to know that something he had taught Naomi took root. Mifuné calmed as he nodded slightly and laid his sword against the wall. He pulled his kimono out from under the sash that secured it and began to remove it. Naomi stood up and bowed before him attempting to leave the room. She prayed that she avoided him seeing her blush again.

Before Naomi closed the door, she peeked through the crack she had left at the man undressing in the room. As his kimono came off, his back was exposed. She admired the chevron-like muscles beneath his neck and the toned roundness of his shoulders. Mifuné's head turned over his shoulder. Naomi's breath sucked into her chest and she shut the door. Her whole face was red as the hood she wore. She could feel her heart pounding in her chest. Once behind the door she turned her back and leaned against the weathered oak. She exhaled. Her heart fluttered out of her chest. She struggled to maintain control of her breath. She smiled relentlessly. After all the time she had spent searching, she had found him. It was just like the old woman said, Naomi mused.

The Soothsayer's words echoed in her memory as she leaned against the door, "You will find the man you are searching for at the Tower of Galahad.

The Fall of Avalon

Be warned, my pet. Wrath burns in his heart. Rage has taken his sight from him. He may not be the man you remember." Despite the grave warning, she could still see in Mifuné the man she had sought after almost all her life. The way he looked after her, Desmond, and Gabrysia every day since his release reminded her of that. As dangerous a man as they knew him to be, Naomi always felt safe around him.

It was not the first time, Naomi had seen his body, as he was naked when she and Gabrysia used their magic to break the bonds holding him— completely exposed. And within him was power unlike anything they had ever encountered. In truth, she feared him then. The way he looked after her, Desmond, and Gabrysia every day since his release reminded her that, as dangerous a man as she knew him to be, she always felt safe around him. Despite his wrath, he was still the same man she remembered.

Naomi brandished a coin from her pocket. One side of the coin was gold, with no distinguishing features to it. Inlaid on the other side of the coin was a purple lotus, once the emblem of the Paladin of Avalon. It was a constant reminder to her of the virtue in Mifuné's heart. In addition, he had developed a relationship with each of them. Their master edified them, not just with their power or skills, but as people. He instructed them on the principles he lived by, and the code to which he was honor bound to adhere. Naomi admired that about him, they all did.

Carl Houston Roach IV

Rather than continue down the long cylinder of stairs, Naomi grabbed the rope Desmond had tethered to a low point in the ceiling of the main chamber and slid down to the floor below. As exhilarating as she found using all those stairs, she preferred to spend her time elsewhere. She decided to join Gabrysia to see what she was up to.

Just as she had mentioned to her Master, Gabrysia was outside meditating in the heat of the midday sun. Naomi noticed the ground her fellow student sat upon seemed extraordinarily level and she was focused, as if she was in another world. Gabrysia did not sweat, even with the heat of the day bearing down on her. She had been deeply engaged honing her magic since before dawn.

Gabrysia was dressed in a black leather figure-fitting cuirass and long pants. Her arms donned a set of vambraces that matched the pair of greaves that covered her shins. Gabrysia could sense Naomi grow closer as she walked casually over to her. Naomi sat in front of Gabrysia, and she decided it was time for a rest. There was a significant change in Gabrysia's power. Before, Naomi had told Mifuné she could hardly sense it, however in that moment, she was nearly suffocated by it. She could even see a gleaming sphere of cerulean aura that flowed around her friend.

"Gabrysia, it seems you have been busy today."

Gabrysia placed her hands on her knees and oriented her head at Naomi. The shining magical energy that enveloped her vanished immediately. "There you are! I thought you were going to spend all day in the tower. Did you talk to Master?"

The Fall of Avalon

"I did."

"So, is it finally beginning, after all this time?"

"Yes, I think so. He said he spoke to the Queen. I imagine that means he gave his warning."

"Well, what else did he say? When do we make our next move?"

"That, he did not say."

Gabrysia sighed. "Well, he is a man of few words. Maybe he still has to process the fact that he saw the Queen again."

"A man of few words? Are we talking about Master again?!" a voice shouted from the distance.

A dark-skinned young man with short, curly black hair approached from just over the hill. He wore a black, sleeveless, leather tunic over long, dark pants. Slung over his flexed arm was a net full of fish, freshly caught from the river. Plenty to feed them all for the rest of the day. He smiled as he approached, as if he did not have a care in the world.

"I do not think that is enough fish, Desmond!" Gabrysia shouted.

"Yeah, I agree. You should go back and get more!" Naomi chimed in.

The two young women laughed heartily as their compatriot closed the distance between them. He mockingly imitated their laughter in a high-pitched fashion and bobbed his head from side to side. He persisted by imitating their speech in the same tone, but unintelligibly and incoherently. This only encouraged the young women's laughter further.

"Here I thought you two were hard at work, but as usual, I am the only one taking my training seriously," he jibed. He dropped the net of fish beside Gabrysia.

"Good sir, I will have you know that I have been taking my training very seriously!" Gabrysia retorted, sounding mockingly offended.

"Oh, is that so?" Desmond replied, planting his fists on his hips.

"As a matter of fact, I have been storing power since dawn, while a certain someone still had drool staining his pillow."

"Hey!" Desmond exclaimed, taking a seat between Naomi and Gabrysia, "I do not drool, as you so repugnantly suggest."

"Ooh! What a big word, Desmond. Looks like what Master has been teaching you is taking hold," Naomi jested.

"Clear the way for Lord Desmond!" Gabrysia laughed.

"What makes you so certain I learned that word from Master?"

The two ladies glanced at one another and sneered. "Spell it," Naomi snickered.

"Um…R…e…p... ugh! Never mind!"

Naomi and Gabrysia erupted with more laughter as Desmond hung his head. He smiled still. That was the nature of things. It had always been the way amongst the three of them. If true friends could not jest with one another, what was the point of living? Desmond joined in the laughter before getting back up to prepare the fish.

"Well some of us are not so fortunate to be gifted with magic. Tapping into one's Aikido takes training, skill, and focus," Desmond said.

The Fall of Avalon

"That is the power that Master uses, is it not?" Gabrysia asked.

"Yes," Desmond replied. "What he has been teaching me, is that the greatest of warriors who manage to overcome their own weaknesses, both body and soul, and become one with themselves, can channel their Aikido and do incredible things."

"Is that why you cannot use it?" Naomi sneered.

"Very funny, but I will have you know, Master says he thinks I am close to unlocking my Aikido. I can feel it, too. I can feel it—this power swirling inside of me the more I train."

"I know the feeling, Des," Gabrysia replied. "That is what magic is like, at least for me."

"So, Naomi, have you managed to practice anything this morning?" Desmond asked, tossing fish bones into the bushes behind him. "Or were you too busy fantasizing about Master?"

"I do not fantasize about anything, Desmond!" Naomi shouted. Her face flushed red. Instinctively, she seized her hood and closed it over her face. Is it bad enough that I am struggling with my feelings towards Master, and now it was obvious to the others, she mused.

"Well, that answers that," Gabrysia said, standing up to stretch.

"Answers what?" Naomi replied nervously from beneath her hood.

"I, Gabrysia, formerly of the House Tallhar, do hereby accept your confession," Gabrysia declared as ceremoniously as possible.

"You know, Naomi," Desmond began, "there is no shame in it, if you do."

Carl Houston Roach IV

"What do you mean?" Naomi replied, muffled through her hood.

"He is one of the greatest warriors in the world, if not the best. He is a kind man, to those he lets in. And... he is a fine man. I do not know what kind of man the Queen chose over our Master, but I do not see how he can compare." Gabrysia interjected.

"You know, I understand that. I suppose I should be more surprised if you did not have some kind of a fantasy about him. I imagine even Gabrysia has her own thoughts and feelings about dear old Master," Desmond jested.

"I admit to nothing, Desmond!"

"Come on," he persisted. "The way you just talked about him compares to how I talk about the women I have chased. You cannot deny you have, at least once, had thoughts and feelings?"

"Shove it, Des!" Gabrysia laughed, pushing him away from her.

From high atop the tower, Mifuné watched his three young disciples play about. He longed for days like that. The days when life was simple, when life was easy, and everything made sense. Once Mifuné had completed his training, when he finally stood before Argus Nox, not as a disciple, but as a fellow Master, they often had days where they would jest and jab with one another. They would share food and drink, and they would plan their next adventure for the future. The sting in his chest reminded him every day that those days were long gone. The sword he held fast in his grip served as a constant reminder that any chance of living a life like the three of his students was lost to him, taken from him by the one he had sworn to protect.

The fun began to settle down, and an ominous feeling, like a specter in the night, nestled into each of their souls. The group fell morbidly silent. The thought of cooked fish and salted rice was no longer appealing. Their eyes sank to the soft grass beneath them, grass that might soon be burned to ash.

"So, this is really happening?" Desmond asked.

"The man is nothing, if he is not a man of his word," Gabrysia replied.

"Are you really okay with helping him tear down an entire civilization? A lot of people are going to die…" Desmond said again.

"I don't have much choice," Gabrysia replied. "Returning to my family's graces from exile affords me few options. I do not like it much, but Avalon has never exactly been a friend to Eramar or House Tallhar during our long histories."

"And that justifies you helping Master kill all those people, even the innocent ones?" Desmond asked.

"I did not say that, Des." Gabrysia's tone was terse. A scowl twisted her face. Her eyes were sunken, and her spirit had waned. She exhaled audibly and lowered her chin to rest on her forearms. "Well what about you? Since you seem so sure…"

Desmond's eyes dimmed. His voice was heavy, and his heart weighed on him. The gravity of the situation he had placed himself in so willingly was now becoming inescapably clear. He searched for the words to say to rebuke Gabrysia. He could only muster up: "I do not know."

"Desmond, Gabrysia..." Naomi spoke up. "Neither of you have to do this. You can still walk away. Master is a good man. He will understand. He would not ask you to follow him where you do not want to go."

Gabrysia stood up and walked beside Naomi. Some light had returned to her eyes. She caringly placed a hand on Naomi's shoulder and offered her as genuine a smile as she could offer. Desmond got up from his sitting place and did the same.

"No matter what happens, we are in this together," Gabrysia reassured her.

"It might get ugly," Desmond admitted, "but there is nothing we cannot do if we stick together."

Naomi stood up with them. She placed each of her hands on theirs and smiled in return. For Desmond and Gabrysia to stay beside her in the face of the malicious retribution their Master intended for the city was a testament of loyalty Naomi had never experienced in her young life. She could see no lies or reservations in their eyes.

"No one on this world has ever had better friends than I have found in you," Naomi said.

"Naturally," Desmond sneered proudly. "Besides, if I left, the three of you would never eat." Gabrysia and Naomi laughed and pushed him away. "I mean it! The two of you never cook. I doubt Master even knows how..."

֍

In the Ivory Palace of Avalon, Queen Titania lay beside Virgil. The heated, stirring passion and

The Fall of Avalon

physical bliss had settled, and they lay there in that moment, naked, on the carpeted floor. Virgil stroked her cheek gently with his thumb. Though the Queen looked into his eyes with a happy demeanor, he could sense she was still afraid. He felt ashamed of himself for failing to defeat Mifuné the previous night. He broke eye contact with her and looked away.

"What is it?" she spoke softly, caressing his handsome face with her hand.

"I failed you, last night. I should have stopped him, but I did not."

"You did your best, love. You did all that you could."

"He could have killed you. He could have taken you away from me."

Titania pulled his head against her breast and held him close to her. She kissed the top of his forehead and stroked his hair down to the back of his neck. She felt his grip at her back tighten. Softly, the Queen whispered into his ear: "I am okay. And I am here with you now." She continued to hold him like that, as she had many nights before. She could feel his spirit ease.

Virgil pulled his head away and looked into her eyes. "I vow this to you now, my love. I will defeat the Samurai. He will never set foot in this palace ever again."

Titania kissed his lips tenderly, cradling the back of his head. Before saying another word, she stood up and recovered her gown. He watched as she dressed herself again, captivated by her serene beauty. Her petite figure with such generous proportions called to him every day and night. He waited until her frock was fully adorned to get up and dress himself.

"My darling, I do not know if even you can defeat him," the Queen confessed.

The Queen's words stung his heart like a poison tipped arrow. "What do you mean?" Virgil asked as he contended with the pain of her insult.

"You are a descendant of Arthur. His blood runs through your veins. And from him, just as the many Paladins before you, you inherited the Light of the Paladin, the source of your great power." the Queen continued. "You became the Paladin when you awakened the light,"

"Yes, I know that."

"What you do not know is, around the time Arthur was Paladin of Avalon, there was a man named Himimaru Tahaka. Few people knew his name, because most people called him the Dragon Emperor. He was the leader of the Lotus Tribe, and they were protected by the Lotus Order."

"Why are you telling me this? Who was he?" Virgil asked.

"He was a man even Arthur could not defeat. He was a man whose strength and skill set him apart from all others. And his blood flows through Mifuné's veins." Titania sighed. "And though I hate to admit it, Mifuné lives up to his lineage. Before he left Avalon to face the Ravana years ago, Mifuné was the greatest disciple of Argus Nox. No one in Avalon was a match for him."

"Who was Argus?" Virgil asked. "Why have I not known about any of this?"

The Fall of Avalon

"Argus was my advisor before you became the Paladin. Last of the line of Merlin, and the most powerful sorcerer in Androma. He was the one who led the Company of Heroes that fought Ravana. There was even a time I considered marrying him. But he would have had me relinquish my throne to him. That, I would never have done."

"This man trained Mifuné, and Mifuné…"

"Became the greatest swordsman since Arthur. He was best known for his unbelievable speed and striking power. I witnessed it first-hand. He was the perfect candidate for Paladin when we did not have one."

"If he has returned, then that means he did slay Ravana. He was strong enough to defeat one of the Lords of Evil. If that is true, he may even be stronger than Arthur ever was," Virgil thought aloud.

"I thought the same thing. And that is why I do not want you to fight him," Queen Titania said.

"If I do not, he will come back."

"He will come back anyway. No one can stop him." The Queen began to sob. "I have failed my people. I cannot protect them!"

Virgil marched to her side. He turned her to him. He cupped her face with his hands and wiped away her tears as they fell.

"You have not failed anyone. We have not lost yet. And if that man thinks he can threaten the woman I love, he has made a grave mistake."

Queen Titania could see determination in Virgil's eyes as she had never seen in him before. The challenge Mifuné presented to him made his

Carl Houston Roach IV

body yearn for battle. The threat Mifuné posed to the Queen, and his life with her, lit a fire in his heart. She could feel the power of the Paladin coursing through him as she traced her fingers down the side of his face.

"Last time we fought, he got lucky. He will not be so fortunate next time." Virgil avowed adamantly.

The Queen did not speak. She only looked up into his endearing, shimmering emerald eyes. She absorbed that moment, taking in everything she could: the feeling of his hand on her waist; his gentle touch on her face; the softness of his skin; the sweetness of his voice. She studied him in that moment, memorizing every last detail of her lover, as if it were to be the last time she would see him again.

"Let us go," she said just above a whisper.

The Fall of Avalon

An army of hundreds marched against him. Alone, they could not hold back his wrath. He felled them like wheat in a field.

The sun neared the final leg of its descent through the sky as the second day drew to an end. Queen Titania made her way to the balcony of the palace that overlooked the courtyard, with Colabion in tow. Her General, four knights, and her militant advisor, lined the gold painted railing, and waited for her. She stepped out to the edge, placed both of her hands gracefully on the rail, and scanned the courtyard below. Rows upon rows of heavily armored soldiers had formed ranks prior to the Queen's arrival. Each carried with him a scutum in his right hand, or a targe, bearing the crest of Avalon. Each odd numbered row carried in his left hand a black iron pike twice his height. Each man in the even number rows carried a long bow that rivaled his height. Every man's belt held a sword. They wore heavy steel armor, purposed for front line battlefield operations. The style of armor had been tested against heavy axe swings, bludgeoning from morning stars and war hammers, and strikes from the sharpest of swords. Each man and his equipment tested true time and time again. This assembled force impressed even Virgil.

At the forefront of this mass of troops were two warriors on horseback: a man of strong stature and

Carl Houston Roach IV

build. Dusty brown hair sat coifed upon his head. He donned armor akin to that of the knights of Avalon – sterling silver, lightweight but sturdy. Though he was in the prime of his youth, no more than thirty years of age, his eyes seemed hardened by the art of battle. Beside him was a woman. Her armor matched his in style and resilience, though it possessed more feminine qualities. She seemed much more excited than the man beside her. It appeared that a battle was going on in her own mind between excitement for this assignment and her military bearing.

Behind the garrison of soldiers, the citizens of Avalon were gathered as well. They seemed frightened and confused in mass. Many communed amongst themselves and speculated as to the purpose for the noteworthy muster of soldiers. The look in some of their eyes said that they knew, or at least, they thought they knew what was going on.

"Behold, my Queen," the General began, "our finest troops from the city's defense, as well as the strongest men we could assemble from the countryside."

Colabion beamed as bright as the sun above, hearing this news. He smiled ear to ear as he surveyed the small army gathered below. He staved off the urge to hang over the rails of the balcony, fore a garrison of such quality and potential had never been assembled for his, or his wife's service, in his time as King Consort. He was like a child who had held his father's sword for the first time.

"How many, General?" Titania asked.

"Five-hundred strong."

The Fall of Avalon

"Five-hundred seems a bit... excessive, General," the advisor chimed in.

"No," Titania interjected. "It may not be enough."

Her grave tone sent chills down their spines. The small group surrounding her could not comprehend how just one man could pose a threat to a militant group that magnitude.

"Even if he did defeat the dreaded Ravana seven years ago," the advisor retorted, "no single man, besides the Paladin of Avalon, could contend with an army of hundreds, especially an army such as this."

"My love, how can you say this?" Colabion asked, placing a hand on her shoulder.

The General dismissed her concerns and stepped forward. "Worry not, your Majesty. My troops will dispatch this man and set your fears at ease. They are being led by Captain Lysander, my personal protégé, and Lieutenant Riley, his second in command. He will not fail you."

There was air of pride in the General's voice. The Queen found it reminiscent of the way Argus once spoke of Mifuné. She could not stop her thoughts from transitioning to the days when it was Argus standing beside her, assuring her that things would be okay. During those times, Mifuné would have been the one down below, readying troops for battle, raising the morale, and marching off to destroy her enemies. Argus always had the answers, the strategies, and the technical knowledge to address and resolve any situation with which he was confronted. Beside him, Mifuné had the skill and the power to eliminate any threat that stood against him. Argus was gone, fallen prey to the Ravana. The Queen could still scarcely believe that, now, Mifuné was the enemy troops were being assembled against. It was truly a nightmare.

Queen Titania steeled herself. All eyes were on her. She could show no signs of weakness. She could not allow her soldiers–or her people–to see that she was afraid. No matter what she believed the outcome would be, her men needed to believe that she believed in them. She took in a deep breath and spoke, "People of Avalon, hear my voice! I stand before you, not only as your Queen, not only as the leader of Avalon, but as a citizen of this great country. A country that has been threatened by a dangerous, powerful man, who will stop at nothing to see our glorious civilization reduced to ash and dust. I will not hide the truth from you. The rumors you may have heard are true. The lion at our doorstep today is named Mifuné Tahaka. Seven years ago, this warrior slayed Ravana, one of the twelve Lords of Evil."

Murmuring and whispers arose out of the garrison. The crowd of civilians stirred. They were frightened, she could see it in their eyes. Queen Titania allowed them a moment to have the truth sink in, so that they might realize the reality of their situation.

"The fight ahead of us will be a difficult one. Some of you may even think it impossible to achieve victory. Hear me when I say this. All throughout Avalon's history, we have faced evils that threatened to swallow us into the ultimate

The Fall of Avalon

depths of blackness from which there is no escape; time and time again, it is you, our soldiers, who carry the mantle; who rise to the occasion and fight back! It is you, the soldiers, who preserve our lands! It is you, the soldiers, who possess the fighting spirit of Avalon!"

The soldiers cheered at the Queen's words. Some even thrust their spears in the air and shook them. A feeling of valor surged among them, and infected them with a sense of pride that defied the situation they found themselves in. Even the civilians behind them were moved.

"To my loyal subjects, fear not. This garrison of soldiers are the finest in all of Avalon. And with them, the Paladin of Avalon shall march. Their combined strength shall make safe this city and make safe this nation!"

The people cheered at the Queen's words. They threw fists into the air, garments, flowers, whatever was light that was on hand. Titania's face was unmoved, despite their praise. In one voice, their cries rang out, "Hail to the Queen! Hail to the Queen!"

"Soldiers, take your fighting spirit, gird your hearts with it, and vanquish this enemy, for victory and glory! For love and family! For all that you hold dear! Soldiers, to battle!" Titania, the Queen of Avalon, proclaimed and raised a fist into the air.

The soldiers cheered mightily at Queen Titania's words. They struck the butts of their spears against the ground rhythmically, like a war drum. Some bashed their vambraces against their shields in tempo with the spears striking the ground.

Carl Houston Roach IV

All cheered. All were motivated. All were prepared to fight.

"That was quite the speech, your Majesty," her advisor said.

"Your faith is not misplaced, your Majesty. My soldiers will return with Mifuné's body in tow. You will see," the General said, stepping beside his Queen.

Colabion led Titania away from the balcony and back into the hall, where Virgil was waiting, poised and prepared for anything. He noticed her attention immediately went to Virgil as if he was not even there, evidence enough to him that her fears on this matter had not been settled. From behind her, he took hold of her bare arms as gently as he was able and pulled her against him.

"You need not be afraid any longer, my love. By nightfall, they will arrive at the Tower, and in the morning, everything will be as it was."

Colabion's touch consoled her. Though she had not fully given her heart to him, his touch always seemed to calm her fears. She leaned her head back against his chest. She could feel his chin rest on the top of her head. His hands caressed her arms, and his fingers interlocked and released with hers. Her heart fluttered every time he would do this with her. Even this could not prevent a tear that freed itself from her eyes. His love was not a force that could protect her from what lay just outside their doorstep.

"My dearest love," she whispered to him, "there is much you still do not understand."

The Fall of Avalon

Colabion turned his wife so that she faced him. Seeing the tear that had stained her face, he brushed it away from her cheek gently with his thumb. She gripped his hand with both of hers and kissed it softly. He wrapped his free arm over her and held her close. She nearly melted into him. The back of his hand brushed the side of her face caringly.

"Tell me what it is that I can do to take away your fears. Anything, and it shall be done."

Queen Titania looked up into her husband's eyes. Earnest brown eyes stared back down into hers. No matter what plagued her mind, he was always there to do what he could. Though he had no prowess in battle—no great skill at anything for that matter, he always made her feel safe. She knew he would do anything for her. She also knew, that, in that instance, there was nothing he could do. She shook her head in silence. Rather than turn from him, the Queen reached her face up towards his and pressed her lips against his. Fire ignited in her heart, as well as his. He cupped the small of her back with one hand and ran his fingers through her silky hair with the other. She wrapped her arms behind his neck as they continued their embrace of the lips.

Virgil watched on, the image of the perfect sentinel. His countenance was stone, his composure iron; yet within himself, he felt his heart bleed, as if a knife had stabbed it. He could hold her to no fault, though. The man before him was her husband, after all. Virgil had sworn to protect Colabion just the same as he had sworn to protect the Queen, the day he had become the Paladin. To see them like this, though, was almost more than he could bear.

58

Carl Houston Roach IV

At the end of their passionate moment, Queen Titania looked into the eyes of her husband. In that moment, she was convinced Colabion could be right, that when her fears were resolved, life would return to the way it was the previous day; the way she had always been. He could see she intended to say something, but The Queen hesitated. With a look only, Colabion assured her whatever it was she wanted to say, he would hear it.

"Colabion, I love you with all my heart, but this is not something you can protect me from." The Queen cupped his cheek with her petite hand. "This battle is mine to fight. I need you to let me do this."

Without another word, Queen Titania slid slowly away from him. Colabion kept his grip loosely around her hand, as long as he could, before she slipped away. All he could do then was watch as she hurried away from him to prepare her next move. Virgil followed her, confident that his power was sufficient to her needs. Colabion knew this. A spark of rage rose up in his heart. He took to one of the hallways opposite the direction of Queen Titania's path and vanished into the palace.

Virgil proceeded down the stairs away from Titania without permission or request to leave. His heart beat like a warm drum, louder with each step. His valor churned within his mighty chest at the chance to prove his might against his worthy adversary.

"Where do you think you are going?" Queen Titania asked. Her voice was ice.

"To join the Garrison, as you said. I am going with them to fight Mifuné."

The Fall of Avalon

"You are not going anywhere, Virgil."

Virgil turned his head and scoffed. "You know as well as I do, those 500 men will not be enough to defeat the man that I faced last night."

Virgil was still haunted by his humiliating defeat at Mifuné's hands. He fell upon Virgil as quickly as the night overtakes the day. Before Virgil could even draw his sword, Mifuné had beaten him down and flung him off the wall surrounding the citadel. Virgil could hardly process what had happened before he struck the ground and fell unconscious.

"No." The Queen turned and faced Virgil. Her face now mirrored the grave tone in her voice. "If they stand and fight, they will all die."

"Then with your permission, let me go with them. They will need my help."

"No. I need you here with me."

"Those are our soldiers. Our countrymen. I cannot just stand by when I know that we are sending them to their doom!"

Virgil had never sounded so intense. He had always spoken softly with his Queen. He had never demonstrated such command or presence to her. In a way, it impressed her. Alas his attitude in conjunction with the attitudes of her advisors and Generals being so dismissive of her concerns began to frustrate her.

"Do not be coy with me, Virgil. This is not about the wellbeing of the soldiers or the opinions of the council and the General."

"What are you talking about?"

Carl Houston Roach IV

"You feel ashamed of yourself because you did not defeat Mifuné the first time you fought. You are the Paladin. You have a responsibility here, just as much as I do. We cannot afford to lose you. Let it go and do as I say!"

Virgil stepped off the stairs and faced her. His face resembled the sky during a storm. His brow was tense. His teeth clenched behind his sealed lips. His hands had balled into fists. Queen Titania could faintly sense heat coming off him. The queen remained steady where she stood.

"Is that all that I am to you, your Majesty? Am I a dog in chains for you to let loose at your convenience?" Virgil asked indignantly.

"Why would you say something like that?" the Queen protested.

"I wish to defend you, yet you stay my hand. I say that I love you, and you in kind say that you love me. Yet you can so easily display your affection for another man in front of me, as though I were not there."

"Another man that is my *husband*, Virgil!" the Queen correct. "That is not something we need concern ourselves with right now. Avalon is faced with the greatest threat since my father Oberon turned against my mother and began the War of the Fae! The war that all but wiped out my kind! And you worry over the little man who clings to me like ice clings to tree bark in the winter?"

"No, Titania. I worry that I have merely become an instrument for you to use and stow as you please."

"How can you say that?"

61

The Fall of Avalon

"How easy it must be for you to ask me that, being surrounded by countless men who adore you. Not a single one of them does for you what I do for you every day! Yet, I am last of any of them!"

Before Virgil could say another word, he felt his Queen's lips connect with his. A wave of love and affection washed over him, taking with it his animosity and rage. The kiss was short, but enough to bring him back to his senses.

"Virgil, everything I have told you is true. I know you desire more than anything for us to be together, but the time is not yet right." The Queen took his hands in hers. "I am asking simply that you be patient with me only a little longer. I have faith that, when this is over, you will be victorious. You will stand above your fallen enemy, and they shall call you the Hero of Avalon, even greater than Arthur. And on that day, you and I can be together, just as my mother and Arthur were. Can you wait, just a little longer, my love?"

Virgil released her hands and knelt before the Queen of Avalon. Though his heart stirred for her, he tempered his desires once again, in order to fight for the newfound hope, she had instilled him. Upon his bended knee, he looked up into her eyes and said: "It shall be as you say."

Queen Titania placed her finger against his right cheek. "You must go to your tower. Wait there until tomorrow. Then come to The Queen's Chamber."

"Yes, my Queen."

࿓

Outside the palace, Captain Lysander marched the troops outside of the city toward the Tower of

Carl Houston Roach IV

Galahad. From atop his horse, he observed his garrison. Pride beamed forth from him like the amber rays of the evening sun. No greater moment had presented itself to him in his military career than to command such an impressive force on a mission of such tremendous importance. Beside him rode Lieutenant Riley, a woman of small stature, but fearsome fighting ability.

This would be her first combat deployment in her career, and she could not have been more excited. She knew Captain Lysander and his reputation for battlefield tactics. He was an inspiration to her throughout her training. While riding beside him, she could not keep herself from smiling.

Lysander had broken the troops into two companies which he and Riley would command. Riley was to remain in the rear with her company, only moving to reinforce as needed. Though she would have preferred a more active role in the battle, she still considered it an honor to have command over half of the force.

"Welcome back Riley," Captain Lysander greeted the Lieutenant. "How was the honeymoon?"

"It was beautiful Captain, like a fairytale," she beamed.

"You chose well. He is a good man." He stated confidently. "You returned early, did you not?"

"Yes sir, but when I heard the call to arms I had to leave. My husband understood my duties to Avalon comes first."

"As expected of one of Avalon's finest."

The Fall of Avalon

Riley sat proud in the saddle and rode along for a moment before continuing, "Captain, how do you think this battle will fair?"

"Difficult to say, Lieutenant. The way Queen Titania spoke of this man, especially if he is who I think he is, we will have our work cut out for us."

"And who is that, sir?"

"Mifuné Tahaka. He was supposed to be unbeatable, at least in swordsmanship. He was a master of a lost sword style, the Dragon Emperor's Sword, I think it was called. And he was the last disciple of Master Argus Nox."

"I do not really know who that is either."

"That does not surprise me. You are young. He was the greatest military leader in the history of Avalon. I served under him when I first became a soldier. You have never known a man with such command presence. When he spoke, you knew it was going to be as he said. When this is over, you should read over his works in the archives. It would be enlightening for you."

"I will, sir. So, this Mifuné, have you ever seen him before?"

"I want to say I met him, at least once, when I was a Sergeant."

"What was he like?" Riley inquired further.

"He was fast, unbelievably so. His strikes were precise. Even if he fought against a group, nobody could touch him. It was as if he could read everyone's movements before they even happened. I have never seen anything like it."

Carl Houston Roach IV

"Do you really believe it could be possible that this one man slayed Ravana those years ago Captain?"

"I do not believe a man could defeat something like Ravana, the Lord of Chaos. The ancient writings tell us that he was a titanic monster that created the demons; that possessed unmatched wisdom of Arcane Arts, magics and the like, as well as mastery over any and every kind of weapon. No one man could defeat that alone. Perhaps Mifuné felled Ravana, but not before the Company of Heroes had sufficiently weakened it first."

"Yes, that makes sense to me. Then this unmatched power of his…."

"Is likely nothing more than pure superstition Lieutenant. I see no reason why we cannot accomplish this task with the force that we have been provided. Especially if we have Virgil as a reinforcement."

"Why is he not marching out with us? That is a bit odd, would you agree?"

"Riley, the thing about Virgil, the man loves to make an entrance. He will catch up."

"Would it be more favorable for us to set up an encampment and wait for him, or will we stage our attack first?"

"We will begin our attack as soon as we arrive. I assured the General we would return by daybreak."

"Yes sir."

Riley noticed a small bird sailing overhead through the air: a red lark with white feathers on its underbelly. She raised an eyebrow at the sight. That type of bird was exceedingly rare in that region, especially in the midsummer season. Watching the bird soar over the garrison filled her with hope.

"Captain, I think fortune is with us," Riley grinned.

Unknown to them, the bird belonged to Naomi. Using her magic, she could see through the bird's eyes. She observed all that the bird saw: the soldiers, their weapons, their numbers, and their leaders. She smiled to see how much of a threat Mifuné posed to the civilization that claimed to stand above all others.

"You will not believe the response she had to your threat, Master!" Naomi giggled.

"How many?" Mifuné asked. His arms were folded over his chest, and his voice was low.

"It looks to be a few hundred, not including the Captain and Lieutenant. They have pikemen, archers, heavy infantrymen, and every one of them is carrying a sword."

Mifuné scoffed and said nothing else. Desmond and Gabrysia could not help but sense that Mifuné felt insulted. The look on his face told it all. His eyes rolled in such a way that begged the question: Could she not be bothered to send her full strength against him?

"What about the Paladin? Is he with them?" Desmond asked.

Naomi scanned through the army one last time as the last of the light sank beneath the horizon. "No, I do not think so."

"The Queen would not send him now. Not in the first attack," Mifuné said.

"Why, Master?" Desmond asked.

Carl Houston Roach IV

"She knows he lacks the strength to defeat me, and therefore she is biding her time."

"She thinks she can weaken you, Master?" Gabrysia asked.

"The best way to remove a mountain from your path is one stone at a time. Argus taught me that, long ago. I have no doubt she learned the same."

"So that is her strategy then? Force you to fight to diminish your strength so that the Paladin can finish you off before you can follow through with your threat?" Naomi asked.

"Titania is a master manipulator. She believes she knows my strengths and my weaknesses, as well as those of the ones who serve her."

"Nevertheless, she does not know your strength, does she?" Gabrysia asked.

An ominous wind swept over the encampment. It brushed the loose sleeves of Mifuné's garb with it. The area suddenly felt cold, like ice. Gabrysia she could see her breath. Each disciple tensed as Mifuné's grip tightened around the handle of his sword. "She has no idea the power I possess." Chills went down their spines. He had never sounded so murderous.

"And that is what tonight is about, is it not? To show her the power of your Aikido," Desmond added.

"No. Tonight will be just a taste, for her, and for you."

Each of the three disciples went silent. Those words he said only validated that he knew of their doubts. The faintest feeling of shame rose up out of each of them. It would taste a lie for any of them to say they did not have at least a touch of doubt that their Master was as powerful as he claimed to be.

"There is no need to blame yourselves, my young disciples. For none of you have seen, but tonight you shall." Mifuné cast his gaze away from the three and towards the horizon from which the army marched. "And so, will she."

Mifuné sat cross-legged with them in a circle. All of them fixed their gaze on him. He seemed so calm, so sure of himself, while simultaneously having no condemnation for them. He raised up his hand and extended and extended it to Desmond. "Desmond, please prepare a fire for us. I suspect it will be cold tonight."

"Yes, Master," Desmond replied.

He darted into the woods to collect suitable firewood. While he did this, Mifuné looked intently to Naomi and Gabrysia. "I have a task for you two."

"I will do whatever you ask of me to the best of my abilities, Master," Gabrysia said.

"Whatever you need of me, I will do, Master," Naomi replied.

Mifuné nodded to their earnest answers. He softly said to them, "I need you to protect me tonight."

Their eyes widened at this request. Mifuné was the mightiest swordsman in the realm. He was strong enough to best the Paladin of Avalon, with no aid. He was insulted by the notion of fighting 500 soldiers by himself. What protection could they provide for him that he could not provide for himself?

Carl Houston Roach IV

"While I am fighting, I have no doubt the Captain will have his rear linemen loose volleys of arrows to strike me down from afar. I cannot deflect these while I am fighting the linemen. I will need you to shield me from the arrows. Can you do that for me?"

"Yes, Master!" they answered excitedly.

"Master!" Desmond called, finally emerging from the wood line. In his possession, he carried a bountiful bundle of logs and sticks suitable for burning, as well as a bundle of twigs for kindling. "What will my task be for the battle?"

Mifuné chuckled at Desmond's eagerness. "You, Desmond, will have the most important role of all."

"What is it?" he asked as he prepared the fireplace.

He set the thinner pieces of wood in a carefully linked stack like a cone. Naomi sent out a small stream of fire that ignited the kindling. As the cone burned to coals, Desmond began to diligently place the larger pieces of wood and logs atop the coals. He watched carefully, making sure the coals were not smothered by the wood.

"You shall be my voice this night. You will deliver my message to the warriors descending upon us."

The weight of that request sat upon Desmond like the weight of the thick logs upon the burning twigs beneath. He could not bring himself to speak to his master's request. He had never spoken on someone's behalf before, save his own. He had only

The Fall of Avalon

ever spoken as a thief to a store holder, or a prisoner to a judge.

"Master, how can I speak for you? I am not a great warrior like you are. What message could I deliver that they would listen to me?"

"You can speak for me, my disciple. You are more than what you believe yourself to be."

"What will I say to them?"

"I will teach you what to say. And when you speak, speak as though my sword is in your hand. As though my strength is yours to command. Do not tremble. Do not run."

"Will I be on the battlefield with you?"

"Yes." Mifuné placed his hand on the young man's shoulder. "You have my solemn word as a warrior, I will not allow any harm to reach you." His gaze turned to Gabrysia and Naomi sitting across from him. "Any of you."

Desmond clenched a fist tightly. "What is it you want me say, Master?"

Mifuné looked into Desmond's eyes intensely. "Listen closely."

❧

As the moon reached the precipice of its ascent through the Western to Eastern sky, Captain Lysander and his garrison arrived at the Tower of Galahad. Riley looked upon the mighty stone tower, and her heart sank. She imagined that, at one point in its history, the tower must have been a mighty stronghold, yet now, it was a monument of the past only, overgrown with moss and ivy. She wondered silently if that was why the enemy had chosen this place.

Carl Houston Roach IV

Captain Lysander kept his forces at a safe distance, in case of ambush or an open volley of arrows. A sizeable fire burned in the open, yet no one sat around it. There was no one anywhere to be seen.

"Where are they?" Riley asked, scanning the darkness for any signs of life.

"I do not know. Be on your guard," he said quietly to her. "Front line, shields up!"

A row of fifty soldiers raised their suctums up and covered themselves completely. A wall of solid metal was formed. From small gaps between the shields, black, iron pikes extended forward. Behind them, archers prepared arrows in their slings. Behind them, swordsmen drew their blades and prepared to charge at a moment's notice.

"Mifuné Tahaka, come forth! Let justice fall upon you for your crimes against Avalon!" the Captain demanded.

The frontline soldiers peered through the eyeholes of their shields for any signs of movement. The world in front of them, save the whipping fire beside the tower, was still as a graveyard.

"First Company, forward!" Lysander commanded.

The army advanced towards the fire beside the tower. A chilling wind swept over them, kissing the sweat at their faces and necks. Something was not right. Each man desperately scanned through the darkness to find something, anything, they could prepare themselves for. Then, something came into view; something small, and far away. A young man stood in the path of their advance. The light of the

The Fall of Avalon

fire behind him barely illuminated him. He wore no armor. He carried no weapon.

Realizing this, Captain Lysander called as loud as he could: "Halt!"

"Soldiers of Avalon, my name is Desmond Ul'rukk, Disciple of Mifuné Tahaka! I stand before you to speak on behalf of my Master!"

Captain Lysander was taken aback by the apparent authority in the young man's voice. He rode to the front of the formation, leaving behind Lieutenant Riley, to address the man speaking to them.

"Who are you that thinks he can speak to a Captain of Avalon, boy?!" Lysander replied.

"My Master has agreed to spare your lives and release you should you renounce your loyalty to the false queen and leave the doomed city of Avalon forever!"

"Tell me, who is your Master to make such claims but a relic swordsman from a generation of the dead?!"

"Soldiers! You will not be held accountable for the actions of your leaders should you decide to leave. You, your families, and your loved ones shall be spared. The choice is yours. So sayeth Mifuné Tahaka!"

Captain Lysander turned his head over his shoulder. None of his soldiers had moved a muscle in retreat. They all remained behind him, behind their Queen, in service to their country. The Captain sneered as he cast his gaze back to Desmond.

"Your master is a blasphemous fool, boy! Tonight, he will eat his words, and drink them with his blood." The Captain drew his long sword, which shimmered from the glint cast by the fire, and raised it up over his head. "Forward! Take back the tower!" he ordered. The soldiers continued their march on the tower at a quickened pace.

"Hold your position!" Riley shouted to the Second Company. She watched eagerly, keeping her attention fixed on the Captain, waiting to see how the battle would unfold. She could not explain it, but something was wrong. Their adversary was nowhere to be found, yet he claimed he would be present.

Desmond remained where he stood as the oncoming tide of armored soldiers drew near. His face showed no sign of terror. Not an ounce of fear. His Master's promise echoed in his head: No harm shall come to you. "No harm shall come to you," he said aloud. He closed his eyes as the distinct sound of an arrow being loosed from a string whistled through the air.

There was another sound, like metal pinging against metal. Desmond's eyes opened to the sight of his Master slashing the arrow out of the air just before it could pierce Desmond's heart. Mifuné then positioned himself between Desmond and the approaching army. Desmond was awestruck by the feat Mifuné had just displayed. Something told him that was only the beginning. There was no time to revel.

"Get ready," Mifuné whispered over his shoulder to Desmond.

Desmond drew his sword and stood behind his master. He held his sword in reverse in his left

The Fall of Avalon

hand. The blade aligned along the back of his arm. He observed the situation carefully, as Mifuné had taught him, waiting for his moment to strike.

Mifuné crossed his sword horizontally in front of himself. His stance widened until his feet were shoulder-width apart. He watched the approaching soldiers from over the edge of his blade patiently. He could almost see the whites of their eyes through the eyeholes in their shields.

Desmond's thoughts circled through his head as he watched Mifuné. If he was going to act, he needed to do so, soon. It would not be long until the garrison overran the tower. His composure was beginning to wane. His sword slightly shook in his hand.

"Archers!" Lysander called out, "Loose!" He swung his sword down through the air as he gave his command.

Hundreds of arrows soared through the night sky, invisible in the darkness. They arced in the sky well past the linemen and descended upon Mifuné and Desmond like a plague of locust to a field of wheat. Before they were riddled with arrows, a brilliant cerulean sphere encompassed Mifuné and Desmond. Some shattered, some fell useless to the ground. From atop the tower, Gabrysia had generated a protective barrier to shield them from the volley.

"What sorcery is this?!" Lysander exclaimed.

In the moment of shock, Mifuné vanished. In the blink of an eye, he was no more than a stone's throw from the frontline men. His stance was the same.

Carl Houston Roach IV

Mifuné called out in a voice like thunder, "Dragon Emperor's Edge!" and swung his blade down.

From the blade emerged a gigantic ball of what appeared to be purple fire. The formation had no time to react. They planted in place and hoped their shields would deflect the attack. The purple ball of fire connected with at least half of the shields in the line. A massive explosion encompassed most of the soldiers in the first company and consumed them. The soldiers in the front line were incinerated immediately. The force of the blast struck most of the soldiers behind the front line, throwing them back and scattering them.

"Captain!" Riley exclaimed in horror.

The second half of the garrison with Lieutenant Riley shirked back away from the carnage. The heat from the flames could be felt even by the men furthest to the rear. Few of the soldiers of the first company remained, less than one hundred. The Captain and his horse were nowhere to be found.

Mifuné did not relent. He maneuvered into the formation and, with his blinding speed, cut down the disoriented soldiers one by one. Whether they raised a sword, a shield, or a spear against him served them little good. He appeared in front of them before they could think and struck them down before they could act.

The Captain, who had managed to survive Mifuné's first attack, forced himself to his feet. Blood spilled from his nose and a laceration on the back of his head. He felt as though his chest had been crushed by a heavy blow. He wheezed as he tried to breathe. Before him stood the young man, Desmond. The fearsome look in his eye told Lysander everything he needed to know. The Captain smiled, chuckled even, at the boy's stalwart desire to fight. The Captain raised his sword and held it beside him.

"Do you think this wise, boy?"

Desmond's brow hardened. "You call me boy?!"

He rushed in for an attack. His blade twirled and spun in his grip. The cold edge of his steel crashed against the Captain's sword. Once, twice, three times he parried. His strikes were not heavy, but they were fast. His blade was like a flash of light through the darkness. He locked blades with the Captain. They pressed against each other, wielding all their might. The strength of their will pushed them even harder. Their blades shook against one another. Sparks flew into the damp grass beneath them.

"I fight for my Master!" Desmond shouted. Desmond turned the Captain's sword down into the dirt. As quick as a flash, he maneuvered behind the Captain, lifted his sword and slashed the back of the Captain's heel. Lysander cried out in pain as he fell to a knee. "I fight for my family!" Desmond slashed across the Captain's back.

Once again, Lysander cried out in pain. He fell forward and fully collapsed to the ground. In his weakened state, he lost his grip on his sword. Burning pain coursed through his whole body. Desmond rolled the Captain over so that their eyes met. Lysander desperately reached for his sword, but Desmond kicked it away from him. "What is it you fight for?" Desmond said contemptuously.

"I fight for my kingdom, my country, and my countrymen! What would a man like you know about loyalty!?"

Desmond scoffed. He pointed his blade to the battle behind them and the Captain's gaze followed. "You call this loyalty?"

Fear clutched the Captain's heart with an unbreakable grip. He watched helplessly on the ground as Riley attempted to gain control of the situation. The remaining men under his command fell one by one; as their cries of fear and pain rang out in the night. Tears welled up in his eyes the more his numbers dwindled.

"You are a foolhardy man playing soldier for a tyrant!" Desmond said.

"The Paladin is coming! Tonight, it ends... for all of you!"

"Then, where is he?" Desmond replied, orienting the tip of his blade at the Captains chest.

Lysander's head fell back. His eyes scanned the darkness over the planes behind him. Any moment now, he expected Virgil, in a shining victorious light, to come to the rescue. The more looked, the more he came to realize... Virgil was not coming. They were alone. We were never going to win this, were we, the Captain thought. Without another word, Desmond plunged his sword into the Captains chest. Lysander felt the white-hot pain in his chest overtake him. Blood filled up his throat and spilled out of his mouth. The images of the battle flashed in

The Fall of Avalon

his mind's eye until his vision went dark. He released one last breath.

Carl Houston Roach IV

CHAPTER 4   UNQUENCHABLE RAGE

He spared the lives of those who fled from him. He allowed them to collect their dead. Yet, in their eyes, he was evil.

The early light of dawn crept over the horizon, faint red and pink trickled over the distant eastern hills. Birds chirped and sang their lovely tunes inside the sleepy city. Gradually, the citizens of Avalon emerged from their homes and the normal daily routine began. Bakers set out their freshly baked loaves to cool in the morning air. Potters set out their newest works, and vendors opened their shops and stands for business before the morning rush began. All of them blissfully unaware of the massacre that befell brave soldiers of Avalon, as they slept.

Queen Titania woke to the sound of chirping at her window sill. She removed the covers from her naked body and walked to the beautiful sound. She felt the sun on her bare skin at first light. She could feel it replenish her soul and restore her vitality. This baptism always seemed to give her newfound life. She breathed in deep the morning air and felt it rejuvenate her. She smiled at the sight of birds collecting on a branch near her window.

As Titania ran her brush through her thick, gorgeous raven hair in front of her vanity, she could feel a lightness in her chest. In the mirror, she could see the reflection of her husband, sound asleep like

The Fall of Avalon

a baby, cradling the mass of blankets, he thought to be her, in his arms.

Mifuné's threat looming over her head and crept into her mind. The Queen's thoughts turned to Virgil and she smiled. Sweet, devoted Virgil, whose life was hers to do with as she pleased. She thought of the prosperity of her nation, the glorious civilization her forebear had established, and its continued greatness, and finally came to the realization that her fear of Mifuné was unfounded.

Nothing could bring down the great kingdom of Avalon. Her mother had done all that she could, Arthur had done all that he could, Merlin as well. Even she herself, had done all that was required to eliminate Avalon's enemies to ensure the survival of the kingdom. The situation she found herself confronted with would amount to nothing more than a footnote in this nation's long and prosperous history. It was nothing more than an inconvenience. At the end of it, she would still have it all, and be known as the country's greatest ruler.

The Queen smiled incessantly as she dressed herself for the day. She selected, from a vast assortment of dresses, a personal favorite of hers: a magenta gown with ruffled cuffs and a long train, trimmed and girdled in black. The dress, by design, hugged her body and exemplified her features, especially her breasts. She tied her hair back in such a way that the tail hung over her right breast to her waist. Her heart fluttered while she admired herself in her dressing room. She had not felt so confident, so happy, in a very long time. As a final touch to her attire, she slung onto her waist a sword belt. She then retrieved from its keeping place a magnificent saber, the Sword of Avalon. Queen Titania pulled the sword from its sheath and held it out in front of her. Power from the ancient world flowed forth from it. She eyed the sword carefully, she observed every detail of it.

The blade was long and slender, made from a mysterious ancient metal—long since lost. Gold engravings written in the language of the Fae adorned the sword from the center of the blade to the hilt, which gave it specific magical properties. The pommel and guard were made of the same gold. Adding to the regal, elegant design of the sword, the handle was wrapped in violet leather. It was a gift given to Queen Glorianna of the Fae over 2,000 years ago during the Great War. It was forged by the legendary smith Fomorian, one of the Lords of Light. The sword was Glorianna's only weapon against her arch nemesis: The Lich, one of the greatest of the Lords of Evil.

Glorianna would say, the Lich was a greater evil than Ravana. Titania shuttered every time she thought of that name. Though she had never seen him before, the way her mother described him gave her nightmares for many years. She always dismissed the existence of the Lich as nothing more than a horror story her mother used to frighten her. Regardless, having that sword in her possession made her feel more confident. Her mother enchanted the sword, that it might be an efficient weapon to bring to bear against the Lich. After the Lords of Evil were defeated at the end of the Great War, it was later used to defeat Titania's father,

The Fall of Avalon

Oberon, when he betrayed his wife, the Queen, and attempted to wipe out those who would not kneel to him and his rule in the War of the Fae, before the founding of Avalon. The history of the kingdom was written with that sword.

Lacing the sword in the belt filled Queen Titania with a sense of power she had not felt in seven years. She felt more like her mother with it: strong, brave, elegant, and powerful. She felt in control of her life once again. She felt the power to protect herself, her husband, her beloved Paladin, and her kingdom from anything. She felt truly connected to the unbreakable will of her bloodline.

Prepared to begin the day with a restored sense of self, The Queen exited her chambers without waking her husband, and set out to begin another day of running her kingdom. She pondered very seriously the notion of her soldiers' return and what news they would bring from the confrontation with Mifuné. As elated as she felt, there was no longer any doubt in her mind the outcome would be favorable. Nothing could shake the resolve she carried.

By the Queen's Chamber, she saw her council gathered in full. They talked amongst themselves, low mutters that were hardly audible. She could not make sense of what any of them said, but it mattered little to her. With the way she felt, it could be nothing but good news.

"Good morning, my Queen," said one of her council members.

"Good morning to you," she answered in kind.

Carl Houston Roach IV

"How fairs the morning, your Majesty?" another asked as he opened the doors for her.

"It fairs well. Perhaps the finest day Avalon has seen," she replied optimistically.

The council collectively felt an enormous weight lifted from them. Seeing their Queen's demeanor so uplifted was a relief. Her frightened attitude and lack of composure from the day before shifted the tone of the whole council. Queen Titania was back on this day. The storm had passed, and all was returning to the way it was. They gathered in her Chamber and discussed the important matters at hand.

"Council," Queen Titania began, she took her seat. "What is the news for the day?"

The council was silent. Each of their faces seemed unsettled for one reason or another. The Queen scowled, but only slightly. It was not anger that infested her cheery mood, but annoyance. Why could my council members not face the day in the same manner that I do, she mused. She clicked her fingers against the arm of her seat rhythmically and scanned their faces.

"Will someone say something? I woke up in quite a good mood today, but I feel that beginning to wane." The Queen's words became terse.

One of the councilmen stepped forward from the rest. He coughed to clear his throat. He knew the news he bore would only agitate her highness further, but he also acknowledged that it was a situation that needed to be dealt with. He lifted some papers he held in his hand and read from them. "In light of the recent threat issued to Avalon,

The Fall of Avalon

our alliance with Zolabar has been suspended... until the Samurai has been dealt with, and the threat looming over these lands has been resolved." He paused. "They are also demanding reparations for the death of their Grand Inquisitor, Isaac Rhitrick, and his two subordinate Inquisitors, Jemehet and Vonen. Until reparations have been paid, Zolabar will suspend all trade and diplomacy with Avalon, signed King Venemor, Lord of Zolabar." The councilman continued urgently, "My Queen, I have received similar tidings from Kilbin. They, too, lost their Grand Inquisitor, and two subsequent inquisitors in the aftermath of the Samurai's attack. They do not require reparations of us. They have requested only that the head of the Samurai be delivered to the palace on a plate of gold. So sayeth King Balthazar, Lord of Kilbin... And my Queen, Eramar ..."

"I understand that Eramar feels the same way, do they?!" the Queen interjected harshly. "King Gregory mistrusts my abilities to stand as a viable ally to him and demands some reparation of sorts?"

"No, your Majesty." A councilwoman spoke out as her head sank into her shoulders. "Eramar has... permanently revoked all peace and diplomacy between themselves and Avalon. So sayeth King Gregory, Lord of Eramar."

Titania lowered her head and covered her face. Her mind raced: This could not be happening. These nations had long been allied with Avalon, even before she claimed Lordship when her mother ascended to be in the realm of the gods. A fire of malicious intent awakened in her heart. Mifuné was wrong if he thought he would burn me down. I will turn the tables on him just as I had all those years ago.

The Queen lifted her head defiantly and faced the council. "What word do we have from Captain Liam?" she asked.

"Captain Lysander, your Majesty," her militant advisor corrected.

"Whatever. Have they returned yet?"

"No, your majesty. Still no word."

Queen Titania rose out of her seat and made her way to the window. She peered over the wall but could see nothing but the open verdant fields stretching out to the tiny wood line in the west. Even the Tower of Galahad was out of sight. She clutched her hand at the window sill. The sound of the birds chirping only irritated her further.

"Why must I do everything?" the Queen sneered.

"Your Majesty?"

"You are all incompetent!" she yelled. She swung about. "All of you are my chosen council, and yet you cannot seem to do the jobs I have assigned each of you to do! Lord Donovan!"

"Yes, my Queen!"

"Tell me, how many mercenaries did you assemble to hunt down the man who threatened your Queen?"

"As you commanded, I went out to my contacts in the guilds from all over, but none of them would offer a single man to undertake this quest. They said the danger would be too great!"

The Fall of Avalon

Queen Titania marched towards him and seized him by his collar. He cowered away from the flames erupting from her prismatic eyes. It felt as if she was burrowing into his soul, scraping away the walls of his mind and heart. The other council members backed away, equally as frightened as Lord Donovan.

"I have had enough of your excuses, Lord Donovan. You have wasted enough of my time."

The Queen turned and flung him back across the room as though he were a doll stuffed with feathers. Lord Donovan shouted as he soared through the air. He yelled out as he collided with the wall behind her seat with a painful thud. On the ground he lay, grunting in agony, clutching his now injured shoulder. Titania glided across the room until she towered over him, her eyes still ablaze. Lord Donovan could not bring himself to look up at her. He trembled on the ground, huddled into himself with his face covered. She turned her head over her shoulder. The rest of the council had moved away from her. None of them would look her in the eye.

"Council members," the Queen began, feigning calmness, "it has become apparent to me that none of you are capable, at all, of assisting me in dealing with diplomatic affairs, so the burden falls to me. Each of you get out of my sight! I will devise a solution to the problem we face."

The council members hesitated for a moment. It seemed any slight movement would rouse The Queen's anger further. They even stifled their breath, hoping to avoid being heard.

"Now! All of you! Out!" she screamed.

Carl Houston Roach IV

The council members waited no longer. They stampeded to the door and exited as quickly as they could, practically trampling each other in the process. Lord Donovan struggled immensely to crawl out the door without being crushed by the pounding feet of his colleagues. Once he made it out the door, the others helped him to his feet and departed.

Queen Titania stood in the middle of the Queen's Chamber and oriented her gaze at the illustrious painting on the wall in front of her. It depicted Queen Glorianna's rise to power, gallantly wielding the Sword of Avalon. Arthur kneeled in front of her, his golden sword struck into the ground, as acknowledgement of her sovereignty in the land. She was the picture of divine majesty and grace, dressed in gold and enshrined in silver. Platinum blonde hair cascaded down her back nearly to the ground.

Queen Titania shook her head. "How did you make it look so easy?"

There was a knock at the door. Then a second, and then a third. Virgil entered the vacated Chamber. He could sense Queen Titania's fury from the door. The blood on the wall beside him only confirmed that point. He approached with caution, knowing full and well anything could set her off. The last thing he wanted to do was present her with something that would feed her anger.

"My love, I am here, as you requested."

"I would much rather be alone right now, Virgil," she replied dismissively.

The Fall of Avalon

"Some of the soldiers returned from the battle. The leader is with the General now. He wishes to speak with you."

"Do we know what news they bring?"

"No. At least, I do not. We can soon find out." He touched her waist softly. "Come. We will accomplish nothing staying angry in here."

"This news had better be good. I grow tired of constant failure."

The Queen exited the room immediately, without returning to Virgil any gesture of affection. He sighed. She had become more distant, and not just from him. If that was how she behaved on the third day, he shuttered to think of what the days to come would bring. Queen Titania and Virgil made their way to the palace's war room. White doors led into a wide room with crimson carpet that covered the entire floor. A tremendous, round mahogany table took up most of the space in the room. About 20 chairs were tucked under the table. In them, two people were seated, her General in his armor, and a young woman.

The General and the woman rose out of their seats as The Queen came into the room. Queen Titania surveyed the woman. She was battered, barely clothed, she trembled, and her face was pale. Most notably, though, she was missing an arm. A blood-soaked gauze filled up the place where her left arm had been severed from her body. Her voice quivered when she spoke such that she could hardly finish a sentence.

"Who is this? Were you one of the garrison who marched yesterday?" The Queen asked.

Carl Houston Roach IV

"Yes, your Highness. This is Lieutenant Riley. She accompanied Captain Lysander as his second in command," the General replied.

"Then tell me, Lieutenant, what happened out there?"

Riley flinched. She could sense The Queen's frustration. It filled the room with unease, tension, a fear that she would unleash her anger on any one of them at any moment. Only Virgil was unafraid.

"Y-Your Majesty…" Riley stuttered, "I… we... the tower." Her words were mixed between gasps of air. "He was there. Everyone." Images of the night before flashed through her mind. "The fire. The explosions. The screaming. He killed everyone."

Virgil winced. Just the yesterday Riley was among the finest assembled group of soldiers he had ever laid eyes on. Riley herself stood next to one of the most capable captains in Avalon's army. Though Virgil was not surprised with the outcome, he was surprised at the condition he found the lieutenant in. It made him think about his fight with the Samurai, and whether Mifuné spared him out of mercy, or pity.

"Are you the only survivor?" Queen Titania asked, planting a fist on her hip next to the sword.

Riley only shook her head. Her arm began shaking violently. In an instant, she was back on the battlefield. The Samurai was coming for her. She drew her sword and charged. With just a flick of his wrist, he knocked the weapon from her hand, and with the next, his blade sliced through her arm as easily as it sliced through air. Mifuné's eyes were full of fire, like a beast on the hunt. Possessed by

The Fall of Avalon

passion. Devoid of mercy. He was like a monster with an insatiable appetite for carnage; a demon they were all too ill-equipped to confront, much less defeat. It was the stuff of legends—the stuff of nightmares. Riley clutched her side in an attempt to control her convulsions. Hot tears streamed down from her eyes. They spread wide as images of the previous night's savageries passed in front of them. Her nails dug into her arm until it bled. Her teeth rattled as her jaw clenched.

"Got away," Riley stammered. "Handful of others followed."

"You fled?" The Queen barked. "You abandoned your duty and ran?"

The frightened lieutenant looked up. Her gaze immediately locked onto Virgil. The sight of him in his armor, clean and intact, forced her to weep. Her shoulders bobbed as more tears poured out of her eyes. "You never came…" Riley said quietly. "Captain… said you would come…" She choked on her tears as she wept. "Bu,,, but you never came," she wailed uncontrollably.

Virgil looked away from her. His hand curled into a fist. Her words stung him like poison. It was as if a serpent injected venom directly into his heart. He should have been there. He could have saved them. He could have helped…

The frightened look in her eyes melted away, replaced by an indignant fury. Her brow furrowed and shook. Tears continued to stream down from her eyes and stain her cheeks. Her teeth were clenched and brought to bear as she hissed, "What Hell have you brought upon us!?" Riley stopped shaking and seized Titania by the bust of her dress. "What evil did you conjure that this fate should befall us who serve you!?"

"Take your hand off me!" The Queen demanded.

"Lieutenant!" the General chimed in, "release her majesty at once!"

Riley was fixed on Queen Titania. The anger in the Queen's iridescent eyes did not compare to the fury that burned within the lieutenant. "No, sir! I will not! You sent hundreds of us to our deaths! They died because of you!" Riley pushed the Queen back, releasing her from her grip. "What did you do!?"

"That is enough, Riley," the General insisted, attempting to hold her at bay.

"No! She did this! She brought this upon us!" Lieutenant Riley thrust her finger at Queen Titania. "No one can stop him! No one! We are all going to die!" Riley screamed at the top of her lungs. "You!" she shouted, pointing an outstretched finger at Virgil. "You!" she said again, this time orienting her finger at the General. "And most of all," the Lieutenant paused, taking her time before pointing her finger at Queen Titania. "You, she uttered vehemently.

The Queen had heard enough. Without a word, she unsheathed the Sword of Avalon and ran it through Riley's chest. Her majesty's eyes were full of self-righteous indignation. "We shall see," she muttered over her burning rage.

Accompanied by the sound of choking on blood that filled her lungs, Lieutenant Riley began to

The Fall of Avalon

laugh. She clutched the blade that pierced her and pulled herself toward Queen Titania. Her hand bled from contact with the sword. Pain was nothing to her now. All there was for her anymore was the end. Riley thought about her loving husband at home, they would never see each other ever again. About the life she could have had, a life she was now robbed of by her Queen. Though the taste was bitter, she laughed. "Bury yourself in this anger, Titania," she said, coughing up blood. "Nothing will save you from The Samurai. Not your armies. Not your Paladin." Riley paused. "Nothing."

"Silence!" The Queen ordered.

"Mifuné is coming for you. Mifuné Tahaka is coming for all of you."

"Silence!" Queen Titania shouted yet again.

"And nothing you can do will stop him."

"I SAID BE SILENT!" Titania, The Queen of Avalon twisted the blade into her lieutenant, a citizen of Avalon, and pulled it upward with all of her might. The saber tore through Lieutenant Riley like a scythe through wheat ready for harvest. Blood spirted from her body. Titania felt it soak her face and bust. Virgil and the General were splashed in it as well. The light faded from Riley's eyes. Her body fell lifeless to the ground. Having silenced the lieutenant, the Queen recovered her composure. She removed a handkerchief from her dress and wiped the blood from her face.

"Virgil, General."

"Yes, your Highness," they each answered in kind.

Carl Houston Roach IV

"No one is to hear about this, under any circumstances," The Queen said, as she cleaned away the blood from the sword. "The soldiers who survived will be rounded up and executed as traitors to the crown. General, you will attend to that. Virgil, I need you to ready yourself. We must announce your return to the people."

There was no response. Virgil and the General cast a glance at one another. Queen Titania's actions extended past her right as Queen, but as men of duty and honor, they could never defy the one they served. Rather than object, having seen how quickly her temperament would change, they each took in a deep, breath and exhaled heavily.

"It will be as you say," they each uttered reluctantly.

"Good. Sound the bells and gather the people." Queen Titania said.

"Give me a moment to wash off Lieutenant Riley's blood my Queen."

"No, leave it. After all, you just returned victoriously from battle."

As the General collected Riley's remains and carried her out of the War Room, Virgil stood at attention with Lieutenant's blood on his face and armor. He and the Queen made their way to the balcony. Knights and guards in the palace saw Virgil and spread the word throughout the palace that he had returned. Without being told, the guards made their way to the bell tower and sounded it.

The citizens of Avalon gravitated towards the palace, like moths to a flame. They could see the Queen and her advisors on the balcony,

The Fall of Avalon

accompanied by four knights. They stood at attention, shoulder to shoulder, as the Queen gracefully passed between them. She stood above them all, looked down upon them, and spoke:

"People of Avalon, hear your Queen!" she exclaimed. "The battle is over. The great evil that has beset our lands has been vanquished! Mifuné Tahaka has been defeated! Behold, your Paladin has returned."

Virgil strode from the shadows of the palace into the light. The harshness of the sun forced his eyes shut for a moment. He stood sternly, masque with pride, by the rail of the balcony. His cape whipped in the wind.

"It is with a heavy heart that I must inform you all, our brave soldiers, our mighty warriors have been lost, but their sacrifice shall not have been in vain. Our people, our city, our kingdom will live on!" Queen Titania reassured.

The people of Avalon went wild with praise and jubilation. They shouted and cheered for the triumphal return of their great protector. From within the crowd, they began to cry out in one voice: "Hail the Paladin! Hail the Queen! Hail the Paladin! Hail the Queen!"

"What comes next, Titania?" Virgil sniped softly.

The Queen offered him no answer. She stayed on the balcony for another moment to soak in the peoples' praise. Then, without a word, she turned from the people and entered the castle. Alone, she trudged through her magnificent palace halls. Though the morning started with such promise, it crumbled so quickly around her, like a castle of sand at high tide. It is all because of their incompetence, she thought to herself as she stormed through the halls. The garrison failed me. The General failed me. Virgil failed me.

To calm her wound nerves, Queen Titania went to her garden, which was where she would go when she wanted to be alone. As a Fae, she felt a profound connection to nature and her natural world which surrounded her. Yet, even the garden her mother planted for her centuries ago; filled with flowers ranging from violet to radiant blues and reds and yellows, the lush green shrubs and vines overtaking the trees; could not ease her mind.

It was here Colabion found her, adrift among the plants and ivory marble walkways. She cradled herself with one arm and stroke the petals of the blossoming flowers with her free hand. The slowness of her movements indicated to him that she was distraught. The weight of the world was on her shoulders, and she wished to carry that burden alone.

It was more than Colabion could bear. He knew his uses were few, and he could tell from her expression that little could be said to console his wife, but he had something to share with her. Something he hoped would be enough to lift her spirits and bring back the light to her smile.

"My love!" Colabion said.

The Queen did not answer.

"I have something to tell you. I hope it is enough to change your mood."

The Fall of Avalon

"I think I have had enough news for one day," she sighed.

"Titania, my love," he said as he placed his hands on her waist, "I may have found a solution to our problem. Last night, I dispatched a group of knights to recover a famous mercenary from Eramar. They call him the Boar of the East Hills!"

Titania showed no reaction to the announcement of the man or to his title. Instead, she shifted away from Colabion and caressed her seemingly lifeless plant further.

"They say no man or beast in the realm can match his physical strength. They say he caught a great boar and killed it with his bare hands. I trust that he can accomplish the task of turning Mifuné into nothing more than a footnote."

Queen Titania leaned her back against her husband's warm embrace. The news he just imparted on her carried little weight, but it warmed her heart to watch him try for her. In the end, if nothing else, he could at least do that much. For some reason, that felt like it carried more weight than the failures of those who were competent. She closed her eyes and allowed herself to be still. His presence beside her reminded her that all was not lost. Not yet. There was still time to devise a solution for her problem and set everything back to the way it was. The way she had worked so hard to make it.

"Would you like to meet him?" Colabion asked.

"Yes. Have him brought to the Throne Room."

From the holding room deep in the depths of the castle, two knights—followed by two others—clad

Carl Houston Roach IV

in shimmering armor, capes dangling from the shoulders that whipped about in their march, hauled the burliest man to have ever set foot in the halls of the Ivory Palace. They managed to restrain him, though not without a fair amount of struggle. He was at least twice each knight's mass, but approximately the same height. A generous, well-groomed, black beard adorned his haggard face. His hair was crew cut. He wore a long, heavy, brown coat over a black tunic and dusty brown pants. Fingerless gloves covered his thick, meaty hands.

The knights released him at the lowest step from the throne. Each positioned himself near him in a box formation. The man looked up to see, perhaps, the most beautiful woman he had ever seen, seated upon a winged golden throne. Her countenance would have shined like the rising of the sun over the hills of his home were it not for the menacing scowl that twisted it.

Most frightening of all to him were the nacreous purple eyes that pierced through him like a hunter's arrow pierces the side of a doe. He had never seen such eyes in his life. To the core of his being, they frightened him more than anything he had witnessed before.

"I must admit, I am more accustomed to finer accommodations, but I am here now, your Majesty, Queen of Avalon." The man rendered an insincere bow. "I am curious, though. Why is it you have brought me here?"

"Tell me your name," The Queen ordered callously.

The Fall of Avalon

The man before her returned her scowl with one of his own. "Why should I answer to someone who had me dragged out of my own home for no reason?"

"The Queen asked you to your name!" one of the knights barked.

"Answer her, now!" the other demanded.

"And another thing, Highness: if you want to have a meeting with someone, consider sending a messenger next time, leave the dogs at home."

"How dare you!" The knights at his back drew their swords.

The man sneered and raised up both hands. The level of severity in their tone made him chuckle. Especially the overwhelming displeasure he received from the person seated upon the throne. "I will ask you again," the Queen's voice was incredibly perturbed, "what is your name?"

"Sergei," he answered. "Sergei Meisner."

"And tell me, Sergei Meisner, why should I entrust the task at hand to you?"

Sergei scoffed and quickly turned his head away from her. "Entrust a task? You had your dogs drag me from my home, when I sat to supper with my family, to give me a job?" He took a step forward. "I'll tell you what you can do with that job. You can take it," he pointed at Queen Titania, "and shove it up your…"

One of the knights buried his gauntleted fist into the side of Sergei's face while another kicked him behind his knee. The force of the blows struck him to his knees. Despite this Sergei did not bleed. He laughed at the sensitivity revolving around the throne room. To avoid being struck again, he kept his head down, eyes to the floor. It was his own curiosity that subdued him more so than the guards.

"They tell me you are a great hunter of men, as well as beasts. Is this true?" Queen Titania said, shallowly disguising her impatience.

"Some may say that about me," Sergei answered.

The Queen rose out her throne elegantly. Her dress spread out from underneath her as if it had been caught by the wind. She drew the Sword of Avalon from its sheath and descended toward Sergei. Once in front of him, she nestled the cold face of the blade against his cheek. Huh, this sword is far sharper than the edge of my shaving razor, Sergei mused.

"I have no patience to appeal to your *prowess* as a mercenary, nor do I have any tolerance for your disrespect. I promise you no gift of wealth, no riches, nor jewels, as would have been the agreement. No, your reward shall be your life, which is now just as much mine to take as it is to give."

Colabion shuttered as he watched from beside the throne. He had never seen his beloved wife, the light of his life, so cold. It seemed to him that she herself were made of the same steel that rested in her grasp. Even the knights were taken aback. The Queen was always composed, always so lady like. This was utterly and profoundly unlike her.

"You can take my life if you please, I cannot stop you," Sergei replied.

The Fall of Avalon

Queen Titania hesitated for a moment. "No." She lowered her blade and returned it to its sheath. "I will not take your life. I still have use for you." She cast her gaze to the knights behind Sergei. "Knights, go and collect his family. Bring them here, unspoiled."

"What!?" Sergei's head shot up from the floor.

"It shall be as you say, your Majesty."

The knights bowed and departed immediately. Sergei shot up to his feet and attempted to stop them. Before he could make his next move, a mighty hand fell on his shoulder and held him in place.

"Thank you for joining us, Virgil," The Queen said, walking toward the throne.

Though he struggled against it with all his might, he could not escape Virgil's grip. With just the strength in his hand, Virgil could restrain him with far greater success than the four knights that had escorted him to the throne. Tears welled up in his eyes as he cursed and struggled to break free. In the end, all he could do was watch as the knights exited the palace toward his unsuspecting family.

"Sergei, this is Virgil, the Paladin of Avalon," the Queen announced. He will escort you to the armory. There, you will collect the equipment you will need to accomplish your mission. Your reward, if you succeed, will be the lives of your family. Keep that in mind, before you defy me again."

Sergei, who had finally stopped struggling, glared intensely at Queen Titania. His clutched fists shook by his sides. "Mark my words, Highness, and mark them well. If any harm comes to my river lily or my little ones, nothing in this world will keep me from you."

"Consider them marked," The Queen said dismissively.

Queen Titania gestured dismissively with a light wave of her hand. Virgil nodded and escorted Sergei down the hall to the armory with a mighty shove. He pushed Sergei along like a master pushing a slave. Colabion could hardly watch.

Colabion feared to even look in his wife's direction. He did not recognize the creature that sat beside him. The woman he loved, the woman he had given his heart to, could never have been so cruel to an innocent man who had committed no crime. This thing, this sharp-eared, fanged, sword wielding tyrant, was not her. Without a word, he dismissed himself from her side.

"Where are you going?" Queen Titania asked sweetly.

Colabion looked over his shoulder to his Queen. His heart sank into the pit of his stomach. The look on her face had changed dynamically before his eyes, so drastically from an evil queen back to his loving wife. Who are you, he thought as he glared back at the two-faced Queen. You are not my wife. You are not the beautiful woman who told me that you loved me last night. It was as if what had just transpired had never happened at all. He shook his head. Shaken to his core, Colabion continued walking away. He could not bring himself to speak. Quietly and slowly, he exited the throne room, and the Queen found herself alone, seated upon her winged golden throne.

The Fall of Avalon

૬ঌ

Outside the Tower of Galahad, the morning brought with it a substantially different sentiment. Mifuné and his disciples watched the handful of soldiers, who had survived the onslaught, retreat at full speed back towards Avalon. The battle was over. Mifuné, sprayed with the blood of Avalon's soldiers, was victorious. The image of victory was gruesome. The battle field was littered with bodies, verdant grass was stained with gallons of blood and scorched by fire. The miniscule panicked group of survivors screamed as they ran to the safety.

Mifuné exhaled and swung his sword out. More blood flung from the shining steel onto the grass before he returned it smoothly to its sheath. He silently strode past his disciples like a phantom and sat beside the tower in a meditative posture.

Naomi looked past the carnage of the night before and focused on Mifuné. His shoulders hung lower than normal. His eyes were downcast. His face would not rise to greet the sun. The burden of each man he killed weighed on his weary conscience. His demeanor broke her heart. She made her way over to his side and reached out her hand to him to console him, but he would not budge.

Several tears liberated themselves from Desmond's eyes as he stood witness to the aftermath of the battle. Gabrysia wept as well. They had resigned themselves to follow Mifuné to the ends of the world. He was their Master, and he was a good man. The carnage, the tragic loss of life, pressed their minds and their hearts and surpassed the scope of imaginings and expectations. They looked at one another, as they shared the same thought, and then cast their gaze to their Master.

Desmond looked down at his own hands. Though they were clean, he could see the Captain's blood covering them. His heart sank into stomach. He fell to his knees and closed his hands into fists.

"Desmond," Gabrysia said.

"Yeah. I know," Desmond replied.

"I cannot do this," Gabrysia said. "I cannot be a part of something so terrible if I know not why. I cannot follow him down this war path if I am being kept in the dark."

"You are right," Desmond replied. "If I am going to continue to fight for him, I need to know why all of this is happening."

Together, they walked over to the fireplace where Mifuné sat with Naomi. One by one, each of them took a seat, facing him. The question pounded in each of their minds like the beating of their own hearts. Finding the courage to ask their master felt just a bit out of reach, especially seeing the grief in his downcast eyes. It seemed that he clung to the sword in his hands like it was the only thing helping him hold it together.

"They will come for their fallen, in time. Make them ready." Mifuné's voice shook.

"Master..." Naomi said.

"Make them ready. Soldiers who die in service to Avalon earn a proper burial. I will not deny them that."

"We need to know why!" Gabrysia blurted out. "Why is this happening? Why did these men die?

The Fall of Avalon

Why are you so set to destroy The Queen? To destroy Avalon? I do not understand, and I need to know!"

"Please, Master. Tell us the truth," Desmond persisted.

"I will reveal to you the truth, in time. You have my word. For now, make them ready."

Desmond, Naomi, and Gabrysia reluctantly left their Master's side to clear out their encampment of stray weapons and gear. Using their magic, Naomi and Gabrysia arranged the bodies of the deceased soldiers into rows as neatly as they could, in the event Avalon came for their fallen warriors, as Mifuné predicted. Throughout the day, several caravans came to collect the bodies. They flew white flags and carried no weapons. Each time they came, Mifuné stood tall beside the tower. He took no action against them. Though the servants of Avalon and Mifuné were enemies, respect for the fallen was more important in that moment. The Samurai stood conspicuously as he watched over them collected their dead. Blatantly, he deliberately allowed himself to be seen by the emissaries of Avalon.

Desmond took it upon himself to remain as the lookout for the day. He alerted them when a new caravan came and he watch for danger. As the sun began its descent through the amber evening sky, each disciple sat around the fire Desmond made for them. It had been a solemn, quiet day.

Mifuné looked up at his disciples seated around him. He knew they could hardly bear the weight of what he had done the night before. He could see it in their eyes. He knew they had questions they wanted answered. And he knew he owed it to them to shed the light on the circumstances in which they found themselves.

"I know you must be wondering what could have led me to do what I did last night," Mifuné said, finally breaking the silence. "And what would lead me to continue my campaign against Avalon."

Hearing his voice was a welcome change to the shivering silence he had given them all day. Their eyes were open wide, and their attention fixed onto their Master.

"It could not have been easy for any of you to see the things you saw. If tomorrow wills it, I shall tell you everything. You will know all that I know. For tonight, rest. There has been enough suffering for one day."

"Yes, Master," they each replied.

Mifuné stood up slowly and proceeded to the tower. His disciples watched him until the door closed behind him. Finally, they were going to know the truth, the true legend behind the man to which they had pledged their loyalty. As the sun finally sunk below the horizon, so too did the three young followers of Mifuné sink into a deep slumber, a much needed sleep.

The Fall of Avalon

The Boar was called forth the fight the son of the Dragon. On that day, he saw the terrible power hidden within.

Dawn, the beginning of the fourth day crept over the planes as it had the day before. With it came a light breeze that swept over the encampment outside the Tower of Galahad. Though it was not strong enough to wake everyone up, Naomi found herself unable to resist it. She shivered slightly, and it felt as though the gentle morning rays weighed a ton on her weary eyes. She propped herself up on her arms and surveyed the encampment. Desmond was fast asleep on his side facing the vast, open field. Gabrysia had curled into a ball facing the woods behind them. She shivered as well after the sweeping breeze caressed her body, but she did not wake. Naomi smiled. In her heart, she hoped they would have many mornings just like that one.

There was still something missing. Their Master, lingering in his room at the top of the tower, alone, and away from everyone. Her heart became heavy at the thought of him greeting the day by himself, especially after the battle. The heaviness in his eyes was still seared into her heart. Naomi picked herself up as quietly as possible, so as not to disturb Desmond or Gabrysia. She snuck to the tower door like a thief in the night, scanning her surroundings as if desperate to avoid being detected.

Carl Houston Roach IV

As she prepared to enter the tower, she took one last look over her shoulder at her companions, and she smiled.

Naomi began her ascent up the tower steps as quickly as she could. She had grown accustomed to the several-hundred step staircase that spiraled along the walls pass the rooms of the tower up to the top room. Her heart beat more wildly as she drew closer and closer to the top. Once she stood before the Samurai's door, her breath froze in her chest. Slowly, cautiously, she reached for the wooden door to pushed it open. Something stopped her, though. Something familiar, but frightening. She could hear Mifuné speaking to someone. His voice was just above a whisper. It sounded distressed. Or perhaps angry. Naomi could not make sense of it. She pressed her ear against the door in hopes to gain a better understanding.

"I did not want this!" Mifuné whispered aloud.

"This is what you came for."

The voice that responded was not his. Despite the voice being muffled by the closed door between them, Naomi could discern that much. It was monstrous, guttural, and deep. Naomi had never heard a voice like that in her life.

"I told them to leave. I gave them the chance."

"You are lying to yourself. You wanted to fight."

"That is not true. It is *not* true..."

"You cannot hide the truth from me. I know you. I know your heart. You did not come to show them mercy. You came to shed their blood; to make them suffer as you did."

The Fall of Avalon

Naomi pushed forward, although she did not announce herself or ask permission to enter. When the door fully opened, a crack ran down the very center of her heart. Mifuné was seated on the bed, just as she had found him the morning after he confronted Queen Titania, but something was different. His kasa was on the ground. His kimono was hung on the foot of the bed, and his sword was laid across his lap. He was hunched over, facing the window. His shoulders shook, and his head would not raise. His white knuckles squeezed the handle of his sword and another part of the sheath by one of the golden seals that adorned it. The muscles in his body were tense. His breath was stifled. Tears stained the sheath of Mifuné's sword.

My Master has always been so strong. His will was unshakeable, even in the face of an entire army. From what I saw the night of the battle, he was as fearless and as powerful as he had professed to be, Naomi surmised. That Mifuné was reduced to such an overawed emotional state meant the weight on his soul was beyond anything she could imagine. Tears welled up in her own eyes seeing him in such pain. Naomi could not speak.

In his mind's eye, Mifuné watched the battle unfold step by step. In each soldier he killed, he saw the faces of each warrior from the Company of Heroes that had ventured with him to face the Ravana. Faces that he would never see again. Just as the citizens of Avalon would never see these soldiers alive again. Just as she had done before, The Queen of Avalon had sent hundreds to face a monster in her name, only this time, Mifuné himself was the monster.

"Why did not they listen?" Mifuné muttered as a whisper repeatedly. "I did not want this. Why did not they listen!?"

Naomi clearly heard him then, drowning in his lament. The demons in his head gnawed at his heart like a pack of wolves ravaged prey they had killed. The well in her eyes dissolved and gave way for tears to stream down her face. The longer she watched her Master, the more she felt her heart fragment. She rushed into the room with reckless abandon. Without invitation, she threw her arms around his waist and lay her head against his bare back. Naomi could sense that, even for just that moment, his soul settled. She closed her eyes and smiled, and light shined through her heart.

"I am here, Master. I am here for you. I will not leave you all alone," she whispered to him. Several of her tears fell on his skin and roll down his back.

Mifuné's weeping slowed. His breath slowly returned to normal. The tension she had felt in his shoulders alleviated with a long, heavy exhale. His body became completely still, and tranquility returned to his mind. Mifuné let go of the shaft of his sword and took hold of one of Naomi's hands. He held her fingers in his grip gently. Despite the callous on his hands from years of swordsmanship, his hands felt serene and tender. She closed her fingers around his thumb and savored the moment.

Sunlight poured into the room and chased away the nighttime shadows. The warm light washed over them and the cold tower. Naomi felt as if her soul were renewed. Her resolve to stand with Mifuné, no matter what lay ahead of them, had solidified. No matter where the journey they took led them, she would never let him face it alone.

Mifuné released Naomi's hand. She, in turn, released her embrace and stepped back from him. She watched him rise from his bed, a mirror of the sun taking to the sky from its descent below the horizon. His shoulders locked back as steady as they had ever been, cementing the muscular curvature across his back. He held his head high as he looked toward the sun.

Though Mifuné was a smaller framed man by general comparison, every facet of his body exuded tremendous strength. Round shoulders served as sturdy anchors for the toned, powerful arms that wielded his frightening blade. His back was like a work of art; each muscle group proportional to the one with which it connected. Mifuné turned and faced Naomi. What his chest lacked in size, it made up for in density and definition. His abdomen was more perfectly segmented than a symmetrical cobblestone road. Every muscle was proportionate, in scope and mass, to his frame.

Beyond just his physical strength, Naomi could sense the deep power within him. It was not magical, like hers or Gabrysia's. Mifuné was the product of years of self-discipline and training. His aforementioned might was the manifestation of his will, the greatest force a person can possess.

Mifuné leaned in towards Naomi. His fingers effortlessly brushed her short hair behind her ear, and he gingerly cupped the back of her head. The

Carl Houston Roach IV

look in his eyes was intense, much like how they would be in a battle. There was all the passion, but none of the malice. All the vigor, but none of the intent to kill. She had never seen eyes like those in her life.

Naomi trembled. Her eyes slammed shut. She had no idea what to expect next, or what his true intentions were in that moment. She was not afraid, though. If Mifuné asked, there was nothing she would not do for him. A warm feeling arose in her chest and spread through the whole of her body. She was ready to welcome whatever would happen next. A new sensation stilled the yearning in Naomi. Her eyes peeked open to see his face only inches away. Mifuné leaned in closer still and closed his eyes as he rested his forehead against hers. For the first time since she had met him, he seemed completely at peace. His soul was still. The overwhelming presence he normally gave felt calm and gentle. She could stay in that moment forever.

Mifuné raised his head from hers and lowered his hand to his side. "Come," he said softly. "Let us wake the others." He dressed himself quickly and secured his sash around his waist. He slid his sword into the sash and reached for his kasa. Mifuné exited the room without waiting for a reply. He would not have received one had he waited.

Naomi was lost, so taken by that moment, she fell against the wall to soak it all in. Any other man would have taken her in that moment, either right there against the wall or thrown her onto the bed with aggressive fervor. She wondered, secretly, silently, if she had sensed any sensual desire in his touch. There was something in the way his head rested against her that sparked her curiosity. Mifuné's touch was soft, yet so powerful. It fueled the fire raging within her.

The old woman's voice came to her again. Hers were the words Naomi had held onto for so long, the words that she had placed all her faith in: "If you stay true to your course, you will have what you most desire." The smile the matron offered was so assuring, her tone so serene and promising, Naomi could not help but believe her.

$$\mathfrak{S}\!\!\!\!\bullet$$

"Desmond, Gabrysia, get up!" Mifuné ordered.

Desmond and Gabrysia rose immediately from their slumber. Though their eyes were still mostly glued shut, they feigned alertness. It reminded Mifuné of his days under Argus's tutelage. Before drilling him over his lessons or challenging him to an early morning sparring match, Argus would always wake him by dousing him with water or striking him with lightning. Mifuné's disciples were fortunate that he could do neither of these things to them.

"Disciples," Mifuné began, "our enemy has launched an attack against us. We cannot allow ourselves to become lax. You must stay vigilant!"

"Yes, Master!" Gabrysia and Desmond sat cross-legged in front of Mifuné.

Naomi poked her head quietly through the doorway of the tower. She smiled at the sight of Mifuné giving instruction to Desmond and Gabrysia. Their faces were so focused, so attuned to every word he imparted onto them. Naomi always found that quality about them adorable, especially Desmond. He admired Mifuné more than any man he had ever met, and for good reason.

Before they met him, Desmond was nothing more than a common thief with just above average skill with a blade, short or long. To be cast out, to be imprisoned, to be beaten and battered and spat upon, was common place to him. It seemed to him that the world held no place for him. Mifuné took him under his wing. He taught Desmond, mentored him. As a Master to an apprentice, Mifuné guided Desmond along the path of the warrior. He trained him to wield his blade as an extension of himself, to tap into energies within himself he never knew existed, and to meditate about his place in the world and what he might do to contend with it. He had been transformed from a talentless thief into a warrior of exemplary caliber in just four months.

Gabrysia was an exile from her homeland in the eastern kingdom of Eramar. One of the most prominent families, the Tallhars, banished her from Eramar because of her affinity for magic. She was a prodigy with a proclivity for witchcraft. Mifuné often said that Argus would have been honored to teach her. Despite this, she had been disgraced, and stripped of all her rights as a Duchess by her family. Mifuné welcomed her with open arms. He taught her how to feel her power as a part of herself, and how to focus it. How, through meditation, practice, and determination, she could draw out what she had repressed for so long to please her family, and that she could come into her own as a powerful sorceress.

The Fall of Avalon

Despite his partisans' misfortunes, despite the varying grotesqueries of the lives they lead before they freed him from his prison, Mifuné never judged them. He had no condemnation for them, nor did he chase them away. He took them in as they were. He taught them, he trained them, mentored them. He brought them all together, and for the first time for each of them, especially Naomi, they felt like they had a family.

Naomi knew, and she wondered if Mifuné would remember, that she had met him before. As a young girl, she attempted to rob Mifuné, not knowing at that time who he was or what he was capable of. She remembered that day better than any day in her life; the warmest memory she would never let go of, no matter how horrible her circumstances ever became. Naomi was just a poor girl who lived alone in Avalon, who pickpocketed to get by. Her hope was to steal enough to get a loaf of bread for a day. Some days she was fortunate, other days, she was not. It was when she found herself at her lowest point, at her most desperate, that she would encounter the man she called Master.

Mifuné caught her attention walking through the Merchant District in Avalon. He was dressed much finer than the people around him. His kimono was crimson red with goldenrod trim. A chartreuse sash secured his kimono to his torso. He wore ash gray hakama, similarly to the kind he wore now, though those were of finer quality, with thin black stripes symmetrically segmented around each leg. His kasa was made of a finer material than straw, and colored dark to contrast his kimono. In his sash, Naomi saw

Carl Houston Roach IV

a sack tied with a white thread. She could tell, even from a distance, that it was full of gold, more than she had seen anyone carry in the district. It was her opportunity that she could not pass up. She imagined the gold in that pouch would tide her over for weeks, maybe longer. When she tried snatching the gold sack from his sash, he caught her hand and raised it high above her head. Naomi thought she had been subtle, she thought she could avoid being detected in such a heavy crowd, yet he snatched her hand away from the pouch as though she had told him she was planning to take it.

The guards patrolling the area took notice of the situation. They began pushing their way through the crowd to seize Naomi and take her away. In Avalon, the penalty for theft, especially from a Nobleman, is the removal of the thief's hand. Naomi knew that, if the guards caught her, that was what they were prepared to do, along with a vast array of punishments she had already endured at their hands. She desperately pulled and tugged against his grip in an attempt to escape, but it was futile.

Naomi was terrified. She pleaded and screamed and begged for mercy, though she expected none. Men were always cruel to her. They had subjected her to whatever torment they deemed fit. At the young age of thirteen, she had already been beaten, pierced, burned with hot irons, and raped. Finding herself at a man's mercy yet again made her sick to her stomach.

Then, something happened that Naomi did not expect. Something that had never happened to her before. Mifuné raised his hand towards the guards. "No!" he called out. Authority permeated his command. The guards stopped in place. "It's the Paladin!" one exclaimed. The guards fell to a knee, and with them, the entire populace in the District knelt as well. The area was quiet, so quiet, a feather touching down would have produced an echo.

Mifuné knelt down and looked into Naomi's frightened, tear-filled eyes. He slowly lowered her hand and released it without force. His eyes were full of compassion and care. The warmest smile was painted across his face. From his sash, he drew a gold coin, slightly larger than the average gold coin. On it was an engraving of a purple lotus flower. "A thousand apologies, my Lord, Mifuné," the Sergeant of the Guard began, "this little rat has been a perpetual thorn in our side. With your permission, I shall remove her from your presence. She will bother you no further."

Mifuné presented the coin to Naomi with great care. She hesitated to take it from him. Slowly, she reached her hand forward and closed her trembling fingers around the coin. Then he said something to her. She remembered his words clearly: "Never steal again, little one." Mifuné placed his hand on her head, then sent her on her way without charge. "My Lord, you let her go?" the Sergeant asked, perplexed. "Sergeant," Mifuné answered him, "stand these people up. They do not need to kneel to me. I am a citizen of this kingdom as much as any of them." Without another word, Mifuné departed the Merchant District back toward the palace.

Carl Houston Roach IV

Naomi never did steal again. As it turned out, the coin was more than just a keepsake from a kind man who had shown her mercy. It was a voucher she could use to receive a full meal from any vendor in the kingdom or any of its territories. Mifuné had given her his crest, the crest that had become the symbol of the Paladin before the days of Virgil. Naomi treasured that memory more than she treasured any riches or wealth she had ever obtained. She still carried the coin with her even after it lost its value with the rise of Virgil as the paladin. She promised herself one day, that she would find Mifuné again. In the end, without the coin, she never would have found him in his hidden prison.

ε•

"Desmond," Mifuné inquired. "What is the most important thing to remember when engaging an opponent?"

"To know your opponent. To know yourself. And to know the outcome of the battle before it begins," Desmond answered studiously.

"How is it a warrior to accomplishes this?" Mifuné pressed further.

"By uniting his mind, body, and spirit. This is the key to Absolute Focus."

"Very good, Desmond. You have learned well."

"Thank you, Master!" Desmond replied, bowed his head. The grin on his face beamed with pride.

"Gabrysia, when summoning magic for use in battle, what is the most important thing to remember?" Mifuné asked.

117

The Fall of Avalon

"To know where your enemy is. To know where your allies are. And to know what force is required to defeat your enemy with precision."

"And what is the key for harnessing your power?" Mifuné asked again.

"Finding resonance with myself and the world around me, to feel the natural energies that flow from everything."

"That is very good. You would have made my old master proud."

"Thank you, Master."

Gabrysia could not help but to blush. Argus Nox was well known and highly respected in the kingdom of Eramar. Gabrysia herself had even dreamed of meeting him one day when she was a young girl. To hear those words from the man who knew him best was the greatest compliment she could ever hope to receive.

"Naomi!" Mifuné called without glancing in her direction.

Naomi nearly jumped out of her skin when he called her name. She had been so lost in thought that she did not realize, she hid behind the door still. She bolted through like a frightened cat running from a loud sound. She skirted around the group to face Mifuné. She rendered a short, reverent bow and took her seat between Desmond and Gabrysia.

"Yes, Master?"

"What is the greatest principle of the Arcane Arts?"

Naomi hesitated. The Arcane Arts was the most complex form of magic a mage could attempt. Though it was Naomi's specialty, she was far from proficient. Even with Mifuné's guidance, her skills and abilities with the Arcane Arts extended little past her ability to manipulate animals. She tossed around different principles in her mind, but she knew none of them were correct. She hung her head and pulled up her hood.

"I do not remember, Master."

Mifuné nodded. He folded his arm behind his back and faced the eastern horizon. The sun was well over the divide between the earth and sky, it cast golden light onto the world below. A light breeze brush against his face akin to a woman's touch. Mifuné breathed it in, soaked in the sunlight. A light breeze brush against his face akin to a woman's touch. His pupils could feel, simultaneously, as a surge of power and wisdom coursed through him.

"The Arcane Arts are unique, Naomi. Argus taught me that they were developed by ancient sorcerers during the Great War as the earliest form of magic. The powers and abilities gained by the first users of the Arcane Arts made the impossible possible and gave the mortals that used them the power to fight against evil." Mifuné paused to face her. "The most important principle, Naomi, is that anything is possible." The Samurai drew his sword and held it up into the sky. Sunlight glinted off the sterling steel, making the blade shine. He could see his own reflection in the sword. He had always found something truly magnificent about such a simple thing. "With this blade, I slew the Ravana seven years ago, a feat which should have been impossible." He lowered the blade so that it crossed

The Fall of Avalon

his body. "I did not possess the talent that you have, Naomi, or even that you have, Gabrysia. Therefore, I know that, once you hone your gifts, there is no limit to what you can accomplish."

Mifuné sheathed the blade and sat with his disciples. They were fixed on him, like children listening to an elder's story. It never ceased to amaze them just how strong his will had proven to be. And he never spoke of that day with pride. Most men would boast of such an achievement and lord their strength over others, but not Mifuné.

"My pupils, if you believe in yourselves, if you remember everything I have taught you, if you push yourselves to achieve something, you will. I have faith in each of you, remember that."

"Well, is this not just a moment to savor?" An unfamiliar voice interrupted the moment Mifuné shared with his disciples. "Just sets a warmth in the heart, would you agree?"

Desmond shot up to his feet, about-faced, and drew his blade. A burly, bearded man of tremendous stature stood before them. He had an impressively large broadsword slung on his back. Daggers and knives of varying sizes and function were strapped to his belt. Naomi and Gabrysia positioned themselves in front of their Master. Blue fire erupted in Gabrysia's hands, as scarlet red fire ignited in Naomi's.

"Which one of you is Mifuné?" the interloper asked rhetorically.

"If you want to get to our Master, you'll have to walk over us first!" Desmond shouted.

Carl Houston Roach IV

"I only came for the Samurai. I have no quarrel with you, boy," the man replied.

"You came here to threaten my Master, no doubt at the Queen's bidding! That is plenty quarrel for me!"

The man stepped forward, and each young warrior flinched. He was not even the slightest bit intimidated by the swift swordsman and two magic users. After his second step, Gabrysia hurled a ball of blue fire as large as he was straight toward him. It struck the ground in front of him and exploded with tremendous force. Searing blue flames were left in its wake. The trespasser drew the large broadsword from his back. Undaunted, with a single swing, he swept the flames away from him. His determination was resolute.

As the beastly man approached, Naomi stepped into the fray. She joined her hands and formed a triangle within which he was in focused. A stream of furious fire launched from her hands. The intensity of the flame's heat could be felt even behind her. Surprisingly, the man knocked it away effortlessly with the sword in his hand. As Naomi's scarlet fire disappeared, Desmond closed the gap between himself and the encroacher. In the blink of an eye, he swept his sword diagonally from his right shoulder down to his left side. Before the blade connected with its target, the oncoming warrior stopped Desmond's blade mid swing. Desmond's eyes widened when he saw some form of runes illuminate across the length of the blade. They faded almost as quickly as they had appeared. That must be how he was able to deflect Gabrysia and Naomi's spells, Desmond concluded.

Before he could make another move, the invader balled his free hand into a fist and launched it against Desmond. Titanic force connected with the young man's face. Pain shot through his entire body from the impact. He crashed against the ground beside the advancing man. He struggled to get up and continue the fight. Every muscle in his body fought to push off the ground, but the throbbing pain in his face deterred him.

"Enough," Mifuné said. Gabrysia and Naomi turned their heads to their Master. He stood up and walked towards the stranger. Without question, they closed their hands, extinguished the flames, and stepped back. Mifuné and the foreigner faced one another. The man was a mountain compared to Mifuné. He stood over a head taller and was nearly twice as wide. He had a fearsome look in his eye, much the same as the look in Mifuné's.

"You are very brave to come after me alone. Foolish, but brave. Who are you?" Mifuné asked.

"My name is Sergei Meisner, and I have come seeking Mifuné Tahaka."

"Sergei Meisner, the Boar of the East Hills," Mifuné replied.

"So, you have heard of me?" Sergei asked.

"I have. Your hunting skills were fast becoming legend. Years ago, I intended to make you a Knight of Avalon."

"On what authority could you have made me a knight of any kind?"

Carl Houston Roach IV

"Because I was once Avalon's sharpest sword. I protected the kingdom as the Paladin."

"I heard different. They told me you were a criminal. A monster who had intended to usurp the throne of Avalon and massacre its people." Sergei paused. "Though, I do not see what the concern is. How could a man so small create such a stir?"

"It is not size that makes a man strong," Mifuné replied. "It is the manifestation of a man's will that makes him strong."

"That is tough talk, coming from a man who fights in pajamas."

Mifuné gripped the handle of his sword. He was growing frustrated with the outsider, and more so with the Queen. He was not surprised though. She was as predictable as ever. If she was going to receive any assistance against him, it would inevitably become necessary for her to lie yet again.

Sergei looked at the sword in Mifuné's sash and sneered. Though it was comparable in length, compared to his own bulky, heavy sword, Mifuné's katana was slender and small.

"And you call that a sword? It looks like the kind of blade you give a child before he is ready to call himself a warrior." Sergei erupted into laughter. "I would wager your sword breaks as soon as it hits mine!"

"Enough. If we are going to fight, then let us fight."

Sergei ceased his laughter. He raised the colossal blade in his hand over his head and swung is down against Mifuné. Mifuné stopped the attack well above his head with a lightning fast parry. His arm strained mightily to keep the blade from continuing down towards the top of his head. Both their brows tensed. Their clenched teeth could be seen through the lining of their cheeks. They were gritted nearly to the point of breaking. Sergei pulled his sword away and stepped back. He could not hide the look of surprise on his face.

"It has been many years since I faced a man as strong as you. You are truly worthy of your title, Boar of the Eastern Hills," Mifuné said.

Sergei shook off his surprised expression. "I have only just started!" He lunged forward with a mighty roar and swung his blade.

Mifuné blocked precisely and countered with his own swing. Sergei altered the position of his blade to stop Mifuné's attack. One attack after another, Mifuné continued his assault. Sergei struggled against Mifuné's speed. His blade moved so swiftly through the air, it was practically invisible. Sergei rapidly deduced that he could not afford to make a single mistake. It very well might prove to be his last. Their swords locked against one another. They each pushed forward with all their might. Sergei's heavy feet dug into the ground; Mifuné's in kind. From an outside perspective, they appeared to be evenly matched.

"I have to hand it to you, you are stronger than you look," Sergei said.

"You have yet to see my full strength," Mifuné grunted.

While Mifuné fought Sergei, Naomi rushed to Desmond's aid. Though he was hurt, with a little support from her, he was back on his feet. They carefully and quickly maneuvered away from the battle back to where Gabrysia stood.

Gabrysia had crossed her arms as she watched the fighting. She tapped her fingers impatiently against her arm. Her brow tensed, and her face twisted into a scowl. Her displeasure became evident to Naomi, as well as Desmond. She shook her head.

"Gabrysia, what is it?" Naomi asked.

"I do not believe this!" she said perturbed.

"What is the matter?" Desmond replied.

"I do not believe Master is really trying. I think he is playing with him."

"Are you sure?" Desmond asked. "That man is strong, there is no question." He rubbed the side of his face, which still throbbed from the force of the punch.

"Watch closely."

Sergei pushed Mifuné back and continued his assault. His swings were heavy, and while they lacked the same speed as Mifuné's, there was no shortage of danger behind them. Mifuné seemed to prefer evading the swings with his superior agility rather than to contend with parrying the swings. Most noticeably, he had plenty of time between each evasion to strike Sergei down.

"I see what you mean," Naomi replied. Desmond nodded in agreement.

"Not only that, we saw what Master did against that small army the Queen sent. Why does he not just do that now and end this?"

Gabrysia was right, Naomi and. Desmond thought. This fight was pointless, at least from

The Fall of Avalon

where they stood. It was not clear to them what their Master stood to gain from drawing it out. That never seemed to be a point of interest for Mifuné as far as they had observed. What reason could he have had to draw this out, they wondered.

Their battle went on for hours. Mifuné and Sergei went back and forth between who was dominating the fight, and who was on the defensive. Their fighting styles were so dynamically different. Whereas Mifuné fought silently, calculatedly, swiftly, Sergei fought with brute force, tenacity, and boisterous fervor.

Desmond began to understand what Mifuné was after. Oh, I see now I know why Master did not just wipe this beastly man off the face of the Earth, he thought. This man has talent, and genuine skill that set him apart from the kind of warriors we have contended with from Avalon, Desmond mused further. Little did he know how right he was. He was completely blown away by this opponent's swordsmanship. Even after training with Mifuné for four months, Desmond was still unable to hold his ground against his Master. Sergei Meisner, the Boar of the East Hills, managed to last for hours against the man who each of the three disciples believed was the greatest warrior in the world.

About three hours past noon, the two warriors stopped clashing with one another. Their shoulders rose and fell heavily with each breath they sucked in. Sweat drenched their tattered clothes. Sergei's hair was a mess, and Mifuné's bangs stuck to his forehead from under his kasa. Sergei looked determined to win the battle of his life. All the while, to Mifuné it was a just an accommodate match. Mifuné swung his sword out in front of him, orienting the tip downward, and smoothly placed it back in its sheath.

Sergei's eyes shot open as the guard of Mifuné's sword clicked against the sheath. Sergei knuckles went white around the handle of the blade in his hands. His lips separated, revealing his clenched teeth. "We are not done here!" Sergei screamed.

"Yes. We are." Mifuné stated flatly. "You are a formidable opponent, and a worthy swordsman, but you will never defeat me."

"Is that so? You think you are so powerful that a man like me cannot defeat you?! Who do you think you are!?" Sergei bellowed, outraged.

Mifuné went silent. He reached under his kasa and slicked his hair back into place. His refusal to answer enraged Sergei more so than if Mifuné would have replied.

"I do not care about this 'true strength' you say you have! The runes in this sword are powerful enough to repel magic! To kill demons and vanquish evil! If you are as powerful as you think you are, let's see you stop me from driving this blade through your heart!"

Sergei charged Mifuné, sword raised over his head. He roared like a lion about to devour its prey. The mass in his arms swelled to an unprecedented size. The sword came down against Mifuné, who, despite the danger, was completely still. The blade struck an invisible sphere that surrounded Mifuné. Purple energy erupted around the sphere that encompassed Mifuné's whole body. It began slowly and increased in speed and intensity with each passing second. There was a flash of white. The sword in Sergei's hands shattered into hundreds of tiny metal shards, and he was blasted backward as if by some spell.

Dark clouds encircled the sky above Mifuné and spread until they completely blocked out the sun. Winds as intense as a hurricane howled, shaking the trees behind them. Horrible flashes of lightning jolted across the sky, and thunder rang out overhead like the stomping feet of the gods. The ground began to quake as if the world itself quivered. The tower beside them groaned, as if it was going to collapse.

Caught up in the ensuing chaos, Mifuné disciples struggled to maintain their footing. The wind pulled and pushed them. They grunted as they resisted it. As the ground shook, Gabrysia took hold of Naomi and Desmond. She focused her power, and surrounded them with a cerulean barrier. From within the barrier, Desmond and Naomi continued to watch. Fear crept into their hearts all the while the chaos ensued, and as the power erupted from their Master, but nothing could prepare them for the terror they would witness next.

Sergei struck the ground and rolled through the grass until he stopped on his belly. He struggled to raise his head. When he had lifted it, he shuttered to see the environment had changed so drastically. What Sergei witnessed was beyond any man or beast he had ever encountered. He covered his head with both hands from the howling wind. As he felt the ground beneath him shake, he quickly scanned

Carl Houston Roach IV

his surroundings, seeking a safe place to retreat to. Although, there would be no safe place, he quickly realized. For when he looked up, Sergei saw Mifuné with glowing white eyes that pierced though the vortex of power erupting from him.

Beyond that, an apparition took form which Sergei had never seen before. It manifested above Mifuné, as if it were rising out of the vortex of power which surrounded him. It matched the purple aura, though it was darker. A black aura wisped off of the monstrosity as it took form. The grotesque, ethereal thing he saw towered over the trees. It had one head. Its two eyes glowed white, exactly like Mifuné's. Four powerful arms extended from its human-like torso. Each hand held in it a different weapon of enormous size: a spear, a mace, an axe, and a sword.

Sergei discarded his pride and fell upon his hands and knees. As loud as he could, over the rumbling of the ground beneath him and the shrieking winds above him, he cried out for mercy. Tears poured down from his eyes and dripped onto the blades of grass. "Spare me! Please, have mercy!"

"Why have you come here!?" Mifuné demanded. The volume of his voice was that of a tornado, the tone of which echoed in Sergei's very existence as if thousands of voices spoke with him all at once.

"She has my family! My river lily and my two little beagles. I had to. Please! The Queen threatened to kill them if I did not fight you! I beg you, Mifuné, if you must kill me, spare them."

The Fall of Avalon

Sergei beseeched. "They're all that matters to me in this world."

Mifuné approached Sergei, and the ethereal figure above him moved synchronously with each step he took. His footfalls were heavy enough to break the ground beneath him. Sergei flinched when he heard Mifuné draw his sword once more. He knew brandishing any of the other weapons he had would be meaningless. There was nothing beneath the heavens above that could match the power he was pitted against. This is the end, Sergei believed.

"Please! Have mercy! I have no allegiance to anyone but my own. I did not want to be here in the first place! Titania, Queen of Avalon dragged me here from my home and threatened my family!"

Naomi and Gabrysia's hearts dropped, and even Desmond's did. Suddenly, this man was no longer an enemy. Suddenly, each of them had something in common. And it was then within that very moment in time that they understood why Mifuné did not simply wipe this man off the face of the earth as he had done with so many others.

"You hold no allegiance to Titania of Avalon?" Mifuné asked.

"No! None at all," Sergei assured.

Mifuné's gleaming white eyes closed. One by one, each terror erupting from him vanished. The horrific image above him faded away to nothing. The ground ceased its tremors. The winds settled back to a calm summer breeze. The gray clouds that had overtaken the skies cleared away. The vortex of power which encircled Mifuné faded away, and Mifuné's eyes opened in their normal state.

Carl Houston Roach IV

"Then let us strike up an accord." Mifuné put his sword back in its sheath. "Join with me. Fight alongside me and my disciples against Titania, and we will help you save your family."

Sergei was silent. Everything the knights had told him, every word the Paladin who sent him to this fray breathed about this man, was true. Mifuné was as much a monster as they had claimed. The nightmarish image he had witnessed rise out of this man would remain etched into his memory for all his days. With that same power, though, it was possible that he could help Sergei save his family.

"What say you?"

"How can I trust the word of a monster like you?"

"I swear on the honor of the Dragon Emperor: Himimaru Tahaka, and the honor of his bloodline, if you stand with me, I will help you recover what you have lost. What say you, Boar of the Eastern Hills?"

"Yes. I will join you."

"Then rise."

Sergei slowly rose to his feet. His body was already sore and aching. Apprehension still lingered in his heart, as he stood face to face with Mifuné, yet he faced him anyway. Mifuné bowed slightly for a moment and Sergei returned the gesture.

❧

Meanwhile, in Avalon, Queen Titania had finally convinced Virgil to meet with her in his room atop the Paladin's Tower. It had been several months since she had been in this room. Every time she walked through that door, she remembered the first time she felt his skin on hers. The ecstasy, the pleasure, the power. Bringing up that memory would be useless now, as she could see a change in Virgil's eyes.

"Thank you for agreeing to see me here, Virgil," the Queen said shyly.

"What do you want, Titania?" Virgil asked. His voice was empty, like an echo in an empty corridor.

There was no love, no anger, no trace of any feeling in him at all. The Queen gritted at this lack of expression. Virgil was hers to do with as she pleased, such was the place of the Paladin. Nothing she had asked him to do in the past few days was beyond his scope to accomplish, or beyond her scope to demand. Despite that, she could sense a schism forming between them. Queen Titania knew that it would only continue to grow with time. She could not go on with this gap between them. She closed the door behind her and fell against him.

"I am so sorry, Virgil," the Queen uttered softly. "I have asked so much of you since this started. I have said such cruel things to you. I have treated you so poorly, the most important person to me." Tears streamed from her eyes and stained her cheeks. "I cannot bear the thought of strife between us."

Virgil wrapped his arms over his Queen and held her close. He laid his cheek against the top of her head. Her hair smelled sweet, as it always did. The Queen's feminine wiles did very little, if anything, to chase away the demon of failure that haunted him, the direct result of her collaring him like a dog. The way he lied to the people to sway their thoughts. The way he abandoned the garrison like sheep to a slaughter. He could still see the faces of the deserter soldiers he and the General put down. Their shrieks of fear and helplessness rang in his ears. Their blood stained his hands still, metaphysically. Virgil hardly recognized himself anymore.

"Are you still with me, Virgil?" Titania asked. "Please do not leave me. I am losing everything and everyone. I cannot lose you, too."

Virgil wiped away the Queen's tears and kissed her lips. She returned his kiss passionately, wholeheartedly, with as much affection as she had ever shared with him, or with anyone for that matter. When their lips parted, they stared deeply into one another's eyes. Tears dripped out onto his face.

"You will never lose me, my love. Until my last breath, I will be yours and yours alone."

Titania smiled and leaned her head against his powerful chest. Virgil cupped his hands on her waist. A mix of emotions swirled in his heart: guilt; love; joy; pain. He knew it was not going to get easier. The final day of Mifuné's warning was drawing near. He and his queen each knew the man they sent to dispatch him would not be enough. Even an enchanted Runic Sword was not going to be enough to turn the tide.

"Virgil," the Queen said softly.

"Yes?"

"There is something I need you to do for me."

"Name it, and it shall be done."

"The mercenary's family…"

The Fall of Avalon

Virgil immediately released her from his embrace. He was still, cold, like a tombstone. He stepped past and pushed open the door. His face was devoid of any emotion. He stopped before the descent down the stairs. His hand rested atop the railing that would lead him down. Virgil turned his head over his shoulder to the beautiful woman still standing in his room. The Queen turned her gaze to him, sorrow deeply embedded in her eyes.

"I am your shield," he said softly, "I am your sword." Virgil's last words were terse, tinged with pain.

Without another word, he set forth to the deepest descent of the palace, down to the dungeon. This was far from the first time he had made this descent in his time as the Paladin. He aptly described it to the other knights, once when they inquired of him what it was like. "It is like descending from Paradise into the pits of the Underworld," he stated. Those words rang in his ears as he descended. The further he moved away from the light in his room atop the tower, the more he began to wonder: What Paradise, if any, could await me when this is all over, for all that I have done, and still am to do.

Carl Houston Roach IV

His was the blade that felled The Lord of Chaos.
To him, Ravana was bound for all eternity, but
there would be no reward for his sacrifice.

The Samurai's disciples and new guest finished their meal just as the sun began to set. Gabrysia had prepared the fire that night, while Naomi collected drinking water from the lagoon in the woods. They made idle chat amongst themselves while the meal was prepared. As accepting as the young warriors were, they still knew nothing about Sergei and thereby had little to say to him.

"What is your wife's name?" Gabrysia asked politely after she completely swallowed a mouthful of fish and rice.

"Amelia," Sergei replied as he took a bite out of the fish he gripped between his fingers. His mouth was full when he spoke, and bits of food embedded themselves into his beard.

"Is she pretty?" Desmond asked, curiously.

Sergei only returned to him a guarded look. His eyes squinted, and his brow furrowed slightly. The delicate fish bones in his grip snapped under the tension between Sergei's fingertips.

"I meant no offense, just making conversation." Desmond inched away from him after hearing the faintest sound of growling.

"What about your children? Surely you could tell us about them," Naomi asserted.

The Fall of Avalon

"I have a son who is five years old, and a daughter who is four," Sergei replied firmly. He discarded the bare fish bones simultaneously.

They had hoped Mifuné would join them to break up the awkward tense silence. Unfortunately, after the fight, he confined himself to his room atop the tower without any explanation or indication of return. It seemed that the closer he drew himself to the situation with The Queen of Avalon, the more he withdrew from the rest of them.

"Is he always this sociable?" Sergei asked, chomping on his final piece of fish.

Naomi shot a piercing gaze at him. Of all the people, she thought, you have the least to say about being sociable. Sergei was boorish, rude, and uncaring. They had welcomed him, yet he acted as if he did not care whether or not he had been. The worst for Naomi was his apparent disdain for Mifuné.

"To be honest, this did not start until he confronted the Queen," Desmond answered.

"I... we... think that it did something to him, seeing her again," Gabrysia inputted.

"Right... And you said she had something to do with locking him away, right?" Sergei inquired, orienting his fish bone at Gabrysia.

"That is what he has told us," Gabrysia answered.

"And you have no doubts about this? None at all?"

"The restraints on him were beyond anything we had encountered before." Naomi responded. "We had to utilize Gabrysia's and my combined magic to break them, and it almost killed us to do so." She continued to glare at Sergei from where she sat. He dismissed her potent stare with little acknowledgment.

"Why does he hide out in that tower by himself?" Sergei asked Gabrysia. "You seem to be the smart one, so why don't you tell me?"

Gabrysia lightly shook her head. "I do not know. I do not know everything my Master thinks and feels."

"And you?" He pointed to Desmond. "You carry a sword, so assume he has mentored you. Maybe you can shed some light on what he does up there."

"I cannot say for sure. I think he meditates, practices Absolute Focus, but I could not say with certainty," Desmond replied.

Sergei nodded and feigned interest in the answer. "What about you, Red?" he asked Naomi. "What do you think he does up there all day?"

Naomi did not reply, nor did she dignify his nickname. Her nostrils flared. Her eyes were lit ablaze with indignation. She could feel her heart pounding out of her chest as though it were attempting to lash out against the brutish Sergei of its own accord. She stilled herself just enough to say: "He has his reasons. What he needs us to know, he tells us."

Gabrysia and Desmond looked at one another. They took the same oath that Naomi had when they freed Mifuné from his bonds, but even they had doubts. There was more than enough information that they did not know to substantiate a healthy level of uncertainty that their Master's temperament was solely stemmed from his being imprisoned. There might really be nothing more to it, both all surmised, but they waited patiently for him to share with them the full truth before casting their final verdict. The waiting, however, made them anxious about the truth, and why he might have withheld it from them for so long. Naomi was unwavering, nonetheless. Desmond and Gabrysia could not understand why that might be. Perhaps it was her love for the man, perhaps it was something else. The more they talked to this skeptical man who sat on the outside of the situation, the more their doubts compiled.

"So, you three are telling me, you have absolutely no quarrel with a man whose ambition is to rip down an entire civilization?" Sergei's blatant skepticism resounded in his voice and mannerisms. "And you are willing to take part in that endeavor?"

"Master might be mysterious and cryptic about things, but he always has a reason for what he does," Desmond replied. "He has been that way for as long as I have known him. He is not just some cold-blooded killer."

"He is a man of honor," Gabrysia added. "Probably one of the most honorable I have ever met. How a man like him could serve a Queen like her is beyond me."

"Make no mistake, I understand his grievance with the Queen. If she were standing here now, I would cut her throat myself," Sergei said.

"I think any of us would, just on principle at this point," Desmond said.

Carl Houston Roach IV

"I do understand what you mean, Sergei," Gabrysia replied. "There are innocent people between us and her."

"And how many are going to die undeservingly before he gets to her?" Sergei asked. "Surely you have put some thought to that. Why should he get to decide who lives and who dies?"

"How… How many do you think, Des?" Gabrysia asked.

"I do not know."

"Thousands," Mifuné answered, standing just outside their circle.

Desmond and Gabrysia shot up from their seats. It was one thing to express their concerns amongst each other, but to think their Master had possibly heard them expressing doubts about him with someone they hardly knew shamed and embarrassed them. "Master…" Desmond searched the farthest and deepest recesses of his mind for something to say, something that might spare them from his wrath, a wrath with which they were all too familiar. Before he or Gabrysia could speak, Mifuné raised an open hand to them.

"I know you have questions." Mifuné began, "I know you have doubts about what I am here to do and why." He took a deep breath. He then sat beside the fire. Into his hand he scooped a heavy wad of dirt, which he then cast into the flames. "It is time you learned." Mifuné began to tell his tale, "Seven years ago…"

&❧

A terrible calamity, The Lord of Chaos, from the time of the Great War awakened in the land of

139

The Fall of Avalon

Androma. Ravana was what it was called. It rose up in the lands between the southern kingdom of Kilbin and Avalon. Its power was so destructive and chaotic, that its very presence was a plague on Avalon and its neighbors. The four kingdoms were beset with horrible plagues. Cattle died in catastrophic numbers. Crops failed at an alarming rate. Innocent people suffered and died from demonic onslaughts brought on by Ravana's hordes, and by Ravana himself. Something needed to be done to stop this monster's rampage, or all would have been lost.

The leaders of the four kingdoms convened and discussed possible strategies to deal with the problem we all shared. For the first time in the history of the four kingdoms, all past grudges were set aside in order to focus on the future, or there would be no future for any of us. I, and my former master, Argus, were present. We stood beside Titania to advise her during the deliberations. Argus had proposed to her, before the meeting, that the best chance the kingdoms had of defeating the Ravana was to assemble the realm's greatest champions—warriors and magicians—and combat The Lord of Chaos head on..

Days went by, and Ravana continued its rampage. Everything in its path was destroyed. After enough of Kilbin had been laid to waste, Ravana turned its attention to Avalon. After continual pushing and arguing, a decision was finally reached. Titania brought Argus's proposal to the council's attention, and it was accepted eagerly, which led to the formation of the Company of

Carl Houston Roach IV

Heroes. As rapidly as we were able, Argus and I gathered together the strongest and wisest of the warriors and mages in the four kingdoms and brought them to Avalon. The rulers of the kingdoms bestowed command authority to Master Argus. His proficiency and knowledge of magic and warfare made him the prime candidate for leader.

One-hundred warriors, each were experts in their discipline, gathered in Avalon for a feast of generous proportions. The best meats, finest ales and wines, fresh bread from only premier bakers, and women and men of the most desirable appeal, were available to them, to us, that night. The next morning, we would embark on our campaign against the ancient evil, and possibly never see home again.

Never had such revel been had by so few. They danced, they sang, they drank, and they laughed. They traded stories, played games, and competed in areas of their specialties. Argus himself sat amongst the wisest and most powerful of the sorcerers from the other kingdoms. I presume they spoke about the highest orders of magic and their purposes. He always found bliss in sharing his knowledge with others and hearing out what they had to say.

I spent that night with Titania. She was the love of my life, my hope for a future, my very world. She was everything I fought to protect. To this day, I still remember the taste of her lips against mine. The feeling of her skin. Her whispers in my ear. All of it.

That night, I asked her to be mine, and only mine. I asked her to marry me on the day that I

The Fall of Avalon

should return from doing battle with the great evil that threatened our home. I presented her a ring with an opal center stone and shimmering accent gems. She accepted the ring with tears in her eyes and kissed me as though it were her dream becoming reality. And in the morning, with that promise in my heart, I set out alongside the others.

While the other warriors dreaded what lay ahead of us, I looked beyond that. I looked to the future I believed would be mine. I motivated them to take heart and have courage. I assured them we would be victorious. That we were the greatest and the strongest in the realm was no small thing, and certainly was not something to forget. One by one, their spirits illuminated, I could see it in their eyes. I even saw my former Master smile at my optimism. I realize now, he only jested at my folly.

The Company of Heroes intercepted the Ravana before it arrived at the river Bahtal, the waters that separates Kilbin from Avalon. This was where, Argus launched the assault against the Ravana and its demons. With all our strengths and skills combined, we pushed back the demonic horde from the river and vanquished them in the Field of Nalatsil. Our hopes had grown from a candle in the night into an unstoppable wildfire. We wasted no time surrounding the Ravana and commenced our attack against it.

The battle against the Ravana lasted three days. On the first day, we attacked, hoping to overrun the monster with our full strength gathered. Arrows flew, spells were cast, sword skills were brought to bear, far greater than what you have seen me unleash. It seemed like we would take the day. On the contrary, as great as we were, what we faced was a massacre.

The Lord of Chaos shrugged off the assault as easily as one of you might sweep a few ants from your sleeve. After withstanding our greatest efforts, the Ravana retaliated. I had never known fear until that day. I watched as the greatest warriors in the four kingdoms were obliterated by the power of the Ravana. Not one by one, but in droves. The greatest of armor, the mightiest of shields, the most powerful of protection spells, nothing proved a match for the Ravana, The Lord of Chaos's unrelenting power.

By the second day, only ten of us remained. Argus, and I, and a few others lingered on and continued the fight. Argus took on the mantle of healing the injured, myself included, using Arcane healing magic. Those of us who could continue to fight did all that we could to bring the Ravana down. I mustered the strength to use the most powerful of the techniques of the Dragon Emperor's Sword style. It helped nothing, to my eternal dismay. Before the sun set that day, the Ravana ran his gigantic spear through Argus's chest. I held him in my arms as I watched the light leave his eyes. There was nothing I could do to save my former Master, my friend.

By the dawn of the third day, I was the only one left. Corpses littered the battlefield. My sword shook in my hands. My body quivered in the face of the Ravana and his overwhelming power. He mocked my presence and my fear with a haughty

The Fall of Avalon

laugh. Then, he assembled to himself a legion of demons too numerous to count, more than what the Company of Heroes had felled at the beginning of the battle. They echoed his laughter at my plight. They eyed me with a hunger for my flesh and bones and a thirst for my blood.

The Lord of Chaos' laughter stopped, suddenly. He lowered his guard, and spread each of his four arms open. He tempted me, dared me, compelled me, to attack him. If I had any courage as a man, if I had any strength as a swordsman, if I had any pride as a warrior, I would attack. His jests at me coaxed his demonic hoard into laughter—laughter that still haunts my memory to this day.

I steadied myself. I became as the water that flows in the river—calm and still. My body then hardened like a mountain. My lungs filled up with air, and my heart ignited with fire. I mustered my full strength, my will, my very being, and channeled it all into one final attack. The Ravana did not defend against it. He only laughed as my blade came for him.

In the battle of will against might, I had proven victorious. As much a surprise to me as to him, my blade cleaved him in twain. When his massive torso crashed against the ground, a fountain of black blood poured out of his body and pooled beside his hulking mass. The demonic horde scattered in terror, like cockroaches exposed to light. I could feel it, though. The battle was not over.

The Ravana's spirit did not move on as most things do when they die. Instead, I felt its presence filling my body. It was suffocating. I could feel my

Carl Houston Roach IV

own life being choked away. A burning sensation covered every inch of my flesh, as if my body had been set ablaze. Darkness crept over my eyes. The end was near, yet I refused to yield to this evil.

Although, its spirit was pressed down into my chest. Power swirled around me as I had never felt before. I gripped my sword tight with both hands. It shook wildly from the pressure. I screamed as I forced Ravana further and further away from my heart and my mind. With all my will summoned up and brought to bear, my sword began to shine. I forced The Lord of Chaos out of my body, and then, I managed to force the Ravana into this blade which erupted in black fire. Before the Ravana could escape, I closed the sword in its sheath and sealed it away.

Ten gold emblems suddenly appeared across the length of the sheath. Each one is a symbol from my ancestors, the greatest dragon emperors of my people. The first symbol is Himimaru Tahaka, the founder of the Lotus Tribe, and the last is the symbol of Satoshi Tahaka, I believe their spirits reached out to me from beyond to help me seal the Ravana away. Since that day, Ravana, The Lord of Chaos exists within this sword. No one can ever touch it, lest they be corrupted by Ravana. I am the only one who can bear this burden.

I was able to send word back to Titania that I had endured. That our campaign was successful, and that the Ravana had been vanquished. I was grieved to inform her that I was the only one who survived. She requested of me that I meet her here, at the Tower of Galahad, so we might be alone. I

The Fall of Avalon

agreed and made my way here. I thought nothing of it, only that my dearest love wanted time to see me alone before my triumphal return to the city.

When I arrived, *she* was there, at the entrance to the tower. She wore a scarlet dress that she knew I fancied. She smiled and kissed me when she greeted me, as sweetly and lovingly as she ever had. My sorrows were lifted, just for a moment. Without much effort, she enticed me to follow her inside the tower to the antechamber. I slowly noticed that she seemed different, somehow.

When I stood in the center of the room, all expressions of joy or love or care vanished from her face. She snapped her fingers, and from all around the room I was struck with beams of light. I fell to my knees under the crushing pressure building upon me. Pain coursed through my body. I was unable to move. I screamed, but no one outside of the room could hear me. I fought against the light as hard as I could, but I was too weak. I still had not fully recovered from my battle with Ravana.

I asked her why, why she was doing this. I did not understand why this was happening, I could not fathom any plausible, compelling reason. I had been faithful to her. I had fought her enemies, protected her, and protected Avalon. I had loved her as best a man could love anyone.

The last thing Titania said to me was this: "I have no use for you anymore, Mifuné. So, I shall keep you here, under this tower, for the rest of your days. No one shall know you ever came back." She stepped closer and continued, "No one came back. It took all of your lives to destroy the Ravana!"

Carl Houston Roach IV

With all the strength I could manage, I raised my head. Titania stood over me. I could see her face, but I could not believe what I saw. Her eyes were wide open. Her pupils were dilated and focused, like a predator's. Her tapered ears seemed less elegant and more like razors. Her lips and mouth spread wide across her face, bringing all her teeth to bare in a wicked smile.

There was glee in her. I could hear it in her voice. I could see it in her eyes. That was the last thing I saw before her mages sealed me in a cage of light and moved me under the tower. She wanted that to happen, and she was happy to do it. It is as clear to me now as it ever was.

Before Ravana appeared in the southlands, Argus was Titania's personal council and advisor. We did not have a Paladin then. The Paladin who came before Virgil, Jacob, had died, and the next Paladin had not yet awakened. Argus recommended me to Titania as a candidate for Paladin.

I had been under his tutelage for thirteen years as his disciple. During that time, I became a sword master. Through rigorous training and effort, by the end of those thirteen years, I achieved Absolute Focus, an ability not seen in mortals since the Great War. Shortly thereafter, I was able to achieve a decisive victory against Argus. I was no longer his disciple, but his equal.

Titania decided that the decision ought to be made through a tournament. In the final round, I was the victor. I had proven my strength to her. I gained the title and position of Paladin, and I would serve as Avalon's elite guardian until the next

The Fall of Avalon

Paladin awakened. With this new position, it became necessary for me to travel around with Titania and Argus. Argus was an honest man, wise, and powerful, worthy of his ancestors and the pride of his lineage. I had known him since I was a young boy. As I said, he was my Master. He trained me, made me the warrior that I am today.

Titania was not like him. She was much like a child, always obsessed with having her way. She always found a way to make that happen. Whether through persuasion, or force. Argus knew how prosperous Avalon was, but he began to wonder if this prosperity was the result of favor with gods, or if it was at the expense of the other kingdoms. Over time, he began to suspect Titania might have been making deals with prominent members of other kingdoms to prosper Avalon.

Corruption could only be by way of their Inquisitors; those men and women have prominent political standing and heavy sway on the decisions made by the Kings and Queens of the realm. They also typically serve as ambassadors to other nations. Argus, himself, met with several of the Inquisitors from the other kingdoms on multiple occasions. He told me he would only ever trust them as much as he must.

Argus analyzed the ledgers in The Queen's Chambers to find evidence of transactions that may have transpired between Titania and any of the Inquisitors. As he suspected, the data he collected from the ledgers was inconsistent with what he saw in the official records of the city. There was always more money missing from the treasury than her ledgers recorded. Less troops had been deployed in support of our allies during times of war than the ledgers indicated.

Argus needed answers, so he continued to dig. Several letters turned up in his search, that detailed dealings between Titania and at least three different Grand Inquisitors from the other three kingdoms. Some dealt with war, some with payments. Several of them were old, and nearly turned to powder when he touched them. Titania's dealings had been going on possibly for centuries. His visits to the three other kingdoms were the final proof he needed to confirm his suspicions, especially Eramar, the one kingdom who could rival Avalon for military might. The political division caused multiple factions to form against King Gregory, factions which challenged The King's regime.

It was not just the aristocracy that suffered as a result of the Queen's double dealings. The upheavals that the royals dealt and unleashed upon each other gravely impacted those below them. The general depravity of the citizens in the towns and villages near the capital horrified him. People were starving, dressed in rags, begging and praying for a miracle.

Argus recorded his findings in a journal that he kept with him. It detailed the inconsistencies in Avalon's transactions in comparison with the other kingdoms, along with the letters listing transactions between Titania and the Inquisitors over time. He thought it prudent to keep the information as accurate as possible.

The Fall of Avalon

Argus thought to take his findings to Eramar and inform King Gregory of his Inquisitors' betrayal. He urged me to come with him, to see for myself the truth about what Titania was really doing. He wanted me to see what he had discovered her to be, and how she was hurting everyone outside of Avalon.

I would not listen, though. I was so enamored with her; I was so ensnared in the promises she gave me, and the love she poured out to me, that I would not see the truth. Or, perhaps, I ignored it. I just did not want to believe something as beautiful as her could be corrupt.

Argus meant to set out on his own. He would not be stopped, not by me, not by her. Somehow, she caught wind of his plan and left the city, for a day or so. She pleaded with me to stay and watch over Avalon in her absence. I insisted that I should go with her. I feared for her safety without me. She promised me that she would return to me swiftly, so I agreed to stay in the city and watch over the people.

When she returned, she was quiet. Something had changed, but I did not know what it was or why. She had lost the spring in her step. She seemed weaker. Her hands would shake from time to time. She struggled with mundane tasks, like opening doors, or feeding herself. I worried she might have become ill. I stayed by her side every moment that I could.

Just as Argus had finished his preparations to meet with King Gregory, and set out to leave, we received word that something terrible had happened. A monster, Ravana, The Lord of Chaos, was ravaging the southlands. What no one knew then was, only Titania had the power to do the unthinkable... but I know it *now*. Titania herself summoned Ravana to that place.

&

"What!?" Gabrysia interrupted.

"Titania brought that thing to Androma?" Desmond added.

"Why? Why would she do such a thing?" Sergei inquired.

Mifuné raised his hand to them. As painful as it was for him to relive the events of his dark past, he maintained his composure. At that point he was the only one who seemed able to. "Let me continue," he said patiently. "As I told you before, Argus had caught wind of Titania's dealings with the Inquisitors from the other three kingdoms. He suspected treachery on the parts of each of them and meant to bring this to the attention of the other rulers. If Argus had figured this out, it stood very well to reason that others, as prominent as he, would have as well. Fearing the consequences of being exposed, Titania held a meeting with the Inquisitors to discuss how they might take care of their problem. If Argus had figured this out, it stood very well to reason that others, as prominent as he, would have as well."

"The Company of Heroes?" Sergei asked, eyes wide.

Mifuné nodded.

"So that means that...." Desmond began.

The Fall of Avalon

"To protect herself and her cohorts from being exposed for treason." Naomi cut in. "Sh, she…"

"The Queen summoned the Ravana," Gabrysia interjected. "Next, she gathered the most powerful, elite, men and women of Androma to fight it"

"The very men and women who could expose her—bring her to justice." Desmond chimed in again.

"No…" the three called out in disbelief.

"Yes! Titania created the Company of Heroes just to exterminate us." Mifuné finished.

Sergei leaned his arm against his knees and said, "That makes sense, Ravana was a means to an end. But it does not answer how she and a bunch of politicians figured out how to summon and control something like that."

"Make no mistake, Sergei, she never had control over Ravana." Mifuné paused. "Titania is a Fae who inherited tremendous power from her mother, Glorianna. Even Glorianna's power was nothing compared to Ravana's."

"If you believe in all of that," Sergei began.

"You have seen the shadow of Ravana for yourself," Mifuné answered him.

Sergei fell quiet as the memory of the horrible aberration sprang to mind. In the same moment, the image of the monstrosity he witnessed above Mifuné flashed before his eyes.

"Do you know how she did it, Master?" Gabrysia asked.

Mifuné took in a deep breath, then exhaled. "Ravana is one of the greatest among the Lords of Evil. He is the creator of the Demon race. He possesses knowledge of the universe, of magic, of science, and of weaponry. In order to summon him, one must sacrifice to him the blood of six mages, each of which must possess a mastery of one of the magics or sciences. In addition to four warriors who need to be a master of the spear, the mace, the axe, and the sword."

"Oh… Is that all?" Sergei scoffed condescendingly.

Mifuné shook his head. "Power as great as his is only enticed by other great power. Titania had to give up her magic, which far exceeds the Light of the Paladin, and use it as a catalyst for the summoning. It was not until she ripped out her magic and combined it with the blood for the summoning that Ravana appeared."

"That was the reason for her sudden weakness when she went back to Avalon," Desmond said.

"Master," Naomi asked, "how do you know this?"

"Because Ravana told me, himself."

The group was shocked to hear this specific revelation. It was chilling to think of that monster's voice called to their Master. Naomi thought back to earlier that morning: That second voice I heard was Ravana's, it must have been.

"And he talks to you too…?" Sergei asked.

"What you all saw after Sergei and I battled was no illusion; it was real. It was a portion of Ravana and his power, his shadow, manifesting itself through me. He speaks to me, sometimes as whispers in my mind, and sometimes as though he was sitting in the same room with me. While we were locked away in that cage, we had nothing to do and nowhere to go. Rather than battle and struggle against one another, we talked. Because of him, I know more about the ancient world than anyone."

The disciples and Sergei were all dumbfounded. Suddenly, the Samurai's every action, every step and every word made sense. Queen Titania had made so many more than just Mifuné suffer. Thousands, of innocent people suffered and died because of her desire to rule above all others. Gabrysia clenched her fists until her nails dug into her palms. Desmond stood up and walked away from the fire pit. Naomi moved closer to her Master and rested her head against his arm. Sergei remained where he sat.

"Tell me then, Mifuné. If Titania is truly as evil as you say she is, how do we know my family is even alive right now?"

Mifuné's countenance was stone. It had been for the duration of his discourse. His own heart felt like the tempered steel of his sword, beating ice cold blood through his veins. He turned a steady, hardened gaze to Sergei, who winced at the sight of it.

"There is no way to know for certain. They are at her mercy now."

"Evil witch!" Gabrysia muttered through gritted teeth.

Mifuné cast his gaze back to the fire. In it, he saw glimpses of what he was sure was to come. The soldiers fell by the thousands. The great walls surrounding the city shattered and collapsed. Fire consumed everything that would burn. It would only be a few days more before the shining civilization was reduced to nothing more than a pile of cinders and ash. The more he looked into the fire, the more he could feel the spirit of Ravana stir his own spirit into a malevolent frenzy. "And soon, she will be at mine."

Sergei's resolve became like iron. He thrust aside any notion that harm had come to his children or to his wife. If he was going to see them again, he knew in his heart he had to first believe that. Having seen Mifuné's true power, and now with the understanding of Mifuné's connection with the Ravana, he had no doubt that that man would deliver on his promises.

"Master!" Desmond shouted. "What about the Inquisitors? What will we do about them? Will they not come to her aid if we attack the city?"

"They are already dead." Mifuné responded mercilessly.

"Those must have been the people the Paladin told me you murdered," Sergei added.

"The first night of my return to Avalon, they were celebrating the destruction of Ravana. How convenient for me that they should all be assembled there together. I did not recognize them all, not at first. Once I did, I wasted no time cutting them down." Mifuné drew his sword part way from its sheath, exposing the bottom half of the blade. He looked down on it intently, almost with hunger. His eyes were wide, and his breath was loud and heavy. "Every person who is cut down by this blade is taken by Ravana. Their souls feed him now, and they will remain within him for all time. That is their punishment."

Desmond balled his hands into fists. "It is nothing less than what they deserve."

"How do you know that, Master?" Gabrysia asked.

"Because Argus told me. His soul, and the souls of the other heroes, are trapped within Ravana as well. During my time imprisoned, I learned that I can commune with any of the souls within Ravana, so long as I know their name."

Mifuné returned the blade completely to its sheath. The sound of it closing shut sent chills down Gabrysia's spine.

"Makes me wonder, though. Is that your plan for Titania, when this is all over? To have her trapped in there with all of them?" Sergei pondered.

Fury came over Mifuné, evident in his eyes. His brow tensed such that lines formed across his forehead and under his eyes. Naomi backed away from him. She, as well as all the others, could hear the whispering from the sword clearly. She could feel the hatred swirling in Mifuné's heart. The rage and the pain that fueled his ambition set on them all like the tide against a beached stone. Mifuné stood up and walked away from the fire. He faced the eastern horizon, and gazed out to the stars and the moon. He held fast to the sword in his sash, as if it were a part of him. His disciples and the mercenary watched him carefully.

"Before this is over, Titania will wish death was the only thing I came to impart on her. she will watch all that she has built, all that her mother had built, and everything she ever held dear burn to the ground in front of her. I will take from her what she robbed me of, and what she took from all those who did not have the power to stand against her."

A thousand thoughts raced through Naomi's mind as she watched the man for who she cared so deeply. How did you stay so strong? How did you hide it all for so long, she wondered? She could sense his will was fading, as darkness crept into his heart.

"When I first took up the art of the sword, I swore I would be an instrument against evil, no matter what form it may take. Now, there is an evil in this world. And I will destroy it, so it may never harm another innocent life ever again."

"What about the innocent people still in the city? Are they going to share their leader's fate?" Gabrysia asked.

Mifuné shook his head. "No. I have a plan for them."

"And what plan is that?" Sergei asked again. He rose from his seat and marched over to Mifuné's left side.

Mifuné turned and looked Sergei in the eye. Rare was it for him to be challenged in his persuasion of thought. Yet, Sergei was unafraid to challenge him. He stood before him, not as a subordinate, but as an equal.

"In due time, Sergei. In due time."

Desmond quickly took to his Master's side. "No matter what happens, we're with you, Master."

"All of us," Gabrysia said, joining the group.

"To the very end," Naomi added.

The Fall of Avalon

Mifuné turned from the group and faced the eastern horizon. The others followed suit. For a moment, there was solidity amongst them once again. Sensing this, Mifuné said, "Three more days must pass. When the sun rises on the eighth day, we take Avalon, forever."

❧

Colabion managed to steal away from the castle. As he approached the Soothsayer's door it swung open. He was warmly greeted by his lover, Sabastian, and ushered inside. They shared a tender kiss. Sebastian gazed into Colabion's eyes just as a tear escaped them.

"Tell me everything." Sebastian demanded protectively.

"Titania is cheating on me with Virgil. I have no proof but I know it is true."

"How can you be sure?"

"I know I am being pushed to the side. They are closer than ever and she has been mercurial and cruel as of late."

"Then you must prove yourself as King. Your moment is coming..." Sebastian kissed Colabion playfully. "I know exactly what you need to do. But first come, lay with me."

"Do we have time? Where is the soothsayer." Colabion asked tempted.

"We have an hour my love, exactly one hour and let us not waste it." Sebastian said as he gently ran his fingers though Colabion's hair. "Come, join me my King." He continued as he led Colabion by the hand to the bed chamber.

Carl Houston Roach IV

An hour later as they playfully dressed one another and smiled loving into each other's eyes, Sebastian took pause.

"What is it?" Colabion asked taken aback.

"I promised I would make you a king and now I am promising you your moment will come," Sebastian stated seriously. Watch for it," He continued. "And whatever you do, do not trust Virgil.

᪥

That night, Queen Titania woke from her sleep, startled. She trembled tumultuously in her bed. As she cradled herself to calm her fears, Colabion was fast asleep beside her. She rocked herself back and forth, and breathed rhythmically with her movement, nonetheless, her heart rate increased as the images from her nightmare haunted her.

In her dream, she saw Ravana, the titanic evil entity she encountered years ago. It cornered her in her bedchamber, which was completely empty. She heard it haughtily laugh at her powerless state. Its laughter faded, and his entire body erupted into a vortex of purple fire. It swirled and spiraled around him like a tornado. Titania shielded her face with her arms and prayed with all her might that he would leave her be.

When the fires cleared, Ravana had transformed into Mifuné. His sword was drawn. The steel glowed like the moon in the dark of the night. She watched him approach her slowly. The Queen attempted to flee, but her back was to a stone wall.

The Fall of Avalon

Colabion appeared from nowhere to defend her, but Mifuné cut him down effortlessly. Virgil, too, attempted to stop Mifuné, however, with a single swing of his blade, Mifuné lopped off his head.

Titania fell to her knees, begged and pleaded with her former lover, desperately trying to make him come to his senses, but her voice was stolen from her. Every sound she had heard before was suddenly silenced. The last thing she saw was Mifuné, eyes like fire, raising his sword above his head. The room went black. The dream ended.

"What am I going to do?" Titania cried woefully, hot tears streamed down her face. "What am I going to do?"

Carl Houston Roach IV

He could not be bought. He could not be swayed.
His fury could not be tempered even by the promise
of what was taken from him.

Queen Titania found herself unable to rest that night. The fifth day was upon her, and she had not yet devised a way to deal with Mifuné's looming threat. She had lost her allies in the neighboring kingdoms, and was very quickly losing favor with her Paladin, as well as with her husband. The Queen paced back and forth in her bedchamber until the skin on her feet was all but raw. She searched the recesses of her mind for a solution to her plight. Problems such as these once seemed so simple when Argus and Mifuné were at her disposal, they always had a solution, especially Argus, and Mifuné had the power to carry out his will.

A few hours before dawn, an idea came to the Queen. It was a far cry from a solution, but it would perhaps buy her much needed time to develop another plan. Without the aid of any of her knights or guards, Queen Titania departed from the palace into the city, wearing only a dusty brown cloak with a hood to cover her face. The Queen moved as quickly as her feet would carry her. She shivered as the early morning gusts brushed across her petit figure. She lamented the situation, but it was preferable to the cold grip of the grave. To avoid that, she would go to the ends of the earth.

The Fall of Avalon

Queen Titania arrived at a doorway of a small house near the southern square in the city. She looked down the street to the left, and then to the right, carefully scanning for any signs of life—anyone that might see her go in. She raised her hand, slowly. Her heart pounded in her chest and accelerated her breathing as her knuckles drew closer and closer to the door. Her breath suddenly became like ice. She could see it rise out of her as she exhaled. She clutched her torso as her body convulsed from a fierce shiver. After two sharp exhales, she raised her hand to the door again. The wooden door creaked open slightly just before the Queen could touch it. A small figure lurked in the doorway behind it. The body was nearly half Queen Titania's height and bundled up in a dirty, dusty brown coat. Long, pale, bony fingers with crusty, chewed off nails wrapped over the outside of the door. Titania winced at the sight, as she was repulsed.

"What brings so fine a lady to my humble abode?" the figure spoke. The voice was old and eerie, the kind of voice an adult uses during a scary story to frighten small children around a campfire. The hairs on the back of Queen Titania's neck stood up, and her skin crawled.

"I have come seeking revelation," she answered.

"Yes, of course you have. Come in, come in."

The inhuman hand pushed the door open further. Queen Titania hurriedly made her way in to escape the cold morning. Strangely, though, it was colder inside the tiny, dark house than it was outside. Queen Titania could feel her insides

Carl Houston Roach IV

freezing solid with each breath she took. She could see nothing, not even her hand in front of her face. The lurking figure snapped its fingers, and instantly, dozens of red-wax candles lit throughout the tiny abode. It was dusty and plain. A single wooden table sat in the middle of the room beside a stone fireplace shaped like a pit. Above the fireplace was a polished, black cauldron with four legs. The feet stood out the most, crafted like a dragon's talons.

The entity dropped its hood, revealing a decrepit old woman with one shimmering blue eye. All color had faded from her other eye. Strands of thin white hair, similar in consistency to weathered yarn, hung from her head. Her nose was long and curved like a crow's beak. Warts decorated her decrepit face in an irregular pattern. The color of her skin matched the pale gray of her lifeless eye. Beneath her beak-like nose was a warped smile. Several of her teeth were missing. Those that existed were rotted, stained brown, as though she lodged pieces of wood into her gums. They were disproportionally small, as if worn down by decades of neglect. Some were filed down to a point. The crone was truly haunting to look at. The stuff of nightmares of the youth of the city, and an enigma of mystery and terror to the citizens of Avalon. As every citizen in Avalon came to understand, if there was something you wanted, you went there. You came to see the Soothsayer to make a deal.

"I must admit, I was not expecting her Majesty, the Queen of Avalon, to grace my humble abode with her presence this morning. Had I known, I would have cleaned up a bit."

The Fall of Avalon

The Soothsayer snapped her fingers once again. A broom leaning against the wall swept away the dust on the floor. It moved as though spirit maneuvered it. She smiled and looked at the Queen, but Titania was hardly impressed.

"No, that is quite alright. I have come to ask your help."

"My goodness. You have not come for my help in, well, was it seven years ago? Just before I came to live in Avalon?"

"Yes, that was the last time we spoke."

Queen Titania lowered her hood. Dark circles had formed under her eyes. Her hair was a mess, lacking any form of dressing or care. A rasp had developed in her throat, altering the normal, sweet sound into a crass, corrupted tone.

"What troubles you, your Highness?" the Soothsayer asked. With a flick of her finger, a chair moved itself out from under the table.

Queen Titania's eyes went wide. As gracefully as she could manage, she took a seat in the clunky wooden chair. She tried desperately not to look into the Soothsayer's eyes, or at her gangling form. She took in a deep, quiet breath to slow her beating heart.

"The Ravana was vanquished, but now I face another foe. One I fear the Paladin cannot hold back."

"Yes. Yes, I have seen this; the son of the Dragon has returned to Avalon. If he succeeded in defeating the Ravana alone, then he is undoubtedly strong." The Soothsayer chuckled. "Perhaps it

Carl Houston Roach IV

would have been fortuitous to have kept him in your employ."

"You said the ritual you gave me would destroy my enemies. You said I would have nothing left to fear if Ravana was defeated; yet here I am. Perhaps bringing you into my employ was my fatal mistake," The Queen said, spitefully.

"You presume too much. One is not an enemy simply because you decide that they are, your Majesty." Her tone turned harsh. "It would be wise to examine yourself before you impugn the work of another." Queen Titania sat back in her seat, unsure of how to reply.

"Then what is to be my fate?" the Queen asked. "What does the future hold for me... for my kingdom?" she stuttered.

The Soothsayer shuffled over to a series of boxes on a shelf and sifted through them. Glass jars and metal trinkets clinked and clanged against each other as she assembled some seemingly random assortment of ingredients. With the flick of her wrist, the fireplace erupted with a fresh flame. The Soothsayer skulked over to the cauldron. Carefully, studiously, she examined each ingredient she had assembled with her good eye. She then placed each ingredient rapidly into the cauldron. Queen Titania was reminded of chef tossing the ingredients of a stew into a boiling pot. As these ingredients melted down and meshed together, a foul odor filled the room. Though the stench disgusted her, the Queen was unaffected by the procedure. A weak constitution would have spewed out bile and bled

The Fall of Avalon

from the eyes. She watched carefully, and waited for the results.

"One more thing, your Majesty."

"What is it?"

"A simple lock of hair. That is all I require of you," the woman said, and extended to Queen Titania a small, straight blade.

Titania quickly severed a piece of her hair from her tangled locks and presented it to the old crone. With the final ingredient added to the concoction, a plume of black smoke exploded out of the cauldron that sounded off like a cannon blast. The old crone clutched at the brim of the cauldron with both hands, as if she were under some sort of spell. Her head reared back, and she inhaled. All of the smoke rushed into the crone's nose and vanished inside of her. Her body shook and convulsed as if she was possessed. Her fingers wrapped around the burning rim of the cauldron and seized a tight grip. Queen Titania could hear the sizzling char of her hands. She flinched away from the process. The candles extinguished simultaneously.

Suddenly, the Soothsayer's chaotic episode stopped. The candles reignited again, as if of their own volition. The Soothsayer faced Queen Titania. Both of her eyes were closed, and her arms hung down at her sides, as if the life had been drained from her antiquated body. In an instant, and without warning, her gray eye opened and released brilliant white light.

The crone's voice exploded from her like an echo in a grand hall, "From the ashes of hate, a Warrior of Darkness has risen. With Wicked Blade in hand, he shall cut down all that opposes him. Though all shall be brought to bear against him, none shall prevail. The Light of the Paladin shall rise to quell the nightmare; but shall be swallowed by the Darkness. The Dark Swordsman's mission is a quest of Retribution, which begins, and ends, with you. There will be no escape…"

The old woman's eye closed, and the light that beamed forth from it vanished. Her face was devoid of any expression. Queen Titania found her stone countenance more unsettling than her normal, eerie smile.

"Tell me, Soothsayer, is there nothing I can do? Nothing at all?"

"I may have something that can help, my dear, though the price may be higher than you are willing to pay."

"I will pay whatever price I must! Please. I do not want to die!" Queen Titania beseeched as a tear streamed down her face.

A monstrous smile curled across the Soothsayer's face. Her eyes gleamed with glee but buried beneath it was unmistakable malevolence. It persisted only for a moment and was gone in the blink of an eye. The Queen blinked away her confusion and focused on the task at hand. The Soothsayer maneuvered through the little home to a shelf completely full of books, varying in size and age, thickness and content. She dragged her elongated finger across the spines of the volumes until she came upon a large book with an ash gray cover. She wrapped her gangling fingers around it and removed it from the shelf. Dust fell off it and

The Fall of Avalon

covered her hair. Queen Titania flinched when she dropped the book on the table with a mighty slam. The book itself was massive, comparable the Queen thought, to the book in her library regaling the history of Avalon. The cover looked like it was some old cloth. There was no inscription, no sign of an author, and no indication as to how old the book was. It was old, yet ageless, as if it existed outside of time. The Queen was both curious, and a bit frightened.

"What is this?" the Queen asked.

"This, my dear, is the Book of Shadows. An ancient collection of the most powerful spells and incantations. It is very powerful. Very dangerous."

"How did you acquire this?"

The old woman said nothing. Instead, she cackled sinisterly, as if she carried a dark secret. "In this book, I'm sure there is a spell with enough power to protect the kingdom. I may not be able to help you defeat this warrior, but it may be possible to prevent him from entering."

Queen Titania peered over the pages of the book as the Soothsayer ran her fingers over the various spells and scribblings. Some of the language she recognized, there was the common language of humans, and the language of the Fae on some pages, but she was unable to identify several inscriptions. They were older than me, possibly languages lost in the Great War, Queen Titania pondered. The longer the Queen looked in the book, the more she felt drawn in by it. She felt as though she could hear the book whispering to her. Unconsciously, she reached for it slowly. The closer her hand came to the book, the louder the whispering became, and the more her own consciousness faded. The old crone slammed the book shut. Queen Titania snapped out of her trans and shook herself awake.

"I have just the thing!" the Soothsayer exclaimed.

"What is it?"

"It is an ancient protection spell. Your mother used a similar one to prevent the Lich from entering Avalon. This spell is different, but it should do."

"How long will it take you to assemble the ingredients?" Queen Titania asked.

"I have all of the ingredients I need already, but there is one thing I will need for you to acquire."

"Name it, and I will find it," Queen Titania declared.

"I need something that belonged to him, something precious."

The Queen hung her head. Mifuné was a man of few possessions, he had always been that way. Nothing he owned was still in Avalon, and there was no way he would agree to simply hand her something of his. She covered her face with one of her hands and sulked in her seat.

"Is there nothing you can think of?" the Soothsayer asked.

"No. I have nothing of his, and since he is set to kill me, I doubt he would freely offer me something of his."

"He already has, my dear."

The Fall of Avalon

The Queen looked at the old woman curiously. She had no idea what she had implied. Mifuné had given her nothing but threats, violence, and death.

"The ring."

"What ring? What do you mean?"

"Seven years ago, he presented to you a ring of silver with an opal stone. That should suffice."

Queen Titania searched the corridors of her memory to the night when he first gave her that ring, the night he asked her to marry him. They were naked, alone, in her chambers. The Queen's eyes suddenly grew wide in shock and horror.

"How did you..."

"Oh, I see more than you know. I see everything. That ring he gave you was his heart, the manifestation of his love and devotion for you. Bring me the ring, and I shall prepare the spell."

"And what will be the price, this time?"

The old crone cackled but did not respond. She merely fluttered about her tiny abode. There was a noticeable spring in her step. Queen Titania had never seen her so unmistakably joyous.

"The price for the ritual to summon Ravana was citizenship and residence in Avalon. What is it that you want this time?"

"You need not concern yourself with that now, my dear. I will come to collect my price when the time comes," the Soothsayer replied, hunched over her cauldron.

Queen Titania departed the Soothsayer's home and made her way back to the palace. An eerie chill rattled her bones. Not only did the Soothsayer bring up the Lich, the one thing in the world that truly frightened her, but the last thing the crone said haunted her. The memory of her slowly stirring the ladle round and round in the cauldron turned her stomach. Queen Titania returned to the palace before the sun broke past the horizon on its ascent through the sky. Immediately, she opened every jewelry box, every drawer, searched every nook and cranny in her bed chamber to find the ring. It had never been as important to her as it was that day. The irony was not lost on her. At last, the Queen opened a blue porcelain box with white borders given to her by her mother for her ninth birthday. Buried beneath the clutter and mess of childish belongings she had stored in the container, she found it. The sterling silver ring, with an opal stone of significant size, was in her possession at last.

In that moment, Queen Titania realized what the Soothsayer had said. It was not just a ring clutched between her fingers. She held Mifuné's heart, which at one point, was all hers. She remembered how soft his eyes were when he looked into hers. How his hands of iron and will of steel turned to velvet and silk at any time they were alone together, especially in her bed. This moment of reminisce sparked an idea in her head—a last-ditch effort she could attempt to save Avalon from imminent destruction. The Queen shook her husband awake from his deep sleep. His eyes peeled open to see his disheveled wife standing in front of him with a most peculiar look in her eyes.

"Colabion, get up. I have something I need you to do."

The Fall of Avalon

"What is it, my love?" he stammered. "Why are you awake so early?"

"I need you to take this ring to Virgil. Tell him to deliver it to the Soothsayer."

"The Soothsayer?"

Colabion shook his tired head and rubbed his eyes. He took the ring from her and inspected it curiously. It was a fabulous ring, but it was not a ring he had gotten for her. The longer he held it, the more his tired eyes realized he had never even seen it before. He yawned as he sat up in bed.

"Why do you need me to take this to the Soothsayer at this hour? Come back to bed. Let us rest before…"

"My love," the Queen interrupted, "I know you are tired, but I need you to do this for me. This could be our only chance to save the kingdom."

"How is this supposed to save Avalon?"

"Just trust me," she said, hurriedly dressing herself.

"Where are you going?" he asked, finally getting out of bed.

"I have a meeting with someone who may agree to help us, so I need for you to do this for me."

During that short exchange, Queen Titania managed to dress herself. She wore a gorgeous red dress that exemplified her breasts and hugged her figure tightly. The train split along the side to expose one of her legs, which was bare and without blemish. The length of it stopped just above her ankles. Rather than arduously attempt to tame the beast that was her hair, she tied the excess back and hung it over her right shoulder. Emerald earrings adorned her lobes, and black bands covered her wrists.

"You are going to a meeting like that?" Colabion asked.

"There is no time to explain. My love, I know it is hard to see now, but I am doing this for you. I am doing this for Avalon. I wish there was another way, but there is none. I must go."

"What are you saying?"

The Queen walked over to her King Consort and kissed his lips. He reached to wrap his arms over her, but she ended the kiss and walked straight away from him. Colabion's heart sank into his stomach. Something was wrong. Everything was wrong. More than anything, he wished he knew who this man, Mifuné, was, and why he was so bent on destroying everything.

As Colabion watched his wife's hurried departure, he eyed the ring in his hands. This is the moment Sebastian said would come, he mused. "Do not trust Virgil," he hissed. In that instant, he decided he would not impart the task to Virgil. He would see to the delivery of the ring himself, as he was sure Sebastian would be there.

მ

As sunrise met the encampment at the Tower of Galahad, Mifuné had awakened before everyone else. He looked over them from the entrance of the rooms, as they slept peacefully, with one thought in his mind: struggle is coming for all of them, a struggle each of them would have to endure, alone.

As powerful as he was, there was only so much Mifuné could do to shield each of them from what

The Fall of Avalon

was to come. Mifuné knew he could not protect Sergei from his family's peril. Knowing Titania as well as I do, they are probably already dead, he surmised. Sergei was so hopeful, though. Mifuné knew he could not take that away from him. He could not rob Sergei of his will to fight.

Mifuné knew he could not guard Gabrysia from the fact that her family would not easily welcome her back. After all that had transpired, her redemption was not guaranteed. Even returning with the treasure of Avalon, and playing a role in its destruction, might not be enough to ensure her return home. Old wounds cut deep, and some are without remedy.

Mifuné knew he could not protect Desmond from Virgil if the Paladin challenged him. Though he defeated Virgil the first time they fought, Mifuné knew his surprise attack was what won him that battle so easily. Had Desmond attempted the same thing, he would most assuredly have died. His young disciple was so eager to prove himself but was completely unaware of the gap between his power and the Paladin's.

Mifuné knew he could not protect Naomi from the uncertainty of the future ahead. It became more apparent to Mifuné, with each day that passed, how Naomi felt about him. That was a dangerous thing. For with each day that brought them closer to the attack on Avalon, Ravana's voice became stronger. Scarcely was there a moment when Mifuné did not hear the voice of the sword. He wondered how much longer he might be able to resist the Ravana's call.

Carl Houston Roach IV

Mifuné knew it was possible that, by the end of his campaign against Avalon, Ravana could take full possession of him. If that happened, Naomi would certainly be destroyed. Every single one of them would be destroyed. The thought of it frightened him, but he had set his course. There was no turning back.

"Wake up, all of you!" Mifuné declared is voice echoed through the tower.

Heavy eyes and sleepy faces all turned to face Mifuné at the early morning hour. Reluctantly, each one emerged from sleepy states. They rubbed their eyes and set aside their yearning for rest as they descended the stairs to meet Mifuné. There was something distinctively different about his demeanor. It was as though he knew something unexpected was coming. As though they would face an impending challenge greater than one army of 500 men could pose.

"It is time to resume your training."

Desmond and Sergei faced off against Mifuné. He had given Sergei a new sword from the armory in the tower with which to train. For hours he clashed with them, displaying drastic differences in swordsmanship. All the while, he offered critiques to their forms and strikes.

Sergei fought, he attempted to win with brute strength and heavy swings, as he had before. Naomi and Gabrysia noted distinctively more powerful strikes from him than from Desmond, or even Mifuné. They were slower but controlled. From any point of attack, Sergei was able to transition back into a defensive posture when needed. No matter from what position or with how much force Sergei struck, Mifuné could always parry or evade the attack. It was just as it was when they fought the day before. The added advantage of Desmond fighting with him still was not enough to close the gap between them.

Desmond attempted to outmaneuver his Master and strike with a decisive blow. Despite the quickness in his step or his swings, even when Mifuné was not facing him, Desmond's sword could never make contact. Mifuné would either step out of harm's way or flick his sword through the air and stop Desmond's blade mid-flight. Hours of this drained Desmond and Sergei. They panted heavily as they stood on opposite sides of Mifuné. Mifuné had hardly broken a sweat. His breath was light and steady. For Desmond, his master's calm was nothing new. Sergei could hardly stand it.

"This is the level you can attain when you have achieved Absolute Focus," Mifuné began. "You will be able to surpass the limits of an ordinary warrior. You will be able to read your opponent's moves and react before they can harm you."

"We are not going to reach that level in a few days, Mifuné, so do you mind telling me what the point of this is?" Sergei asked indignantly.

"Your current ability in battle is insufficient for the task at hand, both of you. Though you might not see it, you have been improving, even during this training."

"I appreciate your concern, Samurai, but I think I have what it takes to brush aside some errant soldiers."

Carl Houston Roach IV

"Hear me, then, when I tell you this." Mifuné's gaze became cold and hard as steel. "Fighting against the warriors of Avalon like that, you will die before you save your family."

"How dare you!" Sergei exclaimed. He oriented the tip of his sword at Mifuné. "I will save my family, Samurai! Not even the likes of you will stand in the way of that!"

"Sergei, Master is only trying to teach you what he knows. I have fought against soldiers of Avalon my whole life. They will take any avenue they can in order to win!" Desmond declared.

"And there is still the Paladin to contend with. During our siege, he could challenge any one of you at any time. You must be prepared to hold out against him until I can take him on," Mifuné interjected.

"I have my way and you have yours! Paladin or no, no one is going to keep me away from my family."

Sergei's voice was ferocious. The expression on his face even more so. His breath was loud and heavy. Every muscle in his body flexed under the tension coursing through him. Sergei looked like a predator ready for the kill. As if he would attack Mifuné, and take his life at a moment's notice.

Mifuné vanished from where he stood and immediately appeared in front of Sergei. The burly man hardly had time to process Mifuné's move. He raised his sword as quickly as he could into a defensive position just in time to intercept Mifuné's attack. The force of the impact of Mifuné's sword against Sergei's was enormous.

The Fall of Avalon

Sergei was flung from where he stood. He careened through the air and struck the ground. He stopped in place before he collided with the tower. The tip of his sword dug into the ground as he forced himself back onto his feet. He scanned for Mifuné, but he was nowhere to be found. A cold shiver crawled over Sergei's body as something lightly touched the back of Sergei's neck. The unmistakable, cold edge of Mifuné's sword rested against his flesh. Sergei was once again dumbfounded by the unprecedented speed and power Mifuné possessed, though he was half Sergei's size. No man can move like this! How in the world could he have this much power, Sergei thought?

"Tell me, do you think the Paladin has less strength than me?" Mifuné asked. "It stands well to reason that he may be even stronger than I am! Do not be so arrogant as to underestimate our enemy. Do not make the same mistake I did when I underestimated Titania's treachery."

Mifuné sheathed his blade and extended a hand to Sergei. He accepted and hoisted himself to his feet. He stood face to face with Mifuné, not as a student to a master, but as one man to another. We are after the same thing, Sergei reminded himself. He exhaled and released the tension in his body.

Sergei sighed. "You are right. We are on the same side. Forgive me, I was wrong to be angry with you."

Something in the air had shifted. Mifuné's attention turned toward Avalon, something was headed their way. He was silent as the grave on the outside, but on fire within. The disciples recognized the look all too well from the night when the army of 500 came for them. Though, there was something different. There was an expectant look in his eye.

"Something is coming," Mifuné stated quietly.

"Master, what is it?" Gabrysia asked.

"Naomi," Mifuné said, "send your birds out."

"Yes, Master."

Naomi closed her eyes and focused her magic to her chest. She began to glow with a blood red aura. An incredible whistle rang out from her lips that carried into the woods behind them. The echo was intense, yet the sound was soft; and as the sound settled, a flock of ravens emerged from the trees and perched themselves in the grass in front of her. Naomi stood to her feet and observed the ravens carefully. Each one of them was concentrated solely on her. She waved a glowing hand over them. The blood red aura passed into each one, and as it did, they succumbed to her will. The red aura illuminated in their eyes.

"Fly now. Share your sight with me."

The birds cawed, took flight, and scattered forward towards Avalon. Through their eyes, Naomi could see everything that they saw. After a few moments, she realized what had garnered Mifuné's attention. His senses were impeccable if he could detect that something was approaching them, given how far away it still was.

"What do you see?" Mifuné asked.

"It looks like a caravan. I can see four knights, one at each corner and... at least a dozen horses carrying it."

The Fall of Avalon

Mifuné crossed his arms and started in the direction of the approaching convoy. The disciples shot up after him, eager to join him. He extended out his arm and stopped them dead in their tracks.

"Stay here. Continue your training. I go alone."

"Master, let me go with you!" Desmond pleaded.

"No, Desmond. I must face this wickedness alone."

"But…"

"You did well against the Captain, but this enemy you cannot protect me from." Mifuné turned his head over his shoulder to his faithful disciple. "Have faith. I will return before the sun sets."

Sergei remained where he stood. Though he did not have the same kind of presence sensing as Mifuné, he had a heavy suspicion about what was going on. If he was right, it did not make any sense, at least, not to him.

Without another word, Mifuné continued forward toward the oncoming caravan. His left arm rested on the hilt of his sword, his right swung naturally at his side. The gusty breeze that swept over the fields kept him pleasantly cool. From a distance, he seemed to be on a casual stroll, or perhaps as someone returning home from a long journey. His face was as calm and clear as the cloudless sky above. On the contrary, within him, a storm of wind and fire and fury raged.

After about an hour and a half of walking, the caravan came into view. About a dozen Clydesdales of varying shades of brown, and each with white socks, pulled behind them what can only be aptly described as a humongous tent. The tent was certainly royal property. The art embroidered into it was ornate, decorated with cardinals and blue birds backdropped by a sea of yellow and gold. Roses blossomed from verdant, intertwining vines along the baseline of the tent, adding a sharp contrast to the backdrop.

One of the four knights leading the caravan raised up his hand. The coachman pulled the reigns and the Clydesdales came to a steady halt. Reluctantly, the knight leading the caravan approached the warrior in front of him. He had personally known Captain Lysander, as well as several of the soldiers who had gone to face Mifuné days before. Seeing the man who laid them to waste made the hairs on his neck stand on end.

"The Queen of Avalon, Titania, wishes to meet peaceably with you. As such, she has requested that you relinquish your sword to me until such time as the meeting has been completed. So sayeth the Queen."

Mifuné's head tilted curiously to one side, as a beast's might when confronted with prey attempting to bargain with it. He surveyed the man, head to toe. The knight was clean shaven, as every knight was, with a strong jaw. He had cropped, brown hair, ocean blue eyes hardened by combat, and he spoke with pronounced authority. His shining armor shimmered in the afternoon sun. Mifuné took a slow step forward. Then a second. The fear in the knight became more and more palpable as Mifuné approached.

"What is your name, knight?" Mifuné inquired.

The Fall of Avalon

The knight looked perplexed at first, but he shook it off. "I am Sir William Kant, of the Order of the Knights of Virgil."

"Do you know who I am?" Mifuné asked again.

"You are Mifuné Tahaka, sworn enemy of Avalon and its crown."

"That is correct." Mifuné continued to steadily close the gap between himself and Sir William. "And I will tell you something you may not know, Sir William."

Sir William immediately reached for his sword... but felt unable to draw it, as a fear swallowed him, fear as he had never before experienced. Albeit, he was a knight of Avalon, and a powerful, capable warrior; the man before him was something else entirely. Mifuné stood face to face with the trembling knight. His piercing eyes cut straight to the combatant's core. Every instinct in the knight's body pleaded with him to draw his sword and attack or to flee; every muscle fiber in his body demanded action. Despite the demands his mind placed on his body, he could see in those eyes, apart from him, the truth. One wrong move would mean certain death.

Mifuné leaned in close to Sir William, inches from his face. Sir William could feel his breath brush against him. "If I wanted to kill anyone, I would have done it before I allowed you to speak." Mifuné stepped past the knight without another word, and kept his sword slung in his sash. Slowly, Sir William released his grip on his sword. The look in the Samurai's eyes, the surety in his voice... Sir William knew there was nothing he could have done to stop that man. He shuddered to think he nearly shared in the same fate as the army of 500 sent against him.

Mifuné marched up to the caravan with that same, steady, stoic demeanor, but in his chest, his heart pounded like stampeding horses. He took in a deep breath through the nose. His pulse slowed slightly. With force and presence, he pushed aside the drapes which covered the doorway to the tent and entered.

As Mifuné stepped into the tent, something shocking caught Sir William's attention. A single raven had perched just away from the tent. It cawed annoyingly; to Sir William, the caw sounded more like laughter, like it mocked his frightened demeanor in the face of Avalon's enemy. For a moment, the knight could have sworn he saw a flash of red over the raven's eye.

Mifuné took no notice of anything inside the tent. He had little interest in anything the Queen had brought with her. To think, he allowed himself to be there forced the vortex in his heart to transition to his stomach. His anger only built up stronger. And at last, he was standing face to face with *her*. She wore a familiar red dress, he was well aware it was the same red dress she wore years ago when she locked him away. Though it was evident how pronounced her breasts were, the Queen noticed Mifuné was hardly enticed.

"You came," Queen Titania said softly. "I did not think you would."

"Why are you here?" Mifuné replied. His voice was like ice.

The Fall of Avalon

"I wanted to talk. Just you and me. The way we used to." The Queen's tone was persistently soft and suspiciously innocent. Her eyes seemed heavy, as though they were burdened with remorse. Mifuné was silent. His piercing stare monitored her every move, awaiting the serpents to fly from her and ensnare him. "I brought you a gift." The Queen gestured to a bottle on a small table to her right. "I remember how much you loved the rum we imported from Zolabar. I actually only kept buying it to make you happy."

"You think it is that easy to soothe me, Titania?"

"I was only thinking of something I could do for you. You suffered so long, I was unsure how you would react seeing me this way."

"Do not be coy with me. What do you want?"

Queen Titania fixed her most timid, longing expression on Mifuné's enraged countenance. Slowly, sensually, she unfastened her red dress and let it fall to the floor. Her body was as ravishing as he had remembered; though her breasts were noticeably larger than when last he was with her. She drew nearer to him, slowly, carefully. Delicately, she reached out her hand and placed it on his chest.

"I want you. I want for things to be as they were between us. Come home with me…"

The Queen could feel the rapid beating of his heart over his muscular torso. Incomparable heat radiated from him, but he did not tremble. He remained motionless, like a mountain faced against a storm. His heart continued to beat faster, and with it, the heat from his body continued to rise. Queen Titania pulled back her hand, such that only her fingertips remained in contact with him. She gently traced a line up and down the center of his chest. From his chest, she lightly ran her finger up towards his neck, and finally towards his face.

"Do you remember, how it felt when you would take me in your arms, Mifuné?" the Queen giggled and turned so her backside aligned with him. "How much passion, how much strength, how much ferocity you put into it." She pressed her rear against his pelvis and stirred about as she traced lines up and down Mifuné's neck. "I could never forget. No man ever could do to me the things that you did."

Queen Titania's fingers traced the base of his jaw up towards his face. She could feel goosebumps on his neck, and imagined he had a similar reaction all over his body. Tenderly, she rested her palm against his face. Her head rolled back into the nook of his shoulder and neck, her eyes closed, her lips pursed, and she leaned up to kiss him.

&

"I am going to kill her!" Naomi exclaimed from the encampment. Red aura erupted around her like a volcano. She continued to watch over their master through the eyes of one of the ravens that answered her call. Never before had she been so furious in her life, to see the Queen try to take her Master away from her.

"Calm down, Naomi!" Desmond pleaded.

"What is it? What do you see?" Gabrysia asked.

The Fall of Avalon

"I'm going to march over there and burn that whole caravan to the ground! How dare she!? That evil witch!"

Sergei seized Naomi by the hood and effortlessly pulled her back and away from the caravan's direction. Despite her flailing, she was powerless to escape his grip. Naomi's passionate reaction only confirmed his suspicions about the goings on, but it failed to answer why the Queen thought her plan would work. However, the tiniest seed of doubt planted itself in Sergei's mind. What if it did?

Queen Titania felt a force around her wrist that pulled her hand away from Mifuné's face. He had locked a white-knuckle grip around her arm. The look in his eyes dynamically changed from cold and unfeeling to enflamed and furious. His brow furrowed, and his face twisted into a scowl.

"Do...not...touch me," Mifuné growled through gritted teeth.

Mifuné threw her arm away from himself and lowered his hand to his side. His countenance was steady, yet stern and serious. Queen Titania scoffed and turned her back to him.

"You really have changed. I do not even know who you are anymore."

"Tell me something," Mifuné began, "did you really think I could be bought so easily?"

"I came here to offer myself to you, so that we could be together again. Colabion is nowhere near the man you are, and Virgil... Virgil is a boy who does not even know what it means to be the Paladin.

Carl Houston Roach IV

My intention was to set things right, to show you that I still care. And you throw it in my face!"

"Do you think I am a fool? Do you honestly think I still do not know what really happened all those years ago?"

Queen Titania was silent as she continued to dress herself.

"You think I still do not know that you summoned Ravana, yourself?" Mifuné stated intrepidly.

The Queen shot up. Her arms fell lifelessly to her sides. The room closed in around her, the air felt suffocating. An icy sensation crept into her heart.

"I know the truth now. I know that you summoned Ravana to kill off the members of the Company of Heroes to protect yourself and the Inquisitors who were working with you. I know that you and the Inquisitors gathered together ten innocent citizens of your own country for a sacrifice! 'Sacrifice them like sheep,' is that *not* what you said that night?"

The Queen of Avalon remembered that night well...

❧

The Soothsayer had led the Queen and the Inquisitors to an ancient stone antechamber hidden in the north. Along the walls were inscriptions of the ancient primordial beings, both of Light and of Evil.. Ten masters had been led there and had been sacrificed. Their blood flowed from them to the center of the room. Even that proved not to be enough to accomplish the task at hand.

The Fall of Avalon

"Why is this not working?!" The Queen pressed the Soothsayer viciously.

"Methinks, your Majesty, the summoning may require… more."

"What more can we do? We have already given the blood of ten masters? What more could Ravana require!?"

"A being like Ravana, your Majesty, is only enticed by power akin or greater than his own."

"Then take mine," The Queen said as she spread her arms out.

The Inquisitors looked to her in shock and confusion. They understood the situation was dire, but Queen Titania was acting rashly. Her power was of great use, not just to her, but to them.

"Your Majesty," one Inquisitor uttered, "be reasonable. Perhaps we should seek an alternative solution. The powers you have inherited from your mother are invaluable, precious beyond measure. …"

"It matters not! They are my powers, and I decide what to do with them!" the Queen proclaimed. "Soothsayer, do what you must! Complete the ritual!"

The Soothsayer responded with a wicked grin: "As you wish."

The Soothsayer took ahold of Queen Titania, and stilled her in her grip as she wrenched out every last ounce of her majesty's power—the catalyst for the incantation. The pain the royal experienced in that moment was beyond her ability to describe or even comprehend. From within her, a swirling, amorphous light emerged. The Queen's magic was

Carl Houston Roach IV

birthed in a sea of agony. Once every trace was delivered, the Soothsayer then thrust the ancient powers into the circle of blood. Though the cost was great, the ceremony was successful. In a burst of chaotic power, Ravana emerged from the depths of the Underworld.

Queen Titania had only ever been told tales of the Lords of Evil. In her library, there was a book dedicated to them, full of stories and rudimentary illustrations of their wicked forms, and basic descriptions of their powers and histories. To see one first hand, to be dwarfed in the shadow of one of the mightiest of them, was an experience the Queen, or any of the Inquisitors, could never forget.

Ravana was gigantic, over 200 feet in height. His skin was ash grey. His eyes were like glowing stars buried into his face. Most unforgettable, though, was his voice, a calamitous voice that was as though a mass of people, women and men alike, spoke in unison.

"I am Ravana, Lord of Chaos and the King of Demons. Who is it that has summoned me?" Ravana declared.

Reluctantly, against the wishes of the Inquisitors, the Queen of Avalon stepped forward. She used the remnants of her strength to maintain her composure as she faced the giant of the ancient world.

"I am Titania of the Fae, Queen of Avalon. I have summoned you from the Underworld. You are bound to my will, Ravana," the Queen proudly answered.

The Fall of Avalon

"The Fae? I have only ever known one Fae… That tiny speck of light that hid behind far greater beings. Why she was made a Lord of Light is beyond me."

"How dare you insult my mother, beast!?"

"I, who have awakened. I, who have boundless knowledge of the universe and the powers it contains. I, who have created the Demon race. I who have mastered the weapons and martial arts of the mortal and immortal races, those past, present, and yet to be. You call *me* beast? You, who has no power at all! You are less than your mother was!" Ravana's voice grew in volume and intensity as he spoke. His last words were beyond deafening.

"Regardless. I control you." The Queen drew the Sword of Avalon from her belt and pointed it at Ravana.

Ravana snorted through its nostrils. "For the moment," Ravana replied, sensing the fleeting power of the bonds constricting him.

"Ravana, I compel you! You will go to the Southlands of Androma, between Avalon and Kilbin. Destroy all that you see!"

Ravana hesitated for a moment. "Very well; but know this, Fae: I am not one to take commands from mortals. I will return to your kingdom, and I will lay waste to it." It paused, and looked curiously at the Soothsayer. There was a flash in its eyes, as if it recognized her. "Unless another arrives before me," he stated knowingly.

"We shall see," the Queen replied defiantly.

§

Carl Houston Roach IV

"You are a fool, Titania," Mifuné declared, bringing Queen Titania back to the present. "What would you have done if the Company of Heroes had failed? What if I had fallen against Ravana? What would you have done to protect your people then?"

"I would have figured something out!"

"NO! This is exactly what happened when we went to war against Eramar before I was made Paladin. You did not listen to your advisors, to Argus, to anyone! If not for Argus's strategy, and our willingness to fight on the battlefield, you would have lost the war!"

"How could you understand the decisions that I have to make as a ruler? As a Queen! Everything I do, I do for the welfare of my people!"

"You throw your people's lives away on a whim! You care for no one, but yourself. Argus trusted you. I trusted you! And you tried to have us killed!"

"You know nothing! You do not know anything!"

"I know this!" Mifuné pressed her against the side of the tent with his arm across her chest. "You have no power anymore. You sacrificed your power, along with ten innocent lives, to summon Ravana." He moved his face closer to hers. "You cannot escape what is coming for you. You cannot stop me." He released her and stepped back.

"Virgil will defeat you! He is a greater Paladin than you ever were!"

"Listen to yourself. Even you do not believe that."

The Fall of Avalon

Queen Titania swung her open palm as quickly as she could. With all her strength and rage gathered, her hand struck Mifuné's cheek. The force of the connection shook the tent itself. Hot tears streamed down her face as she glared at the man who once loved her. He turned his face back towards her, unfazed by her strike.

"We are done here," Mifuné scoffed.

"Yes, we are," the Queen replied.

Mifuné stormed out of the tent, ablaze with fury. The knights retreated from him, terror abundant in their eyes. Mifuné hated them. He eyed each one of them carefully, calculative. They were an extension of her, of her will. He gripped the handle of his sword tightly.

"Titania!" Mifuné yelled.

In a flash, Mifuné drew his sword and cut down the knights that escorted her, one by one. He shredded them like a fox devours a bundle of baby rabbits. They screamed in shock and fear, but they felt no pain, as death came too quickly. Not a single one had sufficient time to even draw his sword. The coachman met the same fate in the wake of Mifuné's wrath. The horses whinnied and kicked to get away from the assailant. Several broke their restraints and fled back to Avalon. Mifuné cut the rest free. They stampeded away as fast as they could for home.

Mifuné flicked the blood off his weapon into the grass. Expertly and stylishly, he returned his sword to its sheath. He composed himself, and returned to his typical, stoic demeanor. Looking at the mangled corpses of these once brave warriors, even the innocent caravan driver was not enough to quench the burning hatred in his heart set ablaze by the Queen. Mifuné looked back over his shoulder to see her cowering in the entrance of the tent.

"Start walking!" Mifuné commanded.

The Fall of Avalon

CHAPTER 8   UNCERTAIN FUTURE

The task before him weighed down his soul. Never did he wish to harm an innocent. Through his disciples, he warned the people of the city's impending doom.

Mifuné returned to the tower grounds as the hue of the sky shifted from blue to amber. Dusk was only a few hours away. His scowl had yet to ease from his face. His aura blazed around him intensely. No matter how he tried to settle himself, he could not get the image of the Queen out of his head.

"Master! You are back!" Naomi exclaimed.

Naomi ran to him to greet him with a gleeful smile on her face, but she stopped dead in her tracks a few feet away. The burning hatred seeping out of him was too intense for her to even approach. His face—his eyes had changed. There was no trace of mercy, or kindness, or gentleness as she had always seen in him. In that moment, her beloved Master was gone, and someone else had taken his place. Mifuné walked straight past as if he had looked right through her. To him she was not even there.

Desmond was lost for words. He had seen his Master's face change in the heat of battle. How significantly different his expressions were when he brought his sword to bear against an enemy, determined to take his life. Nothing, nothing he had seen compared to the present fury, the pure hatred, that shot forward from his eyes. As Mifuné drew closer to him, Desmond quickly and eagerly stepped out of the way.

Gabrysia was the furthest away from Mifuné. Though she was equally as intimidated by his demeanor, she could see deeper past it. She could see the enormous pain he felt—his anguish and the undeniable feeling of betrayal as well as the weight of the shame that hung on his heart. She walked over to Sergei's side and watched Mifuné enter the tower.

Sergei gently patted Gabrysia's back and turned away. He recognized the look in Mifuné's eyes. Those were the eyes of a man who once held the world in his hands. A man without want, who was at peace with himself and the world, alas that happiness, that peace, was stolen away from him.

"Betrayal is not an easy thing to recover from, Gabrysia," Sergei said.

"No. It is not. Of all people, I understand that," Gabrysia replied.

"Do you, now?"

"Yes. When I was a little girl, I discovered my ability to use magic. I was so excited. I could do so many wonderful things, like make plants and fruit grow, heal injuries, turn water to ice with just a touch of my finger. Anything I wanted, I could do. When my parents found out, they forbid me from ever using it again."

"You must be from Eramar, then. The use of Magic has been taboo in that kingdom for a very long time."

"Because of what happens when someone becomes too powerful. Royalty feels threatened by power they do not control. Knowing what I know now, that edict must have been a result of their longstanding troubles with *Titania*, Queen of Avalon."

"King Gregory would have made an enemy out of your family, especially if your power came anywhere close to the Queen's."

"Exactly, but magic is a part of me. It is a part of who I am. I could not keep myself from using it. The older I got, the better I got at using it. And the better I got, the more powerful I became. One night, I was seen using magic in the back lot of my home. I was taken before the elders, and it was decided that I should be exiled from the clan. That was six years ago."

Sergei dropped a hand on her shoulder. "I'm sorry, lass."

"I was angry for a long time. I felt alone, abandoned. It was not so long ago that I found Desmond and Naomi. They have been like family to me since then. And even though we have only known each other for a short time, I feel very close to them. There is *nothing* we would not do for each other. And Mifuné, he watches over all of us."

"How is it that you three managed to find Mifuné?"

Gabrysia took in a deep breath, and prepared to respond, however Naomi's face in the light of the setting sun caught her eye. She was focused on the tower, waiting for their Master to come back down and commune with them. Gabrysia knew the tale was Naomi's story to tell. She mused, none of this journey would have been possible without her.

Carl Houston Roach IV

Gabrysia sighed pleasantly, still focused on Naomi. "Ask her."

Sergei and Gabrysia joined Desmond and Naomi around the fireplace. Sergei quietly clasped his hands and twiddled his thumbs together, unsure of how to initiate conversation, as Mifuné's wrath was overbearing, they all felt it. Sergei's patience, however, did not hold out.

"Naomi," he began, "how is it that you found Mifuné here?"

Naomi did not answer. She was lost in thought, in memory. In her hand, she held the coin Mifuné had given her all those years ago. It was her most precious possession. That single coin meant more to her than any amount of gold or silver in the world. She turned it round and round between her fingers and imagined his smile.

"What is that you have there?" Sergei asked. He gestured to the coin in her hand.

After a brief moment, Naomi answered, her voice was soft. "Never steal again." There was unmistakable nostalgia in her intonation, a resonating joy carried in it as well. That answer raised everyone's brows. In the months that they had known her, Naomi had never given Desmond or Gabrysia a straight answer about that coin. She would always try to hide it or evade the question entirely. The new development about the coin only raised more questions than it answered. "When I was thirteen, I was caught stealing from someone in the east trade district in Avalon. I remember that day like it was yesterday. The man caught my hand and held it over my head. Dozens of guards swarmed over us. There were so many of them, and I did not know why. I begged and pleaded for mercy. I was so afraid I was going to die."

"Who was it that you stole from?" Desmond asked.

"I think I know," Gabrysia added with a smirk.

"It was him. It was Mifuné. This was when *he* was the Paladin of Avalon. He raised his hand and halted the guards. After he released my hand, I was still shaking and crying. I was so afraid. He knelt down and handed me this coin. He dried my tears and patted my head. Before he left, he told me those words: Never steal again. And he smiled. There was no anger, or frustration, or cruelty in his eyes. Only kindness and mercy."

"That is our Master," Desmond nodded with a smile.

"I had never known men to be kind. All I have ever seen in them was cruelty and wickedness." Naomi's tone was sharp, like the edge of a blade. "I have been bullied, I have been struck, I've been...." Her eyes filled up with tears. There was pain inside her, pain born from a long, dark history. The more anguish reflected in her eyes, the firmer her grip became on the coin. "I never believed a man could show kindness." She looked intently at the coin in her hand. "Until I met him." The shift in her tone was so noticeably soft, so drastically relieved of slights from her past. "For years, I watched him show that same kindness to so many others. He visited the lower districts as often as he could. Mifuné clothed the needy. He brought food to the hungry." Naomi giggled. "I even watched him help a man repair the roof for his shop. When the man tried to pay him, he refused. Mifuné even paid for all the materials himself. The man could hardly believe it!"

"All this talk about vengeance and destruction, battle and carnage, I can hardly believe him to be benevolent in any kind of way," Sergei said.

"Battling Ravana changed him. I know that. It is just like she said it would be."

"Who is she?" Sergei interjected.

"The Soothsayer," Gabrysia answered.

"Who is that?" Sergei replied.

"They say, she is an old witch-lady who lives in Avalon," Desmond replied. "No one really knows where she came from, but they say that if you need anything done, or if there is something you need to know, you go to see her,"

"She is not a witch-lady, she's sweet." Naomi clarified. "It was only after news of Ravana's destruction reached Avalon, and Mifuné had disappeared, that the Soothsayer came to live in Avalon. It was actually because of this coin that she and I met."

"Is that right?" Sergei asked. Desmond and Gabrysia drew themselves closer in to Naomi. They knew most of the story, but they had never heard that part before.

"It had been three years since Mifuné disappeared; I was nineteen. I wandered through the streets, lost, adrift among the vagabonds and the harlots. Whenever I heard the people shout: The Paladin is here! I went running, hoping to see

The Fall of Avalon

Mifuné there. It was never him, it was always Virgil."

"Virgil had awakened and become the new Paladin for close to a year. He never came to the lower districts of the city the way Mifuné did. Whenever he left the Citadel, he rode on horseback, wearing his shining armor, and he held himself up above the people. He was always followed by an coterie of flag-bearers and trumpeters. He only ever seemed concerned with receiving their praise and cared nothing for the suffering within his own kingdom. It sickened me to see him instead of Mifuné." Naomi said, disgusted. "Then one day, after I watched Virgil ride through the city with his party, I took a turn down an avenue I had not been down before. I turned the coin in my hand as I walked. Then, a door opened as I passed, and a voice behind it called to me."

"That coin is very precious to you, is it not?" a sweet voice asked me.

"I turned and faced the cracked door and answered, "Yes.""

"And the one who gave it to you, he is precious to you, yes?" she asked again.

"I answered again, yes."

"Would you like to see him again?" she asked.

"I asked her who it was that I was speaking to. The door opened with no answer. I could not see inside the house. It was pitch black, as if no light could enter. I had to know who this person was. I had to know what she knew about Mifuné."

"As soon as I stepped through the entrance, the door closed behind me on their own. Immediately, red candles ignited all around the room. It was unsettling—frightening even. I felt as though I had walked into a dungeon of some kind, full of books, and a black cauldron with dragon talons for feet. My heart pounded out of my chest. It felt like, at any moment, I was going to be eaten by some terrible thing that I would be powerless to stop." Naomi continued lost in the memory. "The figure in the room with me was tall, slender, hooded and cloaked. When it lowered its hood, I saw that it was a woman. She was old, but elegant, lovely even. She had one gray eye, and one shimmering blue eye. Her face was clean and well groomed. Her gray and white hair was neatly tied atop her head. She smiled a genuine, clean smile, with teeth like pearls. She told me to call her the Soothsayer." Naomi continued, "The Soothsayer told me she could help me find Mifuné and asked me for my coin. I did not want to let it go. I was afraid she would steal it away and I would lose the only piece of him that I had. She assured me she would give it back to me once she had done her work. I reluctantly agreed, and she gingerly took the coin from me." She persevered, adrift in the past, "The Soothsayer's eyes slowly closed. Her gray eye reopened, brilliant white light shined out from it. She said she could see him, she could see Mifuné. He was alive, in a deep place, not far from Avalon, in a cage of light. Her eye closed and she returned to me my coin." Naomi relived that moment as she told the tale. "I wanted to leave right away. I yearned to set him free, but when I got to the door, the Soothsayer stopped me. She told me that, in my present condition, I would not have the power to release him from his prison. I fell to my knees and I pleaded with her. If there was a way for me to save him, that she would reveal it to me. The Soothsayer caringly helped me to my feet and promised me she would help me find a way." Naomi persisted, "The Soothsayer placed a single finger against my forehead. When she touched me, she told me she could sense great magic within me, power like nothing I could ever even imagine. She urged me to remain with her, to be her pupil, and she would teach me how to use the magic within me so that I could save Mifuné. For the next three years, she trained me to harness my magic. In that time, I learned how to move things, I could heal wounds, and I could manipulate animals." Naomi shook her head as the present returned to her, "After those three years, the Soothsayer sent me on my way. She said I still would not be able to accomplish this task alone. I would need help. She urged me to head west toward Zolabar. There I would find someone who would be able to help me. Once I found that help, my coin would lead me to where My master was."

"And that is when she and I met," Gabrysia inserted. "When she arrived in Zolabar, we met in a tavern just inside the wall. We got to talking about our situations and came to an understanding. I could help her get what she wanted if she would help me find a way to return home."

"Makes sense. So, how did Desmond get caught up in of all this?" Sergei asked.

Carl Houston Roach IV

"I was set to be executed!" Desmond chimed in. He seemed more elucidated than he ought to have been, given the subject. "I had been condemned for the crimes of theft and murder of Duke Romasov of Zolabar, neither of which were true. The Inquisitors of Zolabar built a case against me, and the courts sentenced me to die. On the day of the execution, Gabrysia and Naomi saved me. I promised to help them until I had paid back my debt."

"I would wager that you are happy with your end of this arrangement?" Sergei inquired.

"Definitely. I thought I could fight before I met Master. I thought I was a warrior worth reckoning with. Then I met him, and he... well, my Master showed me just who he is. No tricks, no sleight of hand, no technique I had learned or developed gave me the upper hand against him. Every time I failed to defeat him I hung my head in shame, after which, he took me under his wing, and taught me how to be disciplined. He trained me, made me stronger." Desmond paused to stifle tears that welled up in his eyes. "Mifuné gave me someone to believe in. I believe in him, and thanks to him, I believe in myself."

"He really brought the three of us together," Gabrysia said.

"Well, how was it that you three found him?" Sergei asked.

"We returned to Avalon this past winter. I expected the tower to be heavily guarded and maintained. What we found was this empty building you see right now. We searched it high and low, room by room, but there was nothing that matched what the Soothsayer had told me. That is, until Desmond…"

"Until I leaned against some part of the wall," Desmond interrupted. "A stone shifted behind my back, and the floor began to shake. Part of it shifted down and slid under the rest of the floor. That revealed a stair that led down to something that was glowing with white light."

"And that was where Mifuné was bound?" Sergei asked.

"Yes," Naomi answered. "Just as the Soothsayer foretold, he was trapped in a cage of light that was impossible to see through. I was not even sure that he was in it."

"I had never seen anything like it," Gabrysia stated.

"Me either," Desmond echoed.

"It took almost all of our magic combined to set him free," Naomi continued. "When the cage shattered, he came into view. He was naked. There was practically nothing to him, nothing but skin and bone, yet we could sense that there was power— raw power radiating from him. When he looked at us, his eyes were feral, like a starving animal. He drew his sword and lashed out. His blade flew through the air, uncontrolled, unfocused. Desmond managed stopped him, and I went to him. I touched his face and tried to calm him down. That was when I saw, it was not rage in his eyes, it was terror."

"I held him against me to comfort him. He trembled terribly. There was tension throughout his whole body. Even though it grieved my heart to see him in that state, I was so happy to finally see him again. I was so happy that he was alive."

"I take it, that is why he did not start his plans for revenge until now," Sergei asked.

"Yes. It took four months, day in and day out, of training and meditation, as well as, food and rest, for Mifuné to be restored to his former self," Desmond replied. "While he trained himself, he trained me." He chuckled. "I have never seen someone push himself so hard, with such determination. That is why I know my Master is the best."

"And the stronger he became, the more I could see him as the man I remembered... the man I hoped I would find for so many years..." Naomi's voice trailed off. Her smile, the glow in her eyes, the brightness in her countenance outstripped the fire of its light.

"Do you love him?" Gabrysia asked, though she already knew the answer.

Naomi finally changed her point of focus from the coin in her hand to the group around her. She did not blush. She did not shy away. She did not block or evade the obvious any longer. Though her heart pounded wildly within her chest and her pulse raced like wild stallions, she brought it to heel. With a soft, steady voice, she answered, "Yes."

"So, go to him," Desmond encouraged.

Naomi shook her head. "Not yet. He just saw the woman he loved with all his heart, and she smeared the memory of his love across the ground. He needs to be alone now."

The Fall of Avalon

"The time for that is passed," their master interjected.

Every head turned in the direction of the tower. Mifuné stood just outside of the circle. Naomi looked at him longingly, desperately hoping to hear some manner of reply to her confession.

"My disciples, I have a task for each of you." Mifuné said.

"Yes, Master!" they all chimed together.

"You must go into Avalon under the cover of night. Tell the people the truths that I have told you. There are those who would leave the city if given the choice, those who would forsake Titania as their Queen if they were aware of the danger. For those who leave, I will spare them. I entrust this task to you."

"And the ones who stay?" Sergei asked.

"They will seal their fates." The cold expression in his eyes removed the sensation of warmth provided by the fire.

"Master, how will we get them to listen to us?" Gabrysia asked.

"Good point," Sergei interjected. "Mifuné, the Queen has made the whole kingdom believe you are dead."

"You will take this." Mifuné produced from his kimono a small book. The cover was brown leather, with three squares embedded within each other. "This is Argus's journal. It has everything you need to show the people the truth. This book will reveal who their leader, their beloved queen, really is. Take it with you."

Carl Houston Roach IV

"How did you get this?" Desmond asked as he carefully took the book from Mifuné.

"Argus gave this to me the moment before he died. His intent was to reveal Titania for the tyrant she is. Now, we shall carry out his intent."

❧

Meanwhile, far away from the tower, Queen Titania finally returned to the city. Guards intercepted her at the wall and escorted her back to the palace. The Queen was extremely disgruntled. The red dress she wore was all but ruined, horribly stained with sweat. The base was torn slightly and dampened with dirt. Her feet nearly started to bleed by the time she returned to Avalon from the rough dry grass she encountered. The guards escorting her kept their distance, afraid that they might become victims of the fury she carried. As the doors to the palace opened, she noticed a servant waiting by the door.

"My Queen! You are safe, thank goodness!"

"Where is my husband? Where is Colabion?" The Queen's voice was terse and sharp as a sword.

"I believe, your Majesty, that King Consort Colabion is in your bed chamber."

"Good. He and I have much to discuss. I should like for us not to be disturbed."

The Queen pushed past the servant and headed straightaway for her chambers. From outside of the door, she could hear something truly peculiar. It was something like sobs intermixed with quiet laughter. She pushed the door open, such that it collided with the wall behind it. Colabion was seated, hunched over on the floor, at the foot of the

207

bed. He was naked, and in his hand, he held a mostly empty bottle.

"Colabion, what are you doing?" the Queen asked.

"Is it true, Titania?" her husband stammered.

"Is what true? Are you drunk?"

"By the gods, tell me Titania, is it true!?" he shouted, and slurred his words.

"Do not yell at me! You are the last person in this world who can yell at me!"

"Did you summon... Ravana... to kill all those people?" he spluttered as he struggled to his feet.

Queen Titania froze. Her heavy heart stampeded in her chest like the panicked horses that fled her caravan. Her eyes went wide, and the blood rushed out of her face. A mix of shame and fury washed over her. "Who told you that, Colabion?"

"Who told? Who told me... the Soothsayer, yes," he lied. He finally managed to stand up straight. "She told me, when I took her the ring," he pointed to her face, "that you finally told me the truth... but, but, but I do not know what she means?" He took another drink. "Then she tells me the *whole* story. How you went to her to deal with your problem. With Argus. And... with Mifuné."

"She is lying! I could never do something that horrible! I cannot believe you would think something like that! I thought you loved me!"

Colabion's eyes narrowed as he thought, Sebastian has never lied to me. He staggered over to the Queen. His breath reeked of whiskey. "I do love you," he said bitterly. "Enough to know when you are lying to me!" He clutched the Queen's face tight in his grip. She raised her hands and gripped his arm. His blood leaked onto her fingers from where her nails pierced his skin. No matter how hard she squeezed, he did not feel any pain, and he would not let go.

"What are you hiding from me? Are you going to get rid of me too!?" His face was blood red with anger. Queen Titania tried to push him away, but Colabion would not be moved. She could feel pain seeping through her jaw and flow through her face the longer he held the pressure down. His grip felt like iron. She had never seen that side of him before.

Colabion finished the remainder of the whiskey in the bottle and raised it over his head. Before he could bring it down on her, the bottle shattered into tiny shards. Colabion was then struck with incredible force that sent him flying back through the room. His back struck the stone wall opposite Queen Titania. The breath in his body audibly exited his mouth. He collapsed to the floor, flat on his face, unconscious.

Queen Titania fell back against a powerful presence that had come to her rescue. Her dizzied eyes looked up into soft, green eyes. She smiled slightly. "Virgil," she sighed.

Virgil picked her up in his arms and carried her away from her chamber up to his own, where she would be safe and away from Colabion. All the while she clung to Virgil, as if he was the only thing keeping her grounded in reality. Virgil pushed the door open and lay his beloved Queen down on his bed. She looked weak and frightened. His heart broke to see her that way. She was always so strong, so steady, so beautiful. And in just four days, she had been reduced to something, less... She reached her arms up to him, beckoning him to lay beside her. Without a moment's hesitation, he removed his tunic and joined her.

The Queen pressed her lips against Virgil's softly, tenderly. He returned her kiss, wrapped his arm underneath her and cradled her head. Gradually, the kiss became more intense, more heated. Virgil ran his hand up and down her body, gripped and caressed her breasts, clutched her waist, and pulled her against him. The Queen lost herself in the physical ecstasy. Her eyes rolled back in her head as Virgil stroked his hand up her leg. Queen Titania grabbed him by his bulky shoulders and rolled him on top of her. The longing in her eyes was matched by the longing in his. He unfastened her dress and exposed her breasts. She pulled his head against her chest and gasped for air as his soul entered and consumed her.

༄

That night, Mifuné and Sergei sat beside the fire, each contemplating his own thoughts and feelings. Despite his new knowledge, Sergei could think of nothing other than his family. His beautiful wife, Amelia. Her long, flowing blonde hair and lovely face that was without blemish. Her lips, like pursed pedals of a rose. Her bountiful curves and dainty figure. She was his river lily, the envy of any man.

Sergei also worried for his children, how frightened they must be. He agonized over what might become of his boy, Lucas, and his precious daughter, Hilda. His worries stirred in his mind like a ceaseless storm. He could sit no longer. He stood up and walked away from the fire. Mifuné joined him a moment later, unable to sit any longer himself.

"The Queen tried to seduce you. That was her intent, right?" Sergei asked.

Mifuné nodded. "Yes."

"And you said no."

"She has nothing to offer me that I want, Sergei."

"You really hate her that much."

"She took everything from me. My Master. My home. My future. Whatever beauty she possesses is lost to me. Nothing will change that."

"Naomi loves you. Do you do know that?"

Mifuné paused before he answered. Naomi was the first thing he saw when he was freed from his prison. He thought about the way she looked at him then, and the way she continued to look at him. The way she reached out for him. How she had held him in his most vulnerable moments. Her words, I will not leave you all alone, resonated in his very soul. He exhaled. "I know."

"Then make her your own! Let her be a part of your future."

Mifuné shook his head. "How can I? How can someone like me ask for happiness with what I have in mind to do, with what I have already done?"

"That is what love is, my friend. The Queen never did love you, so I understand why you have doubts, but, take it from someone who knows. Love makes the impossible, possible. Even if you believe you do not deserve happiness when this is over, she does."

"Naomi knows I mean to destroy the city, and anyone still in it in only a few days. She will be there, watching. More people are going to die at my hand. How will she be able to forgive me?"

Sergei sighed. "Maybe you do not have to. Maybe that does not have to happen." Mifuné looked up at Sergei, whose eyes were calm and steady. He is beginning to sound like Argus, Mifuné thought as Sergei continued, "You do not have to do this. It is not too late, Mifuné. You can still walk away. We can save my family, take your disciples, and get out of here!"

Sergei could see Mifuné begin to process the thought. He began to contemplate the possibility of leaving behind that which had plagued him, that which had tormented his soul for so many years. Mifuné's breath was stifled, as though he had never taken up that thought before.

"The choice is yours, Mifuné." Sergei patted Mifuné's shoulder and walked back over by the fire. He laid himself out and began to drift off to sleep.

Mifuné thought only about Naomi. She was beautiful, inside and out. It would taste a lie to say he did not want to make her his own. She freed him from his prison. She came to him when he needed someone. She stood by him, unwavering in her resolve. Naomi's words rang in his mind, the only thing that could still the storm that ravaged on within him.

Carl Houston Roach IV

"You have your course, Mifuné," Ravana whispered as Mifuné began to calm. "You cannot depart from your path." His voice became harsh. "Will you let their deaths go unavenged?"

Mifuné clutched his sword seated in his sash until his knuckles went white. Images of the great warriors from the Company of Heroes and their screams of terror and anguish tormented his mind. Argus's dying face, his mouth full of blood, flashed across Mifuné's eyes. The Queen face, the frightening, predatory smile she bestowed to him when she imprisoned him, overtook them all. Rage kindled again in his heart, and his heart once again became steel.

᠔

Atop the Tower of the Paladin, Virgil and Queen Titania lay naked in each other's arms. Virgil delicately brushed the side of her face with his fingers. He observed her closely. The gray under her eyes had magnified. Lines became apparent across her forehead and under her eyes. Her breathing was irregular. Even his presence could not steady her to sleep.

"Virgil? Are you afraid?" the Queen asked.

"Afraid of what, my love?"

"Afraid of what might come. Mifuné is coming back. He hates me so much for how things ended between us, and he will not let anything stop him from getting to me." Tears pooled in her eyes, as she struggled on. "I do not know what to do."

Virgil swept his thumb under her eye, wiping away freshly fallen tears. "I will stop him. I have never failed you before, this will be no exception."

The Fall of Avalon

"What if you cannot defeat him?" She placed her hand on his face. "If something were to happen to you, I do not know what I would…"

"Hey, listen to me now." Virgil took her hand in his. "Nothing is going to happen to me. I will never let him hurt you. So long as I am still breathing, nothing will ever harm you. You do not have to be afraid."

"I am afraid, Virgil. I am so scared!"

The Queen pushed her head against his chest and wept. Virgil cradled her as she cried, unable to find the words to dispel her fears. Something began to stir inside of him. His resentment that had built up from her staying his hand began to blossom the more he thought about how she would not allow him to fight Mifuné. He knew in his heart he could end the madness, end the looming threat, and set everything back to the way it was. He began to hear a question rise to his ear from his aching heart: How long will you endure this?

"Virgil, I have to go," the Queen said flatly.

"No. Stay here with me. Please," he replied and kissed her head.

"I cannot, my dearest. I need to go to my husband. He will look for me, and he cannot find me here."

Virgil exhaled deeply and released his hold on her. The Queen got up out of his bed and recovered her dress from where it had been cast to the floor. He watched her observantly as she dressed herself. He imagined running his hands over every inch of her flesh. She was the embodiment of perfection,

perfection no one else could fully appreciate. Only him.

"Please stay. Just for the night," Virgil pleaded.

Queen Titania hesitated by the door. She did not want to go back to face her husband. If the Soothsayer did tell Colabion everything that had happened, he would have questions for her, questions she was not prepared to answer to anyone, let alone her husband. She feared he would tell the whole kingdom what she had done. She feared losing favor with her people, being dethroned, being cast into the dark—the way her father was 1,000 years ago.

The Queen leaned her head against the door. Her fingers dug into the wood until the it groaned. She trembled. Thoughts raced through her mind, accompanied by horrible images of fire, shattering stone, bloodshed, and screaming. She was unaware if the screams were her people's, or her own. She managed to catch herself, still her mind, and steady herself for a moment. She looked back at Virgil for a twinkling, who continued to watch her, and then she proceeded out of the Paladin's Chamber.

߮

That night, Desmond, Gabrysia, and Naomi did as their Master asked and began their mission. They traveled light, carrying only what they needed, including Argus's journal, which detailed the Queen's misdeeds over a prolonged period of time. Naomi guided them to secret entryways into the city she had discovered in her years as a vagabond. They agreed that each night they were dispatched, they

215

should target the three residential districts one at a time.

Door to door, down every street they could manage, to every place of residence they could find, they spread the message, the warning, that destruction was coming to Avalon, an annihilation invoked by Queen Titania herself. By the end of that night, they had reached every house in the East District and many in the South. As dawn approached, they returned to the point where they had entered the city and headed back to the tower.

This would become their nightly mission until every door in the districts was knocked upon. The importance of the task could not be underestimated, and they knew it. They would sleep during the day in the tower, out of the sunlight. Mifuné and Sergei would watch over them and ensure they were protected and well rested before sending them back out.

By the morning of the sixth day, hundreds of soldiers and thousands of civilians had taken their things and departed. It was the largest exodus in the history of Avalon. Queen Titania watched from her golden throne as masses of people continued to leave the city, some by day, and some by night. Word of the impending attack had been spread to them somehow, there was no other explanation, the Queen assumed. The Queen had become irate with her subjects. She summoned her General to the throne room. He was escorted to her by two knights.

"Your Majesty, I came as you requested," the General said as he knelt at the throne.

Carl Houston Roach IV

"General, have you noticed that the population of my kingdom is dwindling?"

The General looked up from the ground. He was shocked at how his Queen's countenance had so drastically changed. She looked like a porcelain doll from the heavy application of cosmetics. The coat of powder on her face was heavier than he had ever seen her wear. The light coat of pink lipstick did little to mask that. Her hair was poorly tied up atop her head. Something had gone very wrong. The General could feel it in his gut.

"I have noticed, your Majesty."

"Can you tell me why that is?"

"Your Majesty, we suspect that word of the impending attack is being spread around the kingdom. This may be in connection with the Samurai."

"You suspect?" The Queen dug her nails into the arms of her throne. "Then tell me, General, have you found the one responsible?"

"We have not found anyone responsible, and no one who we have intercepted can identify who it was that had told them."

"Tell me, how many have left so far?"

"About a third of our civilian population from the Eastern and Southern Districts, and nearly 1,000 soldiers have deserted as of this morning."

Queen Titania rose from her throne and descended the steps to where the General was. She drew her sword from her belt and placed the edge of it against the General's cheek. The edge of the blade sheared some of the hairs of his beard from his face

The Fall of Avalon

just from the initial contact. The flat edge was colder than ice. He slammed his eyes shut.

"I grow tired of your mounting failures, General. Your troops could not eliminate the threat to Avalon. You could not keep the borders of the kingdom secure. You are so inadequate as a leader that you could not even prevent the soldiers under your command from deserting! It seems the only person I can rely on in all of Androma is my Paladin. The rest of you are utterly worthless!"

Queen Titania raised her sword to the ready position swiftly and oriented her gaze at the General's neck. The two knights lunged back. The murderous, malicious look in her eyes removed all doubt that the Queen had gone mad. She was fully prepared to execute the General where he stood for a crime he did not commit.

"General, I find you guilty of insubordination and high treason to the crown, and I sentence you to die."

"Stop!"

Queen Titania turned her head to the East Hall. For a moment, she felt as though her ears had deceived her. She must have had mistaken the voice that dared issue a command to her, for there was no way this man would ever raise his voice to her in such a way, or to be so bold as to assume he could command her. When her eyes moved to identify the person, all doubt was removed. Virgil approached the Queen with a fearsome expression on his face.

"The General is guilty of nothing. Knights! Release him immediately!" Virgil's voice was saturated with indignation.

Carl Houston Roach IV

The Knights hesitated for a moment. They shared a muddled look with one another, unsure of what to do. They heeded Virgil's command and assisted the General to his feet. The General nodded to the knights and to Virgil, before he departed as quickly, and as composed, as he could. Hardened by years of war and conflict, the General had forgotten what fear felt like, until the moment his Queen's blade was aimed at him.

"How dare you!" the Queen spouted.

Queen Titania swiftly swung her sword in Virgil's direction with extreme prejudice. Virgil effortlessly caught her arm at the wrist, with one hand. Her attack stopped midflight, though she continued to press against Virgil with all of her might. It was like a child pushing with both hands against a wall made of mortared stone. Virgil turned her wrist and forced the blade from her hand.

"Enough, Titania! Destroying your subjects will not help you succeed. Compose yourself!" he said as he released her hand.

"What are you doing, Virgil?" Queen Titania said as she rubbed her wrist. "Have you forgotten that I am your Queen!?" she shouted.

"For too long, I have sat idly by and watched this chaos unfold. Too long, I have had a short leash around my neck. And too long, have I been a lesser man's second." Virgil's gaze was cast straight to Colabion, who he could see hiding behind the throne. Virgil seized the Queen by her waist and pulled her against him. He forcefully pressed his lips against hers. She resisted as best she could, but her struggle against Virgil's strength was futile.

The Fall of Avalon

When his lips parted from hers, he continued: "I am taking control of this situation, and I am going to put an end to this, once and for all. When I am done, there shall be a new order in Avalon, with you at *my* side."

Without another word, Virgil left the Queen in her throne room. From a distance, concealed in the shadow of the throne, Colabion scrutinized indignantly. Seeing Virgil's deranged actions, and hearing Virgil's treacherous words confirmed a suspicion he had long carried in his heart about his beloved wife and her closeness to her precious Paladin. He shook his head and raised a half-empty bottle to his lips before vanishing into the palace.

▪

Virgil met with the General at the wall surrounding Avalon. The General had hoped to put as much distance between himself and the Queen as he could. He had faithfully served in Avalon's defense since the day he was old enough to become a soldier. He had carried out his orders to the letter throughout his career. No request the Queen presented him with went unfulfilled. Her accusation broke his heart. He was shaken to his very core, for he was bitten by the beloved hand that fed him. It was refreshing, to say that least, that Virgil came to his aid when his need was most dire.

"Thank you, for what you did back there, Virgil."

"You would have done the same for me, old friend."

"Aye, that I would." He shook Virgil's hand. "So, what is our situation?"

Carl Houston Roach IV

"Titania is no longer capable of leading or commanding anyone. I have taken control, but I cannot do this alone. I will need your help."

"And you shall have it, my friend. Now, what are we going to do?"

"We know the interlopers have infiltrated the East and South Districts. The only one left to visit is the West District."

"Then we should deploy the knights to patrol the West District to watch for signs of trouble. Surely they will be able to intercept the intruders."

"No. The knights are needed to guard the palace. For all we know, this could be a ploy to divert our focus and leave the crown vulnerable to attack. We will pull a platoon of troops from the wall, for a time, and have them patrol the area."

"What if we need them here? What if the Samurai returns before his promised day?"

Virgil and the General felt a chill breeze sweep past them. Something about it felt baleful. The hairs on the back of Virgil's neck stood on end. "If he is as powerful as the Queen's behavior suggests, one platoon will make little difference in stopping him."

The General felt a pit form in his stomach. He looked out over the wall at the beautiful land that was Avalon. He let the image flood his eyes and stain his memory like the glass of a cathedral. Love of his country filled his chest and warmed his newly wounded heart. He memorized every last detail, both new and old, as if it were the first time he had seen it, or maybe the last time he would ever see it, and then he closed his eyes.

The Fall of Avalon

"I will have the troops prepare," the General said, just above a whisper.

"Inform the soldiers, if they capture the infiltrators, I want them brought to me. I will deal with them myself."

Within Virgil's soul, a fire had awakened that he had not felt in a long time. The kind of fire that ignites in the heart of a warrior on the eve of battle; in the heat of the moment when two warriors clash; when one stands victorious over another. The fire burned away all his doubts, and insecurities. The time would soon be at hand where Virgil knew he would be face to face with the Samurai again.

The calm before the storm was not lost on Mifuné either. That day he watched over his apprentices while they slept, he could sense Virgil's presence stirring in Avalon. And on that, the sixth day, he could sense that Virgil was unbound, free to act of his own accord without hinderance or denial from the Queen. This was a development even Mifuné did not expect. His pulse quickened at the thought of Virgil pursuing his pupils back to the tower that night or descending upon them at any moment.

In his mind's eye, Mifuné could see clearly, as he could see the lush grass stretched out before him, the Paladin of Avalon, shield in hand and sword at the ready. The Samurai felt in his bones, the Paladin would come, soon. And theirs was to be an epic battle, unlike any since the defeat of Ravana seven years previously. The thought made Mifuné's heart tick a few beats faster. Once again, the line of the

Carl Houston Roach IV

Dragon Emperor would battle against the line of Arthur in the land of Androma.

The Fall of Avalon

CHAPTER 9   UNIMAGINABLE POWER

And it came to pass, that the son of the Dragon and the line of the King would battle once more to decide the fate of the kingdom.

Dusk was fast approaching. The minutes and hours of the day seemed to pass much more rapidly than they would typically, as if time itself fled from Mifuné's wrath. It was the last night, the final mission to warn the last of the citizens of Avalon of the impending doom that lay just around the corner. As they prepared to leave, Desmond and Gabrysia cast a glance at each other, and then at Naomi. Before opening the door to leave the tower, they each stopped her.

"What are you doing? We have to get going!" Naomi insisted.

"*We* do, Naomi," Gabrysia began, "but Desmond and I agreed that, for tonight, you should stay with Master."

"She is absolutely right." Desmond put both hands on Naomi's shoulders. "We will be alright. Leaving Master alone right now is probably not the best idea, especially after what happened the other day."

"Why me?" Naomi pressed.

"We finally got you to admit how you feel. Now you need to pursue that. That is the task I have for you," Desmond said, as he attempted to imitate Mifuné's lecturing tone.

Carl Houston Roach IV

"Desmond is right. Master is walking a very thin line between light and darkness. You are the only one who can pull him out of the darkness if he begins to stray," Gabrysia said, assuredly.

"And something in my gut tells me he will need you tonight," Desmond added.

Naomi released a heavy sigh and nodded. "Okay. I will stay," she answered reluctantly.

Desmond ruffled her hair and smiled. "Do not worry. We will be back before you know it."

"Please, be careful," Naomi pleaded.

"We will. Desmond, it is time!"

The sixth day was at its end. Gabrysia and Desmond took flight as the last of the light faded beneath the horizon. After that night, and a final day of rest, as the eighth day dawns they would take Avalon at last. Both Desmond and Gabrysia knew Mifuné would finally unveil his full power to bring the kingdom to its knees. Desmond yearned to see the depths of his Master's unrelenting might unleashed, the pinnacle which he would strive to achieve for the remainder of his life. Gabrysia would receive a promised treasure, something so great as to merit her a seat in her home once again. The thoughts made their hearts gallop full speed, as well as their feet, while they ran.

Naomi watched her two dear friends run until they were completely out of sight. She wished that she was going with them. She wished Mifuné was there beside her. She could not place why, but she was afraid. Foreboding of some unseen danger loomed in her heart, though she did not know if it

The Fall of Avalon

was for herself, her friends, or her Master. The chilling cold in the air did little to ease her worries.

The night time breeze swept Naomi's bangs across her forehead like gossamer strands of loose thread. She could feel the fear of the unknown take hold of her, as if her own life was would be choked away. The more Naomi thought of her beloved Master, the worse the feeling became as she knew that darkness swirled in his heart and grew steadily with each passing moment. Gabrysia's words echoed in Naomi's mind. "You are the only one who can pull him out of the darkness..." She produced the coin and held it in her hands. It provided no comfort, though.

Naomi closed her fingers around the coin. "I wish I knew what to do," she whispered. She turned and faced the forest at her back, and she started into the wood line. She carefully made her way through the brush and bramble until she arrived at the still water of the lagoon. It was crystal clear; no portion of the bottom was concealed from sight. Naomi unfastened her hood and laid it out on the ground. One by one, she removed her garments and lay them neatly folded on top.

Slowly, Naomi stepped gracefully into the lagoon. She shivered at the chilling temperature, but she continued forward. After only a few steps, she was waist deep in the frigid water. Her skin crawled; she rubbed her bare arms for warmth. She took in a deep breath and submerged herself. The cold chased away the gripping sense of danger that had bombarded her. The water around her was akin to the embrace of a loved one. She was locked in that moment, focused, yet still and relaxed, despite the pounding in her chest.

Beneath the surface of the water, Naomi thought about all that she had done, all that she had been through that brought her to that place in time. Though there was much to fear, she would not be afraid, not anymore. Mifuné's words, "The time for that is passed," echoed in the corridors of her memory. Naomi burst forth from the depths of the lagoon and deeply inhaled fresh air. She understood finally what her Master, Mifuné, meant when he said those words. The time for fear is passed, she thought. The time had come for her to step forward to fulfill her wish.

ᔗ

Mifuné sat alone in the room atop the tower. Thousands of thoughts raced through his mind and twisted his heart into a knotted mess. He thought about Queen Titania; how he detested her, he hated her with a passion, she disgusted him. It infuriated him to realize how little she thought him to be, and that she would once again try to ensnare him with her body, as though he had no conviction or honor. His brow furrowed, and he gripped his sword with white knuckles.

Virgil, and the inevitable battle he and Mifuné would fight, weighed on his mind. The oncoming clash would be far different than the first. Mifuné would not have the element of surprise on his side as he did before. Virgil would be on guard, and without doubt, would bring his full strength to bear. The Light of the Paladin was a formidable power, Mifuné was well aware. From what he had learned

The Fall of Avalon

from Argus, and what he had studied on his own, he knew the strength it afforded Virgil could be sufficient to defeat him. He could not afford to underestimate the Paladin.

Thoughts of Naomi, Mifuné's precious disciple, fluttered softly in the cuckolds of his heart. Each of my disciples is precious to me, but Naomi is set apart. He could feel himself gravitating toward her. Things had been different between us since she held me the morning after the battle against the 500. That single act was the rise of the sun after a horribly dark night, he surmised.

Mifuné fought against the memories of the time before the chaos that enveloped him, the time when Titania, the Queen of Avalon, was his and his alone. A time when he felt love radiate in his heart. All the while, Ravana, reiterated the fact that their love was never real, and that he had been willfully blinded to the truth of Queen Titania's treachery. Furthermore, Mifuné's delusions of love poisoned him. The Queen's attempt to appease him the day before was evidence of that. She was nothing but wicked and false. She knew how to work her way into the hearts of good men and tear them apart with their own desires Ravana declared maliciously, "Mifuné you were a fool for ever believing in love."

Naomi is completely unlike Titania. She is pure, innocent. She is tender and loving. She is honest and kind, Mifuné championed. In many ways, Naomi reminded Mifuné of his mother, Hina. Naomi shared all of Hina's best qualities, qualities his father assured him a man should seek in a woman. Naomi was something a man with blood on his hands was unworthy of. Mifuné opened his hands and looked into his palms. Though they appeared clean on the surface, deep within himself, Mifuné could see them saturated with the blood of every man and woman he had killed since his return. After several hours of isolation, Mifuné made his way out of the tower.

Sergei had moved inside the tower to escape the chilling winds of early fall. He had stoked a small fire in the fire place and bundled himself up in a cocoon of blankets kept in the tower. The bed he made for himself in the corner of the antechamber surprisingly seemed more comfortable than the commander's bed in which Mifuné slept in atop the tower.

Mifuné passed him by, silent as a grave, and made his way outside. The full moon shone over the land of Avalon like a beacon in the night. The wind felt like ice as it brushed over Mifuné's bare hands. Leaves plucked from their places on the tree branches, fell, and cover the ground in and around the forest. The varying shades of green began to change to hues of yellow, orange, and red.

Mifuné made his way through the dense wood line toward the lagoon. The fresh air eased the tension growing in his mind, and he that imagined the sight of the moon's beaming reflection on the clear surface of the water would settle him further. If he was going to succeed in the battle ahead, he could have nothing weighing him down. As he struggled his way through the bushes and brush, his father's words echoed from the corridors of his memory:

The Fall of Avalon

"My son, look at the water. Its surface is still, yet beneath the surface, currents flow all throughout, just like currents flow throughout our bodies. When your mind becomes like the water, and you can control those currents within you, when your mind can remain still in the presence of chaos, you will awaken Absolute Focus. When you have done that, my son, you will never be defeated."

Mifuné smirked. His father had always imparted similar proverbs to him while he was growing up. As a boy watching men fight, Mifuné could hardly see the application of those principles. As a man, and a master of the sword, those proverbs and principles were perfectly clear. A boy could never understand the thoughts of a man, just as a girl could never understand the thoughts of a woman. It made him think about Queen Titania. Did Queen Glorianna try to teach her daughter things that she never learned?

Regardless, Mifuné did learn the lessons his father, as well as Argus, had taught him. Though it took him over a decade of intense, grueling training with Argus, Mifuné awakened Absolute Focus— the ability to remain still in the presence of chaos, to read his opponents movements as they were conducted, the ability to sense the slightest changes in the environment around him, even without his sight, and the ability to bring all of his strength to bear in a single moment. The Dragon Emperor Sword style he had practiced all his life would be his sword against Virgil's Light of the Paladin, and Absolute Focus would be his shield.

Carl Houston Roach IV

Mifuné finally arrived through a clearing in the thicket to the lagoon. As he expected, the sight he beheld was calming; more than that, it was uplifting. The light of the moon reflected off the surface of the water and filled the area of the lagoon with ambient light. Lightning bugs fluttered about, flashing their yellow-green lights across the surface of the water. The crickets and grasshoppers that played their jittering tunes all throughout the forest were centralized there. All of nature was in harmony around him, and within the complete amity of nature, something far more beautiful than his present environment caught his attention.

There was ample light to see clearly that someone else was at the lagoon as well, a woman. She was washing herself in the water. Her wet, packed hair fell to the base of her neck. Beads of water that clung to her pastel skin glistened in the moonlight. Her figure was beyond any woman Mifuné had seen before, and her body was akin to the titanic mountains and the mighty, untamed wild lands of the West.

The woman's body was not free of blemish, though. Scars of varying shapes and sizes were printed across her porcelain skin. Some were easy to make out in the light of the moon, like the ones on her back near the tops of her shoulders. Some were faded, nearly invisible from a distance. Though these scars she bore were manifold, they did little to dim the glow of her spirit, akin to the full light of the moon in the eclipsing dark of the night.

The Fall of Avalon

The woman in the water looked over in Mifuné's direction as she ran her hands down the front of her body to wipe away an excess of moisture. A powerful magnetism drew them closer to each other. She did not cover herself, and he did not look away. The cold of the night was nothing to the flame ignited between them. Face to face, they looked deeply into each other's eyes, longingly, lovingly.

"Naomi…" Mifuné whispered.

Naomi pressed her right index finger to his lips. Softly, with a hand like ice, she took hold of his free right hand, and placed it on her heart above her breast. Her heart beat was incredibly fast, yet simultaneously steady and consistent. She pulled away his hand from her chest and lay it against the side of her face.

"Ten years ago, I tried to steal from you, the day we met. Do you remember that?"

Mifuné nodded. "I remember. You were very young."

"You let me go." Tears pooled in Naomi's eyes. "You are the only man I have ever met who was kind to me. The only one who never hurt me. You gave me a gift so that I would never want again." She pulled his hand away from her face and tenderly kissed his palm. "I thought about you every single day after, hoping, believing that one day, I would see you again. To stand before you like this. So that I could give you a gift, like you gave me all those years ago."

Naomi slid Mifuné's hand down her neck and chest and placed it back to her heart. Its beat had slowed, but there was more power behind each palpitation. Heat emanated from her chest that warmed Mifuné's cold hand. In her eyes, he saw such strength, such resolve. In that instant, he knew she told the truth. She had waited for this moment, for the chance to show him how she felt.

"This heart in my chest is no longer mine, Mifuné Tahaka. It belongs to you, now. Take it... take all of me." The pool of tears spilled onto her face, still damp from the water from the lagoon. "I love you. I always have. Whether you were the greatest warrior in all of Androma, or just a simple farmer in the countryside, would mean nothing to me." She placed her hand on his firm chest over his beating heart. The heat of his sturdy torso warmed her frigid hand. "I have always loved you for all that you are, and all you will become."

Naomi reached her hand up to the back of his head and ran her fingers through his hair. Mifuné slowly closed his eyes. His breath was deep, calm, relaxed. She could feel his skin goose-bump on the back of his neck down through the rest of his body, a direct result of his sensual desire and the ecstasy of her touch. Naomi's heart fluttered out of control. Cautiously, carefully, she pulled herself closer to him. Mifuné did not resist her. He did not try to hide away from her as he had hidden himself before.

The voice of The Lord of Chaos screamed in protest as Mifuné leaned in toward Naomi. Ravana roared like a tyrant at its subjects, yet produced little effect on Mifuné's desire. His lips met with Naomi's; they pursed against one another, as natural as the tide meeting the shore. A wave of emotion washed over each of them. To Naomi, it was the realization of a long-awaited dream; a hope, a figment she thought may have never become a reality. At long last, she felt what she had always wanted to feel.

Within Mifuné, something broke. A crack shot through the wall that formed around his heart the day the Queen of Avalon betrayed him, a wall formed of bitterness and resentment and demolished it. In his time trapped in the prison of light, the feelings of bitterness and resentment festered. In the time since his release, those feelings were the only things Mifuné could feel. Until, that is, Naomi held onto him in his moment of despair. The hatred that coursed through his veins and engulfed his soul, meant naught the moment he felt the beating of Naomi's heart over her bare breast. When his lips met hers in the most cherished moment he had ever experienced, acquiescence—genuine intimacy, and true love flooded his harsh, tormented existence. Mifuné cupped his right hand at the small of her back and pulled her closer, and Ravana's voice was silenced.

As Mifuné and Naomi continued their passionate kiss, a veil of white light surrounded them. Mifuné could feel the hard layers over his heart peel away, one by one. Naomi's touch, her kiss, her very being, cleansed him of his rage, his wrath. For the first time since before the Ravana had come forth to bring chaos to Androma, Mifuné felt like his old self again. His true self.

Carl Houston Roach IV

The two lovers opened their eyes. Their gazes were locked on each other, as the full moon's face looked down on the world below. Each of them smiled, and when they did, the light around them intensified, outstripping the moon of its splendor. Naomi removed the kasa from Mifuné's head and dropped it to the floor, exposing his short, thick, black hair. He lowered his head to her until their foreheads met. She wrapped her arms behind his neck and held herself against him.

"We could leave all of this behind," Mifuné whispered. Naomi looked up into his eyes. "We could leave tonight, when Gabrysia and Desmond return. Save Sergei's family, return them home. Take Gabrysia and Desmond to Eramar, and then leave. We could start a life together," he brushed his hand over her cheek tenderly.

"What about Avalon? What about Titania?" Naomi asked, bewildered. She could hardly believe what she was hearing.

"None of that matters anymore." The tone in Mifuné's voice was absolute.

Naomi's lips spread, and her teeth flashed the brightest smile she had ever given in her entire life. Her heart surged uncontrollably with joy at the realization that her wish could be coming true, the wish she had pursued for ten years. She kissed Mifuné's lips again, but she could not bring herself to speak. She took in a deep breath to steady herself, but before she could answer...

"MASTER!" A cry of panic and terror shot through the night. The voice was familiar, frightened, and urgent. It immediately drew

The Fall of Avalon

Mifuné's attention, as well as Naomi's. The veil of light vanished immediately, and Mifuné released his hold on Naomi.

"Get dressed," Mifuné ordered. He took up his kasa and put it on his head before darting back to the tower. It was Gabrysia's voice, without question. She had returned far sooner than expected, and from the sound in her voice, something had gone wrong. A pit formed in Mifuné's stomach as he charged through the thicket to see what might have happened. He was extremely grateful that Ravana was still silenced from the moment he shared with Naomi, lest he be plagued by Ravana's incessantly depraved speculation.

Once Mifuné was through the clearing, he could see Gabrysia next to Sergei. Her face was flushed. She held herself up on her knees as she gasped for air. Her hair was amess, and her breath was rapid. She had been running as if Death itself was on her heels. Desmond, however, was nowhere to be found.

"Gabrysia, what happened?" Mifuné asked firmly.

"She said they were discovered," Sergei answered. "They tried to escape, but they ran into some trouble."

"What kind of trouble?" Mifuné pressed. His tone was saturated in severity.

Naomi finally emerged from the woods. She was dressed, but her hair was still wet. She could see Gabrysia, but she did not see Desmond either. She made her way to Gabrysia's side and helped steady her to her feet. Naomi's eyes were full of concern, and the earlier sense of danger that perturbed her had returned.

"P-Paladin. Virgil. He found us. Des-Desmond stayed behind."

"What!?" Mifuné erupted. He tightened his left hand's grip around his sword until his knuckles went white.

Gabrysia shook her head with tears in her eyes. "Tried to run. Did not... get far. You were right, Master. His power... nothing I threw at him even fazed him! I have never seen power like that before..." The trauma from Gabrysia's and Desmond's encounter with the Paladin was evident in Gabrysia's troubled eyes.

"Gabrysia, did Desmond stay to fight him?" Naomi pressed.

Gabrysia only nodded. Mifuné was quiet, and a shroud came over his face. He lowered his head, and his left hand dropped from his sword. He stepped away from the group and faced the West, away from Avalon. He was still, while the others discussed the next move they should make.

"If they have Desmond, then we need to go get him back," Naomi said urgently.

"I agree," Sergei said and drew his sword. "I say we march over there now and..."

All conversation ceased as an amber light rose from Avalon, nearly as bright as the dawn. It was a gigantic fire, like a beacon of light. To them at the Tower, though, it was like a candle in a window. Naomi shuttered. She knew that a fire that blazed bright enough for them to see could only mean one thing, especially if that flame was coming from Avalon.

"Master, is that...." Naomi began.

"A pyre." Mifuné replied. He turned and faced the group. His face was blank, and his eyes were lifeless. "Desmond is dead." Mifuné's voice was hollow. It was as though he was numb to the realization that one of his young disciples, the one most like him, was gone forever. Sergei knew all too well the feeling of failing someone he'd vowed to protect. He could see clear as day, Mifuné's heart was broken, just as he could see the tears Mifuné fought to hold back.

"No... No, Desmond, he... he just..." Gabrysia's eyes let loose unrelenting streams of tears. She fell to her knees and dug her hands into the ground. Screams of agony, loss, and despair reverberated through the trees and soared across the plains. "NO!" she cried over and over. Naomi shed tears of her own, as she did all that she could to console Gabrysia. The two friends held onto one another as they mourned their loss together.

As Naomi held Gabrysia against her, she looked up at Sergei. He was calm, steady, with his gaze fixed on the pyre. His shaky breath indicated he held back tears of his own.

"Mifuné said we were going to leave this behind tonight... when Desmond and Gabrysia came back," Naomi muttered over her own sobs. "We were going to free your family and take everybody home..."

"It looks like no one is going anywhere now," Sergei replied, solemnly.

Carl Houston Roach IV

❧

At the site of the pyre, Virgil and the General looked on as Desmond's body burned up in the massive fire. Virgil smiled triumphantly, as though it was Mifuné he had defeated. He beamed with pride, as bright as the blaze. The General felt a haunting sensation have its way with him, as if they had awakened a caged beast by unlocking the door.

"You really think he can see this?" the General asked.

"I have no doubt he has seen this," Virgil replied smugly. "In fact, I am quite certain he is watching right now."

"It has been my experience that insulting your opponent before battle yields ill results," the General dutifully stated.

"Please," Virgil raised a hand to the General dismissively. "I do not fear him the way you do. The table has been set, and our battle will be legendary. Tomorrow, I shall overcome this enemy, and I shall be forever known as the greatest Paladin in the history of Avalon!"

"You are going out there to face him?" the General asked, with stark apprehension in his voice.

"I am." Virgil crossed his arms confidently.

"I will prepare a contingent to go with you," the General insisted.

"No. I go alone."

"Virgil!"

"To him, our soldiers are paper tigers. They would count for nothing."

The Fall of Avalon

The General sighed, realizing his concerns would go unnoticed. "Have you informed the Queen of your intentions?"

"I will. And I will inform her of a few changes that will greet Avalon upon my return." He patted the General on the shoulder. "Big things are coming, my friend. Great things." Virgil took two steps past the General and vanished in a quick flash of light.

The General turned his gaze back to Desmond on the pyre. Though he had been a part of many pyres lit in his time as Commanding General of the army of Avalon, the pyre constructed for Desmond truly disturbed him, less for the fate of the boy, and more for the consequences that would follow. If Mifuné's intent was malicious before, he would bring down renewed vengeance upon Avalon and its people without any chance of mercy, just as they showed no mercy to that boy on the pyre. "May the gods be with you, my Paladin. We will need all the help we can get now."

Virgil appeared at the balcony just outside the ballroom of the palace, where it all began. As he suspected, Queen Titania was there, alone. She wore a black gown that was, as far as her tastes were concerned, extremely modest. Her hair hung wildly and unkept down her back. She leaned against the railing and looked out toward the moon.

"Titania," Virgil began, "I am leaving now to face Mifuné. I should arrive at the tower by dawn."

"Do what you want, Virgil. I cannot stop you," Queen Titania replied, her voice depressed.

Carl Houston Roach IV

Virgil marched to the Queen's side. He placed a hand on her waist and turned her toward him. Her eyes were encircled with gray. The color in her lips was substantially faded. She felt frail and weak in his arms; her dress hung on her as if she wore one of his tunics. Her face was devoid of expression; a blank slate, without fear or courage, without malice or mercy, without sorrow or joy. Virgil took her hands in his.

"By this time tomorrow, this will all be over. I will lay Mifuné's corpse at your feet. Then I will light another pyre and cast him into it. When I have done that, I will make you mine, and mine alone."

Virgil released her hands and walked away confidently. He balled his hands into fists. His great power surged and swelled in his chest. He could feel it course through his body. Images of the battle he would fight against Mifuné passed before his eyes. Virgil never had the chance to test the full extent of his power against a worthy opponent before. The opportunity was exhilarating beyond normal comprehension.

"Virgil," the Queen called to him faintly, "What about my husband? What will become of Colabion?" It was unclear if her inquiry was proposed from a position of concern, or curiosity.

The Paladin stopped dead in his tracks. In his mind, Mifuné was his only objective, the only thing of consequence that still stood in his way. The weak, timid, powerless, spineless, inferior Colabion was nothing more than a pebble on the pavement of the road stretched out before him. Over his

The Fall of Avalon

shoulder, he replied, "When I return, I will kill him, too."

Virgil vanished from the room in the same manner which he had appeared. In a flash of light, he arrived at the gates of Avalon. The sentinels on guard were startled to see him arrive so suddenly. Virgil smirked, having seen them flinch away. Men like them would be no match for Mifuné. They are not like me, Virgil thought; they do not have power like mine. The Paladin was certain that the next time these guards saw him, it would be as the Hero of Avalon. He would have crushed Mifuné beneath his boot and dragged his body back to the Citadel. Without a word, he began his trek across the grassy plains to the Tower of Galahad.

That night, Mifuné sat alone outside the tower, he faced Avalon. He grieved the loss of Desmond in his heart. The young man's voice played in his head over and over again. Desmond would always beg him to teach him new techniques, teach him the Dragon Sword Style that been handed down in Mifuné's bloodline for generations, anything he might learn to make himself a greater warrior. He could see Desmond's determined face as he pushed himself to be more like his Master.

Mifuné remembered how excited Desmond was when he learned about the existence of Aikido within every living thing, and how eager he was to be able to employ it in battle. Mifuné never told him enough, how proud he was of Desmond, of his accomplishments, and his eagerness to learn. Thoughts of regret, thoughts of how he might have done things differently, haunted his mind. The

Carl Houston Roach IV

Ravana's voice had returned and fed on those feelings of failure and deep regret.

Naomi watched from the window of the antechamber as the man she loved sat alone. She wanted to go to him, but Gabrysia needed her more. Naomi cradled Gabrysia as she wept, bitterly. Naomi could not bring herself to cry, though. For Gabrysia's sake, she held her composure. For Mifuné's sake, she carried the mantle of hope that Mifuné had held up for them until Desmond's death.

Gabrysia wished in the depths of her soul that there was something she could have done to stop Virgil. She wished she would have stayed with Desmond, so at least they would have died together. She was haunted by Virgil's apparent invulnerability. Her magic was utterly useless against him, no matter how hard she tried. He swatted away her most powerful attacks as though they were troublesome flies. With only his bare hands, he demolished the most powerful protective barriers she could muster. As sunrise approached, her weeping finally settled into a numb state.

Early red light of dawn began to leak over the horizon as the sun emerged from beneath the skyline. As the light intensified, a silhouette appeared, and drew nearer. Naomi and Sergei strained their eyes to see who it could be. There was no doubt in their minds, even without seeing who it was, that it could only be one person.

Mifuné's eyes shot open and he rose to his feet. His left hand clutched the sheath of his sword just under the hand guard. He started away from the

The Fall of Avalon

tower as his opponent came into view. The sun glinted off the encroacher's shimmering armor. His red cape flowed gloriously in the wind. In his right hand he carried a magnificent sword of unique construction, and in his left, he carried a powerful kite shield bearing the crest of Avalon in the middle. Virgil, the Paladin of Avalon, had arrived at the Tower of Galahad.

Mifuné and Virgil stopped a fair distance from the tower. They faced one another, each with a fearsome, ferocious look in their eyes, akin to alpha lions competing for dominance. The standoff between Virgil and Mifuné created a heavy atmosphere of pressure and power. Their very aura made them difficult to approach.

Sergei darted out of the tower with his sword in hand. Naomi and Gabrysia quickly followed. Gabrysia, at the sight of Virgil, was overwhelmed with rage. Royal blue aura encompassed her body, as she accelerated toward Virgil. She had intended to strike him with the full force of her power.

"You killed Desmond!" Gabrysia screamed with all her might.

Gabrysia mustered her magic into her hands and prepared an attack, but Virgil caught a glimpse of her before she could. "Stand aside!" he roared.

Virgil swung his arm in her direction, and a tremendous force pushed Gabrysia back and onto the ground. Naomi rushed to her side as quickly as she could. Gabrysia had the wind knocked out of her, but she was not seriously injured. Sergei halted protectively just in front of them.

Carl Houston Roach IV

"This does not concern you! This is between me and the Samurai!" Virgil exclaimed and sneered arrogantly.

Mifuné's attention was fixed on Virgil. He did not even feel the force of the swing, though it brushed right in front of him. The Samurai was firm and unshakeable as the stone tower behind him.

"You killed Desmond?" Mifuné asked just above a whisper.

"I did. And I burned his body atop a great pyre. I do so hope you noticed." Virgil paused, waiting eagerly for a reaction from Mifuné, but there was none. Mifuné's piercing gaze was unwavering. Virgil continued. "You would have been proud of him. He did put up a commendable struggle. Unfortunately for him, I am the Paladin of Avalon. He never stood a chan..."

"Shut up," Mifuné interrupted calmly, but forcefully.

Virgil was astounded. "A man of few words, indeed." He smirked. He could sense the pain he had inflicted by taking away Mifuné's disciple, yet Mifuné still possessed the will to stand against him.

Mifuné turned his head over his shoulder. "Sergei. Gabrysia. Naomi."

They each looked to him, but only Sergei managed to answer. "What is it?"

"If you would rather not die, you should leave this place. Now." Mifuné did not wait for a response. He turned his face back to Virgil. "As for you, Paladin..."

Mifuné's knees bent. His left leg slid back, and his right hand wrapped around his sword handle. He

The Fall of Avalon

bent forward slightly at the waist. Deadly focus came over him and melded with the malice in his eyes. "You made a poor decision." Dense perturbation reverberated in his tone.

Faster than anyone could see, Mifuné closed the distance between himself and Virgil. In the blink of an eye, he unsheathed his blade and swung his sword. A massive blast of power exploded from between the two clashing titans that spread over the whole area to the wood line. Whips of wind, sharp as steel, sliced through the radius of the blast, and sheared leaves and branches off the trees.

Sergei raised his arms in front of his face and steadied himself as best he could to keep from being blown away. Had Naomi and Gabrysia not been behind him, the force of the blast surely would have cast them back into the forest. When he finally managed to open his eyes, Sergei could see Virgil had parried Mifuné's blow with his sword.

The two swordsmen pushed each other away. Mifuné held his blade out in front of himself, dividing himself in two. Virgil raised his sword in the air so that the point was aiming to the sky, and with his shield, he guarded his front. He grinned, and his sword began to glow with white light.

"Prepare yourself, Samurai, to face the Light of the Paladin!"

Virgil thrust his sword to the heavens, and from the tip, a beam of light ascended. Clouds swiftly formed and encircled the sky above Virgil. From within the eye of the clouds, an enormous pillar of white light descended upon Virgil and consumed him completely, merged with him and became The

Carl Houston Roach IV

Light of the Paladin. Sergei, Naomi, and Gabrysia covered their eyes from the blinding pillar. The wind churned wildly, like a twister. The ground trembled under the tremendous pressure, akin to the manifestation of Ravana's shadow above Mifuné. Mifuné was unaffected, though his kasa was blown off his head from the vicious surge of power. The blinding intensity of the white light faded, and Virgil came back into view. The pillar of light had changed him. Head to toe, he was guarded by magic armor composed of pure, white light. His sword and shield were transformed as well, each significantly larger, with new, unique shape, and enveloped in shining white light.

Virgil's sword of light vanished from his hand. He raised his right arm and pointed his index finger at Mifuné. A glimmer of light appeared on the tip that flickered through the varying colors of the color spectrum. "Disappear now!" Virgil exclaimed. "Piercing Light!"

A beam of light fired from Virgil's fingertip at Mifuné faster than a bolt of lightning touches the ground. Mifuné shifted his head to his right before the beam could touch him. It continued past Mifuné and passed into the Tower of Galahad. The stones of the tower illuminated briefly. A horrific explosion, which followed Virgil's attack, blew the tower apart. Mounds of stone cascaded in every direction. The bottom half exploded backward into the forest, crushing multiple trees and plants in its collapse. The upper half came tumbling down over the battlefield. Sergei, Gabrysia, and Naomi took to their heels and ran as fast as they could to escape the collapsing tower. Naomi looked back over her shoulder to see a huge chunk of stone careening down toward her Master.

"Mifuné!" she cried out desperately.

Without taking his attention from Virgil, Mifuné swung his sword backward. The edge of his blade struck the stone piece and effortlessly cleaved it clean in half. The two separate pieces fell away from him to his left and to his right. His eyes were unwaveringly focused, and frightening, filled with the intent to kill.

Virgil rushed in at Mifuné with terrifying speed. A glowing blade appeared in the Paladin's hand. It crashed against Mifuné's sword once, then twice, and then a third time. They stepped across the battlefield, expertly parried, countered, and evaded each other's attacks. At times, they moved so fast, they were invisible to the eye until they stopped and pressed against one another. Those moments were accompanied by explosive connections of their swords.

"Your disciple failed to defeat me," Virgil's voice echoed through his enchanted helmet, as he and Mifuné locked in place against one another. "He called out for you as he died. Your favorite disciple perished at my hands, and you did nothing to save him!" Virgil grunted as he strained against Mifuné's formidable strength.

"Shut up!" Mifuné shouted, enraged. He pushed Virgil's sword up and broke the stalemate. "Shut… up!" Virgil barely locked blades with Mifuné's in time to save himself from the attack Mifuné launched against him. He was forced back away from Mifuné. His heels dragged trenches through the ground. Virgil chuckled, amused at Mifuné's growing wrath.

Mifuné crossed his sword over his chest horizontally. His power disturbed the air around his body and forced it into a spiral. His sword ignited with purple flames. The aikido within his body erupted around him in a swirling vortex of unrelenting power. His kimono rent in half, and his muscles expanded and tensed rapidly.

"Dragon Emperor's Flame!" Mifuné shouted, like a ferocious beast's roar when it overtakes its prey.

Mifuné pointed the tip of his sword at Virgil. From the sword, a massive, concentrated beam of purple fire exploded forth toward the Paladin. Virgil thrust his shield forward as the fire struck, and arcs of fire blazed past his shield. The force of the attack pushed Virgil further back. He strained mightily against the power of Mifuné's furious attack as his feet slid, and dug the trench further back still. Virgil roared as he pressed against the flames. The Paladin of Avalon would not be defeated so easily, he superciliously concluded. With a tremendous effort, Virgil gave one last push forward. The force behind his efforts dissipated the flames completely.

Virgil moved his shield and saw everything between himself and Mifuné had been completely incinerated. After blocking Mifuné's ferocious attack, the Paladin could feel his strength had significantly declined. He was short of breath. He had never experienced power like Mifuné's, yet the Samurai showed no visible sign of fatigue. His

The Fall of Avalon

sword extended out to his right, and his guard was down. Though Mifuné was vulnerable, Virgil was not enticed to strike.

"What… what are you?" Virgil asked. A tinge of fear apparent in his tone.

"My name is Mifuné Tahaka!" Mifuné declared with supreme authority. "I am the last of the line of the Dragon Emperor. I am the living legacy of my people. I am the man who slayed Ravana." He paused, positioned his sword in front of himself, and closed both hands around the handle. "And I am the man who will break the Light of the Paladin." Mifuné's declaration was as powerful as the enormous strength he had demonstrated throughout the battle. Despite this, Virgil would not be discouraged. He girded himself, and continued his onslaught against Mifuné, to no avail.

The battle went on for hours in an effort to spur the full power of the Paladin. The impact of Mifuné's sword against Virgil's could be felt as far away as the gates of Avalon. Each time their swords struck one another, a powerful explosion followed. Even from her bedchamber, Queen Titania could hear the fighting, and see the bursts of light from the battlefield. She and Colabion watched from the window, hoping beyond hope that Virgil would not fail. Despite their grievances with his ambition to rule over Avalon should he return, the Paladin was their last hope for survival. He was the only thing standing between Avalon's prosperity and oblivion.

Sunset was upon them. Although both warriors dripped with sweat, Virgil felt fatigued. Despite his greatest efforts and his heretofore unrivaled strength, Virgil had yet to land a decisive blow against Mifuné. His mastery of swordsmanship made combating Mifuné difficult enough, but his unprecedented speed and apparent predictive ability made the Samurai nigh impossible to strike. Virgil put some distance between himself and Mifuné. He poised himself in a statuesque posture to initiate one of the signature techniques of the Paladin.

"Prepare yourself, Mifuné. This is a technique even you cannot evade!" Virgil confidently proclaimed.

Mifuné glared, ultimately unimpressed. "Do not hold back," he scoffed as he held his ground and maintained his focus on Virgil's eyes. As the Paladin's power shook the ground beneath them Virgil held his sword out to his side, and the blade began to change form. The light of his blade became long and slender and curved significantly.

With a deep, mighty voice, Virgil exclaimed, "Paladin Saber!" Swiftly and mightily, he swept his blade horizontally at Mifuné. As it travelled through the air, it increased in length.

Mifuné gripped his sword handle with both hands and turned his sword so the tip was facing the ground. The Paladin Saber struck Mifuné's blade and immediately broke in two. Virgil stood astonished. Mifuné rushed forward and attacked Virgil again before he could utilize another technique.

The Saber, however, did not completely vanish. The tip continued spinning through the air, far too fast for a normal person to evade. Sergei caught the blade through the right part of his chest. He howled in pain and fell to the ground. Blood spurted out of the wound as the sword of light disappeared. Gabrysia and Naomi rushed to his side as Mifuné and Virgil battled on.

"Sergei!" Gabrysia knelt down beside him as he coughed up blood. "Naomi, we need to get him out of here!"

Naomi closed her eyes and folded her hands. Using her magic, she called out into the woods for a friend to help. To their great relief, a mighty bear emerged as quickly as its lumbering mass could move. Naomi brushed her hand over the side of the bear's face as thanks. The bear dropped down as Naomi and Gabrysia hauled Sergei on its back. The bear hurried away with them toward the lagoon, as it was eager to distance itself from the ongoing battle—it was instinctively afraid.

Once at the lagoon, Naomi and Gabrysia lowered Sergei beside the water and tried to heal his wound. They took turns, each positioning her hands over the bloody hole in Sergei's chest. Though their magic, respectively, activated over the wound, the injury would not heal. "Why is this not working!? It should be working!" Gabrysia cried out.

"It was light magic that hurt him. I do not think either of us have enough power to mend this," Naomi sullenly replied. "We should have listened to Mifuné. We should have done what he said and left…" Tears streamed down Naomi's cheeks.

"Well we have to do something! I will not just sit here and watch him die!" Gabrysia's voice trailed off in tears. "I do not want to lose anyone else…" Sergei took Gabrysia's hand in his. Blood filled his throat. He could not speak. With all his might, he tried to assure her through his eyes that it was not her fault. That it was okay. She took hold of his mighty hand with both of hers. "You are going to be alright! We are going to save you!" Gabrysia desperately urged.

Naomi looked at the bear beside her, as it had remained with them. She then looked down to Sergei, who lay bleeding on the ground. A switch went off in her mind, a sudden awakening, as though she remembered something she had long forgotten. Red aura manifested in Naomi's eyes. She placed the palm of her hand on Sergei's injured chest.

Naomi spoke in a peculiar tone, "To save this life, before it is gone Unite these two, upon this dawn. Bind these souls together in life. That Death this day impart no strife. Spirits bound, until the last. Bear the seal, unsurpassed."

The bear was enveloped in the red aura, vanished into it, and became one with it. The red light then transitioned over Sergei's whole body and seeped into him, like water into cloth. When the aura faded, he convulsed, grunted, and groaned as though he was in extraordinary pain. He rolled onto his injured side and slammed his fist against the ground. His body to changed. The wound in his chest closed up, and he grew. Strength and power like he had never known coursed through his body. Thick, white fur sprouted up across his whole body, even over his clothes. His hands changed into paws armed with blade-like claws. As his transformation took place, his head convulsed from left to right and changed drastically from the head of a man to that of a bear. When it was over, Sergei was a towering bear who stood like a man. His eyes glowed crimson red, just like Naomi's magical aura. On the fur over where his injury was, there was a circle with a series of marks that, together, created the face of a bear.

"Naomi, what did you just do?" Gabrysia asked, simultaneously shocked and amazed.

Naomi came back into reality as though she had been in a trance. She held her head and wobbled for a moment before regaining her balance. She felt tired, as if her stamina had been completely drained, but she was fully aware of her surroundings and what had just transpired. "I am not sure, but I think I saved his life." Naomi said softly. She held her hand in front of her face. "I suppose this is one of the powers of the Arcane Arts."

"What should we do now?" Gabrysia asked.

"I am going back out there," Naomi said adamantly.

Gabrysia grabbed Naomi's arm. "Naomi, you cannot go back out there! Those two are fighting at their full power. What you and I have is nothing compared to that level. If you go out there, you could die!"

"I do not care! Mifuné needs me. I will not leave him alone!"

Without any further debate or discussion, Naomi charged headstrong back to the battlefield. Gabrysia watched, eager to stop her. Sergei gently placed his massive paw on her shoulder. She looked up into the eyes of the beast. He was calm, as if he were his normal self. He shook his head at her and watched Naomi make her way back to the battleground. Gabrysia nodded and watched on. Her own words echoed in her mind: 'You are the only one who can pull him back from the darkness.'

"Okay, Naomi. It is up to you."

The Fall of Avalon

CHAPTER 10   UNMATCHED SWORDSMAN

The Light of the Paladin could not prevail against him. And he descended upon the city with the voice of a Dragon.

Virgil rushed to anchor himself against Mifuné's retaliation. His shield bore the brunt of the assault, as Virgil stretched his arm, extended his damaged sword behind him and channeled the light of the Paladin. Within moments Virgil brought his restored sword to bare. The battle between Mifuné and Virgil raged on into the night. The moon was a pale flicker of light compared to Virgil's shining white armor. His glowing blade continued to crash against Mifuné's relentlessly. Each swing carried with it the strength and the will of every Paladin before him. Though his body ached, Virgil would not submit. I will would destroy this enemy and be the hero who saved Avalon, he vowed.

Naomi trembled as she watched the fight from behind the remains of the shattered tower. Thoughts of great legends, celebrated stories, that regaled tales of epic power such as the resplendence the two warriors displayed. To hear about it was one thing, but to witness it first hand was beyond anything she could imagine.

Mifuné noticed a pattern had developed in Virgil's attacks. His strikes had noticeably less power behind them than when the battle first began, and they were slower. Additionally, the frequency of his attacks decreased as well. The glow of his armor became noticeably dimmer. His stamina had markedly depleted and thus, Mifuné would entertain him no longer.

The Paladin's sword met again with Mifuné's, and they pressed against each other. Condescendingly, Mifuné matched Virgil's strength. The blades quaked in their hands. Sparks ignited and flew from the edges onto the scorched earth. They pushed each other away and planted with both feet on the ground.

"Virgil!" Mifuné began. "I have fought countless battles against men, monsters, and demons alike. Not since the Ravana have I faced an opponent as powerful as you. I, Mifuné Tahaka, declare you the strongest warrior in Androma!"

Virgil chuckled. "You say that like it is not obvious. You have witnessed my power first hand. With just the tip of my finger, I demolished the Tower of Galahad. You know you cannot defeat me, Mifuné, and flattery will not save you. Perhaps in your day, you were the strongest, but now you are sorely outclassed!"

"Yes. I have seen your power. You have brought the full of it to bear against me, yet here I stand."

"Not for long!" Virgil replied. "You are a fool to think I have used the full power against you." He raised his sword in a readied position, but Mifuné halted his advance by extending out his hand.

"Enough! Are you so blind that you still cannot see the difference between your power and mine?

The Fall of Avalon

You cannot defeat me, Paladin. Not with the power that was *given* to you."

"You dare insult the line of Arthur!?"

"All my life I have pursued great strength and power. I pushed myself to the edge of my limits and beyond. I will not be undone by a *boy* with no respect for the power he has *inherited*."

"I have had enough of you Mifuné! You insult my heritage! You threaten my Queen, my love! You kill my countrymen in droves! And you mean to destroy an entire civilization created by one of the twelve Lords of Light! You are an evil plague to this land, and I will remove your threat once and for all!"

"Then come get me, try everything you can." Mifuné taunted, his indignant low rasp resonated like a slap on Virgil's face.

Virgil cast his shield to the side. As it dug into the ground under its enormous weight, he thrust the tip of his blade into the sky. His armor illuminated and a sphere of light concealed him from sight. The Paladin channeled his brilliant power into his sword, and increased its size, length, and width. The intensity of the sphere funneled into the sword and in his hands Virgil held a gigantic sword of light.

Mifuné estimated the sword to be equivalent in size to Ravana. He steadied himself where he stood. He positioned his sword behind him, and aligned the blade along the sheath. With his left hand, he steadied the flat edge of the sword against his waist. He closed his eyes, and imagined the surface of the water, still, and quiet.

Carl Houston Roach IV

"This will be the end of you, Mifuné! I've put all of my power into this attack! The ultimate Paladin Blade!"

Virgil seized the handle of the titanic sword with both hands and prepared to swing. With all his might, he turned his torso and swung the blade diagonally at Mifuné. As the monstrous blade of light soared through the air, Virgil called out with a mighty roar: "Caliburn!"

Mifuné remained steady in the face of the attack. Even as the branches and leaves were scattered to the winds, even as the stones and boulders rolled from their place, Mifuné remained unmoved. Before the colossal blade could cleave him in twain, the steel of his blade stopped Virgil's attack cold. The tremendous shockwave from the connection of the two swords blasted away what remained of the Tower of Galahad. The entire forest behind them was nearly blown away from the blast, including Sergei and Gabrysia.

Sergei shielded Gabrysia from the blast with his body. As a bear, it was significantly easier to withstand the force. His heavy feet dug into the dirt and dragged backwards from the intensity of explosion. Gabrysia clung to his back for dear life. She feared for Naomi, who was out there alone, watching the fight.

Naomi hardly was able to shield herself from the burst of wind and the pressure. She threw her hands in front of her and pushed out as much magic as she could in that moment to shield herself. It felt like trying to hold back an ocean. Her body strained under the pressure. The barrier she had generated cracked and wavered, but it held.

The guards atop the wall of Avalon were flung from their posts as the blast reached where they stood. The torches lighting the wall were extinguished. Anything not secured to the ground was thrown from the top of the wall into the streets of the city. The General woke from the sound. Fearing the worst, he immediately called in the troops to establish a defensive posture in front of the kingdom's gates.

Virgil's Caliburn pressed against Mifuné like the waves of a tide beat against the stones on the shore. Despite its great size and enormous magical power, Mifuné was able to hold it off. Mifuné felt the force of the attack press him down into the ground. A depression formed beneath him that deepened the longer Virgil surged against him.

Mifuné smirked, "So, that is it."

A dark purple aura surrounded his body. He slowly pushed Caliburn away from himself, inch by inch. Virgil was completely astonished. No enemy in Avalon's history, not even Arthur's greatest nemesis himself, the Mad King Mordred, was able to repel that attack. No matter how hard he tried, he could not carry through his strike.

Mifuné inhaled slow; controlled and steadied himself. Like the motionless surface of a lake with currents flowing beneath it, the power coursed through him and magnified immensely, yet he was calm. He continued to move the blade away from his body, regardless of Virgil's struggle to press it against him. When his arms were fully extended out, Mifuné turned his wrists, and swung his sword down.

A sound like shattering glass echoed across the battlefield. Dazzling sparks of white light rained down from the sky. Caliburn was shattered. And as it broke, Virgil's magic armor vanished with it. He fell to a knee. His breathing was quick and heavy. Having exhausted nearly all of his stamina, Virgil could only hold himself up with his right hand, whose knuckles were driven into the dirt. He barely managed to maintain his grip on his sword.

"No!" Virgil cried betwixt panting. "This cannot be. I am the Paladin, do you hear me?! I am the most powerful warrior in the world!"

"You are nothing," Mifuné proudly replied.

Virgil looked up to see Mifuné standing over him. The tip of his blade was pointed between Virgil's eyes. For the first time, since the days before he had awakened the Light of the Paladin, Virgil was afraid. He had thrown the very best he had at Mifuné, but nothing proved effective. He thought about Queen Titania, her soft touch, the taste of her lips, the feel of her skin against his. He clenched his teeth and took up his sword.

Virgil knocked Mifuné's sword away with his shield-bearing gauntleted hand and thrust his sword toward Mifuné's chest, but Mifuné vanished out from in front of him before Virgil's sword could hit its mark. Virgil's eyes shot left and right, up and down, as he scanned the surrounding area. His heart pounded out of his chest, his breath was quick. Mifuné was nowhere to be found. Suddenly, a white-hot pain overtook him from his back that burned all the way through his entire torso.

The steel of Mifuné's sword extended through Virgil's chest. His crimson blood clung to the flat end of the blade and dripped onto the scorched ground. He grabbed hold of the steel piercing his body and desperately attempted to remove it. Blood filled his throat and flooded his mouth. A stream of blood flowed down his face. He felt himself rise upward, and his strength to fight against his imminent demise was robbed of him.

Mifuné raised him up until his feet were just off the ground. When he saw Virgil's arms fall to his side, he immediately retracted the sword from Virgil's body and dropped him to the ground. Virgil's legs folded under his weight and he collapsed to his knees, but did not fall. He pressed his hands against the hole in his armor, desperate to stop the blood from leaking out of him.

Mifuné returned his sword behind him and secured it against his waist with his left hand. He stepped around Virgil slowly, and stopped in front of him. He stood over the defeated Paladin for a moment. A chilling breeze swept over the battlefield. Virgil looked up into Mifuné's eyes, one last time. There was fear in them, as well as despair.

"For Desmond," Mifuné said, quietly.

Mifuné swept his blade through the air. The edge cut clean through Virgil's neck like butter. His severed head fell away from his body and rolled across the ground. His body collapsed backwards where he knelt. Before returning his sword to its sheath, Mifuné held the shining steel in front of his face. In it, he could see Virgil's face, as it was being swallowed into the darkness that dwelled within the sword.

Mifuné flicked his sword out away from him, and flung the blood off his blade onto the ground. He turned the tip of his blade to its sheath and slid it back in slowly, controlled.

Naomi emerged from her hiding place. The battle was finally over, and she could be with her master again. She approached slowly, cautiously. She watched every move he made. There was something about the fight... There was far more depth. The malicious beheading of Virgil was personal and done deliberately as vindication of Desmond's death, and to rid Avalon of their Paladin.

"Naomi," Mifuné said. His voice was low, as though it would have been hoarse had he spoke any louder.

"Yes, what is it?" Naomi said as she joined him.

"Summon your ravens." He knelt down and picked up Virgil's head by the hair. "Send this to Titania." He held Virgil's head out to her for her to take.

Naomi was horrified at his request. Such was not like him. He was not the same man she loved. He was cruel, spiteful, vengeful. A question lingered in her mind, though: Was this aimed to dishonor Virgil, or was this an attempt to hurt Queen Titania more than he already had?

Naomi shook her head. "No," she said. "I cannot do that."

The Fall of Avalon

"You would refuse your Master?" Mifuné pressed. "I gave you an order! DO IT!" Mifuné yelled.

"No!" Naomi forcefully replied. "My Master is a kind man! He is caring and loving." Images from the moment she shared with Mifuné beside the lagoon, the gentle caress of his touch, the feel of his lips against hers, resonated within her like a fire in the dark night. "He would never do such a thing... So, whoever you are, give me my Mifuné back!" she demanded.

"If you will not do what I ask, I will do it myself!" Mifuné's voice became monstrous at the end, akin to when he spoke to Sergei with the voice of Ravana.

Mifuné's eyes flashed white like the stars. He stretched forth his hand and opened his palm to the sky. Black fire appeared in the palm of his hand. The fire began to take form, and became a nightmarish bird-like creature with abnormally large talons, long tail feathers, and a long, thick beak. Centered in its head was a single white eye that was lidless, with a black pupil in the middle.

The creature spawned in Mifuné's hand dug its talons into Virgil's skull and carried the Paladin's head back to Avalon. Mifuné turned his head and watched the creature take flight. When he turned his face back to Naomi, she saw no remorse in his eyes, no regret. He walked past her to go collect the others, and Naomi drifted away from him into the night.

Gabrysia and Sergei emerged from the wood line of their own volition. Mifuné was victorious, much to their relief. He approached them steadily. Though he saw Sergei's new form, he did not seem disturbed or alarmed by it. He stopped in front of them beside the rubble from the destroyed tower.

"Master, Sergei..." Gabrysia struggled to think of how to explain the situation, but Mifuné raised a hand.

"The Paladin is dead. Take his armor and fashion it for Sergei. You should be able to enchant it so that it will stay with Sergei's current form."

"You mean, he can change back?" Gabrysia exclaimed. "How do you know that?"

"Several of the members of the Company of Heroes could take the forms of powerful beasts using the Arcane Arts. I have seen it before," Mifuné replied. "He can return to his human form, but he must first choose to." He looked to Sergei. "Choose soon. Because at dawn, we attack."

Mifuné walked past them and sat on a flat piece of the Tower of Galahad. He crossed his legs, folded his arms over his chest, and closed his eyes. He appeared to be in a meditative state. Gabrysia could sense the power in him that had surged wildly during his fight with Virgil began to settle to its normal state.

Gabrysia scanned her surroundings, and felt sheer horror sink into her soul. Naomi was nowhere to be found. Gabrysia peered into the wreckage and the rubble, and into the forest as far as she could see, but there was no sign of her anywhere.

"Master, where is Naomi?" Gabrysia asked.

"Do not be afraid. She is alive," Mifuné replied.

The Fall of Avalon

"Where is she? Why is she not here with you?" Gabrysia inquired further.

Mifuné hesitated. He let out a long exhale through the nose before answering, "She is not coming with us."

The weight on Gabrysia's heart was almost more than she could bear. First, she had lost Desmond, her fellow disciple, her trusted companion, her brother. During the battle against Virgil, she nearly lost Sergei, too; a man who was once a stranger, but now a friend. To lose Naomi, someone so precious to her, someone closer to her than her own kin, was a loss that grieved her soul.

Gabrysia's took up the task that Mifuné had given her, and used her magic to fashion Virgil's armor into armor for Sergei. She shaped his cuirass into a series of downward facing chevrons to cover Sergei's hulking torso, and utilized the shield as the main back plate. The pauldrons were used to connect the breastplate with the back plate along Sergei's flanks. There was not enough material left over to construct a helmet, but what he had would suffice.

"Done," Gabrysia said, as she wiped away sweat from her brow. She sat on the ground, panting. "How does it feel?" she asked.

Sergei moved around a bit and felt out the armor. It was snug on his body, but he lost no range of motion with his movements. Even in the transitions from all fours to standing on two legs, he hardly noticed the difference. Sergei grunted and nodded his head up and down in approval. Gabrysia smiled. She would never admit it aloud, but, she found his behavior as a bear adorable.

Mifuné rose from his sitting place slowly. He grasped the sheath of his sword with his left hand and started toward Gabrysia and Sergei. Their attention went straight to him. Without him saying a word, they knew what he was thinking. He stopped, faced the two, and said, "It is time."

§❧

At the Ivory Palace, Queen Titania looked out the window of her bedchamber. She thought only about Virgil and his battle with Mifuné. The fate of Avalon, and more importantly, her fate, hung in the balance. The sudden silence from the battlefield was disconcerting for her. She feared the worst. She dreaded that she was right, and that Virgil's power was not sufficient to defeat Mifuné.

The Queen wasted no time readying herself to see the Soothsayer. The spell she prepared was potentially the only hope the kingdom had for survival. Queen Titania prayed to the gods, to her mother, to anything and anyone that would listen, that the spell was ready. She arrived at the Soothsayer's home and knocked on the door. She cared little if anyone saw her.

The decrepit old crone pushed the door open and hid behind its shadows. Her beak of a nose poked through the opening followed by the rest of her hideous face. She seemed pleased to see Queen Titania, and hastily opened the door to grant her entrance.

"You have come for the spell, yes?" the Soothsayer asked. Her voice was distinctly gleeful.

The Fall of Avalon

"I have. Is it ready?"

The old woman revealed a small, clear, glass vial from under her wide, tattered sleeve. It was small enough that she could hold the entire base between three fingers. Within it was a pale blue, transparent liquid. The old hag held it out to the Queen proudly, eagerly awaiting her to take it. Queen Titania snatched it out of her hand, carefully avoiding contact with the fingers that held it.

"Now, all you need do is pour the vial into the fountain. It is not far from here. That will activate the spell."

"And you are certain this will stop him from entering the city?" the Queen asked, skeptically.

"Why yes, my dear. With that spell in place, Mifuné Tahaka cannot enter the kingdom of Avalon uninvited. You have my word."

"And what is your price for this spell?"

A wicked smile stretched across the Soothsayer's haggard face. "Oh, you need not worry about that, my dear. I shall come to collect, in time."

Queen Titania swore her ears deceived her. Those last words, 'in time', it sounded as though the woman's voice changed. It was ghastly, deep, and guttural. The Queen dismissed the thought, though, attributing it to her mounting stress. Without another word, she departed immediately for the fountain just down the road in the square. She removed the top from the vial and poured its contents into the fountain.

The fountain's water began to glow the color of the potion. A beam of green light shot up from the top of the fountain into the sky. It flashed at the peak, and a dome of green light encompassed the whole of Avalon. Once it completely encased the city, the light faded. Feeling confident, Queen Titania returned to the palace.

Much to her surprise, Colabion was awake. She came across him in the throne room on her way back to her bedchamber. He was shaking terribly, as if he had been loosed from the underworld to tell of the horrors he had seen there. He could not speak. His face was pale as death.

"Colabion, what is it?" asked the Queen.

"Bed… ch-ch-ch-chamber... it..."

"Speak plainly, my love. What are you trying to say?"

"G-Go to our bedchamber!" he shouted.

"Very well, I shall."

Queen Titania took him by the hand and led him to their bedchamber. Feeling confident in the spell that protected the kingdom, she saw no reason for him to be as afraid as he was. She opened the door casually, as she normally would. She stepped inside without a care in the world. When she looked on her bed, her very spirit and soul were stolen away from her. There, on the center of her luxurious bed, lay Virgil's head.

The Queen looked into the cold, dead eyes of the man who had tried to protect her. He was the only one with power enough to attempt to match Mifuné, and the only one with the courage. And Mifuné sent her back his head. Her heart sank into the deepest pits of despair. Without a successor, there would be no more Paladins to protect Avalon.

The Fall of Avalon

The legendary power of Arthur's line was broken forever.

Queen Titania turned away and departed her chamber. She said nothing to Colabion, and he could say nothing to her. She wandered through the halls of her palace like a ghost, unable to feel, unable to think. The images of Paladins from the past hung on the walls. They haunted her. She had known each one of them by face, and by name.

Every tapestry portrayed of each Paladin in their prime. They were unique: their armor, their swords, and their shields. They were meant to make the palace a living monument to Avalon's great history, and each tapestry served as a testament to the greatness of each individual paladin, all the way back to Arthur. With a single action, Mifuné changed them into headstones, and the palace into a mausoleum.

Queen Titania found herself in the Queen's Chamber. Her councilors were nowhere to be found. Virgil would not sweep through the door as he had so many times before. She was alone, with only the portrait of her mother to console her. The Queen focused on the portrait, as though it were alive. As though Queen Glorianna's judgment was harshly cast upon Queen Titania. As though Queen Glorianna's beauty, power, success, authority, even her Paladin, were a mockery of all Titania had achieved for herself. Rage burned in Queen Titania's heart, to the core of her being. Hot tears streamed down her face. The Queen screamed in her fury. She drew the Sword of Avalon from her belt and swung. The slicing edge of the blade severed the portrait in two at Glorianna's face.

Queen Titania sheathed her sword and departed, unable to stay in the Queen's Chamber any longer. Her wandering brought her to the throne room. The glorious, winged, golden throne of Avalon seemed like nothing but a chair of wood and slivers. The Queen approached and ran her fingers over the polished gold slowly. She examined the detailed sculpting, as if she had never sat there before. She took a seat and looked out the windows of the Grand Hall. "What should I do? Who will save me now?"

Four knights were positioned at the entrance to the palace, as she had ordered days ago. They had each taken notice of the Queen's presence upon her throne of gold, but were unsure as to whether they should interact with her. Sensing her distraught state, one of the four approached the throne and knelt before her.

"What is it that troubles you, my Queen?" he asked humbly.

Queen Titania observed the man. He was handsome, more like Colabion than Virgil. He was bulkier than Colabion, but not quite as built as Virgil. His hair was raven black and thick. He had it tied back in a warrior's tail to keep it neat. His voice was appealing, as well.

"What is your name, knight?" she asked, sounding absent.

"I am Sir Gaston, master of the Sacred Sword technique, and hunter extraordinaire."

271

The Fall of Avalon

"I see." The Queen paused for a moment. Her expression was still blank. "Rise, Sir Gaston. From this day forward, you shall be the Paladin of Avalon."

Sir Gaston's eyes went wide. He rose up, but was more confused than honored. "Thank you, your Majesty... but what of Virgil? Is not he still the Paladin?"

"Virgil was a traitor." The Queen voice was like ice. "He had in mind to betray the crown and overthrow me. His punishment was exile." She stood up. "And Avalon must have a Paladin. So, I have chosen you."

"Virgil… would do those things? How can this be?"

"The Samurai and his… *antics*, have been having effects on every citizen in Avalon. He is coming here, tomorrow, to destroy everything. If we are to survive this, we must come together, as one, and drive him back to the pit he crawled out of. As Paladin, you shall be my spearhead."

Sir Gaston beat his fist against his chest horizontally. "For my Queen, and for Avalon, I will do everything I can!" he proudly proclaimed.

"Well said, Paladin. Now, there is a task you must perform."

"Name it, my Queen, and it shall be done," Gaston confidently declared.

"Go into the city. Gather the Arch Mages, and bring them here."

"It shall be as you say, your Majesty," he answered ceremoniously, set to task.

Carl Houston Roach IV

Doubts and thoughts of turmoil racked Sir Gaston's mind, as hell was upon them. The overwhelming reality of the dismal situation the people of Avalon were faced with suffocated him. Virgil is no traitor, he mused, I wonder just how responsible our Queen was for this plight.

&❧

Hours before sunrise, Mifuné and his group had departed from the remains of the Tower of Galahad. Under the cover of darkness, they marched on Avalon. Gray clouds blanketed the sky, as if the land of Androma itself mourned the loss of Virgil. It felt as if a storm lingered overhead, yet the sky would not release its sorrow.

Gabrysia walked on Mifuné's left. Cold, fierce determination glowed in her eyes. Her power swelled in her chest and resonated throughout her body. Every inch of her body tingled from the feeling. With the loss of Desmond, she was ready to unleash her power, at last.

Sergei walked on Mifuné's right. Even walking on all fours, Sergei was still the tallest of the bunch. His thoughts were only on his family. After days of waiting, he would be reunited with them again. With his newfound power, nothing would be able to stop him from getting his family back.

The group came to a halt when the city came into view. Avalon's army had amassed outside the city gate to defend from any attack. They approached slowly, until they were just outside of the range of the archers. Mifuné and Sergei surveyed the army, both the soldiers on the ground, and the soldiers on the wall. There were thousands, too numerous to count accurately, that had taken up their formation. Heavy shields like those carried by Captain Lysander's men stacked across the front line. Archers lined the top of the walls. Pikemen and swordsmen were prepared to hold the line.

"I estimate at least 20,000 soldiers, Mifuné," Sergei said in a very deep voice.

"And there's something else," Gabrysia added. "I can sense some kind of magic at work around the city. It might be a protection spell."

Mifuné looked to Gabrysia. "You are sure of this?" he asked.

"I cannot say for sure. It is weak, too weak."

"Can you break it?" Mifuné asked.

"I will try."

"What of the soldiers, Mifuné?" Serge interjected.

"I will handle them. Gabrysia, go."

Gabrysia stepped forward. Cerulean aura flashed over her body. She rounded her fingers as if she were trying to grip something large, and focused her magic to the space between her hands. The growing pressure stifled her breath. The more power she amassed, the more her body strained under the force. When she was finished, she held in her hands a sphere of brilliant, cerulean energy.

Gabrysia raised the sphere over her head and unleashed the power she had stored within it. The blue magic streamlined into the darkened skies and descended upon the city. As Gabrysia expected, her power collided against a thin, green dome. As the last of Gabrysia's spell struck the barrier, the dome top dissolved, as ice melts in boiling water, a wall of green energy that was left surrounded the city. "I was able to bring down a layer but the rest is up to you Mifuné."

Mifuné stepped forward. He was silent, and his pace was steady. "Stay behind me," he said over his shoulder as he continued forward. They could hear the soldiers shouting orders and shuffling their positions as Mifuné approached. He stopped within range of the archers, and drew his sword. Sergei and Gabrysia followed Mifuné at a safe distance.

"Archers! Prepare to fire!" the General called.

Sergei and Gabrysia watched as the wall became lined with ignited arrow tips. Thousands of arrows were poised to descend upon them like a fiery rain. The techniques Gabrysia and Naomi had seen their master use were not nearly powerful enough to destroy an army this size. What could Mifuné be thinking?

Gabrysia watched Mifuné. She could not explain it, but she had every confidence that he could prevail. His aura was calm, and his power rose, she sensed it. It far exceeded the amount of power he had used in his battle against Virgil. With his sword, he traced a semi-circle in the ground around him, and raised the weapon into the sky.

"Dragon Emperor's Wrath!" he roared.

Black and purple flames erupted from the ground around him. Upward and outward they spun and twirled and spiraled into the blackened sky. The soldiers watched in terror as the flames which erupted from Mifuné took the shape of an enormous serpentine dragon. It had a massive gaping mouth and rows of saw-like teeth. It reached up higher into

The Fall of Avalon

the sky than the wall and the width of its snout was wider than the gates of the city.

Mifuné thrust his sword forward and pointed it at the city. The dragon spun and spiraled forward at breakneck speed directly at the formation of soldiers. They screamed and panicked as the monstrous manifestation charged. Some broke formation in a failed attempt to escape. Others hid themselves behind their shields, hoping beyond hope to survive.

The dragon scorched through the soldiers like a wildfire through dead shrubs. Those in its immediate path were reduced to ash upon contact. Those nearby caught fire and burned. Unlike the technique Gabrysia and Sergei had seen him use before, the dragon continued well past the front line. It tore its way through the whole of the army until it reached the gate.

The dragon's head slammed into what remained of the protective barrier created by the Soothsayer's spell. In less than a second, the dragon powered through and collided with the city wall. The ensuing explosion was massive. Soldiers atop the wall were disintegrated. The General himself vanished in the blast. Those not immediately killed in the blast were sent flying off the wall.

When the dust settled, the Army of Avalon was destroyed. Those who survived the attack were dying, burning, or scattered to the four winds. Cries of pain, anguish, and fear rang out from the city as the citizens still within realized what had happened.

Mifuné marched to the broken gates of the now panicked city. He did not wait for the others, or signal them to follow him. He kept his sword in his hand, ready to cut down anything that got in his way. He stepped over the bodies that lay in his path. There was no remorse in his eyes. No pity. No feeling at all.

The Samurai crossed over the rubble and debris of what remained of Avalon's gates and entered into the city. He took a moment to look around at the familiar sights that he had once walked by as a hero. The bitter memories hardened his heart. His face twisted into a scowl and he raised his sword again.

Mifuné swung his blade to the left, and from it, a beam of fire launched and destroyed buildings and homes to that side. What was not immediately destroyed burned in the fire of Mifuné's wrath. After a few steps forward, he launched another attack to his right. The citizens who were not killed by the attacks scattered, in an attempt to escape the carnage. As they endeavored to pass the Samurai by, he cut them down, like wheat in a field. Nothing in Avalon was safe from his retribution.

Sergei charged past Mifuné without any regard for permission or punishment. With his great weight, he easily tackled people and straggled guards out of his way. He roared as he stampeded toward the Ivory Palace. The sight of him frightened every man, woman, and child that he passed on his way. They screamed as they fled from his path into Mifuné's.

Gabrysia watched in horror as her Master continued his onslaught. Survivors who lay in his wake reached to her, desperate to be saved from their miserable plight. Gabrysia shook her head and

The Fall of Avalon

fled from them, fully aware she did not have the power to undo what Mifuné had done. Although, she held no desire to, either.

Gabrysia was hard-pressed, if she were being honest, to feel any sympathy for their suffering. They were the same people she and Desmond had warned, the people who laughed in their faces and spurned the disciples for daring to disturb them in their homes. To the people, Titania, the Queen of Avalon, was a goddess on Earth who could do no wrong. They were kept safe by her power, and by her power, the enemies of Avalon were kept at bay. What a farce, Gabrysia thought.

Gabrysia had made up her mind to follow Sergei. Being near Mifuné was far too dangerous. It was obvious that he was not in control of himself. Moreover, if he defeated the Paladin of Avalon, and destroyed its entire army alone, there was nothing he would need for her to accomplish. She ran as fast as she could to keep up with her lumbering compatriot, as she had resolved to help him save his family.

At the palace, the knights scurried about to distribute their numbers as effectively as possible to defend the Queen. Their strongest area of defense was the steps leading to the entrance of the castle. Forty of the one-hundred knights stood poised, ready to defend their kingdom. Sir Gaston stayed with Queen Titania and Colabion.

"I do not understand! How could he have gotten inside the city?! The Soothsayer created a protection spell, did she not?" Colabion shouted.

Carl Houston Roach IV

"Yes, she did. Obviously, it was not strong enough to hold Mifuné back," the Queen replied.

"How can you be so calm!? He is going to kill all of us!" Colabion seized her by her arms. "He is going to kill you!"

"No, he is not. I have a plan."

"You have a plan? Like letting him blast his way through our front door!?"

Just as Colabion finished speaking, an explosion rocked the Ivory Palace. Knights hurried to the entrance to fortify the defenses there. Colabion joined them. He was unsure of what would happen to him, but he would rather die fighting than cowering behind his mad wife. Clad in his royal armor with a specially made saber, he marched beside the rushing knights to an uncertain fate.

Colabion, and the group of ten knights, joined the defending element of forty knights at the doors. They closed the massive mahogany doors behind them. The knights were all prepared to fight, and if necessary, to die for their kingdom, and for their Queen. Colabion kept to the rear of the formation. His sword shook in his hand. He flinched when he heard a knight from the front call out:

"Halt, Samurai! You stand before the greatest warriors in all of Avalon! Surrender now, or be destroyed!"

Mifuné did not acknowledge the leader. He crossed his blade in front of him horizontally at shoulder level and swung his sword. A massive ball of purple fire rocketed from his sword and blasted away the entire assemblance of knights in the blink of an eye. Smoke and ash filled the air. Colabion

The Fall of Avalon

was all that remained between Mifuné and the Queen.

Colabion pointed his sword, which shook immensely in his hand, at Mifuné, and centered himself in front of the doors to the palace. He could not find it in him to speak, but as best he could, he stood his ground. Even as his adversary approached, he did not flee. Mifuné strode straight past him as though he did not exist.

Colabion was infuriated by the gesture. He threw his sword to the ground and screamed in fury. He beheld the city, which had been reduced to ash and rubble and dust. He heard the screams and cries of his dying people rise from the ruins of the once beautiful kingdom. An unyielding hatred for the Samurai burned in his heart. Before Mifuné could pass through the final ingresses, Colabion shouted, "Look what you've done! Look at all of this!" Tears streamed down his face.

Mifuné heeded him and surveyed the destruction he had unleashed upon Avalon and its people. Not one building was left standing. If any was, it was a shattered remnant of what it used to be. Fire burned everything that was green and good. The water was tainted by the dust and debris.

"Is this what you wanted, Samurai!? To bring this upon us!? And for what? Over some meaningless qualm you had with my wife!?"

Mifuné's eye twitched. His pulse raced. The veins protruded from his neck. "Meaningless?" he said tensely. He took his sword in his hand and aligned the blade along its sheath. In an instant, he vanished, and reappeared behind Colabion. "WHAT DO YOU KNOW OF MEANINGLESS?!"

Mifuné swung his blade with such force that the wind itself was shaken by it. The force caught Colabion and hurled him out into the foyer. His whole backside struck a pillar. His eyes rolled back in his head from the pain of the impact, but he had not been cut. He fell onto his hands and knees.

Mifuné seized him by the throat and lifted him to his feet. "Spend most of your life serving another!" He took his sword and hacked Colabion's right arm clean off at the shoulder. Colabion screamed in agony as blood poured out of his body. More hot tears streamed down his face. "Watch everyone you ever cared for die at your side!" He hacked off Colabion's left leg just below the hip. "Like sheep to a slaughter!" Blood oozed out of him and he fell to the ground.

Colabion cried and wailed in agony. He desperately tried to getaway. Using his left arm and right leg, and all that remained of his strength, he attempted to crawl to safety. He had hoped to reach the stairs, that he might roll down and escape. Before Colabion could steal away, Mifuné's sword tip pierced through the top of his hand. He screamed out in pain once again.

"Sit in a prison, alone, with the King of Demons screaming in your head for seven years, fighting constantly to devour your soul and possess your very being! Then, tell me what has more meaning than this!"

Mifuné picked up Colabion by the neck and hurled him against the door like a ragdoll. The light

The Fall of Avalon

faded, as Colabion's could barely keep his eyes open. In his final moment, he watched helplessly as the Samurai approached. His footsteps gradually became inaudible as his vision continued to fade. The last thing Colabion felt was the cold steel of Mifuné's sword piercing his heart.

&

Queen Titania had taken up her seat on the golden throne. She sat expectantly, focused on the door. She heard the sounds of Mifuné as he demolished the platoon of knights who stood guard. Those knights, Colabion, none of them could hold him back. Nothing would at this point, she mused. It was inevitable, just as the Soothsayer predicted. 'There will be no escape.' This confrontation is fated.

The doors exploded, and a gaping hole replaced what used to be the Grand Entryway. As the dust and smoke settled, Mifuné was there, at the base of the stairs, looking up at the Queen. Between him and the steps to the throne stood the last knight of Avalon. He carried himself proudly and spoke with authority.

"Halt, Samurai! You stand face to face with Sir Gaston, Paladin of Ava…"

Mifuné wasted no time dispatching the would-be Paladin. His blade slashed diagonally through the man's torso. His armor was cut like cloth. His blood spilled onto the floor, pooling under where he lay. For a brief moment, Mifuné and Queen Titania locked eyes. The outside wind whipped Mifuné's loose clothing back and forth. The touch of the wind sent a chill up the Queen's spine. Thunder cracked.

Carl Houston Roach IV

Lightning flew across the distant, dark sky. The moment of reckoning was at hand.

♛

Meanwhile, Sergei managed to reach the West Hall entrance of the Ivory Palace. With his great size and strength, he crushed the group of knights standing in his way. Their weapons were useless against his armor, and their armor did little to protect them from his claws. Sergei pressed one knight against the wall by his chest with one of his mighty paws.

"Do your worst, monster! I am a knight of Avalon. I fear nothing!"

"Where is the dungeon?! Take me there!" Sergei roared.

The knight was silent. A smug smile worked its way across his face. Sergei heaved him back outside. The knight's back struck the ground. He rolled and slid until stopping against Gabrysia's feet. He opened his eyes and saw a young woman with red hair standing over him. She aimed an open palm down to him and unleashed some of her power.

"You should have listened when we asked nicely," Gabrysia said with a smug smile of her own.

Gabrysia's magic shocked and electrocuted the knight. He surged in pain, but was unable to scream. His muscles seized up and his eyes burned until she stopped. Sergei lumbered out and watched. Gabrysia had no sympathy for the knight, or the pain she was inflicting on him. He wondered if she had in mind to kill him.

The Fall of Avalon

Gabrysia ceased her spell and folded her arms over her chest. The knight rolled onto his side. He grunted in pain and stifled tears that fought to escape. A light cloud of gray smoke wafted off of him. He lifted his hand and shook it. "No more," he muttered. "No more. Please. I will take you there," the knight pleaded.

"I knew you would see it my way," Gabrysia replied as she hauled the knight to his feet.

The knight led Sergei's lumbering form through the corridors with Gabrysia in tow and down the steps, to the cavern-like dungeon, whose walls were lined with torches every ten feet. Once there, Sergei began to sniff the air. As a bear, he would be able to locate his family by their scent.

Within seconds, Sergei caught scent of his wife. He hurried down the hall, leaving the knight and Gabrysia behind him. In the process, he reverted from a bear to a man. He would have to explain his monstrous form to them once he saved them, but he did not mind. They were his family, they would understand. At last, he arrived at the cell where he had detected their scent. He could see them huddled together in the dark corner.

"Amelia! Kids! I am here!" he said as he grabbed the bars of the cell.

When Gabrysia finally caught up, she used her magic to break the locks on the door. He pulled it open and took a step in, but his family did not move. They remained huddled in the corner. Gabrysia's heart sank in her chest as she watched Sergei slowly approach his family. No matter how close he got to them, they remained still. A tear streamed down her face.

"Come on! I am going to get you out of here!" he said excitedly.

There was no answer. They sat in that corner, motionless, silent. Sergei could feel his heart sinking like a ship beneath the waves. He moved closer in front of them to look into their eyes.

"No. No. No…"

Sergei fell to his knees and wept. Their clothes were stained with dried blood. Each of them had been run through the heart. They clung to each other in their final moments of life. Sergei inserted himself between them. He wrapped his arms around his two little children and propped his wife against his torso. He kissed her head and pulled them all close to him as he mourned.

Gabrysia did not enter. She waited outside the cell for him to come out. She leaned against the stone wall dividing the cell he was in from another and shed tears of her own. She could not begin to imagine Sergei's hurt as his wails echoed down the corridors of the dungeon, but the sound of his cries of agony and sorrow hurt her as much as losing Desmond.

Gabrysia wondered how many innocent families and people Queen Titania sacrificed to achieve her own ends. How many Mifuné's and Sergei's were left in her wake. Which was what she did. To hear Mifuné's stories about the Queen's cruelty was one thing, but Gabrysia had seen the treachery first hand. She found solace in that after this day,

The Fall of Avalon

Titania, the Queen of Avalon, would never hurt another soul again.

Sergei's cries reverberated throughout the whole depth of the dungeon. There was no solace to console him of his loss. His family was his life, and for no fault of his own, they were taken from him. He would never see his son grow to be a man, never see the girls chasing after him. He would never have the chance to teach his son to hunt, to fight. They would never have their first drink together, when his son was old enough.

Sergei would never see his daughter grow tall. He would never see pursue the dreams the vast, open world held in store for her. He would never see her fall in love, nor would he be able to give her away in marriage. He would never witness his children present him with grandchildren, start a family.

And Sergei's beautiful wife, Amelia, his river lily, they would never get the chance to grow old together. To watch the sun rise and set as the last vestiges of their beauty and youth faded to the wrinkles and gray. He would never hear her whisper words of loving adoration into his ear as they lay in the pasture outside their home again.

The excruciating pain he felt resonated loudly in his voice as Sergei's cries filled the dungeon's corridors. He beat his back against the cold, stone wall behind him as the tears poured down his face. He felt waves of fiery heat and frigid cold seize his heart in a tumultuous storm of rage and despair. As he held the corpses of his beloved wife and children, all Sergei could do in that moment was weep.

The Fall of Avalon

CHAPTER 11   UNTRAMMELED PROPHESY

*Before the sun set that day, the line of Glorianna
ended by his hand.*

Beside the tranquil company of a solitary tree, Naomi sat alone. Her heart had sunken into the deepest pits of her stomach as she watched the recent exchange between herself and the man she loved unfold in her memory. The harsh, monstrous voice that bellowed from his chest. The luminous, starry eyes that burned in his face over the soft brown eyes she adored. The black fire, and the horrid creature birthed from it, with an eye to match its maker's.

Naomi wept bitterly, painfully, to think she had lost her master—her beloved Mifuné, to that terrible, nightmarish monstrosity of the ancient world. The thought was more than she could bear. I failed, she thought to herself; I only ever wanted for us to be together; I thought I could pull you out of Ravana's darkness, I thought I could be the one to set you free, but in the end, I failed.

Naomi felt the crushing, soul-piercing grip of despair sink its claws into her heart as Mifuné shattered the walls of Avalon and marched through its gates. From where she sat, she watched the retribution he had prophesied for the city unfurl. The brunt of his seemingly limitless power unleashed upon the kingdom that was utterly powerless to stop him. The screams of agony and desolation—the cries of death and destruction carried on the winds to caress Naomi's listening ears.

Unable to bear the sight or sounds any longer, Naomi's head fell against her forearms, which weakly rested across her knocking knees. This is all my fault, she thought. Over and over, her guilt tormented her in her isolation. She felt as though poisonous barbs had infected her heart and soul, and before the day was past, she would die on the hill with the tree beside her serving as the only witness to her internal affliction and guilt.

Then, through the chaos and suffering that had enveloped her mind, Naomi heard a voice. It was not a foreign entity, or the voice of a passerby yielding words of wisdom to her. It was her own voice, clear as day, that resonated above the sting, the anguish, the guilt, and self-doubt. She heard the words she spoke to Mifuné in the tower, when he was at his darkest moment, "I am here, my Master. I will not leave you all alone."

Naomi raised her head from her arms and looked out toward the burning kingdom. The image of Mifuné rising with the sun flashed in front of her eyes as she stood to her feet. She restrained the overflow of tears from her eyes as the image of Mifuné confronting Virgil emerged from the depths of the dark which shrouded her mind. The storm within her cleared away. Naomi proudly raised her hood over her head, and a new, resolute expression overtook her soft countenance. Her cape swept heroically in the wind as a strong, swift breeze brushed past her.

The Fall of Avalon

"Hold on, Mifuné. I am on my way," she declared as she sprang into action.

֍

Sergei finally emerged reluctantly from the cell wherein lay his family. His cheeks were saturated by the tears he had shed, and his eyes stained red from his unrelenting sorrow. He was shrouded in despair. Akin to lynched men: his bulky arms dangled at his sides, his shoulders lurched forward, and his head hung down. He dragged his feet beneath him with each heavy step he took. He came to a stop at the wall opposite the cell and propped himself against it with his right arm. Sergei shook as he continued to cry bitter tears, all the while, he attempted to hold himself up against the wall.

Gabrysia went to him and carefully placed a hand on his shoulder. There was nothing she could do, nothing she could even think to say, to console him. In that moment, all she could think to do was be there by his side. Beyond the sorrow, though, she could sense something else stirring inside of him. Something malevolent, akin to the feeling she always sensed from Mifuné, especially after Desmond's death.

"I am going to kill her," Sergei whispered angrily aloud. "I swear, I will kill the bitch if it is the last thing I do!" His declaration of retribution rang down the halls of the dungeon. He pushed off the wall and started down the corridor to the exit.

Gabrysia followed him. Sergei sounds like his old self again, despite the horrible, heart-breaking scene he just witnessed, she surmised. Perhaps there would be a chance to mourn, in time, but the time for grieving had not yet come. The time had come for action, to bring justice to a wicked tyrant.

Justice, Gabrysia thought, was long overdue. "So, what do you intend to do?" she asked.

"I am going to take my claws and ram them through her chest! I am going to rip her heart out!" Sergei roared, his voice became progressively hoarser as a result his wails.

"Master might have already done away with her," Gabrysia dutifully pointed out. "What will you do then?"

"That will be good enough for me," Sergei growled. "If I want her dead this much, I can only imagine what he has in store for her." He paused at the stair that led back to the palace hall and pronounced, "May the gods damn me if I cannot get my chance at her!"

෧

At the throne room, Mifuné and Queen Titania continued to stare each other down. Her gaze was calm, poised, and collected, which was no surprise to Mifuné. While he expected her to show no sign of fear, there was no indication of a plot to escape either. She watched him expectantly, and waited for him to make his move.

Mifuné's pace was steadfast as he ascended the stairs between him and Avalon's golden throne. Each bone chilling footstep, the clack of his sandals against the marble steps, was like a countdown, one by one marking every moment closer and closer to the end. Queen Titania resisted the compulsive urge to flinch with each resounding step he took. The slow, steady pace he had set only fed the

The Fall of Avalon

anticipation of the imminent demise that now lingered over her, or so he thought. At last, Mifuné stood at the level atop the steps before the throne. Just as the Soothsayer foretold, he had overcome everything set before him, great and small. Queen Titania smirked and slowly applauded—arrogant, resentful.

"Well done, Mifuné, you have prevailed," the Queen said, her snide scorn reverberated throughout the room. "You have succeeded in destroying the greatest kingdom in the world and undermining the cornerstones of its founding. Bravo!"

Sword drawn, Mifuné said nothing.

"Answer me something, Mifuné," The Queen continued to taunt. "After you kill me and destroy Avalon forever, what happens next? What else do you have?" The Queen declaimed condescendingly. "Nothing!" Queen Titania's indignant riposte rang out. "You will be lost, a monster, bereft of honor and lordship, adrift in a vast world with nowhere to call home. You will linger on at the corners of the earth, hunted for the crimes you have committed for the rest of your miserable little life. That is the fate you have resigned yourself to… You are aware of that, are you not?" she finished, her tone contemptuous, her eyes stark with bitterness.

"Titania of the Fae," Mifuné began calmly, "you have taken countless innocent lives, fed conflicts between nations, brought evil into your own lands to eliminate your allies whom which you perceived as enemies, and you refuse to admit fault for any of the evil you have committed." The intensity in his voice grew as he continued. "Avalon became an empire of evil the day its crown passed down to you. I may face retribution for my actions here, one day, but today... Today is *your* reckoning." The fury Mifuné bore in his heart for Queen Titania came forth in his final words. Triumphantly, he raised his weapon and pointed the tip of his sword at her.

"I think not!" Queen Titania defiantly replied. A sinister smile stretched across her face. She swiftly raised her right hand and sharply snapped her fingers beside her face. From the shadows behind and around the Queen, beams of light fired out at Mifuné. Each beam struck him simultaneously and engulfed him in a shining field of white light, against which he was powerless to fight. Hooded figures dressed in black robes, illuminated by the light, overwhelmed Mifuné's body.

Mifuné let out a sharp cry of pain as the converging beams of light crushed him, suffocating his strength, paralyzing him within its luminosity. He strained with all his strength to break free, but the mounting pressure of the power against him was too great, even for him, to overcome. Slowly, the attack forced him down on a knee, yet he allowed himself to fall no further.

Queen Titania laughed elatedly as she descended from her throne. "Ten Arch Mages, Mifuné! Each a master of Light Magic!" She knelt in front of him. Her sinister smile transformed into a horrific, predatory grin. "I imagine this hurts you something terrible, yes?" the Queen said, mockingly. "To come so close to your goal, only to be stopped at the final step!" She threw back her

The Fall of Avalon

head and laughed maniacally. "Do you want to know what happens next, Mifuné?" The Queen fixed her eyes on the bound Mifuné the way an assailant's eyes beset its prey. "I am going to seal you away again, but this time, no force in existence will be able to set you free!" she growled, amused at the success of her scheme.

Queen Titania snapped her fingers once again. The mages began to chant in a language Mifuné recognized, as he had heard the incantation before. In his mind, he returned to the night the Queen betrayed him, the night seven years ago when she locked him away. The spell binding him was the same spell she had used then. He watched the reminiscence play out in his mind, yet he was not alone. Ravana stood by his side, observantly. He and Mifuné watched the events of the memory unfold to the completion of the cage of light.

"You must do something quickly, Mifuné. She will seal us both away again if you continue to do nothing," Ravana declared urgently.

"I...can...not fight this," Mifuné growled, still strained by the pressure enveloping his body.

"You may not have the strength," Ravana began, feigning comfort, "but I do. These bonds, they are nothing to me. Relinquish control to me. I can break the power of these mages with ease. I will bring all my powers to bear against your nemesis," Ravana assured Mifuné. He appeared behind Mifuné and placed two of his four hands encouragingly on Mifuné's shoulders. "With a word from you, I will eradicate this entire kingdom from the face of the Earth. You will have your vengeance, and I will be free."

Ravana's temptation insufferably enticed Mifuné. He knew that Ravana had more than sufficient power to exterminate the Arch Mages like moths drawn to the flame that burned them alive. He knew that Ravana would follow through on his end of the bargain and reduce what was left of Avalon to cinders and ash, Queen Titania included. Just as Mifuné was about to give in to Ravana's will, another memory pervaded his mind.

Naomi appeared before Mifuné, in his mind's eye. She was naked, as she was when he saw her the night before his battle with the Paladin. She was surrounded by light. Her bare, fair skin glowed with the luminescence of the full moon. Cool water dripped from the ends of her wet, matted hair. She offered him a smile, genuine and pure, and reached out her hand to him. A tear streamed down Mifuné's face, as his heart cried out for the one he had turned his back on.

"Begone!" Ravana demanded as Naomi's image approached them. Ravana's size increased to enormous proportions. Whips of darkness and chaos in the form of black energy erupted from around him and encircled Mifuné. "You will not interfere this time!" Ravana furiously roared with the voice of a thousand lost souls echoing in unison.

The darkness within the Samurai's heart yearned to feel the Ravana's power course through his veins. With such potency at his disposal, it was possible for Mifuné to become an unstoppable force that could annihilate anything that stood before him.

The Fall of Avalon

The Queen of Avalon, her pitiful mages, even a hundred Paladins of greater measure than Virgil, would be nothing to him. No power on the Earth could stand against him ever again. Despite the temptation of the power offered to him, Mifuné understood what accepting such an offer would cost him.

Through the black flames swirling around him, it was nearly impossible for Mifuné to see Naomi. Amidst the wisps and the darkness, despite the presence of Ravana and the release of his power, Mifuné could see glimpses of Naomi just on the other side of the evil surrounding him. She seemed so far away, and yet, she was there. Mifuné could see, also, unmistakably, that she looked toward him with a smile. No matter how seductive the call of darkness that beckoned Mifuné to yield, the light from within, and the light from Naomi, protected him from the Ravana's devious temptation.

"No..." Mifuné adamantly answered Ravana. Naomi's specter drew nearer and nearer to him, in his mind's eye. "Even if I fall here today, I will not let you be free!" The light from Naomi drove back the darkness with which Ravana had subsumed Mifuné. Her loving arms spread over him, and she closed them around him in a warm embrace. A veil of light enveloped them and completely eradicated the Ravana's essence. The image of the Lord of Chaos itself faded away from Mifuné's mind, and Mifuné found himself alone with Naomi's specter which floated just above him.

Mifuné opened his mouth to speak, but Naomi pressed a finger against his lips. Gently, her hand caressed his cheek, and his soul settled to its normal state. She lowered her incandescent eyes until they were in front of his… She lay her forehead against his. Together, they closed their eyes, and when Mifuné opened his eyes again, he returned to the present moment. His body had stopped resisting the power bearing down against him. It was almost over. The spell was almost complete. In seconds, he would be trapped once again.

6♠

Naomi wandered through the remnants of the once beautiful kingdom of Avalon, with extreme caution. There seemed to be no safe place to step, and no clear path forward through the smoldering wreckage. Familiar sights and places she had seen and visited were overturned and scorched with fire. Bodies littered the rubble, each unrecognizable either from blackened burns or dismemberment. Just a day before, the same people carried about their daily lives without a care in the world, yet now, their beloved home had become a sepulcher for them and their children. While she navigated the demolished streets of the city, she searched desperately for any sign of Mifuné, of Gabrysia, or of Sergei, alas, they were nowhere to be found.

From the edge of where the city met the Citadel, Naomi could see a gaping hole in the entrance to the palace. There was no doubt about it, Mifuné had already arrived and was likely amidst his epic confrontation with the Queen of Avalon at that very moment. A pit formed in Naomi's stomach. Queen Titania was far too devious, far too cunning, to simply allow Mifuné to march through her front

The Fall of Avalon

door unopposed. The anticipation of the Queen's next move made Naomi's heart race. She took to her heels and charged forward as quickly as she could.

When Naomi reached the steps to the palace, she slowed her approach. As carefully and stealthily as she could manage, she maneuvered to the broken entrance to the castle. She hid herself behind any piece of cover she could find in her approach. She expected far more destruction at the palace by the time she arrived, but for the most part, it was still intact, and quiet. Naomi wondered if Mifuné had already dispatched the Queen... If it was already over.

Naomi's pulse raced as she approached the stairs leading to the throne. A strange, deafening sound echoed in the Throne Room and down the main halls. Naomi could not make sense of what was causing the noise, not until she reached the top of the steps. To her horror, she witnessed Mifuné on his knee, overtaken by Light Magic. Queen Titania laughed triumphantly over him. Mifuné was strong, but even he was helpless to fight off ten Arch Mages at once.

Rage swirled in Naomi's heart as she witnessed her love suffer, and even more so as she watched the Queen of Avalon relish in his agony so exuberantly. Red aura surrounded Naomi's body. It grew and spread over the whole entryway to the palace. The entire structure began to shake, a product of her increased power. Naomi levitated through the air and landed behind Mifuné.

"Let him go!" Naomi screamed in her fury.

Carl Houston Roach IV

Naomi thrust out her hands. From each of them, a crimson glowing hand extended towards the assembled mages. Each hand seized hold of one mage, and consequently stopped each of their contribution to the spell. Once they were in her grasp, Naomi closed her grip as tightly as she could, and crushed their bodies, reducing them to ashes. Empty robes fell to the floor as her crimson hands disappeared, eight mages remained.

"You little bitch!" the Queen screamed, enraged.

In a blind fury, Queen Titania drew her sword and lunged at Naomi. Naomi ducked as the Queen's saber sliced through the air over her head. Her attacks were extremely fast. Naomi struggled to evade each assault as they came, nevertheless, she conjured a defense. Before Queen Titania could deal a decisive blow, Naomi encased her hand in magic and caught the Queen's blade just in front of her face. The Queen's strength proved more formidable than Naomi had expected. She coated her second hand in magic and gripped the lower end of the sword as she attempted to push the Queen back.

Try as she may, Naomi could not contend with Queen Titania's superior physical strength. The Queen forced her to the ground with relative ease, and the magic dissipated from Naomi's hands. Her eyes shot upward immediately from where she lay. Queen Titania's smile was the most frightening thing Naomi had seen since a manifestation of Ravana arose from Mifuné in his battle against Sergei. Piercing eyes drowned in blood lust, a

The Fall of Avalon

devouring smile painted across her face, ears as sharp as the saber in her hands, and an overwhelming face of madness loomed over Naomi, poised to devour her.

"It is such a shame Mifuné will not be able to save his little whore!" the Queen maniacally proclaimed. She aimed the point of her blade at Naomi's chest. "As Queen of Avalon, I sentence you to die!"

Naomi covered her face with her hands as the Queen thrust her sword to her chest. A peculiar sound followed Queen Titania's attack. When Naomi moved her hands, she could see, clear as day, a cerulean sphere encompassing her body had stopped The Queen's sword. No matter how Queen Titania pressed against the barrier, it did not yield.

"Not today, your Majesty!" Gabrysia proudly declared, one hand fully extended toward Naomi.

Queen Titania clenched her teeth, and her sinister smile twisted into a scowl. "It seems I have an infestation of vermin in my palace! No matter. I shall take my time exterminating each one of you!" she finished smugly.

Gabrysia folded her arms across her chest. "Is that so?" she asked with a snide tone in her voice. "Then exterminate this."

A terrible roar blasted through the halls of the Ivory Palace. Queen Titania's eyes widened in shock as an armored bear lumbered toward her at a breakneck pace. Sergei charged forward, bearing his teeth, ready to tear the Queen apart. He grunted and snarled as he charged past Gabrysia and entered the fray. Queen Titania fled from him, desperate to avoid his shredding claws and crushing jaw. Sergei gave chase.

"Your Majesty!" one Arch Mage cried out.

"Stay where you are!" Queen Titania commanded as she scurried away from the bear. "Complete the spell, now, you fools!" she ordered urgently as she avoided Sergei's relentless onslaught.

Gabrysia ran to Naomi's side and helped her to her feet. Tears welled up in her eyes to see Naomi again. She took ahold of her hands. "You came back!" Gabrysia exclaimed through stifled sobs. "I thought I would never see you again," she continued as she wiped away some of the falling tears. Unstoppable joy sprouted up from the bottom of Gabrysia's heart, joy that was only compounded by what she saw next.

"Gabrysia..." Naomi said with resplendent hope, "look."

Naomi pointed her finger to their Master enveloped in light. With the sudden decrease in power bearing down upon him, Mifuné was able to move again. He slowly struggled to his feet. His bent knee came off the ground, and his foot planted firmly against the black marble floor. His shoulders shook under the force of the magic as they steadily rose upward, until Mifuné stood straight and tall.

"No!" Queen Titania screamed once she noticed. She rushed toward Mifuné as quickly as she could, but Sergei intercepted her before she could intervene. He roared and stamped his feet against the marble floor, which stopped the Queen in her tracks. Titania, The Queen of Avalon flinched

The Fall of Avalon

back and away from Sergei and watched helplessly as Mifuné powered through her spell.

Gradually, and with no small effort, Mifuné raised up his sword from the ground to his waist, and then to his chest. He moved upward steadily, to his shoulders, until The Wicked Blade was high over his head. His muscles tensed and tightened under the pressure of the spell, and the force that welled in his chest felt suffocating. Though he did strain, the power was not beyond his scope any longer.

A ferocious warrior's roar boomed from Mifuné's core as he brought his blade down with a mighty swing. The envelope of light over his body dissipated. The beams broke away from him and were launched back onto their casters, each of whom were struck and enveloped within the spell they brought against Mifuné. The light consumed the mages, and each was reduced to a pile of ashes.

The Queen's pulse raced to see her final line of defense turned to dust and ash. She wished beyond logic that Virgil would charge in and save her, as he had so many times before. She wished her mother would send some miracle down from the Heavens to rescue her. She wished Mifuné had never escaped the prison she had made for him, alas, Queen Titania was all alone. If she tried to escape, Mifuné would pursue her, and it would only be a matter of time before he caught her. She had no other option than to save herself by force. The Queen of Avalon took up her sword and charged at Mifuné.

The fight was brief. Queen Titania swung her sword wildly and swiftly at Mifuné. Her attack pattern was sporadic, uncontrolled, and desperately aimed to pierce him—cut him down. Regardless of the angle from which she attacked, Mifuné parried her strikes with ease. It was evident that the Queen was no match for him. From where Naomi stood, it was as though he knew her every move before she did.

"Enough!" Mifuné shouted. He swung his blade upward to counter the downward attack Queen Titania brought against him. The two swords met and locked in place, but the Queen's blade did not hold against Mifuné's. The Sword of Avalon broke in two as Mifuné's sword followed through its course. The force of the swing sliced through the air and severed off a piece of the golden throne and one of its wings. Queen Titania was overcome with despair to see her mother's sword, the once thought indestructible Sword of Avalon, break against the Wicked Blade. There was nothing left for her. No defense. No mercy. Only the end.

Mifuné took his sword-bearing hand and launched it through the air. His knuckles crashed against the left side of Queen Titania's face and nearly broke her jaw as the hand guard slashed her cheek. The force behind the blow knocked her to the black marble floor. Her face burned and swelled from the pain. She raised herself up as steadily as she could, and, with the room still spinning, she attempted to flee down the East Hall.

As the Queen's left foot struck the ground, Mifuné flicked his sword through the air. The tip sliced through her Achilles tendon. Searing pain rushed from her foot all the way to her head. Her

The Fall of Avalon

left knee came to the ground as she fell. The same burning sensation erupted from the Queen's right leg as Mifuné sliced the back of her knee. The crippling pain forced her to collapse to the ground. Blood flowed down from her wounds and soaked into her dress. She reached forward with her hands, desperate to get away. She pulled herself a few more feet forward before she felt a grip lock around her ankle.

Mifuné dragged her back, through her own blood, to his feet. He aimed the point of his blade between her eyes. Queen Titania threw her arms up in front of her face as a last attempt to defend herself. Instead of piercing her head, though, Mifuné drove his blade through her left shoulder, until the tip touched the floor beneath her. The Queen screamed in agony as her left arm fell limp at her side. She clutched at her shoulder to stop the bleeding as best as she could with her right hand.

As the Queen locked her right hand around her left shoulder, Mifuné mercilessly, and without hesitation, drove the point of his sword through her right shoulder as well. The pain inflicted caused Queen Titania to cry out in excruciating agony and anguish once again. Tears streamed down her face as she writhed in unrivaled torment. The muscles in her core contracted and expanded as her body lurched upward and downward where she lay. She screamed until her voice became hoarse. The Queen looked up into Mifuné's eyes from the floor, saturated in her own blood, with malignant resentment laced in her gaze.

Carl Houston Roach IV

"Damn you, Mifuné! Damn you!" Queen Titania repeated over and over as she suffered endlessly from her injuries. "Bastard! The gods will smite you for this! You have paved your path into Hell this day! There will be no forgiveness for you, at all!" she bellowed.

Mifuné reached down and gripped the Queen's face where her jaw connected. He violently forced her mouth open, rendering her speechless. He worked her jaw with his fingers until her tongue was forced out. The expression on his face had become even more intense from the firm-browed expression he held prior. His murderous glare carried his malicious intent. With the sharp edge of his sword, he severed her tongue, and with his other hand, he ruthlessly ripped it out of her mouth. Mifuné stood up and looked at the poisonous thing he held in his hand.

"You shall never curse or deceive another living soul ever again!" Mifuné declared, rife with indignation. He threw the Queen's tongue aside in disgust. Excess drops of blood rolled from the palm of his hand and dripped onto the black marble.

Queen Titania spit up the wellspring of blood, that filled her mouth, onto her chest. She pleaded through her eyes that he would kill her. That he would put an end to the horrible suffering she had been made to endure at his hands. The promised retribution Mifuné brought to bear was beyond anything the Queen of Avalon could have imagined, the pain was far more than she could bear. However, her perdition was far from over. She could see it in his furiously vindictive eyes.

The Fall of Avalon

The flat end of the Wicked Blade touched her cheek. Queen Titania winced as her eyes slammed shut. She had no idea what to expect next. She could hardly form a thought through the torture with which her body had been bombarded. New pain erupted when she felt a burning sensation from the side of her head. The pulsing adrenaline compelled her to lift her arms up to cup her ear, which had been severed off, yet she could not. Blood poured from the freshly felled flesh where her ear once was.

The menacing look in Mifuné's eyes became even more intense as he callously sliced off her other ear. This, however, did not add more pain to the Queen's egregious suffering. Rather, the mounting pain dulled. Numbness befell her whole body, as if she had been laid in her grave already. Her vision faded. The ceiling overhead seemed as far away as a dream, displaced from reality. In that moment, the blurry figure that she knew to be Mifuné was all Queen Titania could see.

"The last thing you will ever see in this life is me, just as the last thing I saw when you imprisoned me was you. Your spirit shall wander the afterlife lost; blind, deaf, and mute, and this place, this place shall be your tomb," Mifuné said, as profoundly judgmental as a god. Wrath and fury churned in his eyes.

Whilst the Queen's eyes were open, she could not see the blade Mifuné had positioned over her right eye. She felt it, though, as the tip sank into her once beautiful, prismatic eye. White hot pain consumed her mind completely. With what remained of her voice, she wailed in agony as the blood ran over her face and sank into her skin. Her cries were reduced to grunts of sheer torment. As Mifuné did with the first eye, so he did with the second. the Queen's blood trickled off the edge of The Wicked Blade as he raised it away from her flesh.

Naomi and Gabrysia watched on in unimaginable terror. Even Sergei was taken aback by the incomparable brutality of Mifuné's retribution, such that his beast half returned within him to seek sanctuary from the horror the Queen of Avalon was made to endure. Each of them feared to approach Mifuné, lest they fall victim to his blood lust. As Mifuné raised his sword over his head he heard the voice of Ravana cheering him on, the sole encouraging spectator of Queen Titania's plight.

"Yes, Mifuné!" Ravana applauded. "Pour out your malice. Marr her body, the way she has marred your soul!" He paused, relishing in the delectable barbarism Mifuné demonstrated. Ravana spoke into Mifuné's ear with the most alluring tone he could muster, "Kill her. Cut her throat, spill the rest of her blood. Give into the darkness in your heart. Let it take you. *Feel* the power you fight so hard to resist..." His voice trailed off and allowed Mifuné to continue, that he may revel in what savagery he might next witness.

Naomi could stand to watch no more. She ran to Mifuné with reckless abandon, and from behind him, she threw her arms around him and hugged him tight. "No more!" Naomi pleaded desperately. "Please, Mifuné. It is enough, no more." She nuzzled her head against his bare back, against the tense contracted muscles, readied to unleash his unbridled strength. Vicious, soul-shaking eyes turned to see the tears that poured out from Naomi's bright, innocent eyes. "I love you," she whispered softly. "I want to be by your side forever, so come back to me." She touched her lips tenderly to his back in a soft kiss. "Do not go where I cannot follow, please," Naomi pleaded as she sobbed.

The fires stoked by years of resentment and hatred in Mifuné's heart waned. Naomi's touch brought him back from the edge of the abyss, and he took pause. He lowered his sword from the air slowly. His iron muscles were once again flesh. His free hand rose to meet Naomi's, which were clasped together around his waist. His hand gingerly touched hers briefly before she released him from her embrace, after which, he sheathed his sword.

Mifuné watched as Queen Titania lay on the ground. Her chest lurched up and her head pushed back against the marble floor. Her fingers curled and twitched. Most of her life force was lost to her. Her once beautiful, porcelain skin waxed pale as death. She would not last much longer. Seeing her this way did not fill Mifuné's heart with joy nor satisfaction, with pride or accomplishment. Rather, as he watched her writhe in agony, bathed in a pool of her own blood, Mifuné felt an overwhelming sense of pity.

"I am not sorry for what I have done, Titania, to you, or to Avalon; but I am sorry I had to do it," Mifuné said solemnly. He was calm, yet cold. "For a moment of power and prosperity, you unleashed damnation upon the world, and intended to bring forth hell itself had I not stopped you. Titania, Queen of Avalon, you prospered your kingdom from the suffering of others. You became the very evil Avalon was founded against." Although intensely emotional, no tears formed or fell from Mifuné's eyes. He was steady... as steady as Naomi, Gabrysia, and Sergei had ever seen him. None of them in that room that day would have believed the next words he said, had they not heard it themselves. "I forgive you, Titania. Everything you have said, and everything you have done. I forgive you."

The group converged on Mifuné over the Queen's dying body. Gabrysia crossed her arms over her chest to still the unsettling image that lay before her. She had witnessed Mifuné massacre an entire army alone, she watched as he blew away the vestiges of Avalon's amassed military, as well as its civilian populous, but what she bore witness to in that moment was beyond anything she could describe, for years to follow.

Naomi clung to Mifuné's right arm and took his hand, as though at any moment he might succumb to Ravana's will. Mifuné's hand lingered in Naomi's soft grip. He did not resist her, although he would not take her hand in his as she gently curled her dainty fingers around his.

Sergei's sole attention was focused on the defeated, mangled Queen. While the others held a miniscule ounce of pity for the woman's disfigured body, Sergei looked down upon her, and had nothing but contempt for her. The corner of his lip

The Fall of Avalon

rose as his jaw clenched, exposing his gritted teeth. He balled his hands into fists. Blood leaked from his hands from where his nails dug into his palms.

As drops of Sergei's blood splashed onto the floor, Mifuné looked into his eyes. There was deep agony in Sergei's eyes, clear as day. Sergei cast his piercing glare to Mifuné. In that gaze, Mifuné could see Sergei's desire. Mifuné's eyes shifted to the Queen, who continued to writhe on the ground in a pool of her own blood. He merely nodded and stepped aside.

Sergei reached down and seized the fallen Queen by her blood-soaked hair. She was completely powerless to resist, powerless to retaliate. Defeated, dismembered, and disgraced, Queen Titania could only feel herself as she was dragged from where she lay. Her body had lost any sensation of pain. Her mind could bring no thought to focus. There was no fear. There was no sorrow. Only darkness remained for her.

As Sergei drew nearer to the throne, he saw what remained of the Sword of Avalon, the very same weapon with which the Queen had once threatened him. He took up the pommel, which still housed a fragment of the blade. Using his great strength, Sergei thrust the Queen's battered body onto her broken throne. She lacked the strength to sit in place, and therefore, Sergei held her there. His massive hand pressed her torso against the back of the seat.

"For my family!" he growled.

A bitter tear liberated itself from his right eye as he ran the broken sword through the Queen's midsection with as much force as he could muster. The fragmented blade managed to pierce through her body and into the back of the throne and pin her in place. The gold throne was awash red with her blood.

The group watched as the Queen suffered through her final moments. Her fingers and toes convulsed rapidly and spastically at first. Gradually, they slowed and became more and more infrequent. Her convulsions finally stopped, and her head leaned over to her right. Titania, The Queen of Avalon let out one last breath. Just as Mifuné promised upon his return to Avalon, on the eighth day, Queen Titania, everything she built, and everything she dominated by force, deception, or bargain, was gone.

෴

The reunited group descended the steps of the palace together. Mixed emotions overtook each of them as they continued. It hardly seemed real that the four of them, in a single day, brought down the greatest known civilization in history. Avalon, once the pearl of Androma, was now nothing more than a pile of rubble and dust, demolished beyond all recognition, not even a shred of what it once was remained, save the glorious Ivory Palace.

At the base of the steps, Mifuné turned back. Curious, the others turned back and watched. Mifuné wielded his sword and conjured a powerful dragon. By his admission, the dragon encircled the palace, as a serpent ensnares its prey, and crushed it. The rising towers, the lookout points, and the rooftops of the great halls, caved in on the interior

The Fall of Avalon

beneath. Dust blasted out from the wreckage and covered them all in a dark cloud.

Mifuné smoothly and carefully returned his sword to its sheath. Sergei, Gabrysia, and Naomi could only see his silhouette through the veil of dust. Mifuné emerged, and as the dust cleared, he said calmly, quietly, "It is finished."

Naomi went to his side and wrapped her arms around his right arm. She rested her head against his shoulder and looked up into his eyes. "Then let us leave this behind," she whispered as lovingly as she could. Mifuné nodded in reply.

Sergei led the way out of the city. Gabrysia followed closest behind him. Mifuné and Naomi trailed behind her. Naomi was relieved to see Mifuné the way he was. He had been so ruthless as he unleashed his retribution upon the Queen, she began to fear he might not come back to her from the darkness, yet he was there beside her, as calm and as gentle as she had ever known him to be. There was something lingering in the back of her mind, though. Something she did not understand.

"Mifuné…" Naomi began softly, breaking the stalemate of silence between them.

"Yes?" Mifuné replied, equally as soft, as though any word he might utter too forcefully would frighten her away.

"You said you forgive her, Queen Titania, for what she said, and what she had done."

"I did," Mifuné answered, his voice low and steady.

"Why? After everything she had done, everything she was prepared to do, why would you

312

forgive her?" Naomi asked, puzzled beyond explanation. Mifuné had hated the Queen to the core of his being. He obliterated Avalon and its people, its great protector, and the cornerstones upon which the civilization had been founded upon to achieve his desired end. Forgiveness seemed to be the farthest thing from the realm of possibilities to occur.

Mifuné took in a deep breath. "In my culture, all life is sacred. To take life, even if justified, is to destroy something that is sacred. That is sin." He paused. Naomi seemed confused, but not lost. She could sense the judgment he cast onto himself. "I destroyed all of this. That is the weight of my sin. I have forgiven her, in hopes that one day, someone will forgive me." Though there was despair in his voice, Naomi could sense the faintest hint of hope resonating from deep within him.

"Mifuné..." Naomi began.

At the base of the steps which led from the Citadel to the city, a thick ominous mist settled and shrouded the remains of Avalon. Though it was nearly impossible to see through, the group pressed on. A creeping feeling made the hairs on Sergei's neck stand on end, as if something terrible might emerge from the ruins.

Before the group arrived at the gateway, Sergei saw a figure approach through the mist. It was indistinct, amorphous, lumbering, though not gigantic. As it came closer, and the mist cleared from around it, Sergei could see that it was a bear that stood on two legs and walked like a man. The bear took no notice of him, which Sergei found incredibly peculiar. Its gaze was singularly focused on the palace far off in the distance. Sergei turned his head and watched the bear trod off without struggle or intimidation. Strangely, as suddenly as the bear had appeared, when it passed by Sergei, it vanished.

A fair distance behind Sergei, Gabrysia, was in the middle of the pack. A figure approached her through the mist. It was a woman, clad in shining armor. Her long hair cascaded down her back and whipped gloriously in the wind. She was graceful, yet powerful; confident, yet humble. Her eyes carried within them wisdom, knowledge, and experience without sacrificing their femininity. Gabrysia watched in awe as this magnificent woman strode past her toward the palace, but just as suddenly as this woman had appeared, she vanished, as though she was never there at all.

A very distinct chill ran down Mifuné's spine. His eyes went wide. He planted his feet and clutched the handle of his sword, which broke Naomi's hold on his arm. The look in his eyes was intense, not as it was when he had prepared to fight Virgil, but as if he had witnessed something capable of devouring him.

"What is it?" Naomi asked. She noticed his sudden change. There was a twinge of fear in her voice. Mifuné did not answer. His piercing gaze oriented at something that approached them from within the mist. It was small-framed, no larger than either of them, and its steps were silent.

From out of the mist, Naomi recognized the figure approaching them. It was her, the Soothsayer, as poised and elegant as Naomi had ever seen her. Her long, graying hair was brushed and neatly tied, her face was adorned with a pearly white smile. A mixture of joy and confusion swirled within Naomi. She was delighted to see the kind old woman who had taught her to use magic; but how could it be that she survived the onslaught Mifuné brought down on Avalon, Naomi wondered, and why had she returned?

"Soothsayer, is that you?" Naomi called out.

"Why, yes, my pet!" the old woman replied in earnest. She stopped in her tracks and offered a genuine smile to her old pupil. Naomi rendered a courteous curtsey. "My goodness! Look at you. You have truly come a long way since last we spoke," the Soothsayer said proudly. Naomi beamed from the old mystic's words of encouragement.

Naomi watched the Soothsayer turn her attention to Mifuné, who remained ready to attack at a moment's notice. The intensity of his gaze only increased when the entity he beheld oriented its attention to him. The words it spoke confounded Naomi, and haunted Mifuné, and would continue to do so for years to come. "Your eyes do not deceive you, warrior," it stated unembellished.

Mifuné lowered himself in his battle-stance to brace against an attack while the apparent abomination advanced toward him. It took three slow steps before it stopped. A chilling breeze swept the loose excess of its cloak, as well as the ends of Mifuné's hakama. There was tension in the air, such that Naomi could hardly draw a breath. She felt afraid, deeper than just fear. Something was wrong. How could it be that the Soothsayer, this kind, sweet woman, filled Mifuné with the same kind of terror the Queen did when she imprisoned him, Naomi wondered.

"You have done well, Mifuné Tahaka, Son of the Dragon," the entity stated in a manner akin to the way Mifuné spoke to his disciples. The mysterious abomination continued forward until it stood shoulder to shoulder with Mifuné. Mifuné's sword shook in his hand, as he stood side by side with the nightmarish being.

"You have nothing to fear of me, warrior. Surely Ravana told you that." Unintimidated by Mifuné's aggressive posture, the terror strode past him non-threateningly. Mifuné's eyes widened in shock, and his right hand fell lifelessly from his sword, in complete contrast to Mifuné's readiness bring to bear all the power he could muster to fight.

Bewildered by the exchange she witnessed, Naomi was lost in thought, chasing questions for which there were no answers. "Who are you, really?" Naomi whispered to herself. She watched the Soothsayer closely. How in the world does the Soothsayer know who or what Ravana is, Naomi pondered. The final, and most haunting questions that lingered in Naomi's dizzy mind regarded what the Soothsayer had said to Mifuné, "You have done well." What did she mean by that? Naomi wondered: Did the Soothsayer want Avalon and its Queen to be destroyed, and if so, why?

Naomi continued to observe the Soothsayer as she trekked back toward the palace and disappeared into the mist. Her dizzying inquiries came to a halt when she looked back to Mifuné, still frozen where he stood. Shortly thereafter, Gabrysia and Sergei emerged through the mist to where Naomi and Mifuné were. They panted, as if they had been running after something. They searched around, and scanned their surroundings as best as they could manage. They could not find whatever they sought after.

"Gabrysia, Sergei, what is it?" Naomi asked.

"I cannot see it," Sergei replied, still scanning the mist.

"She is gone," Gabrysia answered, mimicking Sergei's search.

"Everyone!" Mifuné said urgently. His body still seemed paralyzed from his earlier exchange. "We need to leave, now!"

The Fall of Avalon

CHAPTER 12   UNPARDONED SINS

From that day forward, the son of the Dragon became known forever more as the Dark Swordsman.

Inside the remnants of Ivory Palace, Titania's spirit lurked through the darkness of the chasm. She was lost within the shadows, anxious and confused. Incapable of sight, her spirit felt its way around the wreckage, desperately seeking a way out. The silence was abundant, much like a tomb. The late Queen felt completely alone, which only frightened her even more. Then, something, somewhere, made a sound. Although it was faint, she could feel the vibrations, which sounded oddly like hollow humming.

"Hello!" Titania called out instinctively as she followed the sound. "Is someone there?" Fear abounded in her helpless voice.

There was no answer. Titania continued, she loomed in the direction of the tune, which drones along, yet she never seemed to get any closer to the source. Moving around exhausted her. She sat and rested for a moment as she lamented the hopelessness of her situation. The humming continued and advanced in on her. It grew louder and stronger, and more distinct, as it got closer. Titania could feel a presence drawing near.

"Is someone there!?" she exclaimed as she shot up to her feet.

"Oh, why yes, my child."

Carl Houston Roach IV

There is no mistaking it, it is the voice of the Soothsayer, she thought. Titania had never been happier to hear her voice. Though the old crone's appearance had repulsed her in the past, Titania had never been happier to hear her voice. Hearing her voice, however, raised many questions in Titania's frightened spirit.

"Soothsayer?" Titania pleaded, desperate for an answer, a comforting word to console her in her dark domain.

There was no response. Only laughter. That same, familiar cackle Titania had heard a time or two. The kind of laughter that seared itself into her memory so that she could never forget it. The laughter she heard in the depths of the darkness, however, became radically different. It warped, the same way the Soothsayer's voice changed the last time she heard it. The deep dark terrifying laughter surrounded the spirit of the trembling former Queen from all directions and grew deeper and more sinister.

"What do you want from me!?" Titania shouted into the abyss.

The laughter ceased. Silence loomed in the air once more. Titania frantically turned about seeking some clarity, some sign of something other than the inescapable tomb of darkness. Robbed of her sight, though, her blind search was fruitless. Her spirit pulsated with fear. Despair's cold grip locked around her as she awaited some manner of response.

In an instant, Titania's vision was restored, as if by some mysterious magic. She could see a clearing

The Fall of Avalon

through the wreckage into a pale light off in the distance, an illumination that was sure to be the way out of her dark prison. She charged towards the glimmer with all her strength. Just as she was about to reach the light and escape, however, pillars of pale green flames, hotter than any fire she had ever felt in the thousand years of her earthly existence, erupted from the ground between her and the passage to salvation.

Titania quickly turned to her left, but another explosive pillar of green flames cut her off. Then to her right, the same anomaly occurred. More pillars spouted out of the ground, two at a time, and created an aisle leading back into the deepest depths of the darkness in which her spirit awoke. Slowly, carefully, Titania turned and looked down the aisle of flames.

In the distance at the end of the aisle Titania witnessed the Soothsayer, just as she had expected: her hideous, wart infested face, beak of a nose, the long, gangling fingers attached to old, decrepit hands, and a hunched back completed her haunting visage. The decrepit old hag cackled still, but inaudibly. Her figure convulsed rapidly, almost too fast to distinctly see, and then, she changed. The haunting, stomach-turning being transformed into an elegant, tall, graceful woman with pearly teeth that shined against the darkness. Inexplicably, the entity changed into a gorgeous young woman, clad in the glorious armor of a knight who stood proudly. That image changed to a young man, dressed in a sleeveless tunic. He was handsome, strong-jawed, with wide shoulders and powerful arms. The final image was a bear, similar, Titania thought, to the one that attacked her in her palace before she died. The transformations she saw flickered back and forth from one another. As the transitions flashed from one to the other haphazardly, they accelerated akin to the persistence of vision of a thaumatrope.

Titania felt terrifyingly confounded. She could not understand how or why she witnessed what she saw. Who are these people, Titania wondered, and what is their connection to the Soothsayer? As the images flashed in front of her, Titania realized she recognized the woman in armor. Her stature, her proud expression, the power that was evident in her eyes... There was an uncanny resemblance to the red-haired woman who fought alongside Mifuné before Titania died. With that thought, Titania mused that the old, elegant woman could have been a parent to the blonde woman in the red cloak, or that woman herself, in her older years. A grave realization that she had been betrayed set into Titania's consciousness as she contemplated what she watched, and the perpetrator stood right before her. Rage erupted within Titania's spirit.

"Who are you!?" Titania called out brazenly, desperate to bring the chaotic transformations to an end. Little did she know her situation would become progressively worse.

The decrepit, old mystic took the solid form Titania best recognized. It was then the true horrors began. Smoke smoldered around the hag's bare feet causing her flesh to bubble and boil away as the haze slowly ascended her decaying body. Chunks of her skin fell from beneath her dusty brown cloak,

The Fall of Avalon

splashed onto the ground, and evaporated into forest green smog. Her long, gangling fingers stretched out, and shrank down to bone. The nails filed to a point. Piece by piece, her bulbous mass fell away and her dusty brown cloak incinerated into a cloud of smoke, revealing a shrunken slender, bony figure draped in a deep green cloak.

This new entity's stature elevated to the blackened sky. The green mist continued its upward rise, spiraling and floating about her head. The skin on its face peeled back and away, the meat beneath sizzled and burned off; the eyes melted into a horrifically bloody paste that streamed down the entity's cheek, leaving behind an inhuman skull. Long, curved, antler-like horns protruded from the sides of the skull, three on each side, and reached nearly double the shoulder length of the towering hunch-backed skeletal entity.

Titania's soul trembled in terror, as before her, manifested the single most terrifying thing she had ever seen. This being was not nearly as massive as Ravana, although, its presence was far more menacing. More than that, it was as if despair itself flowed forth from this being. The late Queen fell to her knees. She wished she could no longer see as her eyes fixed on this monstrosity before her.

"You... this cannot be... you cannot be here!" Titania stammered and shouted in defiance of her own fear. Standing before Titania, to the fulfillment of her worst nightmare, was the one thing in the entire universe that she truly feared. The one entity so powerful, her own mother fled the mortal plane to inhabit the realm of the gods to escape its return.

Carl Houston Roach IV

A figure she had only seen depictions of in old books, that she was sure was sealed away in the deepest pits of the Underworld. Titania covered her mouth and backed away as far as she could from the towering entity before her.

"Oh my Gods…" Titania whispered in tears.

The skeletal entity cracked its neck. It tilted its monstrous head to the side. Its hollow eyes drank, in amusement, the sight of Titania's paralyzing fear. "Not even close," it replied maliciously. There was no denying it, and there was no escaping the truth. All along, the true identity of the Soothsayer was The Lich, Lord of Despair. "Child of my enemy," the creature spoke, its voice was terribly shallow and haunting, yet all encompassing. "I have come to collect my promised price."

"For what do I owe you?" Titania trembled, fear churned her spirit.

"I imparted unto you the knowledge to summon Ravana from the pits of the Underworld. I prepared the formula for the ancient protection spell that would guard Avalon from its enemy," the horrific being answered succinctly.

Titania felt the smallest flicker of courage awaken in her. "The spell did not protect me! Avalon fell, and I perished!" Her voice became malignant in the face of the monstrous immortal which loomed over her. Armed with this truth, she stood to her feet, defiant to the Lich's claim.

"Yes, child," the Lich cackled, "the spell was perfect… powerful, too. Some of my best work," it gloated. "How unfortunate it was undone before it could even be cast."

The Fall of Avalon

"What!?" Titania exclaimed. "The ring! It was his heart! You said it had the power to keep him out!" Her spirit shook as the last vestiges of her will dissolved to nothing.

The Lich laughed maniacally as it produced a shining thing that glinted in the glow of the green flames. "Do you mean this ring?" the Lich mocked. It whirled the ring around its left index finger. The metal clinked against its bones as it spun. "The thing I most enjoy about magic," the Lich began, "is playing with technicalities. For example, one who has been invited in cannot be kept out."

Titania hesitated for a moment. She searched the recesses of her memory over the days before she died but could find nothing close to match what the Lich had inferred. "I never invited him back to Avalon. Even if I had, there was no way he would have returned with me," Titania hissed.

"Oh, but you did... during your failed seduction," the Lich rebuked snidely.

"You are a liar!" Titania screeched.

"I want you. I want for things to be as they were between us. Come home with me..." The Lich mimicked her voice perfectly.

Titania fell silent.

"There is no greater invitation amongst mortals than to bed with them. I should know. Your husband was quite willing to open himself to me," it finished. For a brief moment, The Lich's face suddenly shook and turned, transforming into the handsome, strong-jawed man she had seen among the transformations of the Soothsayer, a face she did not recognize.

Carl Houston Roach IV

"By the gods, Colabion? No!" Titania, sighed mystified.

"I assumed this guise," the Lich began, "to gain his trust when he was very young. He told me he wanted to be a King, to be the King of Avalon, but he was the youngest son of a Baron, and could never claim such a right." The handsome manifestation faded. "I promised to help him, I promised I would make him a King, and in exchange, he would one day help me." The Lich took pause, reveling in the successes of his dastardly schemes. "I placed him by your side, just as I placed your father beside your mother; and little did Colabion know, he fulfilled his contract with me the day he handed me this ring."

"That ring has no hold over me! It belonged to Mifuné, it was nothing to me!" Titania shouted in protest.

"This ring was a symbol of the Swordsman's love for you. You received it from him willingly and preserved it for seven years. Even before the spell, you were bound to it as much as he was," the Lich answered.

"I... I...," Titania was lost for words.

"Of course, I always knew the spell against Mifuné would fail," the Lich professed. "Your arrogance ensured that for me. I had to make certain that when you died, your spirit would be trapped here, so that I might claim it. So, I built another spell into the one I gave to you. One that would tether your spirit to this ring in the event the first spell was broken."

The Fall of Avalon

"This cannot be happening!" Titania looked to the sky. "Mother! Please! Save me!"

"Your mother cannot save you, child. My nemesis had already done everything in her power to guard her children from me." The Lich paced around slowly in the darkness. "She placed a warding spell on the city, so that I could not enter without invitation. *You* so graciously welcomed me in," he chuckled in the shadows. "With open arms!" The entity paused again, savoring the mounting despair crushing Titania's spirit before it continued. "The only thing left was that infernal sword, the sole object that prevented me from killing Glorianna during The Great War."

"No!" Titania's eyes went wide in horror and despair as the realization set in. The memories of all that had transpired, every move which brought her to that place and moment in time became ever so clear. The questions became answered. Suddenly, the presence of such a primordial entity and its intentions became self-evident.

"Oh yes," Lich's smug croon all but struck Titania across the face with the truth. "Surely you did not think it mere coincidence that I had you summon Ravana over the other Lords of Evil you could have unleashed. Do you even understand what manner of thing Ravana is?" It took pause. A dark, ominous tone bellowed from within the bowels of the primordial nightmare. "Stupid child. You could not imagine what sacrifices my nemesis, Glorianna," the Lich smiled wickedly and continued, "your dear mother, and the other Lords of Light paid to lock away the Ravana, Lord of

Carl Houston Roach IV

Chaos, King of the Demons, for the preservation of the mortal races; the countless lives lost, the blood that was shed. You freed him from his prison without thought of the consequences that your kingdom, that the world, might suffer. Even I would not risk bringing him out of the Underworld, although," the Lich paused, stroking his chin, "I needed Ravana's strength to break the Sword of Avalon, for Ravana had slain Fomorian, the creator of the sword." The Lich looked upward, as if he strayed away from the moment into its long memory. "I could not bring Ravana from the Underworld of my own power. The gates of the Underworld were created by Ikeyna, the Supreme Goddess of Magic, the only being ever to defeat me. I needed magic other than my own; I needed light magic."

"You used my magic to…" Titania uttered just above a whisper.

"To pierce the gates of the Underworld and free Ravana to the surface!" the Lich laughed triumphantly. "I thought it poetic, to use the power of a Lord of Light to undo the work of another, especially the second-rate power you inherited from your feeble mother, to bypass the protections Ikeyna laid down her life to put into place." The Lich covered its face with its hand to mask its unrelenting joy. "I thought Ravana might reveal me to you. He saw me, when I stood beside you as the decrepit, old crone. He knew who I was. It all unfolded right before your eyes, but you would not bother yourself to notice, oh mighty Queen of Avalon," the Lich mocked. "Then, finally, when

The Fall of Avalon

that blasted sword was destroyed, and its power against me was broken, there was *nothing* left to keep me from you."

"How dare you…" Titania gritted her teeth. Her hands balled into tight, white-knuckled fists. The energy of her spirit swirled with newfound tenacity. Thoughts of vengeance against the Lich raced throughout the core of her soul. "How dare you!" she bellowed with all her might. "You tricked me! You deceived me!" Titania stomped her foot against the cracked marble floor. "I will have my revenge, you will pay for what you have done, Lich!"

The Lich cackled awfully at Titania's defiance. "Tell me, mortal, what can you do? You have no power anymore. Your sword is broken, and your kingdom is fallen." The green flames extinguished all at once, and the ruined halls of the Ivory Palace were pitch black once again. The skull-face of the Lich expanded before Titania and encompassed all that she could see. "Look into my face, child!" Its voice became magnanimously loud, surpassed even the memory of the voice of Ravana. The remnants of the castle shook from the force of its speech. "I am the Lich! I am Despair! You belong to me, *now* and forever."

A gigantic, bony hand reached forward and seized Titania like an eagle grabbing an unsuspecting rodent. The abiding skeleton's opaque, all seeing black pools, eyed her over closely. She screamed and struggled, a fruitless attempt to escape. The Lich chuckled with unbridled satisfaction. It audibly took in a deep breath, the scent of her, as if her fear and despair were aromatic. From within its cloak, it produced a magical perfectly square chest with a cross-bone embedded lid and a keyhole lock along the seam.

"Never before have I found a mortal who, alone, caused such despair." The Lich opened the box and cast Titania inside. "I shall keep in you here. I will find use for you. In time, you, Titania, *dearly departed* Queen of Avalon, shall be the Queen of the Dead. You shall serve me as I see fit and carry out my will." The Lich sealed away the box within its cloak, and with it, Titania's screams. Silence lingered in the air once again.

The Lich skulked through the darkness of its newly claimed palace. It hummed to itself, and traced its hand over the tapestries, ruined and preserved. Green flames burned over them and changed the images from the glorious civilization they once represented, to horrific images of human pain, torment, and suffering.

From within the rubble of the entryway, the Lich exhumed the mangled, dismembered body of the fallen King-Consort of Avalon, Colabion. His skin was devoid of all color, having lost all the blood in his body from where his arm and leg had been severed. The Lich took note of the stab wound through Colabion's torso and nodded his head.

"Colabion, son of a Baron and master of nothing, we had a bargain, once. You have fulfilled your end, and so I shall fulfill mine." The Lich spun its wrist and unleased a wave of magic that lifted Colabion's body into the air. Plumes of green smoke surrounded him and spiraled downward until they touched the ground and enveloped his remains.

The Fall of Avalon

"Oh, I will keep my word, I shall make you a king."
The smoke cleared. What was once a mangled,
mutilated corpse transformed into a bulky, powerful
entity that was hooded and cloaked, and animated
by the power of the Lich. Sharp pauldrons ran
across Colabion's shoulders over the cloak that ran
down to his black. His steel boots tapered to a fine
point.

"You shall be Colabion, King of the Dead!" the
Lich declared. "You shall also be the first of my
Knights. Unto you I shall grant all power and
authority over the dead. You will serve my will, and
you will carry my banner across this world to all
lands."

Colabion turned his hooded face to the Lich. He
knelt before his unholy master with eternal humility
and said in a soulless, booming voice, "Yes, my
Liege."

The Lich stood before the remains of the Golden
Throne of Avalon, his loyal Knight in tow. It raised
its hand, and from behind the ruined golden throne,
a mass of stone and soil and dust rose out of the
ground and was fashioned into a throne. With a
flick of its wrist, bones of the dead citizens of
Avalon flew into the darkened hall and meshed
together to decorate the new throne with horns that
protruded from the sides to match the Lich's own.
The Lich floated through the air and sat upon its
grand and twisted throne, above the seat of
Glorianna, and looked out over the ruins of Avalon.

"This realm shall be mine," the Lich declared.
"The remaining three kingdoms shall fall before my
power. Now that my nemesis and her line have been

eliminated, nothing shall stand in my way." It smiled sinisterly. "For I am Lich. I am Despair."

᪶

By day's end, Mifuné and his group had traveled to the main trade road north of Avalon that connected the four kingdoms. The trek was a quiet one. Each one of them pondered what they had seen walk past them as they made their way out of the city, and each one of them was equally curious as to why those apparitions vanished so suddenly. The grave expression impressed upon Mifuné's face had not left him. Finally, Gabrysia broke the stalemate of silence.

"Master, what was it that you saw before we left Avalon?" Gabrysia asked directly. "We all saw something different, I know, but the way you are acting scares me."

"I agree," Sergei echoed, "and I am not a man who scares easily."

Mifuné did not answer them. In his mind, he was still frozen in that moment, face to face with the evil the others could not see. It mocked his strength, his magnanimous effort, even his very presence through its deep, vacant eyes and in its flippant speech. Above all else, the last words the entity said as it passed him shook Mifuné to his very core: "You have nothing to fear of me, warrior. Surely Ravana told you that."

"Mifuné?" Naomi asked, giving his arm a gentle nudge.

Mifuné looked to Naomi; sweet, innocent Naomi. It was haunting to imagine someone so pure had spent any amount of time near something so evil as the Lich. What was worse was that Mifuné knew, just as the Lich did, that the Lich could have taken Naomi away from him, and Mifuné would have been powerless to stop it. Ravana had told Mifuné, bound as they were together, the Lich could bring no harm against any Lord of Evil, just as the Lich could bring no harm to Mifuné. Such was the pact of the Lords of Evil forged before the Great War eons ago.

"Gabrysia, if you take this road East, you will arrive in Eramar," Mifuné said urgently. "Take this with you." He presented to her the coin with a lotus flower inscribed on the front that Naomi had carried for years. "This will grant you an audience with King Gregory. Tell them what happened here. Tell them an evil has awakened in Avalon, and the people of Eramar, and all the surrounding kingdoms, must leave Androma!"

"What evil? I do not understand, Master," Gabrysia asked, overwhelmed by Mifuné's rattling alarm.

"Mifuné, you saw something evil before we left? What was it?" Sergei pressed.

"Do you mean the Soothsayer? Mifuné, I have known her for years, and she is a kind soul. She is the reason I found you again," Naomi interjected.

"Not everything is what it seems, Naomi," Mifuné answered staidly. He turned his attention to Gabrysia. "This task is of enormous importance, Gabrysia. Only you can do this." He presented her the coin again, his tone much less strict and much less anxious.

Carl Houston Roach IV

"I will!" Gabrysia answered proudly. A powerful gust of wind swept her hair aside as heroically as a cape might whip in the wind. Mifuné observed her closely. Gabrysia had always been a proud woman, strong, confident. Her reservations had always been held for the day she might return home. Mifuné could see none of them in her eyes anymore. His young disciple was ready to spread her wings and take to the sky.

"Look at you. In just four months, you have grown so much." Mifuné paused and breathed in as Gabrysia's eyes watered endearingly. "You are truly worthy of the name of your house. You are going to do great things in this world."

"Thank you, Master," Gabrysia answered, staving off her urge to cry.

Mifuné smiled. "I am not your Master, anymore. There is nothing left for me to teach you." He rested his hand solidly on her shoulder. "You have made me proud, Gabrysia," Mifuné gleamed.

Inundated by the sincerity of his words, Gabrysia threw her arms around Mifuné's neck and hugged him tight. He affectionately wrapped his right arm around her and hugged her back. Naomi could not keep herself from crying, even before Gabrysia could say goodbye to her.

"Thank you, for everything, Mifuné" Gabrysia whispered gratefully.

"Take care of yourself, Gabrysia," Mifuné replied with care.

Gabrysia released Mifuné slowly and faced Naomi. They both welled up with fresh tears as they prepared to say goodbye. Though they knew this

The Fall of Avalon

day would come, it felt as though the time they spent together went by in the blink of an eye. Naomi shook from the sheer emotions, both positive and negative, that swirled within her as she gazed into Gabrysia's eyes for what might be the last time.

"Gabrysia, I have never had a family of my own," Naomi began, fighting back tears. She looked around, to Sergei, to Mifuné, then back to Gabrysia. "You were like the sister I always wanted. I love you," she began to sob, "and I am going to miss you so much!"

Naomi seized Gabrysia with a mighty bear hug and cried on her shoulder. Gabrysia's emotional reserve expended, and she sobbed as well. Though there was pain in the goodbye, neither one of the women would have traded the chance to get to know each other. They separated from their mutual embrace and gave each other one last look.

"Naomi, I am so proud of you," Gabrysia said endearingly. She placed her hands upon Naomi's shoulders. "You are all grown up now," she said as she choked back tears. "You are finally ready to take on this big, bad world without me, and I will not worry, because I know you can do it!" Gabrysia wiped away a tear that streamed down her cheek. "No matter what happens, no matter where you go, you will always be my sister, so do not ever forget about me!" Gabrysia demanded.

Naomi chuckled as she dried her tears. "Same for you," her voice trailed off, heavy with emotion.

Finally, Gabrysia approached Sergei with playful intimacy in her eyes. She approached him, not as though she meant to say goodbye, but as if to

334

say, "I will see you again." Sergei's face nearly reciprocated the same sentiment as he stood tall, powerful arms crossed over his chest, and a smile on his face.

"Good luck, Gabrysia. I hope you find your way home safely," Sergei said as passively as he could muster. Gabrysia threw her arms around Sergei's neck and pulled him down to her stature. "I will miss you too, Sergei." She kissed his cheek tenderly, and he wrapped his mighty arms around his dear friend tenderly. To her surprise, he hauled her off her feet and squeezed her tight, exhaling a delighted grunt before he set her back on the ground.

Mifuné, Sergei, and Naomi waved as Gabrysia began her long journey home. Sergei and Naomi shouted well-wishes and safe travels, and they waved their arms to Gabrysia as she strolled down the path before her. Though the goodbye was bittersweet, the time had come for Gabrysia to return home after so many years. Just before she was out of earshot of Naomi and Sergei, she turned around, one last time, to take in the sight of her former master, her best friend, and her sister waving to her. "I will never forget you. Thank you all," she whispered to them.

As Gabrysia disappeared out of sight, Sergei and Naomi looked to Mifuné. He was oddly silent. There was no tension in him as there had always seemed to be. In that moment, he seemed at peace, as though the warring chaos, in his mind and in his heart, had settled. He looked first to Sergei.

"Well, Sergei, what road is next for you?"

The Fall of Avalon

Sergei breathed in heavily through the nose, then exhaled. "My family is lost to me. Without them, I have no home to return to. So, it seems wherever you are bound, so am I."

"You are a free man. You are not bound to me, or to anyone," Mifuné retorted.

"Free? Yes, maybe that is true, but I am also the Bear who helped sack Avalon. I will have enemies who will want me dead, either for reward or for glory. I would prefer to take my chances standing next to the man who bested the Paladin."

Mifuné nodded and smiled in solidarity. "Very well."

Naomi had already faced Mifuné. He hardly recognized her as she was. No longer was she the same, timid little girl he caught stealing from him, or the bashful woman who was afraid of her own feelings and potential. She had blossomed, like a lotus, into a confident, powerful woman. He was proud to stand before the woman she had become. Sergei noticed their wordless exchange, and quietly excused himself.

"I know what you are going to say, Mifuné," Naomi began. "You are going to tell me how dangerous the road ahead is going to be. How you cannot promise that I will be safe. How you do not know what will happen next." Her knowing gaze peered into his soul as she continued, "What is more, you are afraid of the darkness within you. None of that matters to me. Whatever is in front of us, *we* can face together." She took hold of both of his hands. "Just like *we* defeated Titania, together."

Carl Houston Roach IV

Mifuné nodded. "You are right. The road ahead is going to be dangerous," Mifuné began, his tone low and sullen. "I cannot promise that you will be safe. I do not know what is going to happen next. And so long as I carry this sword, Ravana is connected to me. He will do whatever he can to gain control over me and pull me into the darkness."

Naomi looked down and away. She had hoped he would have stopped her, fired a rebuttal, or made some proverb-like saying in disagreement. The last thing she wanted was for him to agree.

"There is one thing I know," Mifuné continued. Naomi noticed a slight spark in his tone, and she turned her eyes, now full of hope, back to Mifuné. "If not for you, Titania would have succeeded in locking me away. I would have failed. Countless more innocent people would have suffered and died. Desmond would have died in vain," he momentarily relived the loss, "senseless, futile..." Mifuné took Naomi's hands in his. "*I* would not be here now, without you." He paused, and with all of the love and honest conviction a man could muster, Mifuné said, "Come with me. Let us see what this world holds, together."

"Yes! Yes, yes!" Naomi lunged against him, full of glee, and kissed Mifuné. He held Naomi tight and returned her loving kiss. Tears of joy streamed down her face as they looked into each-others' eyes. Mifuné gently wiped away the tears staining Naomi's cheeks, and he smiled even brighter than the warm smile he offered her when she was young. He lowered his head and rested his forehead against hers. Sergei smiled as he watched from a short

The Fall of Avalon

distance away. He stood with his arms folded over his chest and a wry smile on his face. "I never thought I would see the day.

And so, the legend begins...

EPILOGUE

"And that is how I saved the village of Domur from the bandits."

"Wow! Grandpa Sergei, you are a real hero!"

Sergei laughed as he lifted his little five-year-old granddaughter off his lap. She was so tiny, she could take a seat in the palm of his hand. She tugged on his gray beard as he motioned her to his shoulder.

"Alright little one, time to find your papa."

"Aww grandpa," the little girl groaned, "I want to hear another story!" she pouted.

"You know I can get in trouble for that. Your mama does not like it when I tell you children my stories. They can be a little scary for you young ones."

"Grandpa, I am not scared! Maybe Michael is, but not me!" the child insisted.

Sergei peered into her youthful, determined face with his old, weathered eyes. She had the same kind of look on her face that he did when he was her age. It always warmed his heart to see her want so badly to embark on her own adventures one day, just as he had. He set her on the ground and patted her head.

"Sophie, I will make you a promise, okay?" Sergei began.

"Okay!" Sophie eagerly replied.

"One day, when you get bigger, I will take you on an adventure. How does that sound?"

"Yeah! Yes! Yes! Yes! Yes! Yes!"

The little girl bolted through the door into the next room. As she passed through the door, she

I

The Fall of Avalon

nearly collided with her grandmother's legs. The elderly woman chuckled as the tiny child excitedly shouted "Adventure!" as she continued down the hallway and out the front door.

Sophie's grandmother, Sergei's wife, had reddish brown, but graying hair. Her forest green eyes stripped nature of all of its beauty. Porcelain skin robbed the moon of its glamor. She spoke with the softness of an angel and sang like an entertainer of the gods. The smile she granted Sergei every day soothed the beasts within him, both the bear, and the man. Despite having aged, she was just as beautiful to him as they day they had met. Her name was Roxanne.

"You were telling her your stories again?" Roxanne asked. There was slight provocation in her voice.

"Yes," Sergei replied and lowered his head. He sighed as he watched the small child scurry outside whimsically, without a care in the world. "She dreams of adventures outside of this simple life, you know?" he said as he tenderly wrapped his arm over his wife's dainty shoulder. He lay his head against hers and kissed it.

"That is what worries Alexander and Sybil, my love. They do not want the children to know the hardships that you did. You understand that, do you not?" Roxanne asked lovingly.

"I do, but I also cannot blame her for wanting more than this quiet, safe life. There is not a thing I would change about my life and the course it has taken." Sergei stepped away from her and took a deep breath. Memories of adventures, battles, close encounters with death, treasures beyond description, and sights he could never begin to detail or forget, filled his mind and his heart with nostalgia. "Roxanne, I lived an incredible adventure in my life. I stood on top of the world, above the clouds. I discovered treasures and secrets no man has ever seen!"

Roxanne grinned. "And you walked away from all of that for me." She stepped beside him and kissed his powerful, aged arm.

Sergei smiled back at her. "And I would do it all over again."

Sergei and Roxanne took hold of each other, and they shared a tender kiss, slow, soft. She took ahold of his burly hand and held it with both of hers. Sergei could feel her love for him filling his heart, touching his very soul, as she had always been able to do.

Though his journeys took him far from his homeland in Androma, Sergei had everything he had ever wanted. He had a home to call his own again. Good land he could work and farm, and the finest livestock of any of the nearby farmsteads. A beautiful, loving wife, with whom he had three sons, two of whom were out in the world, making their fortunes. Their youngest son, Alexander, who had remained behind to inherit the house Sergei had built, was married with children of his own.

Sergei strode away from Roxanne out the door to his front porch. He rested his heavy frame against the railing that ran around the wooden house and looked out into the field. The sun, nearing the horizon, cast amber light onto the wide fields full of

The Fall of Avalon

tall sawgrass. The early fall breeze swept over the plains, making the stalks of grass sway back and forth in a rhythmic dance.

Roxanne joined Sergei quietly on the porch. They could see their son, Alexander, and his ten-year-old son Michael, playing just away from the big apple tree that stood alone in the meadow. They could faintly hear Michael and Alexander laughing as they wrestled in the grass.

"Do you remember when we planted that tree, Roxy?" Sergei smiled, reminiscent of the not-so-distant past.

"Aye, I do. The day Alexander was born, thirty years ago, you dug out the place to plant the seed. Every day you took such care with it. Just like you did with me, and our boys." Roxanne nuzzled her head against his arm.

A smile painted across Sergei's face as he continued to watch his family. He watched Alexander hold little Michael up over his head and spin him through the air. It reminded him of a time not so long ago when he did the very same with Alexander. Sybil, Alexander's lovely wife, had made her way out there to bring her 'boys' inside for supper.

Sybil was a simple woman from the nearby village called Domur, where Sergei was well renowned as a hero. Her father, Braxton, was an innkeeper who had taken a liking to Alexander more so than his brothers. When Alexander was thirteen, he had taken up an apprenticeship under Braxton, and so met Sybil. After a few years under Braxton's tutelage, Alexander and Sybil fell in love, and they were married when Alexander completed his apprenticeship at the age of nineteen.

Sybil did not possess any of the finer markings of her mother's beauty. Dusty brown strands of hair tangled down to her shoulders. Her eyes, an unremarkable hazel, as common as any woman in Domur, did little set her apart from other women. A voluptuous figure she did not possess, nor could her voice produce a song to please the angels; although, she was a splendid cook. Despite all that she lacked, Alexander loved her with all his heart, and for that, she loved him unconditionally, and was a wonderful wife to Sergei's precious son. He and Roxanne loved her as if she was their own.

As the little family began their return to the house, Michael waved excitedly to Sergei. The little boy beamed brighter than the sun above whenever he smiled. Sergei waved back enthusiastically to him and smiled even wider. Sybil, who had been carrying him, set him down. Michael ran to his grandfather at full speed through the tall grass.

Sergei stepped off the porch and squatted down. He held out his great arms for little Michael to run into. As the boy came into his embrace, he closed his arms around him and scooped him up. The two laughed together as Sergei spun him around in the air before he perched him on his massive shoulder.

"How is my little bear cub? Ready to get some supper? Your grand-mom has made some of her famous beef stew!" Sergei boasted eccentrically.

"Aww, I hate grandma's stew!" Michael bellowed in disgust.

V

The Fall of Avalon

"Oh, you had better not go telling her that, little cub. You might hurt her feelings!" Sergei pressed his finger against the boy's belly.

"Grandpa, grandma's stew is yucky!" Michael insisted.

"Well if you keep that up, I will just have to tell her you said that," Sergei threatened playfully.

"Grandpa, you say it all the time!" Michael began climbing his way around Sergei's shoulders to hang from his neck.

"What? I do not!" Sergei protested.

"Hyaaaah!" Sophie lunged from her hiding place in the shrubs around the house and seized hold of one of Sergei's legs. "Grandpa thinks grandma's food is gross! Ha ha ha-ha ha!" she laughed.

"No! There are too many of them! Help! It is too much..." Sergei feigned despair and raised a hand to his face.

Sergei fell to the ground and rolled to his side. The two children jumped onto his torso and attempted to pin him down. He wrapped one arm around each of them and began rolling through the soft dirt and grass with them. Finally, Sergei rolled onto his back. Each of the children rested on one side of his powerful chest. They laughed loudly, happily, without a care in the world.

"Okay kids, I think you should give grandpa a break," Alexander said, finally arriving at the front of the house.

"Okay, papa!" Sophie replied.

"Yes, papa," Michael answered.

"Now go inside and wash up! Go, go, go!" Sybil urged playfully as she followed them in.

The two children laughed and scurried inside. Alexander stood over Sergei and extended to him a hand. Sergei gripped it tight and hauled himself up. He took a good look at his son. Alexander was nearly a mirror's reflection of Sergei's younger self. He was strong, as strong as Sergei was in his prime, with hands like iron, a sturdy frame, broad shoulders, and thick arms. He was handsome as well, but of course he would be, Sergei always thought. Thick brown locks of hair draped from his head over his steady brow, and a generous beard, years in the making, adorned his chin. He was a good man; a man Sergei was proud to call his son.

"How are you feeling today, papa?" Alexander asked, patting Sergei on his shoulder.

"Well, you know, getting old is no easy thing. Sure, being a Werebear added years to my life, but no man lives forever," Sergei said as he stretched his arms upward. He flinched after feeling a tinge in his neck pull down into his back.

"Please tell me you have not told *that* story to the children," Alexander pleaded.

"No, I only tell them the small stuff. Just enough to put them to bed at night," Sergei assured him.

"Good," Alexander sighed with relief. "Mama finished making supper?"

"I think. It should be just... about... ready..." Sergei's voice trailed off.

"Papa? Are you alright?" Alexander inquired.

VII

The Fall of Avalon

Sergei stepped past his son and looked back out into the field. He could not believe what he saw. He rubbed his eyes to ensure it was no illusion, no trick of the light, or his old eyes making fantasies, that it was not some shadow his aged mind wanted him to see. Alexander turned around and saw him, too. There was no denying it. Upon further inspection, standing under the shade of the apple tree, was a Samurai, whose face was covered by a straw kasa.

"It cannot be!" Sergei whispered as his heart rate accelerated.

"Papa, who is that?" Alexander asked.

Without a word, Sergei began making his way toward his old friend. He had not seen Mifuné since he decided to stay with Roxanne in the nearby village of Doshur over fifty years ago. The closer he came to standing face to face with Mifuné, the faster his feet carried him. His heart raced out of his chest. He could feel tears welling up in his eyes, but he refused to let them fall.

Then at last, Sergei was face to face with his old friend. He still towered over Mifuné, like a bear to a wolf. The two warriors stood before one another with mutual respect and admiration. Mifuné reached up and removed his kasa. As Sergei had suspected, his face had not aged a day. Mifuné smiled, and Sergei smiled back.

"It has been a long time, Mifuné," Sergei initiated.

"It has, my friend," Mifuné responded, heartfelt to see Sergei once again.

"Look at you. You have not aged a day," Sergei chuckled.

VIII

"Side effect of immortality. The Ravana has preserved my youth since the day I trapped him in this sword," Mifuné answered.

Sergei had not taken the time to notice until Mifuné mentioned it, but the Samurai's left hand still clung to the sword in his sash the way it always had, yet the malice that so frequently emanated from Mifuné and pervaded his demeanor seemed lost, as if it was a chain that he had been unshackled from long ago.

"You have changed, my friend. I can see it in your eyes," Sergei uttered endearingly.

Mifuné looked Sergei over. His thick, brown hair had all but faded to gray and white. A short tail of excess hair was tied behind his head. His beard was thicker and longer than when last they saw one another, and matched the color of the hairs on his head. His eyes were heavy and aged. Lines and wrinkles had overtaken much of the space on his face. Despite his age, though, he managed to sustain his muscular physique, with the addition of a round belly.

"I would say you are just as youthful as you have ever been," Mifuné replied in kind.

Sergei shook his head. "Flattery has never been your strong suit."

Mifuné chuckled.

"What brings you back to Istananor? I thought you said you had no interest to return to these lands when last you were here," Sergei inquired.

"That is true. That was after…"

"Naomi?" Sergei interrupted.

The Fall of Avalon

The joy and the light left Mifuné's eye. He turned his face away from the light of the setting sun and stared into his growing shadow on the ground beside him. His tone became sullen and grave, "I have sought her out, every day since we were separated. It has been nearly a century, Sergei. I honestly do not even know if she is still alive."

Sergei scoffed. It was not dismissive of Mifuné's pain, nor was it mocking of his yearning for Naomi. He had seen the love that they shared, the undaunted, undiminishing love she imparted onto him, and the undying, unyielding love he reciprocated to her. It grieved Sergei to think that such love was so short lived, but it did little to discourage his hope for the two of them to be together. "You might think I am mad, but I am confident that she is still out there, somewhere."

"You think so?" Mifuné asked, as though his heart was a leaden weight he could not lift.

Sergei leaned his face right in front of Mifuné's. Their gaze locked, and each of their glances was unwavering. Sergei said with absolute certainty, "I know so. I would even wager she is out there right now, trying to find her way back to you."

"You really believe that?" Optimism sparked in Mifuné's voice, down to his very spirit.

"It is like I told you in Avalon. That is what true love is." Sergei peered over his shoulder to his house. His beautiful wife, Roxanne, walked toward them as they spoke. "It makes the impossible possible. One other thing I have learned is that love never gives up." As Sergei's beloved wife stood by

X

his side, Sergei turned his endearing glance back to Mifuné.

"Mifuné," Roxanne said gracefully as she joined them, "it is so good to see you again."

"Roxanne," Mifuné smiled, and rendered to her a short, polite bow. "You are as radiant as ever."

"Would you care to join us for dinner?" Roxanne asked, invitingly.

With a smile, Mifuné raised an open hand to his gracious hostess. "Thank you, but no. I will not be staying long."

"That woman you were searching for, the last time you were here, did you ever find her?" Roxanne questioned.

Mifuné sighed heavily. The spark of hope diminished along with the remaining light of day. "No… I have not."

The weight of Mifuné's words, the sense of loss that flowed from him set on Roxanne's soul. She, however, did not despair. In the face of the depressive surge that pressed down on the Samurai warrior, the champion who felled thousands of Androma's most fearsome soldiers, who bested the greatest champions that stood against him, who feared no man, beast, god, or demon that confronted him; she smiled. "I have faith that you will." She paused, and lovingly reminisced over memories of her precious husband, whom she loved above all others. "Sergei is the greatest man I have ever met. Beside him, there is no other. No other, except you. For what it is worth, I have faith that you will find her again, one day, and I wish you every fortune in the world for your search."

The Fall of Avalon

Roxanne dipped her head to Mifuné and stepped away. She was free of the chaos, the Hell, that Sergei and Mifuné had encountered most of their lives. She was peaceful, beyond even the most serene natural sanctuaries that either had seen in their many adventures. Sergei and Mifuné watched her walk back to the peaceable house in the field, a treasure neither Sergei nor Mifuné believed they would ever have.

"Of all that we have seen and done together in fifty years, none of it compares to this, I think," Mifuné said with a smile.

"You are right. Having a loving family and a place to call home is more precious to me than the greatest wealth of this world." Sergei turned his attention back to Mifuné. "I am not so convinced that this the reason you came back to see me. I know you, Mifuné. Is there something else?"

Mifuné smirked and shook his head. "That is not the reason I came. I came here to see you, my friend." Sergei and Mifuné locked arms around each other and pulled each other near in a long-overdue embrace. The moment was so moving, so touching, Roxanne shed a few tears as she watched on from the porch. She had known for years that Sergei, more than anything, wanted to see his dear old friend again. He held no man in higher esteem than Mifuné. Despite his faults, despite his connection to the King of Demons, Mifuné walked with honor, spoke the truth, and carried himself with pride and dignity.

Roxanne had heard all the stories and tales of their adventures together. She had even spent time with Mifuné before he departed Istananor. Hearing the way Sergei spoke about him, coupled with the memories she carried of him, Roxanne perfectly understood why Sergei held him in such high regard. That Mifuné could be there on this day to see Sergei after all those years was a wish granted for Roxanne.

The two men released each other. Pools of tears were visible in each of their eyes, but they showed no shame. They felt no fear of judgment from one to the other. No words were said for a few moments. Volumes of emotion and sentiment were expressed through their eyes. They were proud of one another, and the men that they had become 100 years since the fall of Avalon.

"I have come to tell you a grand story," Mifuné said, finally. "The story of the strongest man I have ever known. A man, who did what I could not."

That single claim Mifuné had made was more than sufficient to capture Sergei's attention. The question that excited Sergei's mind was this: What manner of man might it be that could do what the mighty Mifuné, the Dark Swordsman, could not. "Tell me. I must know, who could possibly do what you could not!" Sergei responded excitedly.

"This is the story about a boy who became a King... about a man they call the Burning Sword..."

XIII

Biography: Carl Houston. Roach IV

My name is Carl Houston Roach IV. I grew up in a small house in Miami, Florida. Since I was very young, writing has been my passion. I had a wild imagination as a child, and even now as an adult, I have refused to let it burn out. Consequentially, I have developed my very own world and filled it with life and with people, with legends and lore, mythos and religion, all of which reflect the nature of our own world in creative and fantastical ways.

I aspire to tell stories of heroic triumph in the face of daunting adversity. That is what I believe the quintessential characteristic of humankind to be. We, as people, face battles and struggles and trials in our lives that push us to our breaking points. Some of those battles become floods that wipe us out. We're left scarred, damaged, sometimes cynical and resentful.

Yet, I believe every single one of us has the capacity to recover. Like the Phoenix, we have the capacity to renew and rise from the ashes of complete and utter destruction. We have the power to orient ourselves towards the highest good, to transform ourselves into our greatest ideal through determination, perseverance, and resilience. These are the characteristics of the heroes in the stories I will tell in my writing.

I also intend to explore the complexity of what it is to be a hero. I don't believe the definition of being a hero is someone who always walks the line and does the right thing to the point of a fault.

While characters such as those represent the ideal hero, heroes – even in legends – are men and women with their own faults and flaws, oppression and resentment, trials and circumstances that set their course. They make mistakes, they can lose their way as easily as anyone, the line they walk between good and evil can become blurred.

The foremost question I aim to answer by way of the different heroes I will write about is simply this: what is it that makes a hero? Is it someone who stays true to their convictions through thick and thin? Is it someone who discovers what their principles are through trial and error? Is it someone who makes a hard choice and bares the consequences of that choice? Those who read my books will go on that very same journey of exploration with me, in this world where anything is possible.